For Heathrow, Gatwick, and Baltic —

who swear they write the books

1

Kelly Jax wasn't happy. I couldn't blame her.

"The title of the book is *I'm Into Wellness, Not Hunger!*" she reminded me over the phone, which wasn't necessary at all. I was the agent who sold her book for a hefty sum. It was an easy deal. America cannot get enough of beautiful blonde talk show hosts writing diet books, and *IIWNH* was already a top 10 *New York Times* bestseller.

"Do you know what those *freaking* morons did?" Kelly went on.

Okay, she did not actually say "freaking," but you get the picture. America's sweetheart has a mouth on her. They don't call her Jax the Ripper for nothing.

I knew exactly what the freaking morons had done. Kelly had already texted me a photo of the bookstore window in Chelsea, where her book was prominently displayed in a pyramid of about fifty copies. Normally that would be a good thing for an author, but the store had made an itsy-bitsy mistake. Kelly needed to vent. I understood.

"They put a discounted price sticker in the corner of the book," she continued, in a voice loud enough to carry through the phone to the other tables in the restaurant. "They covered up half the title! So now the freaking title of the freaking book in the freaking window is *I'm Into Well Hung!*"

Do not laugh, I told myself silently. Do not laugh, do not laugh, DO NOT LAUGH.

1

I smothered the phone with my hand, and I laughed anyway.

"Look, I understand," I told her when I could talk without choking. "I'll call the agency. They'll talk to the store and get it fixed."

"Do you know what I'm doing on the cover?" Kelly asked me, as if I hadn't said a word. "I'm eating a hot dog! I have my mouth open, and I'm about to eat a freaking Coney dog!"

"I hear you, Kelly. The stickers will all be moved by tomorrow morning."

"It's too late! People have been posting about it all evening! The top trending hashtag on freaking Twitter is #KELLYJAXLOVESBIG——!"

I think you can guess how that hashtag ended. Yes, rhymes with lox.

Anyway, that's the kind of phrase that gets people's attention. The other diners at da Umberto turned their heads to stare at me. I smiled bravely. Across the table from me, Helmut Mischler sat with a tiny smirk and drank a glass of expensive Dornfelder wine.

"I'll fix it, Kelly," I promised. "Really."

Kelly hung up on me with a final "FREAK!"

Again, that wasn't exactly what she said.

Helmut waited patiently for me to compose myself. He discreetly flagged the waiter, who materialized with another glass of San Giovese for me. Say what you will about Helmut (and many people do), he is impeccably cultured. You can afford to be gracious when you make as much money as he does. A year ago, Helmut was in Tokyo, overseeing the Far East digital music division of Gernestier, the European conglomerate which owns pretty much everything in the media world. Today, he is based in New York, running the company's U.S. publishing interests. He freely admits to knowing nothing about the book biz, but as he likes to say, "*Machts nichts.*"

I think that translates roughly to: "Who cares, I can buy and sell your mother."

I knew Helmut was ready to get down to business. He picked

imaginary lint off the lapel of his chocolate brown suit (Kiton, five thousand dollars). He smoothed his trimmed beard with thumb and forefinger and used both hands to carefully secure his tiny oval glasses on the bridge of his nose. His fingernails are more perfectly manicured than mine. He is an oddly tall, narrow man with an oddly long, narrow face, and he is probably about ten years older than me. In my case, I will turn forty in 617 days. Not that I'm counting.

"Unhappy client?" Helmut asked me.

"Yes, very unhappy."

"Being an agent, you must deal with difficult personalities," Helmut said.

"Oh, no. Most authors are well adjusted and really good with people."

Ha ha ha. We both laughed at that one.

"You have been an agent for a long time, Julie," Helmut went on. "Your whole career, yes?"

"Almost. I was an actress for a couple of years before I went into the book biz."

"Oh, really? I did not know this."

"Well, sort of. My breasts were in acting, but the producers had to hire the rest of me to get them."

Helmut looked confused. The very mention of *die zwei Alpen* made him uncomfortable. His eyes didn't know where to look. "I'm sorry?"

"It doesn't matter. I was an unsuccessful actress. Fortunately, I've been a successful agent."

"That is true, very successful — but now you are a publisher! This is a big change for you. How are you finding it?"

"It's too soon to tell. It hasn't even been a month. I'm still organizing my father's affairs."

"I understand. So you don't know yet whether you will stay on at the helm of West 57?"

"I haven't made any decisions," I said.

"Naturally. You have my sympathies. Sonny is such a loss to the entire industry."

"Thank you."

I brushed my Jane Seymour-length black hair from my face, which gave me cover to rub away the tears that filled my eyes. If you have lost your father, you know that a month is no more than a minute in measuring grief. Maybe it's even worse when he is a force of nature, the kind of man who is so filled with life that you cannot imagine death stealing him prematurely.

Sonny Chavan. My father. Founder and owner of West 57 Publishing. In its heyday, Sonny's publishing house was considered *the* barometer of literary trends (as he would be the first to tell you). Intelligent. Thoughtful. Meaningful. Deep authors saying deep things. If you were a novelist with an original voice in the 1970s and 1980s, you wanted West 57 on the spine of your books. If you were a critic at the *Times*, the advance copies from West 57 moved to the top of your reading list. But that was then, and this is now. Sonny is gone, and the world has changed. I was less concerned with black ink on the printed page than red ink on the balance sheet.

West 57 was running out of money. Helmut was well aware of my predicament.

"To inherit a house like West 57 must be a complicated legacy," he told me. "The brand has a storied past, but in the current economic climate, well, I'm afraid the past isn't much comfort, is it?"

"We have some encouraging prospects," I replied gamely.

His eyebrows arched in surprise. "Oh?"

"Yes, this week is huge for us. King Royal's memoir *Captain Absolute* arrives in stores. It's about Irving Wolfe and the massive Ponzi scheme he ran on the Upper East Side. It's going to be our biggest bestseller in years. Lots of orders. Lots of national media attention."

"Ah, yes." Helmut leaned across the table, and his nose cast a long shadow. He probably knew the advance orders on King's book better than I did. "Your father did overpay for the book, though, didn't he? Four million dollars in this marketplace? Such a cowboy Sonny was. Even if the book is a bestseller, it's unlikely to be profitable."

"Well, we'll see."

Helmut picked at the artichokes in his plate of pappardelle and gave me a condescending smile. He was right, and we both knew it. One book wasn't going to change the fortunes at West 57. And four million dollars for King Royal? Ridiculous. But that was Sonny, throwing big advances at books he liked, demanding re-writes that added months to production times, sniffing at accountants who fretted about money when he was concerned with art.

Now I had to deal with the consequences.

"I have a proposal for you, Julie," Helmut said.

"I figured you did."

"I think it represents a practical solution to your problem."

"What's my problem?"

"Debt. Debt is your problem. Let us not pretend, okay? West 57 is bankrupt. You are proud of what Sonny built, and that is a good thing, but not if it blinds you to sound decision-making. Your father, he was the kind of stubborn man who thought he could get out of a hole by digging to China, but you are not your father. You are smart, tough, mature."

Mature. There's a compliment that makes a girl's knees go weak. You are smart, Julie! Tough! Wizened!

"So what do you suggest?" I asked.

"Let us take over the brand. Gernestier will assume all of your financial obligations. A clean slate, so to speak. The alternative is shutting down, is it not?"

"If West 57 is in such dire straits, why would Gernestier want to acquire it?"

"Because the name still carries weight in the marketplace," Helmut explained. "West 57 is like Rolls-Royce or the Mandarin Oriental or Krug. It carries an expectation of quality, and this is something we can leverage. What the house has always lacked is fundamentals like discipline, budgets, good business practices. This is what we bring. With proper management, West 57 can again aspire to be the premiere name in American literature."

"Again?" said a raspy, cigarette-stained voice that was not mine. "Again? Helmut, you wouldn't know *literature* if it bent over and farted in your face."

I covered my smile with my hand. It was Sonny.

My father towered over our table, all six-feet-four of him, his jet black hair as regal as the mane of a lion, his face fogged by the smoke of his Davidoff Superslims. I was surprised it had taken him so long to show up, but this was Sonny. He was always late. Even when he arrived at a restaurant on time, he greeted everyone at every table like a giant Indian version of Ed Koch. Arm around back. Nicotine breath in your face. Coffee-brown teeth grinning as he whispered a tidbit of gossip or debated the merits of a Cortese Barbaresco on the wine list.

Sonny.

Don't worry, I'm not crazy. I knew he wasn't really there. A heart attack felled Sonny last month like a bullet takes down a bear. He slumped over at his desk into the blue-inked pages of a manuscript he was editing. Garrett Wood, Sonny's protégé at West 57, found him there and called me. My father was gone. Even so, he has shown up in my head ever since that day, same old Sonny, bellowing, laughing, and arguing. Maybe he was a ghost. Or maybe my heart was simply conjuring a fantasy in order to convince myself that nothing in my life had changed. Instead of everything.

"I understand how difficult this is for you," Helmut told me.

Sonny snorted. "Oh, please! Helmut has to pluck a nose hair to work up a tear."

"What I'm offering you is an opportunity to restore and preserve what your father built," Helmut went on. "Gernestier can put West 57 on a sound financial footing, and with that foundation, we can identify important new authors and give them the kind of multi-media backing and economic support that Sonny never could." He snickered, which sounded like an oboe flourish at the Philharmonic. "Not that Sonny ever hesitated to spend money he didn't have."

"Freak you, Helmut," Sonny announced cheerily. Or words to that effect.

I frowned at him. I do not like swearing. Yes, I live in New York.

"Gernestier doesn't exactly have a literary reputation," I pointed out. "Don't you prefer bosom-heaving vampire tomes? That sort of thing?"

On cue, Sonny slapped his big hand on his chest, and his voice boomed like Ian McKellen. "*Artemis swept aside my flowing hair to expose the trembling skin of my neck. As I smelled the intoxicating musk that told me he was as much man as monster, I knew that I wanted him not just in this moment of paradise but through the interminable stretch of ungodly time.*" He laughed so hard that the table shook. Or maybe it was a nervous tic in my knee.

"We do sell many vampire books," Helmut admitted. "I have to say, it puzzles me. What is it about women and these erotic domination fantasies?"

He said it with an arch of his eyebrow, as if to ask: Does that turn you on?

"Bite me, you animal," I said.

No, I didn't say that. Even a year of self-imposed celibacy wasn't enough to make Helmut attractive to me.

"Sorry," I said. "That's not my scene. No vampires, no femporn. I didn't even read *Fifty Shades of Grey*."

"Ah. Well. Anyway, yes, this is a big category for us, but that doesn't mean we do not see the market potential of more literary authors. Hence our interest in rescuing West 57."

Sonny snarled. "Rescuing?"

"I'm not ready to make a decision yet," I told Helmut. "It's too soon."

"Of course. I understand. I'm sure your hands are full."

"Maybe once I get past the launch of King Royal's book," I said.

"Yes, this is a busy time. I know you are concerned with your father's business and your own future. You are probably thinking that you owe it to Sonny to run the business yourself, so you can't imagine selling the house. What I want you to know is that you don't have to make a choice."

"What do you mean?" I asked.

"West 57 has always carried the Chavan name on its masthead. Why change? If we acquire the brand, we would welcome the opportunity to keep you on as the senior executive, reporting directly to me. This way, you would honor your father's legacy."

"Don't trust him, darling girl," Sonny warned me.

I didn't. I knew perfectly well that Helmut wanted me as a figurehead to reassure the book world that the editorial standards of West 57 wouldn't suffer under the green eyeshades of Gernestier. He'd call the shots, not me. I'd be there to do the dirty work, cutting off authors who underperformed. After a year or two, he'd ease me out, or make my life so miserable that I left of my own accord.

However, Helmut was no fool, and he knew how to negotiate.

"Of course, you may be hungry to return to the world of agenting," Helmut speculated. "Is this so?"

"I wouldn't say that."

"I imagine you made a lot of money as an agent."

"I wouldn't say that, either."

"Well, we would naturally want you to be properly compensated for your senior role at West 57 and for giving up your ownership interest in the house. As an executive, you should receive executive rewards. Say, a three-year contract? We can haggle over the details, but we would want your compensation to be in the range of — "

Helmut mentioned a number.

It was a very good number.

It was three times my salary at the McNally-Brown agency, where I'd worked sixty hours a week making money for the partners, rather than me. Gernestier was trying to buy my love, and they were succeeding.

"That's very generous," I said. "I'll think about it."

Sonny wasn't happy with me at all. "Don't think about it! Tell him to go to hell! You can't possibly let this accountant get his hands on my house. West 57 is mine!"

Not anymore, Sonny. It's mine now.

"I'll think about it," I repeated.

2

As I headed uptown after dinner with Helmut, I savored the sights of New York, because it's easy to take it all for granted when you live here. A night-time cab ride in the city is always magical. You can admire the pastel colors of the Empire State Building overhead. A young girl with her head on the shoulder of her lover, strolling past Bryant Park. An out-the-door, after-theatre line for a slice of pepperoni and mushroom at Ray's.

A goateed teenager waving at me as he urinated into the gutter.

Nice.

My phone rang as I stared out the window. It was my mother. If I called my father Sonny his entire life, my mother has never been anything other than "Mother." Her actual name is Cherie. Yes, I know. Sonny and Cherie. I gave mother a special ring tone on my phone, for the same reason that yeomen dug moats around their castles in the old days. You want a little warning when the barbarians arrive at your gate.

Mother's ring tone? *Ride of the Valkyries.* It seemed appropriate.

"Hello?" I said.

"Julie!" Cherie announced. "Where are you?"

She always asks me where I am when she calls. It's her first question. I suspect she wants to confirm that her GPS tracker is working.

"I'm in a cab, Mother."

"How is the weather?"

"Cold. Drizzly." It was April, but spring hadn't sprung.

"It's sunny in L.A."

I checked my watch and calculated the three-hour time difference.

"No, it's not. It must be dark by now."

"Well, it was sunny all day. Seventy degrees. Heaven."

"I'm sure."

"Where are you going?"

"Back to Sonny's office," I said.

It would always be Sonny's office to me. It would look like him and smell like him. I could sit behind the desk, but I would always feel like a little girl visiting Daddy's office for the day. I glanced out the window of the cab. We were nearly at Rockefeller Center. West 57 is located — as you might guess — on West 57th, around the corner from Carnegie Hall. Thirtieth floor. Great view toward the Park. A monthly lease that makes you want to jump out the window.

"You work too hard," Cherie chided me. "It's late. Go home and put your feet up. Go have a drink. Go dancing. Go sleep with someone."

"Mother!"

"I'm sorry, but you've been crabby for months, my dear, and I can only conclude that it's because you're not getting any."

"I'm not crabby."

"Oh, please. What's so important at the office at this hour?"

"I'm up to my ears, Mother. *Captain Absolute* by King Royal launches this week. Sonny left eighteen other projects in various stages of production. If we have no sales, we have no cash."

"You work too hard," she said.

That's rich, coming from a woman with fifty film deals in process at any given moment. She works eighteen hours a day, but it's L.A. work, lubricated by Chardonnay and fueled by edamame and ahi at Malibu bistros.

I was also not telling her the whole story. There was plenty of work to be done at West 57, but I also knew that Garrett Wood would still be at his desk. He's always there, a man like me, with no life, just work. I'd spent a lot of quality time with Garrett since Sonny's death.

More about that later.

"I have to go, Mother," I said.

"Nonsense, pay off Naresh or Hassim or Farouk or whoever is driving you and keep talking as you walk."

I paid off my cab driver, who really was named Farouk, and gave him a big tip to thank him for using the streets rather than the sidewalks. It slows you down, but the tourists prefer it.

I buttoned my London Fog raincoat and tied the belt around my twenty-four-inch waist. Yes, I am small. Five feet nothing, one hundred pounds. Most of that is hair. The coat left my legs bare; I'd worn the power dress for Helmut. If you know me, by the way, you know my mother. We look like twins. Her plastic surgeon, her hair colorist, her dermatological consultant, and her yoga instructor have kept her L.A. young. You wouldn't guess that she is twenty-five years older than me. In another twenty years, she will probably look the same, whereas I will be...mature.

I was half a block from the West 57 building as I left the cab, but I turned north instead and walked two blocks to the park. I crossed Central Park South and sat on one of the benches and smelled the wafting of dung from the carriage horses. My Bluetooth was in my ear. People stared at me, wondering if I was talking to myself. In New York, you never know who's on the phone and who's just crazy.

That should be the slogan in the Bluetooth ads. "Is it Bluetooth or is she nuts?"

"So what's really going on with you, Julie?" Mother asked.

I was quiet. Then I said: "I miss him."

Mother was quiet, too. "Yes, I miss him, too, my dear."

"Don't lie."

"It's true, Julie. Sonny and I had a lot of good years together. We were still friends."

"The last time you were in New York, you hit him with a Jonathan Franzen novel. You nearly sent him to the hospital."

"I can't help it if Franzen is wordy, my dear."

I laughed. For all their screaming matches, Cherie was sincere about how she felt. Love and hate are pretty close on the emotional scale, and Sonny's death was as much a punch to her gut as to mine. Neither of us could imagine a world without him.

"He wouldn't like tears, you know," Mother added, and she was right.

"I'm not crying," I lied.

She changed the subject. "So did you have dinner with *Helmut?*" she asked, drawing out his name so that it sounded like *Hellllmoooot.*

"I did."

"What did he say?"

"Gernestier wants to acquire West 57."

"You should say yes."

"I said maybe."

"Julie, why do you want the hassles of running a white elephant like West 57? This is your chance to get out of dreary New York and dreary publishing, and join me in Los Angeles."

"And do what?" I asked. "Act?"

Mother laughed. It wasn't a particularly kind laugh. "Oh, hardly, my dear. We've been down that road."

That was true. As I told Helmut, I didn't start my career in the agenting biz. No, no. I was an actress. Sort of.

Let me explain. By the time I was in college at NYU, Cherie had relocated to the farthest physical point in the continental United States away from my father. Namely, Los Angeles. There, she set up shop with a large chunk of Sonny's money as an independent film producer. She also set about luring me to join her.

To a college girl, summer on the beaches of L.A. beats summer in New York, and I felt the lure of the camera while I was out there. With Cherie's help, I landed a role in a shampoo commercial (long black hair is a plus) and as a waitress spilling red wine on Jennifer Aniston's blouse on *Friends.* Not much, but I was hooked. I had my future planned in my head: Golden Globes, Academy Awards, Leonardo DiCaprio, Malibu estate.

It didn't work out that way.

As *Titanic* was hitting the box office, my career hit the iceberg. I'm not someone who gives up easily, but I don't wear rose-colored glasses about the future. Two years shuttling around L.A. convinced me that my body was more in demand than my acting. You can still see me naked on Netflix if you're into that sort of thing. Just rent the movie *Kiss Me, Kill Me*, and look for Julie Chavan in the credits as "Hooker With Long Hair."

There was also the little matter of my failed engagement to an up-and-coming actor named Thad Keller.

More about that later, too.

At the peak of my frustration with my acting career and my love life, Sonny proposed an alternative. He said that with my industry connections, I could be a great asset to one of the most distinguished literary publishing houses in New York. I wasn't about to join West 57 and work under Sonny's thumb – I'm no fool – but he was right about the value of my industry connections. As an entertainment agent, I could scout commercial properties and negotiate film tie-ins, endorsements, media placements, all the things that generate lots of money for clients and agents alike. I could do it all fully dressed, too.

So I gave up on Hollywood and joined the McNally-Brown Agency, and until last month, I was in the Flatiron Building doing deals. I grew older and wiser, if not a lot richer. I even met Leonardo DiCaprio once when I was handling a big book-to-movie deal, and although he didn't peel Bar Rafaeli off his arm in order to kiss me, I'm sure that's only because he didn't want to hurt Bar's feelings. At least that's the version of the story I tell.

I stayed at McNally-Brown longer than any rational person would have done. The smart agents go out on their own, but not me. Not until now. God made the decision for me by taking Sonny away, and here I am. My departure from the agency is technically a leave of absence, but I'm not going back.

Not that I have a clue where I'm actually going.

"Work for me," Mother repeated.

"I wouldn't work for Sonny, so why would I work for you, Mother? No offense."

"I can offer you things Sonny couldn't."

"Like what?"

"Sun. Ocean. Blond actors who will screw producers to get a part."

"I live in New York. This is my home."

She tut-tutted me. "Live? Julie, you work, you don't live. You're alone. You stayed in New York because of your father, and Sonny is gone. It's time to move on."

"Helmut offered me triple my old salary to stay on and run West 57."

That stopped her. "Did he?"

"Yes, with a three-year contract."

"You wouldn't want to work for him."

"I wouldn't want to work for you, either, Mother."

"What did you tell him?"

"I told you. I said maybe."

Mother was silent. I could almost hear her mind working. Cherie Chavan doesn't like roadblocks when she is mapping a highway for her daughter's life. "Don't rush into anything, my dear. Keep your options open."

"I intend to. This week is crazy, anyway. King's book is launching."

"Good." She added with a casualness that wasn't convincing at all, "By the way, what are you doing tomorrow night?"

"Nothing." I added pointedly: "Why do you ask?"

"I told an old friend to look you up."

"Who?"

Her laugh was maniacally Machiavellian. "Oh, I don't want to spoil the surprise, but you'll thank me."

"I really doubt that."

"Now go home, Julie, forget about the office. I'm going to strip naked and jump into a hot tub."

"Good for you. Tell me more about this old friend."

"My lips are sealed. Ta, my dear!"

This can't be good.

I hung up the phone. When I glanced beside me, Sonny sat on the bench. Big arms draped behind him. His legs crossed, his shoes shined. Same cloud of cigarette smoke. There was a lumpiness about his face in profile, his nose huge and rounded, his cheeks puffy. He watched the hordes of traffic come and go from the Plaza to Columbus Circle. He wore a black suit, which was taut on his beefy shoulders, and a tie as yellow as a daisy. No coat. I guess when you are dead, you don't get cold. The rain was leaking on me, but Sonny's black hair was dry.

"Do you remember our walks in the Park on summer Sundays?" he asked me.

"Of course."

How could a girl forget that? I was even smaller then, and Sonny was still the same hero-sized father. Young. In his prime. Going places. We were rarely alone on those dazzling days on the Great Lawn. Sometimes Mailer joined us. Sometimes Roth. Or Korda or Hellman or Lenny or Warhol or Ginsberg or Chita. I had only the smallest idea who any of them were, but I remember the waves of people parting for us, and the whispers of recognition, and I thought: My father is somebody.

"The city was glamorous then, darling girl," Sonny said. "They're all dead now, and no one can take their place."

"No."

No one takes the place of the dead. The present is never what it was. Glamour is simply what we remember of the past through a fuzzy lens.

I got up from the bench. Sonny stayed where he was. I thought about West 57, and seeing Garrett Wood, and I knew I should go to the office and spend an hour with him and the books. The trouble is, it would be more than the two of us there. The wood of the desk would be scraped bare where Sonny used to prop his shoes. The closet would smell of Clive Christian cologne. The black-and-white photos on the wall would be scrawled with inscriptions bearing his name.

I couldn't deal with it now.
I walked ten more blocks north, and I was home.

3

In the morning, when my alarm went off before sunrise, Katy Perry was singing about "California Gurls." When she got to the song's rap, it wasn't Snoop Dogg but my mother who supplied the patter about how great it is to live in L.A. Cherie wore Snoop's blingy sunglasses and had a goatee.

Okay, maybe I was still dreaming.

When the alarm really went off, Sinatra was on the radio, crooning about having a crush on me. Much better.

I started coffee percolating in the pot, and in the interim, I took a shower. Afterward, I stood in the steam, toweling off, pulling on a pink bra and pink bikini panties. I sat down at my dressing table and laid out my blow dryer, brush, and makeup. I have no bangs, just waves of thick, long, straight black hair, parted in the middle, down to my hips. It takes me about a week and a half to dry my hair, but blowing and brushing are my substitute for meditation.

My hair created an oval around my gold-toned, Freida Pinto face. Fifteen years ago, I looked just like her, which is a reminder that a pretty face only takes you so far in Hollywood. She found her *Slumdog Millionaire* role, but I never did. However, I am still vain enough to pluck, paint, buff, dust, bleach, and apply until I look almost like I did then. Almost. Anyway, I still have the high cheekbones, the flat jawline, the arching brows, the smoky eyes, the pouty lower lip, the slightly over-large smile. Thank the good Lord, I also got Cherie's pointy little nose and not

Sonny's. Freida certainly never looked in a mirror and wished she had a potato in the middle of her face.

In the kitchen, the coffee waited in the pot. I liked my coffee black and European, the way Sonny taught me. I scooped a bowl of fruit. I turned on the television and flipped the channels to choose a perky host for the morning news. Thinking perky made me think of Kelly Jax, which reminded me of her diet book, *I'm Into Well Hung*. I'd left a message for my former colleagues at McNally-Brown to get those stickers off the books in the bookstore window. Technically, it wasn't my problem, because I don't work at the agency anymore. Even so, Kelly was my client there, and I felt bad for her.

Okay, it was still funny, but I felt bad.

On the cable news, I saw an ad for the Pierce Gorgon talk show. He was cancelled once, but now he's back. I think it's called *America May Have Talent, But We've Got Pierce Gorgon*. Or something like that. Ha ha, just kidding, Pierce. I love him. I especially love him this week, because he is devoting an hour-long interview to King Royal and *Captain Absolute*, which is the spring blockbuster for West 57.

I watched the commercial. Pierce was typically grumpy.

"Tomorrow night, my guest is author King Royal. This is the pretty boy who got four million dollars to do a Kitty Kelley tell-all about Wall Street crook Irving Wolfe. I'll rip him to shreds. I'll make his genitals shrivel like a raisin. Watch my show, you witless gun-loving American cretins."

No, he didn't say that.

However, I'm concerned that Pierce will serve up King Royal like an order of breakfast bangers and swallow him down one bite at a time. It didn't really matter. Even bad publicity is good publicity when it comes to book sales. Besides, I couldn't blame Pierce. I had mixed feelings myself about publishing *Captain Absolute*. It distressed me to make money off a book about Irving Wolfe.

You probably remember Wolfe. He conned rich New Yorkers out of hundreds of millions of dollars in a pyramid scheme big enough to stake a site in Giza. I didn't like the fact that *Captain Absolute* portrayed Wolfe as dashing and romantic, but you don't make it as a con man unless you're part Robert Redford, part Warren Buffett. According to King Royal, who was Wolfe's personal assistant for two years, Wolfe was utterly brazen about his crimes in private. Bragged about them. Laughed about picking pockets on the Upper East Side, even as he seduced husbands and wives. His favorite play was a nineteenth-century farce called *The Rivals* by Richard Sheridan. Wolfe liked to boast that he was the hero, Captain Absolute, wooing his victims like lovers behind a secret identity. Unlike the brave Captain, however, Wolfe's mask hid a thief.

It's a hell of a story, as memoirs go, until you remember how many people had their life savings wiped out.

I've never met King Royal, who wrote the book, but that will change tomorrow. Actually, like most celebrity writers, King probably never picked up a pen. Sonny hired one of his top ghost-writers to do the heavy lifting, and the writer took King's reminiscences about Irving Wolfe and turned them into a cultural biography, like *Midnight in the Garden of Good and Evil*. King was merely the public face of the book, and that was what worried me. The buzz in the media world was that King was a fragile flower, which made someone like Pierce lick his chops.

The real power behind the book was King's London agent. She was the woman who somehow finagled Sonny into a four-million-dollar advance that West 57 could ill afford. She was a woman who'd made a career of stepping in crap and sprouting roses from her heels. A woman who was, once upon a time, my confidant, my sister, and my best friend.

She was also the woman who ruined my life.

Bree Cox.

You may know Bree, because she wrote a bestselling account of her life in the London publishing world called *Paperback Bitch*. It was one of those novels that (wink, wink) claims to be mostly true, with names changed to protect the innocent. For example, *Paperback Bitch* featured a scheming New York agent who was the chief rival out to steal clients from our innocent heroine, Bree.

The agent's name? Julia Charon.

Real subtle.

Bree admitted in *Paperback Bitch* that she slept with "Julia's" fiancé and broke up their engagement. That part was absolutely true, because that's exactly what Bree did to me. Not surprisingly, she and I haven't been best friends since then. In fact, we've been blood enemies.

Bree Cox. I knew she would be in New York this week, chaperoning King Royal. I knew I'd have to see her again.

I sipped my coffee and thought to myself: Focus, Julie. This week is about launching a bestseller. This week is about the future of West 57. This week is about you and the rest of your life. This week *isn't* about Bree.

I took a deep breath, and I was serenely calm. I was in complete control of my emotions.

Oh, who was I kidding?

I was probably going to have to kill her.

My apartment is on the Upper West Side near 69th and Broadway. For a one-bedroom unit in that area, the rent is reasonable, which means that it's the equivalent of buying a used car every month. Of course, I don't own a car. I have nowhere to park it, and I don't know how to drive. Sonny always told me to learn, but I never really saw the value in becoming expert at an activity that I would almost have never an opportunity to practice.

Sadly, I approach sex the same way.

I left for work before the sun was up. When I worked at the McNally-Brown Agency, which is fifty-odd blocks south in the Flatiron Building, I took the subway. For the past month, I've been able to walk. I followed Broadway through Columbus Circle back to West 57th at my typical fast pace. The night security guard was still on duty when I arrived. Lionel likes me. Sonny was an early riser, too, and I think Lionel enjoyed the morning banter with my father about the Yankees. I'm Sonny's daughter, so he has kept up the banter with me. He sometimes brings me pumpkin bread made by his wife.

However, there was no banter and no bread this morning. Instead,

Lionel pointed with obvious suspicion to a man sitting in a chair by the elevator.

"That man there, he's been here half an hour," Lionel grumbled in a low voice. "Says he's waiting to talk to you."

"Who is he?"

"He wouldn't tell me. You want me to roust him?" Lionel looked as if it would be an honor to pitch the man into the street, and Lionel was big enough to do the job.

"No, I'll talk to him."

I approached the elevator, and the man scrambled to his feet. He was small and skinny, though not as small or skinny as me. I figured he was in his late twenties. He wore a brown raincoat that had seen a lot of rain, but his shoes hadn't seen polish in a long while. He had buzzed red hair and sallow skin, with a couple pimples that matched his hair. When he smiled at me, I saw crooked teeth and caught a whiff of mustard and onions; he'd had a hot dog for breakfast. His eyes were beady but sharp – a quick look up and down my body, just enough to leer, not enough to make me scream and run.

His lack of personal hygiene convinced me that he was a reporter.

"Ms. Chavan?" he said, reaching out a sweaty hand, which I didn't shake. "Nick Duggan with the *Post*."

See?

He had the accent of someone who grew up eating salt beef sandwiches and pork pies south of the Thames. He was a British reporter, which is mostly an oxymoron, like "New York Republican."

"What can I do for you, Mr. Duggan?"

"I'm working on a story about King Royal," he told me.

"Well, then I'm sorry, I can't talk to you. Pierce Gorgon gets the first interview with King tomorrow night. Until then, I'm embargoed. Call me after that, and I'll see what I can do."

"Oh, I'm not trying to scoop Pierce," he sneered. "I worked for him in London before he went all Hollywood. He used to call me Diggin' Duggan."

"I'll tell him you said hi."

I reached for the elevator button, but Duggan grabbed my wrist. His fingers were sweaty. I stared at him with a cold face until he let go.

"Touch me again, Mr. Duggan, and I will have Lionel there throw you through the outside windows."

"You really need to talk to me," he said.

"No, I really don't."

Duggan put a finger on the side of his nose. "Look, I know what smells bad, Ms. Chavan, and this whole thing with King Royal stinks."

"What whole thing?" I asked, a little curious.

"The book. The advance. Hey, I knew the Soho scene in London. Everybody knew King. We called him Lord Byron because he had a fancy act, always dressed up like some Romantic poet, singing dirty songs, reciting limericks in the pubs. King had a radar for queer money, hanging out with bankers and execs. Nobody was surprised when he wound up in Irving Wolfe's bedroom."

"Goodbye, Mr. Duggan." I punched the elevator button.

"Think about it. After Wolfe died, King was on his way back to the Soho nightclubs. He was out in the cold. And then, Holy Mother Mary, he winds up with a *four-million-dollar* book deal. Now why would a bankrupt publishing house like West 57 throw that kind of cash at a loser like King Royal?"

"King's book is going to be one of our biggest sellers in years," I said.

"It smells, Ms. Chavan. I'm digging into it. The FBI is looking into it, too. Did you know that?"

I stopped. "Excuse me?"

"That's right. The feds and the government attorneys, they all think King's dirty. He was neck-deep in Wolfe's con game. You know what that means?"

"I have no idea."

"It means your father was, too."

The elevator doors opened. I got inside. My instinct was to slap

Nick Duggan, just like I slapped Bree Cox once. You do not insult Sonny in my presence. You do not lie about my father. However, I also knew enough about reporters to know that violence is exactly what they want. Violence makes headlines; violence hits the gossip pages. I didn't want to see myself splashed across the front page of the *Post*.

"Sonny was a great man, Mr. Duggan," I told him with a patient smile. "You're not."

Duggan got in one final shot as the doors closed. "Great men don't always tell the truth."

4

When I got upstairs, I saw an envelope taped to the West 57 door. It was addressed to me. I opened it and found a single theatre ticket tucked inside. No name. No note.

I removed the ticket and saw that it was for tonight's performance of the new Broadway adaptation of Hitchcock's *Rear Window*. Front row, no less. Five hundred dollars if you can get a seat, which you can't. Bradley Cooper and January Jones had taken over the famous Jimmy Stewart and Grace Kelly roles, but I'd read that Cooper was out because he'd broken his arm while rock climbing. I hadn't heard who was taking over the male lead.

Anyway, I am cynical enough to know that free tickets aren't free. There's always a catch. I just didn't know what it was.

I let myself into the office. I was the first person to arrive every morning, the one who turned on the lights. West 57 occupies an entire floor of the building, but we're really a small publishing house, with only a handful of employees to handle editorial, sales, publicity, and business functions. Sonny and Garrett did most of the editing themselves, and Sonny outsourced production tasks to a stable of freelancers. The result was that West 57 was like a small family, and many of the staff had been with Sonny for a decade or more. A death in the family always brings change. Fortunately, the people here knew me and trusted me, because I was Sonny's daughter.

They would not trust Helmut Mischler and Gernestier.

I went into Sonny's office. I mean, my office. It was big, like him, the corner office with the northern view. The walls were lined with floor-to-ceiling book shelves. You could write the history of the last thirty years of the publishing industry by perusing the first editions. Sonny always said he had one brand: The Great American Novel. That was what he published; that was what he kept in his personal library. The authors all had faces to me, because I knew them, and I'd read their books. It was a list to make you laugh, cry, love, hate, cherish, despair, and marvel at what it means to be human.

I don't think that I'd ever told Sonny how proud I was of what he'd built at West 57. It was just one of the many regrets I had about his life being cut short.

The same desk had been in this office from the beginning. It was cherry wood, nicked, scratched, dinged, and burned with cigarettes. I sat in his chair, which was three sizes too large for me. The leather on the arms had been worn down to the wood as Sonny read manuscripts and buffed the brass studs with oily fingers. I hadn't had the courage yet to dig into the papers stuffed in all of the drawers. I'd kept the surface of the desk mostly the way he'd left it. The scorch-marked ashtray from Paris. Bi-focals that he swore he didn't need. A stack of decades-old West 57 novels; he liked to go back and re-read them and see what he'd missed.

He'd been studying Libby Varnay's *Morningside Park* in the days before he died, and, as always, he'd been making notes in the margins. I opened the book at random. At the end of an early chapter, Sonny had scrawled a note: *Mrs. McCall's reaction? Too mild based on her own past abuse. Intensify and speed up dialogue.* He dated all of his comments; that note had been made only two weeks before he died. This, in a book he'd published almost twenty years earlier, that had sold five million copies worldwide and been made into a movie with Denzel Washington. To Sonny, no book was ever really finished.

I was seeing Libby for lunch today about a new book. I thought she'd be amused, getting Sonny's copy of *Morningside Park* and seeing his notes. Libby was one of my very favorite people, gossipy, elegant, wealthy, and timelessly beautiful.

"Good morning."

Garrett Wood smiled at me from the doorway of the office. He held a monster travel mug of coffee, which he'd brought on the subway from the West Village. Garrett was a creature of routine, like me. He always stopped at the all-day, all-night Turkish coffee shop in the lobby of his apartment building. In his other hand was a paper bag, which I knew contained two cream-filled rum babas. One for him, one for me.

He put my donut on a napkin in front of me and poured some of his coffee into the ceramic mug that Sonny kept on his desk. I'd made the mug for my father as a child in middle school. It was misshapen and atrocious, but to my knowledge, he'd used it every day of his life since I gave it to him.

I'd already had plenty of coffee, but I love coffee, and I always had more when Garrett brought it for me. This may be why I get very little sleep.

I held up the ticket for tonight's performance of *Rear Window*. "Is this from you?"

I was hoping he'd say yes. Instead, Garrett sat down in the chair on the other side of the desk and said, "What's that?"

"Someone left me a gift."

"Lucky you. Sorry, no, it wasn't me."

"I'm trying to figure out the catch."

"Does there have to be a catch, Julie?"

"No, but there usually is."

"Maybe you have a secret admirer." He took a bite of his rum baba. Some of the cream filling oozed onto a finger, and he licked it clean. He meant nothing by it, but I found the gesture erotic. "How was your night?" he added.

"Fine."

"What did you do?"

"Takeout Thai. Yankees."

That was a lie, of course. On any given night, it would be true, but not last night. The meeting with Helmut was my secret. No one knew, other than my mother. I wanted to tell Garrett, but the idea of Gernestier acquiring West 57 would have horrified him. To Garrett, Gernestier represented corporate publishing at its worst. Bureaucratic. Money-driven. Soulless.

I'm a terrible liar, but if Garrett suspected I was being untruthful, he was discreet enough not to say anything. Instead, he asked, "Are you still seeing him?"

I knew who he meant. Sonny. Garrett was the only person to whom I'd mentioned the odd way my father had haunted me for the past month. As if Sonny and I had unfinished business.

"Yes."

"Maybe he's a ghost," Garrett speculated.

"Or maybe I should see a shrink," I said.

Garrett smiled. Some people smile, and you can see all the way down into their hearts, and you know it is a warm place, like a field where you lie down and close your eyes and feel the sun. That is Garrett's smile. "I wouldn't worry, Julie," he told me. "You loved him, and you aren't ready to let him go. That's all it is. It's a gift."

He had a way of making me feel better.

Let me explain. Garrett is a few years younger than me. More than a few, actually. He is about as close to thirty in the rear-view mirror as I am to forty through the windshield, so call it seven years between us. I don't feel the age difference, and he is more mature about life than I'll ever be. As young as he is, Garrett has worked for Sonny for more than fifteen years, going back to when he was a high school intern. Sonny liked Garrett's eye right from the start. In college, Garrett became Sonny's screener on manuscripts, poring over submissions from agents like me, finding the jewels that deserved more attention. Sonny hired Garrett full-time after college, and Garrett has been at West 57 ever since. He obtained a master's and doctorate in literature during his evenings and weekends. If he wanted to leave publishing and teach, he could have done so, but his loyalty to

Sonny was fierce. I think Garrett missed him and grieved for him every bit as much as I did. He felt the same protectiveness for West 57, too.

Yes, I respected Garrett as an editor. However, if you think I'm leaving something out, I am. There is more between us, but I don't know what it is. We have never dated. We have never kissed. He has never said a word to lead me to believe he is interested in me. During that time, I have seen other men, slept with other men, nearly married other men. Well, two, actually. Thad Keller. Kevin Stone. More about them later.

What I mean is that Garrett has never pursued me, and I've never pursued him, but even so, we have danced around each other for years. There have been times when I've sent him manuscripts I knew he had no intention of buying, just so I could invite him to lunch. Whenever I came to see Sonny at West 57, I saw Garrett, too, and sometimes we talked for hours. I think Sonny always believed I was there to see Garrett, not him. Maybe he was right.

He has brown eyes that sparkle with intelligence. His eyebrows wrinkle when he is teasing me. He has unruly black hair, parted on the side, with a cowlick that you want to reach over and gently smooth. His face is kind. It's the kind of face where you notice its parts: his discreet sideburns, his chin scar, his ski-slope nose. He has young skin because he is young. He has long, lean legs; we look crazy together, him as tall and lean as a basketball player, me an Indian leprechaun. He dresses casually but makes jeans and a sport coat look as dressy as a tuxedo.

The maddening thing is that I feel like he knows exactly what I'm thinking when he stares at me. It makes me want to shout: "If you can read my mind, why aren't you kissing me?"

Is that what I want?

I don't know.

"So what aren't you telling me?" Garrett asked.

See? Wherever I'm going, he gets there ahead of me.

I shrugged. I didn't want to tell Garrett about Gernestier or ask him the questions that were in my head. How did you get that scar? What will you do if I sell West 57? Are you in love with me?

"It's a big week," I said.

"Is that all it is?"

"That's all it is. I'm stressed. Sonny never worried about anything. Me, I'm a worrier."

"Things look good for *Captain Absolute*," he said. "Orders are up. Publicity is strong."

"I know."

Garrett watched me run my fingers along the grains of the wood in Sonny's desk. I hadn't touched my rum baba. "How bad is it?" he asked.

"What?"

"Money."

"Bad," I said. "I'm meeting with our banker tomorrow. Sonny was making deals like the business was going to turn around, but it's not. We're running out of time and cash."

"I'm sorry," Garrett said. "I've never been a numbers guy. I'm all about the books. I guess that doesn't help you much right now."

"That's okay."

Fortunately, as an agent, most of my life was about numbers. Unfortunately, I felt like CC coming into the game in the ninth inning, with the score already 10 – 0 against us.

Garrett stood up and gave me that smile again. "If it makes you feel better, everyone here believes in you."

I wondered if that would still be true when they heard about Helmut and Gernestier. Garrett headed for the office door, but I stopped him by saying, "Hey."

He turned back. "What is it?"

"Did Sonny ever talk about why he did such a big deal for King's book?"

"No, but you know Sonny. He made up his mind, and he went for it."

"It just seems over the top even for him."

"Maybe, but it looks like he was right," Garrett said. "We're going to sell a lot of books."

"Yeah. Thanks."

Garrett left me alone. I felt small again, sitting in the big chair. I had a lot to do, but I started reading more of Sonny's notes in Libby Varnay's *Morningside Park* instead. It made my father feel closer, seeing his scrawl on the pages. No more than five minutes passed, with my head down, before I heard the rat-a-tat-tat of fingernails tapping like a machine gun on my door. I assumed it was Garrett again, but when I looked up, I saw multi-colored highlights streaked through a mop of blond hair. The woman in my doorway wore sky-high heels and as much leather as a dominatrix. She'd added a diamond stud in her nose since I'd last seen her. Her cocked arm was balanced on her hip.

She gave me a wicked grin with her vampire-red lips. "The bitch is back, darling."

It was Bree Cox.

5

"I'm sorry, the escort service is located next door," I told her.

Bree slinked her way into my office and sat in the chair across from my desk. She slumped sideways and draped a bare leg over the chair in a not-very-ladylike fashion. "Nice to see you, too, Julie."

I looked her up and down. "You know what would go with that outfit? A dog collar and a whip."

"What makes you think I don't have them?" she asked with a wink. "I rather fancy the occasional spanking."

"Okay, bend over," I said.

Bree wagged a burgundy-nailed finger at me. "As funny as ever, darling."

"What are you doing here, Bree?"

"You're not prepared for my arrival? No champagne? No caviar? Don't worry, I forgive you."

"I expected you later today with King Royal."

"Yes, I flew in a day early. Got here last night. Lots of meetings. Lots of deals. An agent never sleeps. Besides, it's New York. It's my favorite city."

"Naturally."

"I'm a best-selling author now," Bree added. "We sold *Paperback Bitch* in ten languages."

"Congratulations."

"We're doing a film, did I tell you? What a hoot. The hard part is casting myself. I need the perfect actress to play me."

"Is Judi Dench available?"

I was proud of that zinger, but if the insult stung, Bree gave no evidence of it. "Oh, Julie, you are deadly."

"Have you found someone to play me?" I asked. "Or should I say, *Julia Charon?*"

"Do you want an audition? I can get you one. I assume you have no problem with tasteful nudity."

"Well, you've never had a problem with *tasteless* nudity."

"Ouch! White flag, darling. I surrender. You win, you win." Bree looked around the office as if it were an old friend. She'd been here many times; every agent in the business knew Sonny. Her face grew sad. "Hard to imagine this place without him," she said.

"I know."

"There's no book biz without Sonny. It's like the movies without DeNiro. Seriously, darling, how are you?"

"I've been better."

"Of course. You poor dear. Can I help?"

"I don't think so."

She looked at me like a sculptor with a block of marble, as if she were deciding where to start chipping away at the stone. "Still hate my guts?"

"I don't waste much time on you or your guts anymore, Bree."

"I come in peace," she said.

"I really don't care how you come. Or how many times you come."

"Touché," Bree said. "I deserve that, darling, but the Kevin Stone thing was years ago. Can't we get past it?"

"I'm sorry, is there a statute of limitations on screwing your best friend's fiancé?"

"No, but you know me, Julie. It really wasn't my fault. I'm an utter slave to my little man in the boat. It's like a disability. Don't you Americans have to make accommodations for people with disabilities?"

"I'm not sure the ADA covers sluts," I said.

"Well, it should. Imagine if I *hadn't* slept with Kevin and you wound up marrying the son of a bitch. He would still have been a horny horse cheating on you with nineteen-year-old interns. So you could say I was actually doing you a favor by sleeping with him." Before I could slap her for the second time in my life, she leaned across the desk and whispered, "Kidding, darling, kidding, kidding, kidding. You know I feel like a complete and total shit for what I did."

"You should."

"And I do, but the disability thing? Absolutely true. It tingles, and I must obey."

I laughed. You can't help but laugh at Bree. For as long as I've known her, she has been obscene, ruthless, shameless, and very funny. I've hated her for years, but I loved her for even more years.

We go way back. Back when my hair was short. Before we both became entertainment agents on opposite sides of the pond. I've slept in her bed more times than I can count. No, not in an "I Kissed a Girl and I Liked It" kind of way; we were best friends who bunked together whenever we were in the same city. Truly, Bree was my sister. I envied her for her utter confidence. She could waltz into a roomful of strangers and charm the pants off them. Literally. She was the ballsiest girl I had ever met. She used to RSVP herself to in-crowd parties when invitations came for her boss. She used to raid the slush piles for manuscripts when the top agents were out to lunch. She was arrested once for beating up a reporter who trashed one of her clients in the press, and the reporter wound up hiring her as his own agent. That's Bree.

She's right about Kevin, too. Marrying him would have been a disaster. That doesn't mean I wasn't ready to pluck out her eyes when I found out she'd been sleeping with him.

"Did you and Kevin hook up last night when you got into town?" I asked.

Kevin Stone is still an agent at McNally-Brown. He finally got married last year, but I doubted that monogamy was his style. If Bree called, he'd come running.

"No, no, no, fool me twice, shame on me," Bree insisted. "I have sworn off married men forever."

"You?"

"Forever! Or at least until I'm really, really horny. Shame, though. Kevin did have amazing stamina. I mean, after four hours, I would look at him and say, shouldn't we call a doctor or something? But he claimed it was all him, no drugs."

"Shut up, Bree."

"You're right. Me and my big mouth. Although most men like that." She slapped herself. "Ouch, there's a freebie for you. So what's up with you, darling? Are you seeing anyone?"

"No."

Bree sighed. "Look at you, you gorgeous thing. What a waste. What are you saving yourself for, Julie?"

"I'm experimenting with celibacy," I said. "Or rather, celibacy is experimenting with me."

"That's like putting the Mona Lisa behind glass."

"The Mona Lisa *is* behind glass," I said.

"Yes, but her smile would be bigger if she were on her back."

"I'm not like you, Bree. I don't jump into bed for the hell of it."

"Yes, yes, you have to be in a *relationship*. Why add complications to something simple like sex? Look, you were engaged to Thad Keller, and you told me the banging with him was roll-back-your-eyes-orbit-the-moon. As for Kevin, I *know* what it was like to sit on that nightstick. So do yourself a favor, darling, and get some."

"Do you really think I want sex advice from you?"

"Who better than me?" Bree asked. "What about your new office mate? Garrett? He's delicious, and you see him every day. I know you always had a thing for him."

I shot her the evil eye that said, *Quiet!* I got up and shut the door. It's a small office. It's easy to overhear.

"Ah, methinks I touched a nerve," Bree said. "You should go for it, darling. Dating a younger man is hip these days. Everyone's doing it."

"Can we move on?" I said. "I assume you didn't come here simply to talk about my love life."

"Okay, fine. Next topic. Are the rumors true about Gernestier? Are you letting Helmut take over West 57?"

Oh, great. Word about the possible take-over was already on the street. It wouldn't take long for news to spread. The publishing industry is populated by incorrigible gossips. I wondered if Helmut had leaked the offer to put pressure on me.

"Where did you hear that?" I asked.

"The two of you went to da Umberto, right? Vittorio likes me. He tells me everything."

"Well, keep it to yourself, okay?"

"My lips are sealed, darling."

Right. At least until someone sticks a tongue between them.

"Do you want my advice?" Bree went on.

"Like I want an STD."

Bree was unfazed. "Sell the business."

"Just like that?"

"Publishers are dinosaurs, darling. Sonny was the last T-Rex. We all need to reinvent ourselves."

"I love the book biz," I said, which was true.

"There is no book biz anymore. There are hardly books anymore, just bits and bytes on Kindles. We serve the great god Amazon."

"A book is a book."

"Sell," Bree repeated.

"And do what?"

"Work with me."

"With you?" I asked. "Are you kidding?"

"Not at all. I need a partner. We always made an amazing team."

"I don't think so, Bree."

"Well, suit yourself, darling, but you should think about it.

Anyway, if you won't join me, I'm sure your mother can hook you up in L.A., right? You'd look great on Venice Beach."

I'd heard that suggestion before, and when it comes to my mother, I don't believe in coincidences. "By any chance, has my mother talked to you about her plans for my career?" I asked.

"Well, of course, we talk every day. Didn't she tell you? Cherie is producing the film version of *Paperback Bitch*."

Stop. Pause. Rewind. Bree did not really say that, did she?

"*My mother is producing the movie of your freaking book?*" I asked.

It came out more like the sound made by a howler-monkey. I really did say "freaking," by the way.

"Yes, she loved it," Bree said. "She said it was the funniest damn thing she'd read in years."

"That book makes me look like some kind of deranged über-bitch."

"Oh, it's just a novel, Julia. Sorry, *Julie*." She gave me an evil cackle. "Oh, and nice use of *über*. You're already getting in touch with your inner German. Helmut will like that."

"Go away, Bree."

"We haven't talked about King."

"So talk. Make it quick."

"He's flying in tonight. We're both staying at the Gansevoort."

"Is he ready for Pierce Gorgon tomorrow?" I asked.

"Darling, no one is ready for Pierce. The man feasts on children like some kind of Hans Christian Anderson troll. Anyway, King isn't really a candidate for media training. I never know what's going to come out of his mouth until I hear it."

"Great."

"Whoopi wants him on *The View*, too. I love her, but I miss Barbara, don't you? Just as well, though. Babs probably would have brought her little dog on the set. King isn't good with dogs."

"I'm trying to get King on the Kelly Jax show, too, " I said, "but

Kelly isn't very happy with me right now."

Bree shrugged. "Relax. We're golden. The line at the bookstore will be out the door."

My habit is to think about all the things that can go wrong. It's a sickness. I remembered the reporter in the lobby and his insinuations about King and Sonny. "Do you know a *Post* reporter named Nick Duggan? I gather he was in London for a while."

"Diggin' Duggan?"

"That's him."

"Typical tabloid trash. The only thing he digs into is his nose. Why?"

"He's asking questions about King. I'm a little worried."

Bree shook her head. "Forget him. Nothing to worry about. Worrying is a symptom of someone who's not getting laid. You need to get out more. Come on, I've got the evening free. We can paint the town."

"You and me?"

"Sure, it'll be like the old days. We'll have fun. Get drunk. We can see a play together."

Uh oh. Did she say: *See a play?*

I said: "See a play?"

Bree grinned. "Right. See a play."

"Tonight?"

"Tonight."

"With you?"

"With me."

"Any suggestions?" I asked.

I was really hoping she'd say *Kinky Boots. Fun Home. The Book of Mormon. Mamma Mia!* Anything but what I knew she was going to say.

"I hear that adaptation of *Rear Window* is terrific," Bree replied with faux innocence.

She reached into the pocket of her leather jacket and slid out a Broadway ticket and waved it at me. It was a match for the free ticket on my desk. She was sitting next to me in the front row.

See? There's always a catch.

6

I had lunch that day with Libby Varnay, author of *Morningside Park*. Libby is an incorrigible gossip, and she was in fine form.

"Have you seen the new Woody Allen film?" she asked me, her eyes dancing wickedly. "It's about a sexually charged twenty-two-year-old girl who falls passionately in love with a short Jewish man in his seventies." She snickered and added, "I do love these May-December male fantasies, don't you? Think about all those fifty-something university professors who write novels. Have you noticed how their heroes are always fifty-something university professors? And invariably, the gorgeous blond undergrad falls passionately in love with them. I mean, honestly, has that happened even once in the history of the world?"

Libby sipped white wine. I had iced tea. She eyed me across the table, where we were seated near the conservatory windows at Tavern on the Green. She had no trouble reading my face. "I'm trying to cheer you up, Julie," she said. "Obviously, I'm doing a terrible job."

"No, no, it's not that."

Libby took my hand. "Never mind, I understand. Cry if you want. I did plenty of it myself when I heard the news."

I'm sure she did. I love Libby, and so did Sonny.

Libby is the very definition of how to age beautifully. She is around fifty years old, tall, pencil thin, caramel skin. Her nose is pinched, like Lena Horne's. Her short black hair sweeps across her forehead, every strand precisely in place. Her fingers are delicate, with cuticles like crescent moons. Normally, she wears an expensive necklace of gray pearls, with matching ring and earrings, but today she wore a high-necked white silk blouse, giving her the elegant neck of a swan. I doubt she even owns a pair of jeans or flat shoes.

You'd think, looking at her, that this vision of grace must have been born to money, but the opposite is true. She grew up dirt-poor north of 150th. Twenty years ago, while working as a day nurse in a facility for Alzheimer's patients, mostly indigent blacks, she wrote her one and only novel. *Morningside Park* was set inside a fictional version of that facility, where a young psychiatrist illegally uses experimental hallucinogens to unlock and document the visions of his patients. The book skipped across time and geography, evoking the worlds in which each patient lived. Those beautiful worlds stood in stark contrast to the unflinching horror of the facility itself, depicted as a house of such bleak torment that the disease becomes an escape. Like his patients, the psychiatrist begins to seek refuge in an alternate reality, taking the drugs himself, going on longer and longer respites from his daily life until, in the end, he cannot find his way back.

I remember reading the novel for the first time when I was eighteen. I sat on the rocks in a hidden crevice of Central Park on an August Sunday morning, intending to spend an hour with the book, because Sonny told me it was wonderful. Ten hours later, as darkness started to fall, I finally emerged from my hiding place, my face flooded with tears. I had never felt so devastated, so fragile, or so alive. I didn't go home. I walked north to Morningside Park, a stupid thing for a teenage girl alone, but I needed to stand outside the facility where Libby had worked and study its brick walls and broken windows, and feel its hopelessness, and try to see what she had seen there.

It was at that moment that I understood the power of a novel to change your life.

Fourteen publishers rejected *Morningside Park*. It was too frank. Too honest. Too extreme. They wanted nothing to do with it. Sonny was different. He read it and drove to the Washington Heights apartment that

Libby shared with her mother and four sisters and asked her in person for the honor of publishing her novel. They became best friends.

Some people write book after book; some have only one in their hearts. Libby birthed *Morningside Park* into the world and never finished another book. Not that she needed to. The book and the movie lifted her and her family out of poverty and into the exclusive wealth of the Upper East Side. She'd established a foundation in her will for combating Alzheimer's, so that her crusade would live on long after she was gone. So would the power of her novel.

That was exactly how publishing was supposed to work. Or at least, that was what I'd always believed.

"I have a gift for you," I told her.

Libby's eyebrows went up in a question mark. I handed her the first edition of *Morningside Park*, Sonny's copy from his desk. She handled it delicately, like china. She opened the book to the middle and saw the freshness of his notes, scrawled on the pages. Her eyes filled with tears.

"That man," she said with such deep affection I smiled.

Her emotion attracted attention. Outside the restaurant, in the rain, a middle-aged man in a wool suit stared at us. He had curly gray hair, flat on his head, and he looked too prosperous to be a typical gawker. However, he obviously recognized Libby. He stood there with his nose practically pressed against the glass and watched us for so long that it became uncomfortable. Finally, my cold stare drove him away.

I watched as Libby turned each page in her book as if it were brittle. I don't think she'd even been aware of the stranger outside. She was probably used to fans popping up everywhere.

"Sonny told me once he was prouder of your book than anything else he'd put in print," I said.

Libby smiled, and her teeth were ivory white. "Look at these notes. I wish he'd made those suggestions back then. I would have made more edits."

"No, you wouldn't," I teased her.

"No, I wouldn't, you're right." She closed the cover and

reminisced. "Sonny and I were both so stubborn. The battles we had over this book! Sentence by sentence until the early hours for months at a time. I was a pigheaded egomaniac, and I resisted every suggestion. Both of us were so damned sure we were right. I don't even remember how we resolved most of the disagreements. I won some, and he won some."

In my head, I expected Sonny to join us. I figured this was the perfect time for him to chime in, but he didn't. It was just the two of us. Libby felt some of my loneliness, and she looked around at the bustling restaurant and its elaborate chandeliers with dismay. "There are people whose loss simply leaves the world a grayer place," she said.

"I know."

"Thank you for this," she said, holding the book. "It means the world to me."

"He'd want you to have it."

"I'll treasure it, Julie. Really."

Libby gestured at a young black man at another table and waved him over to us. I knew him; he was Drew, Libby's nephew and chauffeur of the past three years. Like me, Libby didn't drive, so wherever she went, Drew went. She'd already lifted most of her immediate family out of poverty, and she was determined to do whatever she could for the next generation, too. It wasn't an easy struggle, even with money. Drew had been hooked up with gangs and drugs for most of his teen years before Libby dragged him off the street corners at Audubon Avenue and into her rarefied circle. I liked him. He was overweight and quiet, but he would do anything for Libby.

Libby handed Drew the copy of *Morningside Park*. "Keep this safe for me, will you, dear?"

"Of course, ma'am," he rumbled.

I smiled at Drew. He didn't smile back – he was too shy – but he dipped his head and shuffled back to his own table. It was one of Libby's traditions. Everywhere she ate, she booked a table for Drew, too.

"Do you need anything, Julie?" Libby asked me. "Is there anything I can do to help? You must have a lot weighing on you right now."

"I appreciate the offer, but no," I said. "It helps just to see you, Libby. I'm glad you called."

She put down her fork and knife. I realized she'd barely touched her goat cheese omelet. "I did want to talk to you about something else," she told me. "Business, actually."

"Of course."

"You know that Sonny and I talked about me doing another novel, don't you? Hard to believe after all these years."

"I know. I was thrilled when I found out. And surprised, too. First Harper Lee, now Libby Varnay."

"Sonny and I kept it quiet. I didn't want the weight of publicity. Everyone would be speculating about it."

"Sonny didn't say a word. I only found out when Garrett showed me the contract."

Libby's face betrayed her discomfort. "It felt like the right time of my life to say something new, but I've struggled. It's been months. The words aren't there."

"They'll come."

"That's what Sonny told me, but so far, I've been dry. Now, with him gone, without his inspiration, I simply don't know if I can do it. It was a mistake even to think about it."

"Take your time, Libby," I told her. "There's no pressure."

I hoped that was true. I didn't know how Gernestier would feel about an open contract with an author who showed no sign of delivering a manuscript. Even someone with the reputation of Libby Varnay. Sonny let his writers go for months, even years, on a long leash. For him, the book was the only thing that mattered, not the money. Helmut didn't share his patience.

Libby squeezed my hand. "Thank you, Julie. I appreciate your confidence. And your discretion."

"Of course."

She sighed as she relished the décor around us. Most New Yorkers are cynical about the Tavern, but Libby made no bones about loving its timelessness. She stroked the crystal with a slim finger. Her eyes lingered on the ceiling design, like a rose window in a medieval cathedral. "I've decided I need a change," she said. "That's the only way to get the book done."

"How so?"

"I'm leaving Manhattan."

I was shocked. "You? I can't imagine you anywhere else."

Libby shook her head. "No, no, it's true. I'm moving. I've finally realized it's the city that has been keeping me blocked all these years. I need something else. Someplace where the energy is different and the pace is slower. I'd also be lying if I didn't tell you that the city feels empty to me without your father."

"Where will you go?"

"Upstate. One of my sisters lives in Ithaca. She's not in the best of health. Drew will come with me, of course. I won't go anywhere without him."

"When?"

"Soon."

I thought about what she'd said. The loss of some people left the world a grayer place. It wasn't just by dying. It was by leaving, too. New York without Libby, New York without Sonny, was a different city than I'd known. I wondered if I could still feel at home here.

Maybe I needed a change, too.

"My mother wants me to move to L.A.," I blurted out.

Libby showed no surprise. "Cherie has wanted you there for years. She's nothing if not determined. Are you thinking about it?"

"I am. Maybe. I don't know."

Libby leaped to the obvious conclusion. "So you'd leave West 57 in someone else's hands?"

"I'm not sure what I'm going to do."

"Gernestier?" Libby asked.

I didn't say anything, but she could see the truth in my face. A faint, ironic smile creased her lips.

"I better start writing if the barbarians are taking over," she said.

"I told you to take your time."

"Don't worry about me, Julie. You have enough on your plate."

"The truth is, I'm torn," I said. "Sonny would hate the idea of my selling West 57."

"You have to do what's best for you," Libby told me. "Not what's best for Sonny, me, your mother, or anyone else." She added, "Having said that, I'll put my nose in where it doesn't belong. The book business needs people like you, more than the movie industry does. I'm old-fashioned. It's lovely that so many people have seen the movie of *Morningside Park*, but the book is all that matters to me. You are a child of the book world, Julie."

That was true. More than that, I was also a child of Sonny Chavan.

I was about to thank Libby for her support, but before I could say a word, her face grew alarmed. She looked over my shoulder and said: "Oh, dear."

"What?"

I heard shouting. I looked toward the restaurant entrance and saw a rain-damp man in a suit. It was the same man who'd stood outside the window, watching us. His arms waved in wild, angry gestures. He ran toward us, but I realized he wasn't coming for Libby. He wasn't shouting at her.

He was focused on *me*.

"You!" he bellowed. "You're the one!"

I watched him come and couldn't move. I was frozen with shock.

"How can you publish that filth? How can you profit off that son of a bitch? Do you know what he did to me? I lost everything! Everything! And now you're putting him on the cover of a book like he was some kind of *hero*. You heartless bitch!"

He added two more words, and he repeated them at me over and over again, louder and louder each time.

I think you can guess what they were.

The man became violent. He threw a butter knife, barely missing my face. It clattered against the conservatory glass. He was picking up a wine bottle to throw at me when Libby's nephew, Drew, hit him with his whole body like a fighting walrus and took him down. Drew kept him pinned under his girth. I saw park security running past the entrance, too, taking hold of the man, who wriggled in their grasp. As they dragged him away, he was still screaming at me.

"He stole my money! Where's my money? I have nothing!"

Then the same two words again. Definitely not "freak."

I felt an arm around me. It was Libby, asking if I was all right, but I found that my brain and my mouth were temporarily disconnected. The people at the restaurant were gracious, everyone wanting to make sure I wasn't hurt. Which I wasn't. Not physically. Even so, I was in shock. My hands quaked. I wanted to throw up.

I heard someone asking what it was all about. The buzz floated from table to table. Did I know him? Did I know who he was?

No, I didn't, but I knew perfectly well what it was all about.

This was about *Captain Absolute*. Irving Wolfe.

I was publishing a book about the devil.

7

I spent the afternoon re-reading King Royal's book.

I told myself not to feel guilty. Authors write biographies of thoroughly horrifying people all the time. So what makes Irving Wolfe special?

First, there's the voyeur factor. Reading King Royal's memoir is like sneaking a peek inside the diary of a Manhattan madam. Every other page, somebody rich and famous gets screwed. The feds have been tight-lipped about Wolfe's investors, and not many high-profile victims have held press conferences to admit they were bilked out of millions. So there's been a guessing game in the media for months. Who got fleeced? Who lost everything? As you read *Captain Absolute*, you keep wondering which of the celebrities traipsing through the book wound up with a goose egg on their balance sheets.

Second, it's not just that Wolfe was a crook. It's the flamboyance with which he ran his scheme. The ego. The cockiness. Most thieves try to run under the radar screen to avoid getting caught, but Wolfe bragged about his wild investment returns on CNBC, as if he were daring someone to catch him at his game. For two decades, no one did. No one ever asked how he could be making so much money for his investors, even when every other fund was underwater. Maybe nobody wanted the truth. All the while, Wolfe lived the high life in the public eye: the top floor condo on Park, the yacht on the Hudson, the limo with his corporate logo crawling along Broadway.

Third, he's dead.

As far as fame goes, it's much better to die young. We have short memories. Celebrities who linger into old age wind up with awkward-looking face lifts and one-sentence obituaries in *People* magazine in the "Wow, They're Dead!" section. No such obscurity for Irving Wolfe. With the feds tightening the noose, and rumors hitting the New York streets that Wolfe's billion-dollar investment portfolio was all a big lie, Wolfe took a final cruise on his yacht into the cold Atlantic waters, with no one else aboard except – you guessed it – King Royal.

And then?

Well, I'll let King describe it. Or rather, King's ghost writer.

Something awakened me at two in the morning. A swirl in the current, moving us side to side. A wave. Looking back now, I wonder if it was the sudden shift in the boat's weight, two hundred and ten pounds shoving off into the sea. I wonder if that was the moment when he did it.

The Captain's side of the bed was unmade. He had never joined me. I'd left him topside at midnight, alone with a bottle of Grgich 1981 Cabernet. He'd failed to offer me a glass, but that was typical of him. For a generous man, he could be selfish about his indulgences. I think, too, it was a way of putting me in my place, reminding me who I was.

I can't say it was unusual to wake up alone. He often stayed up all night. Even so, the sheer stillness of the boat felt different to me, and I knew he was gone. Call it the sixth sense of someone who has known abandonment and recognizes the feel of it and the smell of it. My lifeline had been severed. I was literally at sea. Drifting.

I got out of bed. I was nude. The Captain always insisted I sleep nude for his pleasure. I emerged onto the deck and felt like a god, bare-skinned and tumescent, illuminated by moonlight, the only soul within miles of glassy ocean.

Captain Absolute had fled. He was part of the ocean now. People call it a coward's end, but heroes choose their moment and method to die, and I think he chose well. There would be no pound of flesh for the angry mob. There would be no jail cell, shrinking him to something smaller than he was. In death, he would remain larger than life. An enigma, a legend.

King was right about one thing. With his dramatic suicide, Wolfe got the last laugh on his victims. You can't get justice from a dead man. You can't get answers. It's like a television series that ends on a cliffhanger and then gets cancelled over the summer. Nobody was happy about it.

His death prompted crazy rumors, too. People wondered where the money was. Had he really spent it all? Had he squirreled away millions in overseas bank accounts and island estates? Jewelry in safety deposit boxes? Nothing prompts a frenzy like a treasure hunt, and Wolfe's untimely demise triggered a gold rush behind him. So far, no one had located a dime. Not the feds. Not his bankrupt investors. Not Diggin' Duggan. It was all gone. That didn't stop people from speculating that there was a fortune to be found.

If you wanted clues, if you wanted closure, if you wanted to know *why*, you only had one person who could help you get at the truth. King Royal. Everybody wanted him, but Bree and I, we were the ones who had him, and we were ready to roll him out to the world. The only place left to find Irving Wolfe's secrets was in the pages of *Captain Absolute*.

Sonny had made a shrewd bet. This book was going to be huge. So why was I so uncomfortable with it?

"I always knew what I was doing, darling girl."

It was that familiar voice again. Haunting me. Sonny.

I looked up, and my father loomed over the desk, wearing the same dark suit he always wore in my odd fantasies. He breathed his usual cloud of smoke at me. I felt less lonely, having him back with me.

Sonny paced the office like a caged tiger, stroking the spines of the books he'd published. His hands gesticulated impatiently. "People may hate Irving Wolfe. People may hate King Royal. It's not our job to care about how people feel, Julie! It's about the story."

"The story is immoral," I said.

"Which is why no one can resist it."

"It's not *Morningside Park*, Sonny."

"Nothing will ever be *Morningside Park*."

"I'm just saying, there's nothing here to elevate the human experience. This is exploitation, pure and simple. It's making money off a tragic soap opera."

Sonny scowled. "I published books to sell them! You don't think I opened champagne every time we hit #1 in the *Times*? Of course I did. When did I ever say commercial was a bad thing, darling girl?"

"All the time," I reminded him.

"You're exaggerating."

"You said if we kept down this road, eventually the only thing anyone would publish is books by James Patterson."

I knew how to push Sonny's buttons. He froze, and I expected to see foam gather at the side of his mouth like a rabid dog. The very name made him crazy. "Patterson!" he hissed.

"He sells a lot of books. It's about the brand."

"The brand!" Sonny raged. "Yes, the brand! Let's give out a plastic toy with every Alex Cross book like some kind of freaking Happy Meal!"

No, he did not say "freaking."

Sonny skewered everybody, but popular authors got the brunt of his rants. It was all in good fun, but the writers on the receiving end didn't always appreciate his humor. I heard Stuart Woods took a swing at him once. Janet Evanovich sent him a case of rotting fish heads.

His beet-red face softened as he saw I was teasing him. "You are wicked, darling girl. You know how to rile me up."

"You never change, Sonny."

I wished that were true, but I thought: You do change. You're gone. You're only in my head, and soon enough, you won't even be there. Not like this.

He saw that my laughter was fading to grief, and he folded his arms over his chest, which was as big as a barrel you could ride over Niagara Falls. "I love seeing you behind that desk," he told me. "It's where I always wanted you to be, Julie. You belong there."

"No, you belong here, Sonny."

He had nothing to say to that. He went over to the office window and looked out at the city. It was dark outside. I'd been reading for hours. Manhattan was a carnival of electric light, except for the black rectangle of the Park.

"I used to worry about running out of stories," he mused. "Months would go by, and I wouldn't be excited by anything coming across my desk. I'd think, that's it. We're done. All the great novels have been written. Then I would stand here and think about the streets below this window. I'd think about Libby saying that all you had to do was scratch the surface with ordinary people, and you'd find tales of tragedy, triumph, grace, loss, cowardice, and heroism. You just had to find someone who knew how to write them down. It always seemed like the very next day, something crossed my desk that got me excited again. Something that made it all worthwhile."

"I understand," I told him, because I did.

He glanced down at me, that self-satisfied grin on his face. "That's why you're here in this office."

"I'm here because you did something stupid, Sonny. You died."

"Maybe that was my secret plan," he said. "How else could I get a stubborn girl like you into West 57?"

"You could have asked."

Sonny gave me a belly laugh. "Like my daughter would ever do what I asked!"

He had me there. It was true. The Chavans are all too stubborn to do what anyone tells them to do.

I closed the cover on *Captain Absolute*. Sonny watched me.

"So why did you do it, Sonny? Why did you pay King Royal all that money for this book?"

I waited, but he didn't answer me. That was because, in my head, I had no idea what he would say. Instead, he leaned over the desk and silently crushed out his cigarette in the Parisian ashtray. I was about to chide him, but when I looked down, I saw that the pretty ceramic dish with its painted image of the Moulin Rouge was empty. No ash. No cigarette. Nothing.

I was alone.

It was time to meet Bree.

8

"King's drunk," Bree said.

We were at a swank hotel bar on 47th. I'd never been here before. I've lived in New York my whole life, but Bree always seems to scout the hot places before I do. She is a whore for New York, as she put it so delicately in her own book.

"Already?" I asked.

Bree shrugged. "It was a long plane ride from Heathrow. Our boy was drinking mimosas by the pitcher for five hours. He started reciting *The Canterbury Tales* in middle English from memory, which is actually pretty impressive."

"Shouldn't we be babysitting him?"

"Relax, he's unconscious. I left him in his suite at the Gansevoort to sleep it off. He won't cause any trouble tonight."

We clinked our martini glasses and slurped down the remnants of our first cosmopolitans. I learned my lesson from *Xanadu* that most Broadway plays go down better if they're lubricated by several drinks before the curtain.

"Still hate me?" Bree asked.

"Yes."

She ordered a second round.

We were inside, but Bree wore sunglasses. I remember her telling me that celebs wear shades to avoid being recognized, so if you want people to think you're somebody, keep the sunglasses on. She had her smartphone on the table in front of her, and she was a slave to her text messages.

Me, I hate texting. I like talking to actual human beings.

The drinks arrived. Cold, frosty, pink. They went down smooth. Bree ordered appetizers, and I wondered if I was in a Telluride ski lodge. Hellfire wings. Bison sliders. Rocky Mountain Oysters. For a London girl, she had a redneck appetite. I told her I wasn't going to eat balls, and she grinned and murmured something about "spits or swallows."

Her phone rang.

"Oh, darling, how are you?" she answered. "Yes, I'm here with Julie, actually. We were just discussing the technical specifics of blow jobs."

"Who is that?" I asked.

"It's your mother."

Wonderful.

"Yes, I suspect it has been a while," Bree said into the phone, with a grin and a flick of her eyebrows at me. "No, no, I can't say the same, but this is me, after all. Well, of course, darling, we all like being on the other end."

At that moment, the waitress brought the Rocky Mountain Oysters. I did not want to swallow.

"Have you talked to Kate?" Bree asked Cherie. "Fabulous. Well, that would be perfect, don't you think?" She covered the phone and said to me, "What do you think of Kate Winslet playing me in the film version of *Paperback Bitch*?"

"The poor girl already went down on one sinking ship," I said.

Bree was immune to my insults. "Julie thinks it's a great idea, too," she said. "Do you want to talk to her?"

I was frantically waving my arms to say *No!* when Bree handed me the phone.

"Hello, mother," I said. "When were you planning to tell me that you're producing Bree's movie?"

Cherie's voice crackled through the line. "Did I forget to mention that, my dear?"

"You did."

"Oh, well, whatever. Have you read the book? It's a hoot. Very snarky. Perfect for Kate, she's a ballsy one."

"This is Bree, mother," I reminded her. "Remember? The horny bitch who broke up my engagement?" I covered the phone and said, "No offense."

"None taken," Bree said brightly.

"Oh, you have to get over it," Cherie lectured me. "Ancient history. You can't hold a grudge forever. People make mistakes. Bree's heart is in the right place, even if her vagina occasionally isn't. Besides, I never liked Kevin Stone."

"You weren't the one marrying him."

"Water under the bridge, my dear. I want you and Bree to be friends again. That's why I got the tickets for you."

"Excuse me? You bought the tickets?" I looked at Bree and said, "My mother bought the tickets?"

"Yes," they said simultaneously.

"Why?" I asked my mother. "What are you not telling me?"

"Oh, you are so suspicious." Cherie laughed, which only made me more suspicious. "Go, enjoy, take a night off for once in your life. See the show. Remember, I said you'd thank me!"

Ding ding ding. That was the sound of my warning bells going off.

"I have to run!" my mother went on cheerily. "Call me tomorrow, we'll have lots to talk about. Ta, my dear!"

I hung up the phone and handed it back to Bree.

"What is she not telling me?" I asked.

Bree ate a ball. "Truly, darling, I have no idea. All I know is that the tickets were waiting for me at my hotel when I checked in, with a note from Cherie saying I should corral you by the throat if necessary and drag you to the show. I don't say no to the woman who is producing my movie."

"This isn't just about you and me," I said.

"I wouldn't know, darling. Everything is about me."

"That's true."

"Still hate me?" Bree asked again, reaching for a hellfire wing and licking her fingers.

"More than ever."

She ordered another round.

By the time we left the hotel to walk to the theatre, I was drunk, and I did not hate Bree anymore. We declared a truce, at least for the evening. We clung to each other, laughing like lunatics as we dodged the crowds in Times Square. Her arm was around my shoulder. She smelled like smoke. She was dressed to kill in a glittery, shimmery dress up to her mid-thighs, and I wore the classic little black dress. We were both spilling over with cleavage and not walking a straight line in our heels. We got a lot of attention.

I don't get out to the theatre much. My mother is right that I don't have much of a social life. Sonny would usually pry me out of my apartment two or three times a year to see Shakespeare or something new by Kushner. I went to an off-Broadway show last September with Garrett. It wasn't a date. Not really. We went out to dinner after the show, and he had that look in his eyes that said he approved of what I was wearing, which wasn't much. Later, he walked me home, and I thought he might kiss me. He didn't.

That's my love life.

I felt Bree hanging on my shoulder. We'd gotten drunk together plenty of times in our twenties. Sometimes in New York, sometimes in London, sometimes in Frankfurt during the big book fair. We had big dreams. We talked about going out on our own, leaving our agencies, starting Cox & Chavan, or Chavan & Cox, teaming up on both sides of the Atlantic. Needless to say, her affair with Kevin Stone shelved those dreams permanently. It didn't matter. For me, a dream is a lovely thing, but reality is a big scary animal. Bree, on the other hand, had balls.

"So you finally did it," I murmured into her ear.

"Did what, darling?"

"Went out on your own. Started the agency."

"Yes, I did."

"I will deny saying this in the morning, but I'm proud of you, Bree Cox. I could never do what you did."

"Yes, you could. You're doing it right now."

"No, no, if it were up to me, I'd still be in my cubicle at McNally-Brown. I'd go home every night and swear that the next day I'd quit, but I never would. I can't make a decision. I can't choose. I can't commit. It's pathetic. If Sonny hadn't died, nothing would have changed."

"Darling, I was the same way. We hate our ruts, but after a while, we can't imagine living without them."

I shook my head. The cosmos were swimming between my ears. The drinks, I mean, not the universe at large. "Balls. You have them. Not me."

Bree held me up as I started to pitch forward. We were a block from the theatre, on 50th west of Broadway. I could see the ticket-holders lined up outside, waiting for the doors to open. It was a good thing, because I didn't think I could walk much farther.

"My own boss had to die before I thought about leaving the agency," Bree reminded me. "I'd probably be a bag lady in Hyde Park if Brad Pitt hadn't come through with a movie deal for some much-needed cash flow."

"I love him."

"Brad's a doll. He saved my arse, no doubt about that."

"Any regrets?" I asked.

"Yes, he never asked me out."

"No, no, regrets about going out on your own."

"God, yes, darling. It was terrifying. It still is. Not that I'd ever go back. I couldn't work for anyone else. Never again. Plus, when I make money, I keep it. That's a perk. I like seeing my name on the checks."

"I'm jealous," I said.

"Of me?"

"Of you."

If I hadn't been drunk, I would never have admitted it to her, but I'd been jealous of Bree Cox ever since I met her. She made everything look so easy.

Bree laughed, as if I'd said something very funny. "That's a riot, darling."

I thought she was laughing at me, and I was annoyed. You don't bare your soul and expect your best friend to laugh. Did I just call her my best friend? That should tell you that I don't have many friends. Anyway, Bree saw me stamp my feet like an angry bull, and she leaned in with her hands on my shoulders until we were almost forehead to forehead. "It's a riot, darling, because I've been jealous of *you* my whole life."

"You're kidding."

"It's true."

"Why?"

"Oh, get a clue, Julie. You are the most gorgeous woman I know. You have that annoying hourglass figure and you weigh three pounds. You are smarter than me, you're more decent than me, you're way more loyal than me, and you're as deep as an ocean whereas I revel in being as shallow as a stream. Does that sum it up for you, darling?"

I said, "Oh."

"Yes, oh."

"That's about the sweetest thing anyone has said to me."

Bree shrugged. "I know, it's hard to believe it came out of my mouth, isn't it?"

I didn't know what to do, so I hugged her. I didn't want to cry and ruin my makeup, but my eyes felt watery. I began to think our truce would last longer than a night.

We reached the end of the theatre line, where impatient ticket-holders stretched half a block from the box office. The marquee listed REAR WINDOW in large letters. I thought about the movie: Hitchcock, Stewart, Kelly, even Raymond Burr as a bad egg before he became Perry

Mason. Good movie, but as a New Yorker, I get creeped out by the voyeurism theme. When you live in an apartment like I do, you figure someone is always watching you from behind binoculars. It's usually not Jimmy Stewart.

The line started to move.

"Thank God," Bree said. "I really, really need to pee."

"Did you see the show in London?" I asked.

"I did. Emily Blunt was amazing in the Grace Kelly role. But I'm a sucker for January Jones. So who's in the Jimmy Stewart role tonight? I heard they brought in someone while Bradley Cooper recuperates."

"I don't know."

We reached the theatre as the line crept closer to the door. They had oversized photos of the actors on the wall. Yes, the play had a guest actor in the lead role for a limited engagement. One month only. Final days. How had I missed it? But then, I'd been busy for the past month.

I recognized his face. It was a face I knew all too well.

"Oh, balls," I said.

"What is it?" Bree asked, but then she saw it, too. "Oh, balls!"

There are no coincidences. This was all about my mother. She'd planned the whole thing. She is an evil genius.

I've asked an old friend to look you up.

I don't want to spoil the surprise. You'll thank me!

No, I won't, Mother.

I've been engaged to two men in my life. One was Kevin Stone, and you know how that one ended. The other was an actor named Thad Keller. This was in my acting days, back when I thought I was destined to be a star. I didn't make it.

Thad did.

He made it all the way to Broadway.

9

Thad Keller.

I met him the way actors meet other actors, on the set. You will hear actors boast about fourteen-hour filming days, but the reality is that most of that time is spent waiting to be called to the set for a few minutes with the camera going. Otherwise, you sit in makeup and costume, getting into trouble. Some actors memorize their lines, but for those of us playing "Nurse With Long Hair" (do you see a trend in my credits?), memorizing a single spoken line doesn't require a lot of time.

"Anything you say, Doctor."

Got it.

Back in those days, Thad and I were both struggling. I was in my early twenties; so was he. We'd snagged guest starring roles on *ER*, although I was more an extra than a guest star, and the camera spent more time on my backside than on my face. Thad had a real part, as a medical student paying off his debts as a male prostitute. Trust me, there were plenty of women who would have paid to be with Thad.

If I'd slept with him that day on the set at County General, that would have been the end of our relationship. He was used to trailer courtships, one day, one actress. In the sexual credits in his autobiography, I would have been "Indian Extra with Long Hair." Not that I didn't think about it. If Thad is anything, he is charismatic, like a young Nick Nolte, with wavy blond hair, chiseled jaw, blue eyes that have their own magnetic pole. He was as tall and physically imposing as my father. His personality was also as intense and controlling as my father's. For more self-aware people, this might have been a warning sign about disaster ahead. Not for me. Not back then.

That first day, we talked about politics. His are liberal, like most actors; mine are inscrutable. We talked about the Los Angeles weather. It's great; that was a short conversation. We talked about our dreams, which must be page one of the seduction playbook for men. "If a woman tells you her dreams, she's half-way to bed." We flirted over sushi. He put a hand on my ass; I slapped it away. A couple hours later, the hand came back, and I left it there. We kissed, wet, lots of tongue, but that was as far as it went. Maybe, if we'd had twenty minutes more, my resistance would have crumbled, but instead, I got called to the set to run my line opposite some actor named George Clooney.

"Anything you say, Doctor."

Cut. Print. That was my day. I didn't see Thad again when I was done, and I figured I never would.

I was wrong. Thad wasn't accustomed to wanting something he couldn't have, and I was the one that got away. Truth be told, we had chemistry, and we both felt it. He called me. He took me to dinner at a crab shack on the coast. He probably figured it was erotically barbaric, cracking shells on butcher paper beside the ocean. I'd suck crawfish heads, and then I'd – well, you know where I'm going with this. I didn't. I thought about it, but I didn't. I knew who Thad was and what he wanted. If he didn't want something more with me, he wasn't going to get anything.

Not immediately, anyway. Three dates later, when my own juices were dripping like butter off a lobster claw, I gave in. I'd had sex before, but this was *sex*. "Hang on, my hands are getting carpet burns" sex. "There's a light switch on the wall that's digging into my butt" sex. I learned a new word, namely "orgasm," and I mastered it through repetition. I prayed to God, usually preceded by "Oh, my."

The physical heat between us was fierce, but we all know what we learn about heat as children. Don't get too close, or you'll get burned. We were definitely in a relationship, but the best word to describe that relationship was "tumultuous." We couldn't stay away from each other, but we had trouble being together, at least when we weren't naked. If that sounds a lot like Sonny and Cherie, well, the apple doesn't fall far from the tree. I loved him. I really did. I think he loved me, too, as much as a narcissist can love another human being. He had a Bigfoot-sized ego, but I couldn't blame him for it. Thad was going places. No doubt about it. The easy thing to do would have been to hitch my wagon to his star. For a year, I did.

He asked me to marry him, and I said yes. My mother was thrilled. My father, not so much. When it comes to egotists, it takes one to know one. I'm sure Thad cheated on me constantly, not that I knew about it at the time. You can put on blinders about such things. Hey, I didn't think Kevin was cheating on me, either, until Bree proved me wrong.

Speaking of Bree, she was with me on and off through the whole Thad affair, too, visiting me in Los Angeles. Foolish me, I never asked whether she slept with him. In retrospect, I wonder, but I'd rather not know. She'd probably be honest and say yes, and I'd have to hate her all over again. Back then, she was my rock, watching me career through emotional highs and lows. Thad and I were as hot and cold as a Katy Perry song, breaking up, making up, unable to stay, unable to go. I felt consumed by him. In bed, that was good. Out of bed, he was slowly devouring my identity, re-molding me like a plastic surgeon. If I married him, I realized I would forever lose who I was. Finally, the only thing I could do was cut him out of my life like I was going into rehab. Step one: You are powerless to resist.

I had to travel a long way to escape him. I went back to New York and stayed. Not long after, I gave up my acting career, too. My mother was unhappy with me. She thought I'd given up love and money, and I never could get her to understand that I'd done exactly what she'd done with Sonny. I'd chosen to find my own way.

Don't worry about Thad. He prospered. I knew he would. He landed a supporting role in a brainy thriller that spawned two nine-figure sequels. He's rich. He can pick and choose his roles. I've kept an eye on him over the years, which a therapist would probably tell me is unwise. He flits in and out of the Star Tracks photos in *People* with various bikini-clad models. He married once, a Hollywood marriage that hit the rocks after a year. I thought: That would have been us.

It's funny. You'd think I would have learned something from the experience, but a few years later, I made the same mistakes all over again with Kevin. They could have been brothers, and I almost married him, too. Bree is right. Maybe I should thank her, because left to my own devices, I'm a fool when it comes to men.

Here I was a few more years later, and nothing had changed. I was still a fool. I was going to see Thad again, and I was already forgetting lesson one.

You are powerless to resist him.

Bree and I sat in our front row seats as we waited for the curtain.

I was holding a small note card in my hand. An usher gave it to me in an envelope as we sat down. I knew Thad was going to contact me – that was the point of this whole game – but I wasn't expecting it to happen so quickly. I figured, intermission. Or maybe after the bows. No, Thad was never one to wait.

I read his message for the fiftieth time in five minutes:

I would love to see you again, Julie. Have a drink with me after the show.

Bree sipped her cocktail. She fingered the program and didn't look at me as I obsessed over my note. "So, Thad," she said.

"Thad."

"*Quel surprise.*"

"Yes." Then I said: "Was it really a *surprise*, Bree? Or did Cherie tell you?"

"I had no idea. None. Truly, darling, I didn't know. This was all your mother."

I believed her. This conspiracy had Cherie's fingerprints on it. Even so, Bree looked uncomfortable, like a mouse in a house with seven cats. Maybe it was just the alcohol, or maybe it was something more. I know I said I didn't want to know, but I was drunk, so what the hell.

"Did you sleep with him?" I asked.

"Who?"

"Thad."

"*What?*"

"Back then. When he and I were engaged. Did you sleep with him?"

"Of course not."

"No? What about your sexual disability? You were just as horny in those days."

Bree put her hand over her heart. "Darling, I swear to you, the only fiancé of yours that I ever screwed was Kevin."

I'm sure the people behind us were enjoying our conversation.

"Did he try?" I asked.

"What do you mean?"

"Did Thad try to seduce you?"

Her face reddened to match the highlights in her hair. "Oh. Well. Sort of."

"Sort of?"

"It's ancient history, darling."

"What did he do?"

"He sort of felt me up under the table at dinner one time."

"Where was I?"

"Um, on the other side of the table, as I recall."

"And you never told me?" I fumed.

"We were all drunk that night. When you went to the loo, I told him to get his hands off my knickers. He did. That was that. I figured, one mistake, darling. End of story."

"I'm surprised Thad gave up so easily."

"Well, he did."

"I'm also surprised you had the willpower to push him away. That's not like you."

"Well, that's what I did," Bree repeated. "As soon as you went to the loo, I pushed his hands away. Yes, I did. As soon as you went to the loo, I stopped him cold."

Hmm.

I know Bree. I've known her for years. I know when she's not telling me everything. She's a gifted liar with everyone else and a terrible liar with me. She swells up like an overblown birthday balloon, ready to pop. I just waited, and she felt me sitting there, waiting. She didn't look at me. She knew what I wanted.

"Bree?" I said expectantly.

Pop.

She leaned into me and said in a drunken whisper at an extremely fast pace, "Look, darling, in the spirit of complete candor, and at the risk of spoiling our newfound rapprochement..."

She stopped. I waited again.

I think Bree was hoping someone would yell "Fire," and we would have to evacuate the theatre. No one did. Finally, she gave in.

"...it would have been better if you'd gone to the loo a little sooner that night."

10

I didn't really blame Bree. That's like blaming a puppy for peeing the carpet. It's what puppies do. You can swat their fannies, but they'll still do it again when you're not looking, and in Bree's case, she'd probably enjoy the spanking. If anything, I was glad to know that my suspicions about Thad in those days were correct, because it stiffened my resolve to resist him.

That lasted until the curtain went up, and there he was.

Oh, balls.

He was no more than twenty feet away from me. In *Rear Window*, he is a photographer in a wheelchair, recovering from an injury, and his character is charming and street-smart. It's less a mystery than it is a stage for beautiful people to trade flirty, witty remarks. I had to admit, Thad was well cast. He doesn't need to stand up to be sexy.

He hadn't changed at all. Actors always seem untouched by time, because they have makeup and plastic surgery to wipe away the wrinkles, hair color to erase any gray, private chefs to watch their calories, and fifty-two weeks of Los Angeles heat and sunshine in which to tone their bodies. Physically, Thad could have been twenty-five. It was in his attitude that I could see his new-found maturity. That's where the rough edges get smoothed. He carried himself like a man comfortable in his own skin, empowered by his success. He was even more attractive now than he was when we were engaged.

Damn.

I've been on stage before. I knew he could see me in the front row, regardless of the bright lights. He never acknowledged me directly. When his eyes passed across the fourth wall, they never paused as they met mine. Even so, he saw me, and I felt his stare. I could tell in his face. Oh yes, he saw me. It had an uncomfortably arousing effect between my legs.

Bree grinned at me. She knew.

The play felt long. I think it was ten or twelve hours before the final curtain. At least that's how it felt as I stared at Thad, because he was on stage essentially every minute of the show. He was terrific. So was JJ. I actually felt jealous of their chemistry. It wasn't a good thing. I shouldn't have cared.

When they took their bows, he finally made eye contact. One wink.

Swoon.

The house lights went up, and everyone gathered up their coats. I was a little wobbly on my feet. I debated whether to stay. I was under no obligation to say yes to his invitation, but I knew I would. Yes, I wanted to see him again, because I am The World's Most Stupid Human Being.

"You okay?" Bree asked me.

"Not really."

"Still hate me?"

"Yes," I said, "but no more than I did before."

"Good. I'm sorry." She added unnecessarily, "You know, about the whole diddling thing."

"I get it."

"Maybe I really am a slut."

"No arguments here, Bree."

"I'm going back to the Gansevoort to check on King," she said, "unless you need a chaperone back stage."

"I'll be fine," I said.

She air-kissed me rather than leave lipstick on my cheek.

I waited until most of the audience had left before I worked up the courage to go back stage. Maybe I wanted him to wait. I didn't want to look over-eager. Security was obviously expecting me, because they waved me through with a leering smile. Some of the cast were still in costume in the hallway as I threaded my way to the dressing rooms. I bumped into January. She was still dressed like a vision from the 1950s, looking amazing even in helmet hair, which was also true in *Mad Men*.

"Great show," I told her.

She smiled. "Thanks."

"You did Grace Kelly justice," I said. It was about the highest praise I could offer, and I think she appreciated it.

"That's sweet." She saw that I was aiming for Thad's door and made a quick perusal of me. "Are you Julie?"

"I am."

"Thad mentioned he was seeing an old girlfriend tonight."

Old?

"We were actors together," I said.

"Oh, you were an actress?"

"There's some debate about that."

She laughed.

I smiled at her as I knocked on Thad's door. Part of me wanted to run, but everyone was looking at me. From inside, I heard his voice. I'd been listening to it all evening on stage, but it still made my heart thump. I slipped inside, closed the door behind me, and leaned against it. I was breathing hard.

"Julie," he said.

He'd showered and changed already. He crossed the room in two long strides and gathered me up in his arms. He planted a soft kiss on my lips. Instantly, I was twenty-three years old again. That's not a bad feeling.

"Look at you," he said. "More beautiful than ever."

I caught my breath. "You're looking pretty good yourself, Thad," I said, but he already knew that.

"I'm so glad you came."

"Thank my mother."

"I know, I'm sorry," he said. "You must feel like the victim of a conspiracy. I wasn't sure if you'd see me if I just called out of the blue."

"Probably not. I didn't even know you were in the city."

"Not for long. Only for a few more days. My run's done soon."

"Well, here I am," I said. "What now?"

"Let me take you for dessert and a bottle of wine."

He saw me hesitate.

"I know a little place in the Village," he went on. "It's private. We can talk."

This was more than a drink. This was more than half an hour reminiscing about old times. We were in the present, not the past. I wondered about his agenda and Cherie's. In the end, however, I wasn't going to say no. Sometimes you have to return to old intersections and find out if you turned the right way. If you want to get to the next chapter, you have to turn the page.

"Okay, I'd like that."

"There will probably be paparazzi as we leave. I just want to warn you. Are you okay with that?"

I smiled like a star and brushed my hair from my face. "Oh, they're after me all the time."

Thad was right. There were flash bulbs as we left, but the taxi lost the popzees by the time we reached the little trattoria off Bleecker. He'd called ahead. The Italian owner, florid-faced and barely taller than me, met us in the alley and kissed us on both cheeks. He smelled of garlic. He took us through the kitchen to a secluded room separated from the main restaurant. It was actually the wine cellar, and the walls were lined with dusty bottles of Chianti and prosecco. A single table waited for us, lit by a tall candle, with an open bottle of wine already breathing, and two servings of tiramisu on square china plates.

Nice.

The owner pulled out my chair and placed my napkin carefully in my lap. Music played on hidden speakers; it was Tullio Pizzorno's

Conosco L'Assassina. I'd discovered him on a trip to Italy four years earlier, and I don't know how Thad knew that I'd become a huge fan. Then I realized: My mother again.

This was definitely a conspiracy.

The owner poured wine and left us alone. Just me, Thad, and Tullio crooning over our heads.

"I was so sorry to hear about Sonny," Thad told me.

"Thanks."

"I lost my own father two years ago. I know what you're going through."

"Does the grief go away?"

"No, you just learn to live with it." He reached for my hand and caressed my fingers. I remembered how strong and warm his grip was. "Sonny never liked me much, did he?"

"No, he didn't."

Thad grinned, taking no offense. He knew most people liked him now, and he didn't really need to care about those who didn't. "Sonny was right about me back then. So were you."

"Seems to me I liked you," I said. I added in the silence that followed: "I loved you."

"I loved you, too, Julie. I just meant you were right to break up with me the way you did. I deserved to lose you. I was callow and controlling. My ego ran my life."

"Well, there's nothing like becoming rich and famous to deflate your ego, Thad. Pulling in a few million per pic. Ducking the popzees. Starring on Broadway opposite January Jones."

Thad studied my face the way a painter would, trying to unlock its secrets. I heard the silent message; he wanted me. Or at least, that's what he wanted me to think. It was seductive, seeing those eyes focused on me, not letting go.

"Believe it or not, I've learned a few things over the years," Thad said. "I've matured. It took a bad marriage and some bad relationships to teach me what was real and what wasn't. That's not always easy in

Hollywood." He added, "Looking back, what we had was real. It simply wasn't the right time for either of us."

Yes, what we had was so real you groped my best friend under the table in front of me. Okay, I chose not to remind him of that story. Reality is overrated.

I took a bite of the black-bottom tiramisu. It was divine. Tiramisu is my favorite dessert, a fact that Cherie most certainly shared with Thad. There are no accidents in my mother's world.

The wine was superb, too. Thad always had good taste in everything.

"You've done well, Thad."

"I've had some lucky breaks."

"You don't need to be modest. You're a great actor. Audiences love you. You could feel it in the theatre tonight."

"Plenty of great actors work at Wal-Mart and eat Chef Boyardee for dinner. I'm fortunate to do what I do and get paid for it."

I didn't know if he was sincere, or if he was simply acting again, for my benefit. He was right, though. Talent and success only graze each other in Los Angeles. Otherwise, it's luck and connections.

"Tell me about *your* life, Julie," he said.

He was definitely on his best behavior, talking about me, not talking about himself. Or maybe he assumed I knew all about his life from reading about it in the weekly magazines. Which was true.

"Didn't my mother tell you about it?" I said.

"I think I'm likely to get a different story from you than from her. You know how mothers are. Mine still says I should get a real job."

"So does mine."

"I wasn't actually thinking about jobs," he said. "You never got married?"

"No." My fiancés kept cheating on me.

"Are you serious with anyone?"

"No."

"Neither am I."

"Didn't I see a photograph of you in St. Maarten with one of those *Sports Illustrated* swimsuit models?"

"Body paint, actually."

Right. Now that's a real job, standing there naked while someone paints your privates. Sign me up.

"She's cute," I said.

"Cute. Fun. That's all it is."

"All?" My skepticism was obvious, but Thad wasn't offended.

"I didn't say I was celibate," he assured me, "just that I'm not serious with anyone. I assume you're not celibate either."

Actually, yes.

"Of course not," I said. I wondered where he was going with this, so I asked, "Where are you going with this?"

He took a sip of wine, savoring the mouthful. Studying his mouth, all chiseled with sharp angles, made me think about kissing him. Not a good thing. "Here we are unattached after all these years," he said. "Maybe our timing is finally better."

"It's not. What do you want, a one-night stand? Are you feeling nostalgic?"

"I know you better than that, Julie."

"Then what?"

"I'd like to get to know you again. Who knows where it would lead?"

"I'm not in the market for romance. I've got too much on my plate right now."

"Yes, I know. Sonny. West 57. You must feel like you're wrestling with your whole life."

"Exactly."

"I'm sorry to add another complication."

"There's no complication. We're having dessert. That's all."

Thad put down his wine glass and stood up. I held my breath as he drew closer and knelt beside me. One strand of my hair had fallen wrong on my cheek, and he set it right. His fingers lingered on my skin. "I wasn't sure what I'd feel when I saw you again," he said.

"And?"

"It's like finding a favorite ring I lost years ago."

Damn, he's good. It was a fight not to give in to what I was feeling, which was to start unbuttoning his shirt.

"Why now, Thad?"

"What do you mean?"

"You've had years to look me up. You're in and out of New York all the time. Why now?"

"You said it yourself. You're re-evaluating your whole life. We only get so many windows of opportunity."

"Our window closed a long time ago."

"Maybe it did, but you can't tell me you feel nothing."

"I never said I felt nothing, but I meant it when I said I wasn't looking for romance right now."

"Actually, neither was I, but now I'm not so sure."

"What does that mean?" I asked.

"It means that your mother suggested I talk to you tonight," Thad said, which is not one of those lines that enhances the romantic mood.

"Naturally."

"Not about us getting back together. She wasn't thinking about that at all."

"Apparently you don't know my mother."

"I do. I know her very well."

Uh oh.

"Cherie and I are partners in a new production company," Thad went on.

"Excuse me?"

"We started it six months ago."

Funny how my mother never mentioned it, I thought.

"Funny how my mother never mentioned it," I said.

"Are you surprised?" Thad asked, smiling.

"No."

"We need someone in L.A. helping us find and develop the right properties. We need your eye for the book and movie worlds."

I stared at him. "This is a *job* offer?"

"I know Cherie already talked to you about moving west and working with her. She wants you leading our new project."

"That's what this is all about?" I said. "That's what you want?"

Thad shook his head. "Not just that. Not anymore. That was before I saw you."

I pushed my chair back. I put my napkin on the table. I headed for the door. "I have to go."

"Julie, wait."

He stopped me and trapped me against the wall. Wine bottles poked my back like a body massager. If he was any closer to me, we would already have been having sex. "Let me go," I said.

"Please. Listen. I meant what I said about getting to know you again. I also meant what I said about us making a good team. If you don't feel anything, if you don't think there's something worth exploring between us, personally or professionally, then just say so. That'll be the end of it."

"There's nothing worth exploring between us, personally or professionally," I said.

No, I didn't say that.

I had every intention of saying it, but I didn't. Instead, I pulled him to me across the two inches separating our faces, and I kissed him. I wasn't twenty-three, and neither was he, but it was better than any kiss back then. His body paint model never kissed him like that, no matter what else they did together.

The kiss was so electric that I actually started vibrating. That's what I thought, anyway, but it was really my cell phone. Still breathing hard, I checked the caller ID and saw that it was Bree.

Balls!

"Am I interrupting something?" she asked me.

"Yes."

"Are you naked?"

"Not yet."

"Shame."

"What do you want, Bree?"

"Well, I really hate to kill the mood, darling, but I'm afraid we have a problem."

11

The problem was King Royal.

Bree and I rode the elevator at the Gansevoort to the rooftop bar. We were squeezed inside limb to limb with club-hoppers who were young and mostly naked. At least that's how it looked to me. I felt over-dressed in my shorty dress. I was pretty sure half the couples were having sex in the elevator. The woman who was squeezed against my butt might have been having sex with me.

"So how far did it go?" Bree asked.

"What?"

"With TK."

"Do we have to discuss this here?" I asked.

Bree shrugged and called out, "Does anyone here want to know if my friend had sex tonight?"

There was a general grumble of disinterest. Someone muttered, "Who hasn't?"

Bree smirked at me. "How long has it been, by the way?"

"Is Bush still president?"

"Funny."

"We kissed," I said. "That's all."

"You slut."

"Then you called."

"Sorry. No time for a quickie before you caught a cab?"

I glared at her. Behind me, I felt a hand on my thigh. "Please remove that," I said loudly.

The hand disappeared.

"We're having dinner the day after tomorrow," I said.

"Do you need condoms? I have a variety pack in my purse."

"It's just dinner."

"Of course, darling."

"He's a spy from the House of My Mother," I said.

"How so?"

"He and Cherie have formed a production company. They want me to join them on the coast."

"Lucky you."

"I guess."

Maybe it *was* lucky me. Maybe I was a fool not to jump at it. Maybe I didn't even know why I was hesitating. It didn't mean I was going to jump into bed with Thad, and even if I did, it didn't mean we were re-kindling a relationship. Change doesn't have to be bad, right? Just different.

The elevator doors finally opened at the roof. When I got out, I heard singing.

"That's King," Bree said.

I threaded through the beautiful people drinking multi-colored cocktails in trendy glasses. The doors to the outside loft were open. It was a cold night, but there was a lot of body heat to keep everybody warm. The views of the city and the Hudson were to die for. No one had time for the view, though. They were all watching King Royal serenade the crowd.

It was quite a show.

I met a lass named Assy McHattie
And I asked her how she got her name

She twinkled at me
You'll see, you'll see
But that was as close as she came

I courted a lass named Assy McHattie
And I asked her how she got her name

On our nuptial day
I'll say, I'll say
But that was as close as she came

I married a lass named Assy McHattie
And I asked her how she got her name

Put dicky right here
In my rear, in my rear
And shortly thereafter she came

"Oh, my God!" I said. For good measure, I said it again, even louder: "OH, MY GOD!"

"Well, he has a nice voice," Bree said.

This was a disaster. People had their cell phones out, getting the whole thing on video. I'm sure it was up on YouTube and Facebook by now. It would be tweeted and re-tweeted like a Susan Boyle song, going viral all over the world. By morning, you would Google King Royal's name and get a link to Assy McHattie instead of *Captain Absolute*.

"We have to get him out of here," I said.

"Good luck. I tried."

King stood on a bench by the very edge of the roof. He was tall enough that two-thirds of his body swayed awkwardly above the railing, and he was drunk and skinny enough that I was worried he might blow away in the cross-breeze. His white silk dress shirt was unbuttoned, exposing a long length of flat chest. The sleeves were rolled past his elbows, and a white flap peeked through his undone zipper. A paisley cravat billowed at his neck like a wind sock. He wore pleated trousers that were a size too big and looked like clown pants. His feet were bare. I saw two forlorn dress shoes on the patio floor.

He had thick brown hair styled in tight girlish ringlets. His facial features were soft, no hard lines, no bones. He had a prominent nose and waifish, vulnerable eyes, with brows arched in a permanent look of wonder. His skin was creamy, and I would have sworn he was wearing rouge and lipstick, but I think it was just the cast of his complexion. I understood why his Soho cronies called him Lord Byron. He was probably the most feminine man I had ever seen.

Bree and I pushed our way through the crowd to stand at his feet.

"King!" I called to him, holding out my hand. "I'm Julie Chavan. Why don't you come on down from there?"

"Julie Chavan!" he shouted. "Huzzah!"

"King, please."

"You are the daughter of the great Sonnymonias, and I am the King of Kings. Look on my works, ye mighty, and despair!"

"That's Shelley's Ozymandias," Bree said mildly. "You have to give him credit, he knows his stuff."

"Do I look like I want a lecture on poetry right now?" I snapped.

"Sorry," Bree said.

"Huzzah!" King repeated. He gestured at a scuzzy twenty-something who was holding a bottle of Corona. "Oy, toss me my beer, mate."

The guy threw it end over end. Beer sprayed. King grabbed for the bottle and missed it and nearly went over the edge himself. The bottle headed down thirteen stories for Ninth Avenue. I was really hoping no one was on the sidewalk below. "West 57 Author Kills Pedestrian" was not the headline I needed this week.

"O the bleeding drops of red," King recited, switching to Walt Whitman, "where on the deck my Captain lies, Fallen cold and dead! O Captain! My Captain!"

"You have to admit, he's entertaining," Bree said.

"No, he's not," I said.

"EVERYONE!" King bellowed. "O Captain! My Captain!"

King waited, but no one shouted back at him. They were too amused by the show. He shrugged and spread his arms wide and announced:

"I once screwed a girl named Rhonda
Her hair it was ever so blonde-a
I sucked on her teat
I nibbled her feet
And all in the back of my Honda!"

That was it. I'd had enough.

I yanked on King's belt buckle. He came tumbling toward us like a missile, but I grabbed one arm, and Bree grabbed the other, and we prevented him from going face-first onto the floor of the patio. He was dead weight, and we couldn't hold him for long, so we eased him down, where his nose broke the fall.

"Up, King," I said.

He rolled over on his back. He stared wide-eyed at the night sky. At least he was conscious. "I wandered lonely as a cloud," he recited, "that floats on high o'er vales and hills."

"No more poetry!"

He put a finger over his lips. "Huzzah!" he whispered.

"Let's get him to his room," I said to Bree.

"How? Do you have a winch?"

I gestured at two strapping young men, identical twins, who were drinking chocotinis and were exceptionally well dressed. Is everyone in this city gay except me? I'm sure it's different out in Los Angeles. Ha ha ha.

"Hey, guys, can you give us a hand with Liberace here?"

"Who?" they said.

"Never mind, just help us get him downstairs, okay?"

They shrugged and squatted on either side of King. They popped him up like a Jack-in-the-box, and he looked bewildered to be standing again. The two boys (men, boys, it's a gray area in your early twenties) draped King's arms over their shoulders and hung on to his waist. I think they copped feels on his backside, but I didn't care. I grabbed his shoes. The five of us maneuvered him back to the elevator, which was empty going down. We only needed to go two floors. King was in a corner suite.

He sang more ribald ditties with lyrics that rhymed with words like "pucker" and "blockhead" as he was half-walked, half-dragged down the hotel corridor. Bree and I led the way.

"What do all these rich guys see in him?" I asked Bree. "Couldn't Irving Wolfe do better than King Royal?"

"It's a mystery, darling," Bree agreed.

We reached his door. I wasn't about to fish around in his pocket for his key, but one of the gay twins did that for me without being asked. He obviously found more than the key, because King perked up and said, "Nightcap, boys?"

"No nightcaps," I said.

I gave them each twenty bucks and sent them back to the party upstairs. Bree let King slump on her shoulder, and I opened the door. His suite was larger than my apartment. King squared his shoulders and attempted to walk, and as he did, he peeled off clothes. Shirt. Pants. Bikini briefs. Everything. We got the full rear view. His skin was white enough that his ass had no tan line. Naked except for his cravat, he disappeared through the double-wide doorway into the bedroom, and we heard him throwing up in the toilet. At least I hoped it was the toilet.

Bree collapsed on the sofa. "Wow," she said.

"Pierce Gorgon is going to grind him up tomorrow night," I said. "King is going to look like he went through a wood chipper."

"You can't embarrass the shameless, darling. I'm a perfect example."

"We're putting this guy on national television."

"I've seen King on BBC. You'd be surprised. He cleans up all right. He's actually something of an intellectual. You heard him quoting all the poets."

"In between the girls from Nantucket," I said.

"He's a character. Characters sell."

"Well, we need to keep him on a short leash."

Bree saluted. "Consider it done. I'll sleep on the sofa and make sure he doesn't wander into traffic."

That sounded more noble than it really was. The sofa in King's suite could have slept five. It was as soft and plush as a Gund bear.

"Thank you," I said.

I was about to leave when a voice called, "Julie Chavan!" It was loud enough to make me jump. I spun around and blushed, as much as an Indian girl can blush.

Wiping his mouth, King stood in the bedroom doorway. He was still naked, but we got the front view this time. I tried not to stare, but it was hard. Actually, yes, it was hard. Engorged. Bree licked her lips. I am not a particularly reliable judge of male anatomy, based on limited experience, but I feel confident in telling you that King's equipment was, well, king-sized.

"Now we know what Wolfe saw in him," Bree murmured.

"Hush," I said.

"Julie Chavan," King continued, blithely unconcerned by his nudity, "might I have a word with you in private?"

"In privates?" I said. "I mean, private. Yes, sure."

He turned around, depriving us of our view, and disappeared into the bedroom.

"It's been a while, darling," Bree told me. "You may want to do some Kegel exercises before tackling that thing."

"Oh, shut up."

I followed King into the bedroom. He lay on the bed, hands behind his neck. His eyes were closed. He was absolutely motionless, and I thought he had fallen asleep on top of the covers. I waited, staring at him. I was reminded of my trip to Italy a few years ago. Pisa in particular.

"Julie Chavan," he said again, eyes not opening.

"Just call me Julie," I said. "And please cover yourself."

"Does my robust manhood make you uncomfortable?"

Tell me he did not say "robust manhood."

"Yes, it does."

King sighed and took a fistful of blanket and threw it over his mid-section. The red-striped comforter looked like lava descending from the peak of a volcano. "Better?"

"Thanks."

"I need more money," he said. For a drunk guy, he'd sobered up fast. His eyes were still closed, and he was as frozen as a corpse.

"Excuse me?"

"Another million for now would be satisfactory," he said, "although two would be better."

"We've already paid you a four million dollar advance."

"Mostly spent, I'm afraid."

"On what?"

"Cars. Restaurants. A condo on the Thames. Gifts. I am a generous man. And then, of course, Bree and the government extract their pound of flesh, too. I barely received two million dollars for myself at the end of the day."

Poor baby.

"If we sell a lot of books, you'll get royalty payments," I told him. I didn't mention that we'd have to sell A LOT of books to cover his advance.

"That isn't soon enough. The hotel already called with unfortunate news regarding the status of my American Express card."

"Sell something," I suggested acidly.

"I don't wish to sacrifice my standard of living."

"Well, I'm afraid that's too bad, King. There's nothing I can do."

"Find a way," he said.

"It doesn't work like that."

His eyes popped open, blue and hard. I was startled. It was like having one of those Madame Tussaud's wax figures suddenly move.

"I know things, Julie Chavan," King said.

"Things?"

"Things you want to keep private. Secrets."

"Like what?"

"You know what I mean."

"No, I don't."

He watched my face, as if to see if I were serious. "He never told you?"

"Who?"

"Sonny."

"Told me what?"

He put his finger over his lips. "Shhhh…"

I had no idea what to say. Part of me wanted to press him for details, and part of me wanted to take a baseball bat and go all A-Rod on his robust manhood. When I didn't say anything, King closed his eyes again. He looked relaxed and confident. I thought he was sleeping, but then he spoke again.

"Yes, two million would be better," he said. "See what you can do, Julie Chavan."

I didn't bother with the taxi line outside the Gansevoort. It was two in the morning, but I'd be standing for half an hour behind the clubbers. Instead, I wandered into the streets, figuring I'd catch a late cab trolling through the meatpacking district. The neighborhood was mostly empty. Mostly. I spotted another person a block behind me, but it was a woman in a brown pants suit, so I wasn't nervous.

I wanted to be alone anyway.

I had no idea what King was talking about. Neither did Bree. I didn't like the idea of him keeping secrets, and I really didn't like the idea of him trying to blackmail me. Not that he would be the first author who ran out of cash and came begging his publisher for an advance on royalties.

What secrets did King know? Probably nothing.

I thought maybe Sonny would join me, but he stayed away. There was only me and the brunette woman in the brown pants suit, wandering the district at a safe distance from each other.

I was making something out of nothing. King had learned lessons from Irving Wolfe about how to con people.

I checked my phone and saw that I'd missed a message while I was in the theatre. It was from Garrett. *Call me as soon as you can.* I felt bad that I hadn't seen his note earlier in the evening. It was way too late to call him now. I felt a strange twinge of guilt that I'd been with Thad.

At the intersection ahead of me, I finally saw a taxi. I waved and ran into the middle of the street to get his attention. Fortunately, this was one of the few New York cabbies who actually stop for paying customers. I gave him the address of my apartment uptown and climbed in the back. His name was Farouk. They're all named Farouk. Or maybe it was the same driver I had yesterday. That's pretty likely in New York.

I passed the brunette in the brown pants suit on the street as we drove away.

The funny thing is, she looked straight at me. Almost as if she knew who I was.

12

"How about that A-Rod?" Lionel the security guard asked me when I arrived at the West 57 building the next morning. It was bright and early, as usual; the difference was that I'd only had three hours of sleep.

"What?"

I heard A-Rod, and I was still thinking about King's robust manhood as I swung for the bleachers.

"Ninth inning homer. Didn't you see it?"

"Oh, no, I missed the game."

I staggered for the elevator, but Lionel called me back. "These flowers are for you," he said.

"Flowers?"

Lionel pointed to a gigantic bouquet of two dozen red roses sprinkled with baby's breath. I hadn't even noticed them there. "For me?" I said.

"For you, ma'am. Nice."

I peeled the card off the clear plastic wrapped around the flowers. I opened it and read:

Remember St. Bart's?

Oh, damn.

Of course, I did. How could I forget? Eight months after we began dating, Thad and I took a vacation to the Caribbean island. I'm not sure I've ever had, or will have, days that were more magical. I had never seen water so transparent and green. I had never walked nude on a beach at sunset. I had never been so much in love, or so physically satisfied, that I almost lost myself in another human being. I remember Thad saying: "No one can ever take this away from us."

However, someone did take it away. I did. Not long after that, I ended us. What scared me in the here and now was that I couldn't remember exactly why.

"Julie."

I turned around and found Garrett standing next to me. "Oh! Hi."

"Beautiful flowers," he said.

"Yeah. Thanks."

In the encyclopedia next to "awkward moment," you will find a picture of this encounter.

"You really must have a secret admirer," he said. "First Broadway tickets, now flowers."

"I wish."

This was the point where a question hangs in the air. Yes, he wanted to know who sent me the flowers; no, he wouldn't ask me about something personal and private. It was up to me to tell him. For some reason, I didn't want to. I didn't want him getting the wrong idea about me and Thad. I also didn't want him thinking I was keeping secrets from him. Which, sadly, I was.

"My mother," I lied.

"That's sweet. My mother never sends me roses." He gave me another of his unbelievably charming smiles. I think that was his way of saying: I don't believe you, but it's okay if you don't want to tell me.

"I'm sorry I wasn't able to get back to you last night," I apologized.

"I understand. Bree Cox. 'Nuff said."

He walked with me to the elevator. The three of us got inside. Garrett, me, and my flowers. The bag was almost as tall as I was. The plastic kept crinkling, calling attention to the roses.

"I met King Royal last night," I told him.

Garrett rolled his eyes. "Yes, I've had the pleasure."

"We had to rescue him from the rooftop bar."

"Singing?"

"Yeah."

"Limericks?"

"Yeah."

"That's King." He added, "How was the play?"

"Fine. Good." Don't ask me about the male lead. Don't ask me, don't ask me, don't ask me.

"No cat fights with Bree during the show?"

"No," I said. "We were very civil."

"I'm proud of you."

"What did you want me to call you about?" I asked. "It sounded important."

"It is. We have a problem."

Another one?

Everybody had problems. Sonny was dead. Libby had writer's block and was leaving Manhattan. Bree was Bree, and that's always a problem. Me? I had my ex-fiancé and my mother luring me to a job in L.A. I had my father's ghost badgering me to hang on to a publishing house that was bleeding money and in danger of a blitzkrieg by the Germans. I had a book launch this week with an author who was trying to blackmail me.

"What's the problem?" I asked.

The elevator doors opened at the floor for West 57. We got out. Garrett put a hand on my shoulder as we let ourselves into the office. Whatever had happened, it wasn't good. I had an odd premonition. I rushed past the lobby to Sonny's office – my office – and I clapped my hand over my mouth in horror as I saw the damage.

Someone had broken in. The office was trashed. The books that had lined the shelves were spilled on the floor, many of the spines slashed open. Prized first editions, ruined. Every drawer in the desk and in the file cabinets had been emptied, contracts and documents strewn like garbage.

Worst of all, there was a different smell. I didn't smell Sonny anymore, the smoke, the cologne. He was gone. In his place was a foreign mix of leather, paper, and sweat from someone intruding on my space.

I backed up, bumping against the wall. Garrett's face was dark with concern. He took the flowers from me, as if he knew I didn't even have the strength to hold them. I sank down to the floor, biting my lower lip, wrapping my hands around my knees. My hair spilled across my face, and I left it there.

"It could be my fault," Garrett said. "I went to dinner late last night. Maybe I forgot to lock the office door."

I looked at him. "You didn't forget."

He shrugged. "No, I don't think I did."

"Somebody picked the lock," I said.

"Well, they got in somehow, and they knew what they were doing. I wasn't gone more than half an hour, but I never saw anybody. They were in and out fast."

"They probably had someone on the street watching for you." I added, "Did Lionel see anyone?"

Garrett shook his head. "It wasn't his shift yet. The other guard couldn't tell me anything."

"Police?"

"I called them," he said. "You know how it is with things like this. Not much they can do."

I examined the damage from the floor. I saw the mug that I had made Sonny years ago in school; it had fallen or been thrown, and the handle had broken, and a jagged chunk of ceramic had split from the lip. That was the one that made me cry. It was the most worthless thing in the whole office, and I stared at it, and fat tears formed a parade out of my eyes. It was like losing him all over again and realizing he was never coming back.

Garrett slid down next to me. He wiped my face with his hand. "I'm so sorry, Julie."

I leaned into his shoulder. His arm slid behind my back, pulling me closer. I felt him kiss the top of my head. It was a safe feeling, and I liked it.

"I'm just glad you weren't hurt," I said.

"Thugs know better than to mess with a book editor," he said. "Particularly one with a doctorate in Ralph Waldo Emerson."

I laughed. "You would have quoted *Self-Reliance* to them?"

"While I was kicking the crap out of them, yes."

It was hard to imagine Garrett fighting, but I believe there were things he would defend to the death. Sonny. West 57. The First Amendment. John's Pizza.

Me.

I wasn't sure there was anyone else in my life who would say the same thing.

"Thank you," I murmured.

"For what?"

"For being here." I twisted around in his arms, and I looked into those warm eyes. "I mean it."

"I've always been here."

Suddenly, there was something strange between us. Something new. Or maybe it wasn't new at all. I wanted to kiss him. I wanted to lay him down and make love to him. I wanted to hold on and never let go. I saw his face, his longing, his care, and I knew he wanted all those things, too. I thought: *Touch me. Kiss me. Tell me you love me.* Here I was, only a day after being in Thad's arms, and I didn't care.

We were walking on air, but we were mature (there's that awful word again), and we didn't fall. It was as if we were on that skywalk over the Grand Canyon, staring straight down. I could have made the first move, and I didn't. He could have made the first move, and he didn't. Between us, somehow, there was a wall of glass.

I separated myself. The moment passed. I felt a sense of loss, even worse than when I had first walked into the office. I knew we had made a mistake between us, but I didn't know whether the mistake was doing something or doing nothing.

"I suppose we should clean up," I said. I checked my watch. "I have to meet with the banker in an hour."

"I'll take care of this," Garrett said. "You have enough to worry about. Go take a walk or get some coffee."

"No, I'll help." The first thing I did was pick up the broken pieces of the mug. I simply stared at them in my hands. "Bastards," I added. "Why do this?"

"They were looking for something," he said.

"Are you sure it wasn't just vandals?"

"I don't think so. They were starting to go through files in accounting, too. I must have gotten back earlier than they expected, because they didn't get far. Vandals don't usually bother with financial records. This was a search, Julie."

I heard what he said, but in my mind, all I could think about was King Royal.

I know things. Secrets. Didn't Sonny tell you?

Garrett was right. Someone out there was searching for something.

Something they thought Sonny was hiding.

What?

II

13

I don't like the coffee at Sonny's bank.

It's not that it's bad. No, it's great. They serve me cappuccino with exactly the right swirl of golden foam, with dense espresso underneath, in a Lenox china cup that should have been on display at the Hermitage museum. It is the Oxycontin of coffee. However, I would prefer that my banker serve me brown tap water with a plastic spoonful of Folger's in a Styrofoam cup. I want him to feel my pain.

You have to admire today's banking biz. They've given up that silly old "invest in our community" model. Today they take your money, pay you .00003% interest, buy government bonds with your cash, and go golfing. There are fees for everything today. Checks. ATMs. Doing business at a branch. Not doing business at a branch. Want to talk to a human being? That'll be ten dollars, please. I'm pretty sure they charge the Girl Scouts a percentage for selling Thin Mints on the sidewalk outside.

Do I sound cynical? I'm sorry. I never got my free toaster when I opened a checking account in 1994. It still stings.

Sonny's banker was a small round man with a gray suit and unusually large ears. His name was Gordon Barnes, but I referred to him in my head as Dumbo. When I arrived for my appointment, Dumbo left me alone in his office to enjoy my cappuccino, probably so he could consult on my situation with Timothy Q. Mouse. He returned ten minutes later and buzzed the desk a few times, ears flapping, before coming in for a landing in his chair.

"I'm so sorry, I wanted to have the most current numbers on hand when we talked," he told me.

Flap flap, went his ears.

"Of course."

Dumbo looked uncomfortable. To his credit, he probably also looked uncomfortable when he was kicking eighty-year-old widows out of their houses. Foreclosures are a pain in the backside when you have an early tee time.

"Let me assure you that I feel as strongly about West 57 as you do," he assured me. "Sonny was one of my earliest customers. He and I sweated the ups and downs of the book business together all these years."

This was supposed to be comforting, I guess, because I knew that today's meeting was more of a "down" than an "up." Even so, I was polite. I said, "I know Sonny valued his relationship with you and the bank, Mr. Barnes."

"Thank you." Dumbo scratched his neck with his trunk. I smelled peanuts on his breath. "I wish I could tell you Sonny always took my advice about financial matters."

"Sonny took Sonny's advice," I said.

"Indeed. Well. I'm sorry he didn't listen to me as the market went south a few years ago. I told him changes needed to be made. I warned him of the consequences of inaction."

"I know what my father was like, Mr. Barnes. I don't blame you or the bank." But I still want my toaster.

"Yes, of course. I appreciate that. I know you're handling the resolution of his personal affairs as well as attending to the management of West 57. There isn't much in the way of usable assets in either instance. Sonny had already leveraged most of his personal wealth back into West 57, despite my recommendations to the contrary."

"I understand."

"I don't mean to be blunt, but one thing I always respected about Sonny is that he didn't like me sugarcoating bad news."

"Neither do I."

"Good, good. Then let me fly right to the bottom line, as difficult as it may be." Saying that, Dumbo flapped his way out of his chair, spun around a few times above the desk, and landed like a helicopter.

"Please do."

"West 57 is facing a major liquidity crisis," he informed me sadly. "The house is bleeding cash and will soon be unable to meet its debt obligations or its payroll. I'm very sorry."

"How long do we have?" I asked.

"Two months at the outside. Maybe less. After that, the circus will be bankrupt."

Okay, he may have said "house," not "circus."

"What about our credit line?"

"I'm afraid the credit line is maxed out. It has been for some time. I wish I could be encouraging about the prospect of some kind of bridge financing, but to be honest with you, no one on our loan committee sees a path by which West 57 can return to profitability."

Dumbo blinked sympathetically at me. He had very long eyelashes.

"You do realize we're in the process of launching one of our biggest books in years," I reminded him.

"The Irving Wolfe bio? Of course. The advance orders bought the house a few weeks, but it won't be enough on its own to change the overall financial picture."

"I see."

"Oh, by the way, I loved the Assy McHattie video on YouTube," he said.

No, he didn't say that.

"I wish the situation were different," he said.

"What are my options?" I asked.

"Again, let me be blunt. First, you can declare bankruptcy and attempt a restructuring of the house's debt. I'm not a bankruptcy attorney, but I'm not optimistic that a restructuring would be successful. You would be dealing with the same business relationships as before, and I doubt your creditors would want to take their chances on the future of the house without a more promising business plan. Second, you could simply close the doors and liquidate your assets. Any ongoing cash flow from book sales would be put toward paying down the remaining debts."

"So I could close down the house," I said, "or I could close down the house. Is that it?"

"Barring a significant infusion of cash, yes," Dumbo said.

"How significant?"

"Oh, tens of millions."

That's pretty significant.

"Without that kind of investment, West 57 is dead?" I said.

"Unfortunately, that's the reality you face. I wish it were different."

There must be other options. I thought about robbing the bank. They might have a Renoir in their vault. Or I could kidnap Dumbo and hold him for ransom. Then I realized I'd have to cut off one of his ears to prove I was serious. He'd never fly again. No, that wasn't a plan.

"Do you have any suggestions about how I might go about raising that kind of money?"

"Only one," Dumbo told me, and I knew what he was going to say. "Assuming you can find a buyer, you could sell the house."

"You left me quite a mess," I told Sonny.

I sat by myself at a hole-in-the-wall *dim sum* restaurant in Chinatown, but I wasn't alone. Sonny was with me. This was always one of his favorite places to meet me for lunch. He loved the deep fried chicken feet. Tastes just like chicken, he always said, being funny.

A little Chinese girl pushed a cart of food next to my table. She began whipping the lids off plates and describing the items in broken English. "Pawr dunlin," she said.

Allow me to translate. That means pork dumpling. *Shu mei.* "Yes," I said. They're my favorite, little pasta purses stuffed with ground pork and black mushrooms.

"Shimbawls."

Shrimp balls. This might give me pause, but to my knowledge, shrimp don't have actual balls. These are *har gow*, and they're delicious. "Yes," I said.

"Brawly."

Chinese broccoli in oyster sauce. "Yes," I said.

"Chin feed."

She held the plate of chicken feet so I could see them. When they are fried, they still look like, well, chicken feet. It made me happy that beak is not considered a delicacy. "No, thanks."

"Chin feed?" She was persistent.

"No chin feed."

She grinned at me and made a little claw with her fingers and wiggled them. She knew me, and she knew my father always ordered chicken feet when we came here, over my objections. On the other side of the table, Sonny winked at her, and I half-hoped she would put the plate down in front of him. If she saw him sitting there, that would prove I wasn't crazy. Instead, she punched my bill and pushed her cart to the next table.

"You should really try them, darling girl," Sonny told me.

"No, thanks."

"You need to be more adventurous. You're a Chavan. We're risk-takers." He added, "Tongue. You should try tongue, too."

"I don't like the idea of licking something that can lick me back."

He laughed at that one. A big, shoulders-bouncing Sonny laugh. I liked hearing it again.

I remembered the last time we'd been here together. It was the week before he died. By then, he must have known the truth. Dumbo would have given him the numbers, just like me. He would have realized the end of West 57 was near. His dream was collapsing. If he'd been worried, he hadn't shown it at all. He'd been the way he always was, irrepressibly confident.

"What were you going to do, Sonny?" I asked him. "How were you going to get out of this one?"

He waved his cigarette as if I were talking about silly things. "I would have thought of something. I always did."

"Like what?"

"Don't bother me with details, darling girl! Details are for little bald people who wear glasses. Think big."

I began to get angry, but how can you get angry with a ghost? I was actually angry with myself. I should have been able to think of something. I should have been just like Sonny. Instead, I felt helpless.

"Would you have let the house go?" I asked. "Would you really have let West 57 disappear?"

Before he could answer me, my phone rang.

"Ah, Julie," said a wealthy Germanic voice. "It is Helmut at Gernestier."

Naturally. The timing of his phone call wasn't an accident. I suspected Helmut had a pipeline to Dumbo and all of the financial records for West 57. He knew what I needed. Cash and lots of it. He knew the only alternative to selling the house was liquidation.

"Hello, Helmut."

"I really did enjoy our dinner the other night," he told me. "I hope you did, too."

"I did, thank you."

"I see that your author King Royal is going to be on the Pierce Gorgon show tonight. Congratulations."

"Yes, and he'll be on *Good Morning America* on Friday," I said.

"It's obvious that the book will be a big bestseller. This is good news."

"It is."

"Sonny would be proud of you. You have taken over with considerable aptitude in just a short period of time."

"I don't know about that."

"You are modest, Julie. With your background in the agency, I am not surprised you would have tremendous talent for the business side of publishing. That is what all my scouts have told me."

"I'm glad to hear it."

"Well, the purpose of my call is merely to wish you well on the launch of *Captain Absolute*."

"Thank you."

"I don't want to put any pressure on you regarding our earlier discussion. Take your time. Think about it. Naturally, our offer is still on the table. That goes for West 57 and for yourself, too."

"I appreciate that. I'll be in touch soon."

"I'm glad. Goodbye for now."

I hung up the phone. My *har gow* was cold, but I'd lost my appetite anyway. I looked across the table, and Sonny was gone. I was alone again, just when I really needed his advice, but it didn't matter. All Sonny would tell me were things that didn't help me decide what to do. Be a risk-taker. Think big. That was fine, but none of that paid the bills. None of that changed what I had to do.

As far as I could tell, I only had one option.

If I was going to rescue West 57, I had to sell to Gernestier.

14

As I got out of a cab at the West 57 building after lunch, I spotted Nick Duggan from the *Post* waiting for me. He wore a plaid Goodwill sport coat that didn't fit, a baggy white dress shirt, and wrinkled gray slacks. He'd covered up his red hair with a Yankees cap. He was eating a hot dog, and he'd dripped ketchup onto his shirt like a bloodstain.

Duggan bounced off the wall to meet me, spilling a trail of white onion bits on the sidewalk. "Ms. Chavan."

"Mr. Duggan," I said.

He tugged on his baseball cap, which threatened to blow away in the New York wind. "So His Lordship is on TV with Pierce tonight, huh?"

"That's right."

"Looks like you've been having trouble keeping him under wraps, though."

"Excuse me?"

"I saw the Assy McHattie video on YouTube," he snickered. "Classic King. I loved it when you yanked him off the balcony. You've got some moxie for a tiny gal."

I wasn't impressed with the compliment. "King was jetlagged. He'd had a long flight."

"Jet lag, huh? Is that what you're calling it? I hope you checked his hotel room for rum and coke. And I don't mean the soda." He closed off one nostril and snorted loudly.

I was annoyed with myself, because I hadn't thought to check King's room for alcohol or drugs. That was a mistake. Bree had stayed the night, so hopefully she'd made sure King didn't raid the mini-bar or get a late-night delivery from one of New York's dealers.

"I'm very busy, Mr. Duggan," I said.

"Give me ten minutes. You can call me Nick, by the way. Or Diggin. Some people call me Diggin."

"I'll call you Mr. Duggan. We're not going to be that close."

He put a hand over his chest, fingers spread wide. "Hey, not a word about King Royal, okay? His name won't cross my lips. I promise."

"What do you want to talk about?"

"Irving Wolfe," he said.

"Then I still have nothing to say to you."

Duggan shook his head. "Come on, you don't strike me as a head-in-the-sand girl, Ms. Chavan. People I talk to say you're a straight shooter. Seems to me you'd like to know what's really going on."

I hesitated, and he could tell he'd landed a greasy hook in me. "Do you know what's really going on?"

"I could help you get some answers. I know stuff, Ms. Chavan. It's crap you should know, too. Maybe we can do a quid pro quo. You may know things that would help me, too, huh? We could put our heads together."

My head wasn't going to land anywhere near Nick Duggan's head. "I don't think so."

"This isn't just about me. You need to think about yourself, too. I heard what happened at Tavern on the Green. That guy coming after you? Scary."

"How did you hear about that?" I asked.

"I told you, I know how to dig stuff up. Do you know who he was? That guy in the restaurant?"

"No."

"I do. His name's Walter Pope. Retired top exec at a big insurance company. Bailed out of the biz with a golden parachute five years ago and thought he was set for life. Trouble is, Irving Wolfe shot a hole in his parachute. Pope invested his nest egg with Wolfe and lost everything. Now his wife's got cancer, and he can't afford the treatment."

I closed my eyes and wasn't happy, because I remembered the desperation and fury in Pope's face as he came at me. It tugged at my heart. "I hate to hear stories like that."

"Yeah, well, people have it in their heads that you're aiding and abetting Irving Wolfe with this book."

"That's not what we're doing."

"Are you so sure?" Duggan asked me.

"This book is *about* Irving Wolfe. That's all." I sounded defensive, but that was how I felt. Defensive. Guilty. Confused. With every day that passed, I was beginning to hate this book. You can hate things and still not be able to walk away from them.

"Maybe it's just a book, but King makes Wolfe out like a hero. Even that freaking title. *Captain Absolute*. That's bound to rub people the wrong way. Especially people who lost their shirts to this son of a bitch."

No, he didn't say "freaking."

"I'm not going to debate the memoir genre with you, Mr. Duggan. I'm also not going to defend Irving Wolfe, who was obviously a terrible, terrible human being. However, he's dead. Don't confuse the awful things he did with a *story* about what he did."

"Oh, let's not pretend that's all it is," Duggan said. "King Royal was in bed with Wolfe. Literally. He knew exactly what was going on with the fraud. You know he did. And he did squat to stop it. He could have tipped off the feds. He could have tipped off the media. Instead, he kept his mouth shut and lined his pockets. Now he's getting rich off Wolfe's story, thanks to your father. You really don't have a problem with that?"

Of course, I do.

A big problem.

That didn't change what I had to do. I had to publish the book.

"You said you didn't want to talk about King Royal, and now you're talking about him," I told Duggan. "Have a nice day."

I brushed past him, but Duggan called after me. "Tell me something, Ms. Chavan, do you ever get the feeling that somebody's following you?"

I stopped.

Duggan had an unpleasant way of knowing things he shouldn't have any way of knowing. I thought about leaving the Gansevoort last night and wandering through the meatpacking district in search of a cab. That brunette in the brown pants suit was behind me the whole time. When I left, she was watching me eye to eye. New Yorkers don't do that.

I wondered if Duggan really knew something or if it was just a guess. He came up next to me and took off his hat and rubbed his buzzed red hair with chewed fingernails. "So that's a yes, huh?"

"No."

"Come on, you saw somebody, right? My advice is, keep your eyes open. People are watching you."

"Who would do that?" I asked.

"Could be the feds. You know, either the FBI or the Attorney General or the SEC. Could be lawyers or private eyes working for the victims. Could be reporters like me, smelling a story." He added, "If I were you, I'd assume my phone was tapped, too."

"That's ridiculous."

"Get it checked and then tell me that."

"Someone broke into our office last night," I said, watching his face. "Was it you?"

He smiled. "Me? Hey, I told you, there are lots of people interested in Irving Wolfe. Someone like that brings out guys who don't play by the rules."

"I have no idea what anyone would want with me or West 57."

"That's easy. Money."

I laughed, but it wasn't funny. "Trust me, there's no money," I told him.

"Not your money. Irving Wolfe's money. Everybody thinks he stashed a fortune somewhere before he died. People want to get their hands on it."

"Then they're looking in the wrong place."

He leaned in closer to me, as if all the people on the sidewalk might be listening. "Irving Wolfe had lots of secrets."

"I don't know anything about that," I said.

"Maybe not, but I bet Sonny did." He peered into my face like a palm reader at a county fair. "I think you're starting to believe he did, too."

"Sonny would never have been involved in anything illegal," I said. "Never. That's not the kind of man he was."

Duggan pushed the last bite of his hot dog into his mouth. He spoke as he chewed. "In my experience, good men do bad things for one of two reasons. Love or money. And let's face it, Sonny needed money."

"Sonny made money by selling books, Mr. Duggan. My father went after *Captain Absolute*, because he knew it would be a commercial success. That's all."

"Oh, yeah? What about Sonny's relationship with Irving Wolfe?"

"There was no relationship," I said.

"You're wrong, Ms. Chavan."

"What are you talking about?"

Duggan stared at me and rubbed his chin. "See, I'm not sure about you, you know? I think you're honest, but then I remember, you were an actress, right? So maybe you're acting."

"If I were such a good actress, I wouldn't be in publishing," I said.

"Okay, let's say you don't know."

"Don't know what?" I asked.

"Well, I did some digging," he told me. "Digging is what I do. Back when your father started West 57, he needed outside investors for seed money to get the business going. Guess who one of his biggest investors was?"

Oh, no.

Oh, no, no, no, no.

Duggan saw the horror in my face. He knew I wasn't acting. "That's right. It was Irving Wolfe. He and Sonny knew each other for years. They were partners."

15

Sonny and Wolfe. Partners. I wanted it to be a lie, but in my heart of hearts, I knew Duggan was telling me the truth.

I rode the elevator in a daze. I was so upset that I collided with someone going the opposite way in the doorway of the West 57 office. We crashed together like bumper cars. I nearly fell, but he held me up. I didn't apologize or say "Excuse me!" or anything that polite people do. I was too distracted.

"Are you okay?"

I looked up. The man I'd tried to wipe out in the doorway still held my elbows. He probably thought that if he let go, I would crumple like a doll. Maybe he was right.

"Oh, hi," I said, recognizing him. "Yes, I'm fine."

But I wasn't, and he knew it.

It was Brian Freeman. Brian was one of Garrett's authors at West 57. He writes dark, emotional thrillers. It's great stuff; you should read him if you're not already a fan. His web site is www.bfreemanbooks.com. Bree is his agent, but I try not to hold that fact against him. Honestly, I've always been suspicious that Bree got Brian's help in writing *Paperback Bitch*. I asked him about it once, but he wouldn't rat her out.

I know he does ghost writer work. Sonny used him as the wordsmith behind *Captain Absolute*. That's why the book is so damn good.

"I didn't realize you were in New York," I told him.

"I had an editorial meeting with Garrett about my new thriller," Brian explained. He gave me a boyish grin and added, "Actually, it's just an excuse for me and Marcia to get to Katz's Deli."

"That's good stuff."

Brian lowered his voice. "I'm sure you can't talk about it, but Garrett told me that West 57 is on the block. I know the market is crazy these days. I'm sorry."

Damn. Garrett knew about Gernestier. He was bound to find out sooner or later; he always had his ear to the ground. I felt bad that he hadn't heard about it from me.

"We'll see what happens," I said to Brian.

"Marcia and I were so sorry to hear about Sonny. He was very supportive of me and my books. I'll always be grateful."

"Thanks. I appreciated getting the card from you two. Tell her I said hi, okay?"

"I will."

He was heading for the elevator when I realized that Brian might be able to tell me things I didn't know about King Royal. "Say, do you need to rush off? Could you stay a couple more minutes?"

"Of course."

I led him back into Sonny's office. It was in better shape than I'd found it this morning. Garrett had cleaned up. Books were back on the shelves, but you could still see copies where the spines had been sliced open. Papers were back in the drawers, not on the floor. The broken mug was in a little box for me to take home. It was the smell I missed. I wanted that musky combination of tobacco and cologne, but it was gone forever.

Brian sat down opposite me. He wore a black turtleneck, black jeans, and black dress shoes. I don't think I'd ever seen him in anything else. He's a thriller writer, and that's his uniform.

"Bree is in town," I said. "Have you seen her?"

"Sure. We had dinner the night she got in. My head still hurts from all the wine."

"I saw her yesterday."

His eyebrows betrayed his surprise. He knew about our feud. "Really? Are you two friends again?"

"Well, I didn't kill her," I said. "Despite *Paperback Bitch.*"

"I don't suppose it's your favorite book," Brian said. "Maybe you should think about writing a novel yourself. It would give you a chance to tell your side."

"Oh, I'm not brilliant like Bree. I'd need a ghost writer."

He smiled again, but he still didn't rat her out. If I ever do want to write a book, I'm calling him.

"Speaking of ghost writers," I went on, "you did a great job with *Captain Absolute.*"

"Thanks. Not that I can talk about it in public. Sonny swore me to secrecy. He was pretty generous with the contract, but I had to keep my lips sealed that I was the writer."

"Do you know why he did that?"

"I don't, but I got the feeling that it was for my own protection. Given all the craziness about Irving Wolfe, I guess I'm happier keeping it quiet."

"So how did the project come about?" I asked.

"Didn't Sonny tell you?"

"No, I just assumed Bree brought you in to handle the writing when she did the deal for King."

Brian shook his head. "Other way around. Sonny came to me directly. I don't think Bree was even in the loop at that point."

"Sonny called you in?" I was surprised. "When was this?"

"Everything moved pretty fast. Sonny talked to me right after Wolfe's death. It was one of those books that he wanted to produce quickly because of the media interest. He probably figured half a dozen other books about Wolfe would wind up in the queue ahead of us if we waited. I dropped everything else to get it done."

"So you must have spent a lot of time with King Royal."

"Oh, yeah."

"Was it an experience?"

"Oh, yeah."

"I take it you're not planning to give up fiction for a career in celebrity bios," I said.

"Get me Shakira, and we'll talk," he replied, chuckling.

"I'll work on it."

"Besides, who says I gave up fiction?" he went on. "I'll always think of *Captain Absolute* as one of my best novels."

I didn't like the sound of that. "Novels? What do you mean?"

"I mean the more time I spent with King, the more he drank. The more he drank, the more his stories changed. By the time we were done, I couldn't tell you which stories were true and which were made up. Honestly, I'm not even sure King knows."

"Did you tell Sonny about this?"

"Of course. He told me not to worry about it."

"I guess that's one good reason not to have your name on it," I said.

"I guess."

"You don't know of anything that's actually *false*, though, right?" I wanted reassurance.

"I only know what King told me," Brian said.

"You sound uncomfortable."

"Well, to be honest with you, Julie, it's not really the drunk parts that bothered me. If King exaggerated some of the little details, fine. No one's going to quibble with that. I was more worried about what he told me when he was dead sober."

"Why is that?"

"Because King was hiding things," Brian said. "That was obvious. There were parts of the story that he didn't want anyone to know."

16

Garrett's office was a sea of paper stacked like blocks in a Jenga game. You couldn't see a square inch of wood on his desk. Most editors these days have switched to electronic copies for their work. Not Garrett. He still wanted the feel of paper in his hands and dirty printer ink on his fingertips. He made edits in long-hand in the margins, just like Sonny. In personality, the two men couldn't have been more different. As editors, though, they were both from the old school. Garrett would never change.

I watched him from the doorway. He sat on the floor in a corner with his long legs bent and a bound manuscript propped on his knees. His messy hair needed a brush. He had half-glasses on the end of his nose, which made him look older. He sipped from a bottle of iced tea as he turned the pages.

I'm not sure how long I stood there, unable to take my eyes off him. Finally, he felt my presence and looked up.

"Oh, hi," he said.

"Hi."

"Why are you smiling?" he asked me.

I didn't realize I was. There wasn't much to smile about, but when I put a hand to my face, sure enough, there were teeth between my lips. I think I was smiling because Garrett was in his element. He was where he should be, doing what God had put him on the planet to do. How can you not smile when you see that?

"I was thinking about a joke I heard the other day," I said.

"I could use a good joke."

I sat down next to him on the floor. "An editor writes this really great novel," I said.

"Okay."

"That's it. That's the joke."

Garrett laughed. "Wow, you're mean."

"I got you to laugh."

"Yes, you did."

We sat in silence. Garrett sipped more of his tea. He put the pages of the manuscript he was reading on the floor.

"What's the book?" I asked.

"It's a first novel called *Woodham Road*. It's set in the eighteenth century as a frontiersman heads across the country. Or so we think for most of the book. The reality is very different."

"Good?" I asked.

"Superb. Best book I've read in a very long time."

"Are you going to offer on it?"

"No," he said.

"Why not?"

Garrett looked at me, and his eyes were sad. "I don't want to make promises to a new author that I can't keep."

I felt as if he'd slapped me. "I'm sorry."

"It isn't your fault, Julie. You didn't cause any of this."

"I know there are rumors about West 57 being sold. I should have told you days ago. I didn't want you hearing about this from anyone but me."

Garrett put a hand on my shoulder. I could feel the warmth of his skin through my blouse. "I don't need to hear rumors to know what's going on. It's obvious we're in trouble. You met with the bankers, right?"

"Right."

"Is the situation as dire as you thought?"

"Worse."

"So what does that mean?"

"It means my options are basically shut down the house or sell it to keep the brand alive."

"Do you have an interested buyer?"

"You know I do."

"Gernestier."

He said it like the giant ants were coming over the hill in *Them*. Run for your lives, everyone.

"Yes, Gernestier is willing to invest millions," I said. "It would be a whole new start for West 57 instead of liquidation."

"I realize that."

"If Sonny were alive, he would have faced the same choice," I said.

"I know."

"What do you think he would have done?"

"I wish I could tell you, Julie, but I have no idea."

"You're just being kind. You think Sonny would have let West 57 go under before putting it in the hands of Gernestier. You think that's what I should do, too."

"No, I'm not saying that at all," Garrett told me. "Sonny and I rarely talked about money. We talked about books. He wasn't a savvy business person like you, and I'm not sure he ever faced the tough decisions. He ran the place through the force of his personality."

"I don't have that luxury."

"No, you don't, but that's not a bad thing. You have strategic vision that he never did, and he knew it. That's why he worked so hard to get you here. Not a month went by when he didn't tell me how much he wished you would join West 57. He asked me countless times to persuade you."

"You never said a word to me about it," I said.

"Of course not. I told him I wouldn't try to talk you into it."

"Why not?" Part of me wished he had. Years ago. When we still had a chance to turn things around.

"Because you are the most independent woman I've ever known, and I would never dream of trying to change that."

Oh, damn. Why did he have to say things like that?

"I'm struggling, Garrett," I admitted. "I really don't know what to do."

"I wish I had a magic solution, but I don't."

"I could use Sonny's advice. I'm angry at him for not being here. I'm angry at him for dying. I need him."

"Maybe that's why you keep seeing him."

"Maybe."

I wondered if that was true. To me, Sonny was West 57, and West 57 was Sonny. I couldn't separate the two. That was why everything involving King Royal and Irving Wolfe was so disturbing. I was beginning to feel as if I didn't know my father at all. Until I understood who he really was, until I understood what he'd done, he would keep haunting me.

Of course, I could be nuts, too. We can't rule it out.

"Did you know Irving Wolfe was one of the original investors in West 57?" I asked Garrett.

"No, I didn't. Are you sure about that?"

"Someone told me, but I don't know whether to believe it or not."

Garrett took a long time to reply. "It doesn't really change anything, does it? West 57 opened up years before Wolfe began his Ponzi scheme. He would have been legit in those days. It wasn't dirty money."

"Yes, but it means Sonny and Wolfe had a relationship."

"So?"

"So it makes everything involving King's book feel wrong. Like Sonny was using the book to cover something up."

"Like what?"

"I don't know."

Garrett kissed the top of my head again, like he'd done in the morning. I liked it. I wished he did it more. I wished he'd kissed his way down to my lips. "You're making too much of this, Julie."

"Am I?"

"Yes. *Captain Absolute* is a book like any other book. It's not going to help you come to terms with the death of your father. It's not going to help you decide what to do about West 57."

"You're right," I said, but he wasn't right. Not this time. I needed to know the truth.

I stood up from the floor.

"Tell me something," I said to Garrett, even though I didn't want to hear the answer.

"What?"

"If I decide to let Gernestier take over West 57, what will you do?"

He didn't hesitate for even a millisecond. "I'll leave."

I stood there in shock, thinking: That wasn't painful at all. It was easy, like having surgery without anesthesia. Cut me up some more, Doctor. Remove a few more organs. Start with the heart. I tried to make a joke of it, and it came out lame. "Gee, could you get back to me a little faster? You always think things to death, Garrett."

"I haven't thought about much of anything else lately, Julie. The fact is, I can't work for a corporate machine."

"So it's better for me to shut down the house?"

"I'm not saying that at all. I'm just telling you the truth, because you asked me. When Gernestier takes over, I'm gone."

I noticed that he said "when," not "if," as if it were a done deal.

Maybe it was.

"Helmut asked me to stay on," I told him. "I'd still be in charge of the house. A three-year contract. I'd insist on the same for you. Does that make a difference?"

I hoped he'd say yes. I hoped everything in his demeanor would change. Yes, of course, I'd stay. That makes all the difference in the world, Julie. It would be the two of us together, leading West 57 to new glory.

"No," he said.

I felt a twinge of anger, as if he'd rejected me personally. "Just like that?"

"I'm sorry. Look, Julie, you know there's nothing I'd like more than to keep things the way they are now, but that's not going to happen. When Gernestier takes over, Gernestier is in charge. Not you. Helmut and his bean counters will run the show and no one else. You know that."

I did know that.

"So what will you do?" I asked.

"I'm not sure. NYU has been after me for a couple of years about starting a new literary press. Maybe now's the time."

"You'd starve."

"Starve? No. Get rich? No. But that's not the point. I'm not getting rich now. They'd give me complete editorial control. I'd be able to build my own list."

"It sounds like a dream. Why haven't you already done it?"

"Because I already have a job," he said.

I heard what I wanted to hear, which was unfair. With Sonny, he had a job. With me, he's out the door.

"Well, don't let me stand in your way," I told him.

Did that sound bitter? Okay, maybe a little. I could have apologized, but instead, I left his office without saying anything more. I may even have stamped my feet a little. How mature of me. There were lots of things I could have told him. Lots of thoughts in my head. They all would have made the situation worse.

You're naïve. We all work for corporate machines sooner or later.

Don't be a fool. Small presses are dying.

If you loved me, you'd stay.

The last one was the hardest. It led me to one inescapable conclusion. Garrett didn't love me. Of course not. It was silly to think that way. He'd never given me any reason to believe he did. He'd never walked through any of the doors I'd opened for him. To him, we were friends, and that was all.

There was one other conclusion I didn't like.

Maybe I loved *him*.

Maybe the thought of working at West 57 without Garrett sounded intolerably lonely. Maybe this city of millions of people had no one in it for me, no one to keep me here. That was the reality. I'd been a fool not to see it. I stood in the hallway, trembling with some odd combination of rage and despair, and I realized I felt a warm breeze blowing over my body like a caress on my skin.

It was the ocean. It was the west coast. It was calling me.

No, really, it was the vent from the copy machine, but you know what I mean. I was beginning to get my head around a truly terrifying realization about my future.

It was possible, just possible, that my mother was right.

17

That evening, I met Bree at the CCN studio in the Time Warner building, where Pierce Gorgon was planning to do his Wolverine impression by digging his claws into King Royal. Bree was on the phone when I arrived. As usual. I suspect the day is coming when cell phones will be surgically implanted in our heads, and I'm sure Bree will be among the first to sign up for the procedure.

When she finally hung up, she air-kissed me – mmwha, mmwha – and began primping her multi-colored hair in the reflection of the trophy case where CCN keeps their Emmy awards.

"That was your mother," she informed me as she twiddled her highlights.

"Thanks for not putting me on the phone this time," I said.

"Well, she was getting on a plane, so we had to cut it short."

This wasn't a surprise to me. Mother is always at the airport, coming and going, going and coming. I didn't ask where she was headed. (Note to self: Do not make that mistake again.)

"It's a disaster," Bree went on. "I'm distraught."

"Why?"

"Kate's out."

"Winslet? Why?"

"Oh, you know how it goes, darling. Timing is everything in Hollywood. Kate loves the script, but she's locked in to back-to-back contracts for at least the next ten months. Cherie doesn't believe we should wait."

She didn't ask for my casting suggestions, but selflessly, I volunteered.

"I was thinking, with the right makeup, Jack Black could probably handle the role."

Yes, that was unusually mean of me, but my best insults kept glancing off Bree without impact, so I was forced to dig deep.

"You are funny, darling, but I'm truly upset about this."

"I get it. I'm sorry. Who's your backup?"

"None! Cherie's not worried, but I want it to be just right, you know?"

"I know."

"By the way, she asked about you and Thad. She knows you're having dinner with him tomorrow."

"Of course, she does. My mother knows everything." Then I said: "Here comes our boy."

King Royal was being led out of makeup to the set. Bree was right. He cleaned up well. He wore an expensive suit, tie perfectly knotted, every crease impeccable. His curly hair had been washed, set, and sprayed. His face was even pinker than usual. He nodded at me with the *noblesse oblige* of an emperor.

"Julie Chavan," he said.

I wonder if he thinks that's my first name. JulieChavan. Which would make me JulieChavan Chavan.

"Hello, King," I said. "No singing and no limericks tonight, okay?"

And for God's sake, don't talk about your robust manhood.

"Never fear, I will do the Captain proud," he said.

They escorted him to the interview table and gave him a bottle of water. He sat with the straightest back of anyone I had ever seen. The cameramen started testing. The sound engineers did sound checks. Bree and I stood off by ourselves, well away from the action.

"You realize this is going to be a disaster," I said to Bree.

"Oh, yes, complete and utter, darling."

"So why are we doing it?"

"Because the media loves train wrecks, you know that. King will say outrageous things, and the newspapers will talk about him saying outrageous things, and the tweeters will re-tweet his outrageous things, and the bloggers will be outraged about him saying outrageous things. And tomorrow everyone in America will start buying the book because it's so outrageous."

She was right, of course. Morally questionable, but right.

I had other things on my mind. "I saw one of your authors today at West 57," I said.

"Brian Freeman?" she guessed. "He's tasty, don't you think? The deep ones are very sexy. His books are great, too."

"He told me that Sonny approached him directly about doing the ghost work on *Captain Absolute*. Is that true? You didn't know?"

Bree didn't flinch. She was watching the CCN crew flit around King like house flies. "Yes, that was very naughty of Sonny. Tsk tsk. I had words with him, getting between me and my client. Mind you, the author figures he's saving twenty percent commission, so what does he care?"

I'd been hoping Brian was wrong. I'd been hoping that Bree gave Sonny the green light to talk to him directly. I'd been hoping the entire *Captain Absolute* project, from the moment Irving Wolfe took a leap off that boat, had been cooked up by Bree with dollar signs in her eyes. I wanted to think that Bree had been the one who was pushing King Royal onto the world, because I didn't like the alternative.

The alternative was Sonny.

"When Sonny told me about the deal with King, he made it sound like you were the mastermind," I said.

Bree was surprised. "Me? Oh, hardly, darling."

"King's your client."

"Now, yes, but not then. Sonny sent King to me."

"King had no agent?"

"He was an unsullied virgin," she said.

"Then how did he find his way to Sonny?"

"I have no idea. I assume he sniffed around about a book deal, and someone gave him Sonny's name. King was a babe in the woods. He had no clue about publishing or marketing. Sonny had him in his pocket, but he knew King needed an agent who was savvy about overseas rights and publicity. Me, I nearly had an orgasm when Sonny called. Cash cows don't usually moo their way into my lap without competition. I was so thrilled I cut my percentage in half on the U.S. deal, because King and Sonny had already agreed on a number. I just needed to handle the details of the contract. Easy peasey."

"I figured you were planning an auction," I said, "and Sonny made an offer to preempt it."

"That would have been rather ungracious of me, wouldn't it?" Bree laughed wickedly. "Not that I wouldn't have scrapped the deal in a heartbeat and started all over if I thought I could get more money, but four million was already twice what I could reasonably expect. I decided it made no sense to be greedy."

"Why did Sonny agree to pay so much? Particularly if King was naïve about the business."

She shrugged. "This was Sonny. You know how he was, darling. If he got excited about a project, he threw money at it. I wasn't going to sit him down and tell him to lower his offer, now was I?"

Sonny lied.

He lied to me.

Months ago, he'd told me he was publishing *Captain Absolute*. Even then, I wondered about the numbers. I wondered why he was taking on a project that was so outside the norm for West 57. He said it was Bree who got him to see the light. Bree who painted the book as the hot spring title for every list. Bree who jacked up the price by dangling an auction in front of him.

He could have gotten the book for less. Millions less. Sonny, what did you do? And why?

Bree read my face and misinterpreted my reaction. "Oh, Lord, darling, did I speak out of turn? I have no idea why Sonny didn't send King to you, not me. All I can figure is that he thought the family connection would raise eyebrows. Conflict of interest, that sort of thing."

She was right. Sonny knew the deal would raise eyebrows.

Mine.

I suddenly felt a hand on my shoulder, squeezing me like a ripe avocado. Another hand appeared around Bree's shoulder. A face dipped between us with all the cheery confidence of the sun lifting over the horizon.

"Ladies," Pierce Gorgon announced, oozing his British élan at us. "How are we both tonight?"

"Why, Pierce, you charmer, how long has it been?" Bree cooed sweetly, as if it were a surprise to see him here, on the set of his own show. "Years and years, isn't it, darling? Remember our little tete-a-tete in the Docklands when you kept swearing at me? I think that was the last time."

"I remember you were trying to fuck me over on an exclusive story, Bree Cox," Pierce told her with a smile.

I'm sorry. I could have covered that one with a "freak," but no one would have believed me.

"Oh, but darling, you were just a lowly publisher then," Bree went on. "And now look at you, a big American television star! On CCN! It must be so exciting to have five or six hundred people tuning in to watch you each and every night."

I didn't think it was such a great idea to insult Pierce before the interview with King, but Pierce and Bree obviously had history together. I wasn't going to get between them.

"It must be hard on you, Bree, knowing my life is so much better than yours," he told her brightly. "More money, more fame, a better sex life. You must go to sleep every night hoping you die and are reincarnated as me."

"I'm sure your viewers hope that, too, darling."

I was about to duck before the two of them came to blows, but instead, Pierce kissed Bree squarely on the lips. With tongue. "My God, you are hot as ever," he announced.

"You, too, darling, sizzling and breathless," she laughed.

"Julie, you're a vision," Pierce told me. "So sorry about your father."

"Thank you."

He rubbed his hands together gleefully. "Ladies, I'd like to stay and talk more about how talented and wonderful I am, but I have to go carve up your client like a Christmas goose."

I didn't think he was kidding.

We were two minutes to air. Pierce strolled to his interview table and shook hands with King in a pleasant manner. He settled himself into his chair with the kind of smile that reminded me of Anthony Hopkins wearing that awful mask thing in *Silence of the Lambs*. I saw him wink at us.

Bree, beside me, appeared unfazed. "He's a freaking trip, isn't he? I love him."

No, she did not say "freaking."

I waited silently for the cameras to go on, and I told myself: How bad could it be?

Then the cameras went on, and I found out. Pierce introduced his guest and rolled right on to his first question.

"So, King," he began in his honeyed voice, "you were Irving Wolfe's personal assistant for two years. Now, when you say 'personal assistant,' that's another way of saying 'man hooker,' am I right?"

18

"Yes!" Bree exclaimed drunkenly. "Can you freaking well believe he said yes?"

No, she did not say – oh, never mind. You know Bree well enough by now to know what she really said.

Anyway, hours later, we were still reeling from the interview. Pierce asked his first question, and King calmly replied, "Yes. Yes, that's true, Pierce. Irving Wolfe wanted a skillful young lover, and he compensated me handsomely for the services I provided him."

I don't think even Pierce knew exactly where to go from there. He was actually speechless for five seconds, which may well be a record for him.

"This thing is going to be huge," Bree said to me. "Enormous."

"No doubt about it."

She added, giggling: "Mind you, we both know how huge it is."

"It's robust," I agreed. "Engorged."

"I wonder if he has to have his trousers custom fitted," she speculated. "His poor tailor, the man must get a black eye when doing the measurements."

"Bree!"

She giggled again. We were well into our second bottle of wine and both pretty buzzed. I'd forgotten that most of the time I'd spent with Bree during our friendship was in an alcohol-induced stupor. That was what we did. We drank. We gossiped. We complained about our jobs. I told Bree about my boyfriends, and then she slept with them. Nothing much had changed over the years.

The rooftop patio at the Gansevoort hummed with laughter and the clink of glasses. Bree and I huddled in a corner while King entertained the clubbers. He had returned to the bar at eleven o'clock and been greeted like a knight back from the crusades. People cheered, waved, and whistled. King was a celebrity, and he devoured every moment of it. He sang to them again. He didn't haul out Assy McHattie, but he regaled everyone with the story of "Kelly John Venus, the Girl With a Penis," which was much, much worse.

We didn't try to stop him tonight. That was like trying to put a cork back in a champagne bottle. King had popped.

Bree's phone rang for the eleventh time since we'd started drinking. "Bree Cox," she said, and then she covered the phone with her hand. "It's Whoopi. See? Media frenzy."

"She spoke into the phone as if the two of them were old friends. "Good to hear your voice again, too, darling! Oh, I know, it's Pierce, what can you do? Yes, the *View*, in the morning, King will be there. Well, relatively sober. You don't have a dog, do you, darling? Barbarba had a dog, and King doesn't do at all well with dogs. Right, good. Ta!"

"What is it about King and dogs?" I asked.

"Best you not know," she said.

My own phone buzzed, because someone was texting me. Since the show, I'd been besieged with interview requests, photo ops, tweets, blogs, and journalists looking for quotes and comments. I checked the phone, expecting another query from a reporter. I was wrong.

This time the text was from Thad.

Looking forward to our dinner tomorrow.

I pictured him in his hotel, his fingers on the keys of his phone. It was a simple message, but if truth be told, it shot straight between my legs. I felt flushed. I tasted our kiss again and wanted more of them.

Yes, okay, it had been way too long.

I texted back:

Me too.

Bree eyed me as she put down her phone and picked up her glass of pinot noir. "So, darling, if I hadn't dragged you away, would you have slept with Thad?"

"No." Yes.

Bree grinned, as if she could hear the voice in my head telling her the truth. "How about tomorrow?"

"No." Yes. Damn it, stop that!

"I'm not trying to pry," Bree said. "Well, I am, but that's just me. I'm actually without a reliable male partner myself right now. Too busy for sex. Hard to believe, I realize. Anyway, I'm living through your clitoris."

Yes, she really said that.

"You won't find much excitement down there," I said, which at that particular moment was a big old lie.

"Hmm," she said skeptically. She reached in her purse and extracted a cigarette and lit it. I hate smoking as much as profanity, but when you work in publishing, you become accustomed to both. "How do you feel having Thad back in your life?" she asked.

"He's not back in my life. It's dinner. That's all."

"Yes, but obviously it could be more than that if you wanted. Personally, professionally, or both."

"I'm not thinking about any of that. There are too many other things going on in my life right now."

"Not thinking about it? Darling, he's gorgeous, and he's rich."

"So?"

That was an admittedly lame comeback. Bree shook her head, as if I were beyond help, and maybe I was. We kept drinking. The second bottle of wine disappeared and was replaced by a third. The patio became fuzzy and out of focus in my brain, but gorgeous, like a Renoir painting.

King held court near the hotel wall in the shadows, surrounded by empty martini glasses. The gay twins who'd hoisted him to his room last night were there, along with a dozen other partiers, and no one had their hands on the table. I didn't want to think about what their hands were doing.

Bree and I were both mellow, by which I mean completely wasted. Bree kept texting and phoning her contacts around the city, sounding no worse for all the wine. She'd built up her tolerance, whereas I'd gotten rusty. I heard her talking to someone at HuffPo. It may have been Huff. I heard her talking to Viggo Mortensen, or at least I assumed it was him, because I didn't want to think that she knew two people named Viggo. Actually, I'm not sure if she really knows any of these people. Half the time I think she just dials her own number and makes this shit up.

Oh, my God, did I just say that word? I'm so sorry! I was beyond drunk now. I put down my wine glass, but it was too late to save me.

"I have to pee," I announced with more gravity than it probably deserved.

Bree smiled benignly at me. "You go do that, darling. I'm going to call someone for you."

"Clall summin," I said. Well, that's what it sounded like.

"Yes, I want someone to take you home and put you to bed."

"Zhus clall cab," I said. I believe I meant to say, "That is unnecessary, Bree. I will locate a taxi to return to my place of residence."

"Cab, yes, alone, no. Go pee."

I leaned into her face, close enough that we were in danger of a Katy Perry moment. Bree was very amused at me. She has extremely red lips. I retrieved enough of my remaining brain cells to tell her, "Do not do not do not do not do not do not do not call Thad."

"Shall I call Thad?"

"Freak!" I said, and yes, that is what I said.

"Go pee."

I kicked off my high heels. There was no way I was going to walk in those. I noticed that King was gone, and so were the gay twins. I didn't care where they were or what they were doing. I found my way to the ladies room, with a couple errant stops at the kitchen and what might have been the Warhol room at MOMA. The bathroom was empty. I found a stall, did my business, flushed, stood up, turned around, and threw up.

I flushed again. I threw up again. I flushed again.

I felt much better.

I came out of the stall. Sonny was leaning against the bathroom door. Smoking. Smiling. Shaking his head at me.

"Very nice," he said.

"This is the ladies room, Sonny."

"Nothing I heard sounded too ladylike in there, darling girl."

"I don't want to talk to you," I said.

"You're being petulant."

"Go away."

"You miss me."

"No. No. No. No. Not anymore."

"Oh, come, Julie, don't be like this."

"No. I don't even know who you are anymore. You're not the man I thought you were."

"That's not true at all."

"It is. I'm serious. Go away."

I put my head in one of the sinks and turned on the faucet. I rinsed out my mouth. I splashed water on my face, and it soaked my hair and my dress. My makeup ran. I was a sight.

When I looked up, Sonny was gone.

I started to cry.

Bree had to come find me. I don't know how long I stayed in there. Ten minutes. An hour. I was still sitting on the floor in the bathroom, hoping Sonny would come back to me. He didn't. I couldn't tell Bree what was going on, but it didn't matter. She was very kind. She lifted me up and held me by the waist. She told me everything was fine as she guided me back to the bar.

"I love you, Bree," I told her, because I was still very drunk. "Even when I hate you, I love you. You know that, right?"

"Of course, darling, you can't help it."

"You're a great friend."

"Off and on, but thank you."

"I love you," I repeated.

Yes, I loved her, and then I saw who was waiting for me at the elevators, and I hated her, I hated her, I hated her. I wanted to run back to the bathroom and hide. I wanted to throw myself off the rooftop patio. Bree, how could you?

I think I even said it aloud.

"Bree, how could you?"

She hadn't called Thad. She'd called Garrett.

He stood there by the elevators, looking all sexy and handsome in his torn jeans and a Yankees sweatshirt, with his midnight hair rumpled and his hands in his pockets, and his mouth bent into this tiny teasing little smile, and me, looking like...oh, God, what on earth *did* I look like? I remembered my reflection in the bathroom mirror, but that couldn't be me. That was a villainess in a Disney cartoon. That was someone who jumps out at you in a haunted house.

"She's all yours," Bree said to Garrett. She handed him my shoes, which he dangled from his fingers.

He gathered me up in his arms, making sure I didn't fall.

"Come along, princess," he said, laughing quietly. He took me into the elevator, where the buzz of the machinery was white noise, drowning out my other thoughts. I crumpled into him as we went down. My face was scrunched against his chest.

"Sorry," I murmured.

"For what?"

"I don't know. I'm just sorry."

"Don't be."

"Were you sleeping?" I asked.

"No, I was reading *Woodham Road*."

"I drove him away," I moaned.

He tilted up my face. "Who?"

"Sonny."

Garrett opened his mouth as if to say something, but he caught himself. Maybe he was going to say, "He'll be back," but he knew he couldn't tell me that. Instead, he eased my head into his chest again, and I felt his breath going in and out.

The elevator doors opened. We were in the lobby. Bless him, he had a cab waiting, door open, engine grumbling. One of the Farouks stood beside it, big grin on his face. The idea of sitting in the smelly backseat of a New York cab and going home to my cramped apartment sounded absolutely wonderful right now.

Garrett helped me through the lobby into the cool night air. I shivered. I was still damp from the bathroom. He poured me into the cab and got in next to me.

Through my semi-conscious state, I saw a man on the sidewalk just outside the glowing hotel lights. He was impossible to miss. It was King Royal, and he wasn't alone. He wasn't with the gay twins, either. No, no, no. I wanted to believe I was having visions in my drunken state, but I saw the other man in profile, and I knew exactly who it was.

King Royal was with Nick Duggan.

19

I'm pretty sure I slept in the cab. You know how sometimes you wake up, and you know you've been snoring like a fat man after nine beers? That was me. I was still in the cab, leaning against Garrett's shoulder. Right in his ear, very sexy. There was a damp spot on his sweatshirt, too, where I'd drooled.

"How are you feeling?" he asked.

How was I feeling? My mouth was the dust bowl in *The Grapes of Wrath*. My head was a hip-hop dance club at four in the morning.

"Beep," I said.

"What?"

"Julie's not available right now, because Julie is dead. Please leave a message after the beep." To emphasize my point, I repeated, "Beep."

He whispered, "Hi, Julie, it's Garrett. I'm sorry to be the one to tell you, but you're not really dead."

"Then do the right thing and kill me."

I separated myself from his shoulder, and my head flopped back against the seat. The world went around a few times before stabilizing. I saw the Park on our right. We weren't far from my apartment. I had a vision of my bed, with me sinking into the pillow-top mattress. I had a vision of Garrett in bed with me, with my legs wrapped tightly around his backside.

Interrupting that very pleasant vision, I was nearly lifted off my seat by a loud and lethal burst of gas exploding from underneath me into the cab. It was nasty. Even Farouk in the front seat whiffed the air with displeasure, and I was sure he grew up sleeping with goats.

"Oh, my God," I said.

Garrett laughed as he rolled down the window to rescue us. Or maybe he was weeping from the smell. He didn't appreciate the horror of my situation. I was going to have to move to Alaska and live under an assumed name. My humiliation in New York was complete.

"Why are you laughing?" I demanded.

He tried to stop choking. I'm sure he was breathing through his mouth. "Because you are the most beautiful woman I have ever met in my entire life," he said.

That was not exactly the moment I wanted to hear those words.

I sat and pouted for the last few blocks and kept my butt cheeks tightly clenched. Farouk looked happy to drop us off. I was sure he would go home and tell his family about the stinky lady in his cab. At the outer door to my building, I fumbled with the key fob and kept missing the magnetic plate. Garrett had to help me. I insisted that he leave when he opened the door, but he walked beside me to the elevator, apparently oblivious to the dangers of being in closed spaces with me.

"I'm fine," I said.

"No, you're not."

No, I wasn't.

I closed my eyes in the elevator and hoped I was dreaming, but I wasn't. At my apartment door, I had no better luck than I'd had downstairs. I dropped my keys, picked them up, dropped them, picked them up, dropped them, picked them up, and began crying again like a complete idiot. Garrett gently peeled the key ring from my fingers and opened the door on the first try. I stumbled inside.

It occurred to me that Garrett had never been here before. All these years, and this was the first time he had been in my apartment. I really didn't want it to be like this.

"Thank you," I said. "You can go now."

"You look like you could use some coffee."

"I can make it myself."

"I don't think you should be operating electrical appliances," he said with a smile.

I didn't protest further. I staggered toward my sofa and watched Garrett in my kitchen, opening my cabinets, filling my coffee maker with water, scooping coffee from my mason jar, and clinking my china as he put a cup on a saucer. He found my stash of Pepperidge Farm Milanos on a top shelf. He put one cookie on the plate; it was the last one in the bag. When enough coffee had dripped into the pot, he filled the cup and brought it to me and set it on the table and sat down next to me.

"May I have eighty-six Advil, please?" I asked.

He disappeared into my bathroom. I had no idea what he would find in there, but I knew there were no embarrassing birth control devices, which is one advantage of celibacy. When he returned, he offered me two pink tablets, but I opened my mouth and pointed, and he dropped them on my tongue. I washed them down with hot coffee.

"You're being very sweet," I said.

"I am a sweet person."

"Yes, you are."

I drank the coffee. I nibbled the cookie. The chocolate melted on my fingers, and I sucked them. Garrett looked uncomfortable, staring at me. I wondered if I was sucking my own fingers, or if I'd started sucking his. Crumbs fell on my chest, and I plucked them off my cleavage and ate them. Very dainty, but these are Milanos, and you don't want to miss a bite. Plus, I was still drunk as a skunk.

"You saw the interview?" I murmured.

"Of course."

"I guess we got what we wanted."

"Controversy means sales. I told you, you have the gift."

"I feel like Frankenstein creating a monster."

"You didn't create King Royal," Garrett reminded me. "Sonny did."

"Yeah." I stared into my coffee. I wished I had another cookie, but it was gone. "The whole thing with the book was Sonny's idea. Not Bree. Sonny's. He was the one who signed up King."

"So?"

"So nothing."

Nothing except Sonny lied to me about it. What else was he hiding? I thought about Pierce talking to King on television.

There are rumors, you know. Did Irving Wolfe hide a fortune? Are there millions to be found somewhere? Secret bank accounts?

I wouldn't know anything about that, Pierce.

Is Wolfe alive? Some people believe that he faked his death. And that the money you got was to buy your silence.

On screen, King gave Pierce a dreamy smile. That was the worst part for me. That smile. Frozen, fake, condescending, utterly unconvincing.

No, that's untrue.

Wolfe is dead?

He's dead. It's in the book, Pierce. It happened just like I said. Don't go looking for ghosts.

That was good advice. The trouble is that the last time I went looking for a ghost, I found one. Sonny.

"Go to bed, Julie," Garrett suggested. He was watching me as I sat, lost in my thoughts, empty coffee cup in hand, chocolate on my lips. Go to bed. Yes, I wanted to be in bed, but I didn't want to go alone. I wanted him to hold me and ravish me. I wanted us both to be naked.

"I need to take a shower," I said.

"I'll leave you alone," Garrett told me.

"No, stay, please."

He hesitated. "All right." I could see him wondering about my intentions. I'd been urging him to go, but now I was asking him to stay.

I swayed getting up. Garrett held out his arms as if to catch me, but I didn't fall. I made it to the bathroom and closed the door and turned on the water for the shower. I bunched my dress and pulled it over my head and dropped it in a silky pile on the floor. Bra followed, then nylons and bikini panties, and there I was, the way I was brought into this world. Steam gathered over my nude reflection. I stepped inside the shower and soaped myself until I was slippery with bubbles. I rinsed off, feeling at least partially human again. I thought: I'm naked, and he's a man, and he will want this body.

After my shower, I brushed my teeth and slipped into a black, flowered kimono that reached to my mid-thighs. A lot of damp mocha skin was showing. My hair was wet. I swallowed hard as I opened the bathroom door. I wasn't thinking particularly clearly, and I didn't really have a plan. I sat down next to Garrett, and neither of us said a word. I was very conscious of my clean bare body under the robe, which had traveled dangerously far up my legs.

Let's be honest: I was extremely horny.

He stared at me. I wondered what he was thinking. Was he getting aroused with me here, obviously offering myself to him? Or did he not know what was going on? Men are obtuse about such things. In my mind, I was wearing a neon sign that flashed a message like a downtown parking lot. "Enter Here."

I expected his eyes to wander. I was giving him a lot to look at. I could feel a drip of water traveling in the valley between my breasts. Don't you want to see where it goes, Garrett? Don't you want to reach out and touch it? But no. I may as well have been his ugly cousin.

"How are you feeling?" he asked again.

"Better," I said. "I'm better."

"Good. I should go. You need some sleep."

What did I have to do? Stand up and take off my robe? I could have taken a hint, but no, I had to make it worse. I had to make him explicitly reject me. "You could stay," I said.

There. No games. Stay and make love to me. I tried to sound seductive, but I haven't had much practice lately.

"I can't," he said.

"Why not?" I asked him.

Oh, my God, how much worse can I make this? Stop talking! He doesn't want you, Julie!

"You know why."

"No, I really don't. I'm naked under this robe. You get that, right? I'm saying I think we should have sex. You and me. Is that really such a terrible idea? Can you really say you've never thought about me that way in all these years? What is it? Oh, Jesus, you're not gay, are you? I'm so sorry. Is that it? I can't believe I didn't know. I didn't think you were. Are you? You must think I'm an idiot."

Let's try this one more time.

STOP TALKING!

I finally took a breath and shut up, which is like hitting the brakes after you drive off the cliff.

"Julie, I'm not gay," he said, laughing at me again.

"So you're simply not attracted to me."

"You're drunk," he reminded me patiently.

"I'm not going to claim you took advantage of me."

"And yet that's what I'd be doing," he said.

"It doesn't have to be a big deal. It's just one night."

"I know, and that's not what I want from you, Julie."

"What do you want?"

Garrett stood up. He patted my cheek, and I felt like I was twelve, with a crush. "I'll see you at the office."

He left me on the sofa, and I felt angry and rejected. Hell hath no fury like a celibate who gets shot down trying to break her vow. At least I knew now that there would never be anything between us.

Or did I?

I heard Garrett hesitate in the doorway. I wondered if he was having second thoughts about my offer. He looked at me on the sofa.

"Have dinner with me tomorrow," he said.

A date? I volunteer to spread my legs for a man, and he asks me out on a date?

"Okay," I said.

I tried to sound non-committal and hard to get, which is tough to do when you've already suggested sex.

He smiled at me again, and then he left without saying anything more. We had a date, our first date. At least, I think it was a date, but I wasn't sure. I got the feeling it was harder for him to ask me to dinner than it was for me to ask him to bed. I also got the feeling that saying yes to a night of risotto and wine was a more serious step with Garrett than letting him inside me.

I had no idea what I was doing. As usual.

I'd also forgotten one itsy-bitsy little problem.

I already had a date for dinner tomorrow night. With Thad.

20

It was too much trouble to find my nightgown, so I slept without it. I didn't even make it under the blankets. My alarm went off ten minutes after I closed my eyes – or that was how it felt to my brain – and I staggered out of my bedroom with mussed hair strewn across my bare torso and my lower body neatly trimmed and on full display.

I don't usually sleep in the nude, and I picked the wrong night to start.

"I'm pleased to see you're waxing, my dear," my mother said.

I screamed.

Cherie Chavan sat on my sofa, right where I'd unsuccessfully tried to seduce Garrett a few hours earlier. She had a cup of tea in her right hand, and my apartment smelled of jasmine. Her owlish reading glasses were pushed down her nose, and she had a neatly folded copy of the *Wall Street Journal* in her other hand. She observed my body over the tops of her glasses with a mother's curious interest.

"Three pounds," she said. "I'd say you're three pounds heavier than when I saw you last. Don't worry, though, it gives you the cutest little pooch."

"I do not have a pooch," I said.

Cherie gave me a condescending little smile and returned to the *Journal.*

I ran back to my bedroom, brushed some semblance of order into my hair, and slipped on a sensible cotton robe instead of the sexy kimono that sat in a pile where I'd sloughed it off as I collapsed into bed. I checked myself in the mirror. Definitely no pooch, at least not when I sucked in my stomach. I came back to the living room, and after I kissed my mother's cheek, she poured me tea.

"I prefer coffee," I said.

"Tea is better for you."

"I don't like tea."

"Tea has anti-oxidants, and it reduces stress. You look like you could use both, my dear."

That was probably true. I sank down into an armchair opposite the sofa. I wasn't sure if I was hung over or still drunk. Either way, I felt like road kill. I humored my mother by sipping tea, which tasted like brown water.

"How did you get in here?" I asked.

"You sent me a key years ago," Cherie told me. "Remember?"

"No."

"I told you that if I came to New York and went to your apartment and you were being attacked by some hideous serial killer, I wouldn't be able to get inside and rescue you. So you sent me a key."

I did remember. Sending her a key seemed the lesser of two evils compared to listening to more of those stories. Honestly, I never thought she'd use it. (Note to self: Have the locks changed.)

"I meant, when did you get into New York?" I asked.

"I took the red eye."

My mother is the only person in the world who can get off a red eye flight looking just as good as she got on. Maybe better. Her makeup was perfect. Me, I get bags under my eyes when my noon flight arrives twenty minutes late. Her hair, which is as jet black as mine but much shorter, looked as if she'd stopped at Jeffrey Stein for a blow out on the cab ride from LaGuardia. She wore a red long-sleeved blouse dotted with flowers and a gray skirt, both pristine, like clothes recently unwrapped from a dry cleaner's plastic bag.

I spotted a garment bag hung over my bathroom door.

"You're not thinking of staying here, are you?" I asked. "I don't exactly have room for guests, mother."

Cherie rolled her eyes. "No, dear, don't worry." She gazed unhappily at my apartment, as if she assumed cockroaches were in my kitchen, and added, "What do you pay for this place?"

I told her.

"That's outrageous," she informed me. "Who can afford to live here? New York prices are out of control."

"Yes, and Malibu condos are such a steal," I said.

"Well, at least you get a view of the beach."

I sipped more tea. Little tea bits floated on the surface. I do not like bits of things in my beverages. "So what brings you to town, mother?"

"Oh, this and that. Bree and I need to pow-wow about *Paperback Bitch*, now that Kate is out. Such a shame. She would have been perfect, and she's fine with nude scenes, which is a must. Bree does get naked a lot in that book."

"With my fiancé," I pointed out.

"Water under the bridge, my dear. Cate Blanchett is too ethereal for the part, wouldn't you say? Blunty is young, but she could pull it off, don't you think? I like her, that little spitfire. If we go young, we could get Freida to play you. I imagine you'd like that."

"I want to play me, so I can slap Bree," I said.

Her tongue clucked. "My, you really hold on to grudges, don't you? You get that from your father, cheating bastard that he was, may he rest in peace. You need to be more 'live and let live,' like me."

That comment was so outrageous that my mouth dropped open in horrified disbelief, but before I could protest, Cherie marched on.

"Anyway, Bree and I are having lunch. She's over the moon about all the publicity involving King Royal's book. Nice job on that, by the way. The man is one weird flower, but it will sell well. Bree and I are jawing over film rights. Would you like to join us?"

"No, thanks. You're thinking of optioning *Captain Absolute* for the movies?"

"Thinking about it." My distaste must have shown on my face, like eating an old piece of sushi. "I thought you'd be pleased, my dear. Movie deal equals more book sales."

"Just because I'm selling it doesn't mean I'm a big fan of King or the book," I said.

"No one says you have to like it. You just have to make money off it. My goodness, where did you get all these principles? It wasn't from me. That must be Sonny's influence, too. Mr. Literary Lion. Anyway, *voila*, here I am, in town to see Bree. And you."

Don't forget Thad.

"Oh, and of course, I have to see Thad," Cherie went on, with a just-us-girls wink. "He told you about our little production venture, didn't he? It's not often that actors have two brain cells in their head for business, but Thad is a natural. I hope you don't mind my little conspiracy about the play, but I gather it worked out well. He tells me you're having dinner with him tonight. Excellent, excellent. I'd take you out myself, of course, but I want you two to get to know each other again, and three's a crowd. That's why I came straight here from the airport so we could have breakfast together." She swallowed down the last of her tea and checked her watch. "Shower and make yourself presentable, Julie. Hurry now. I made reservations at Sarabeth's. I don't want to miss the lemon-ricotta pancakes."

"About Thad," I said.

"No need to thank me, my dear. Happy to do it. He's scrumptious. I just needed to get past that stubborn little hide of yours. Once you saw him, I knew you'd melt. What a team we'll all make! It's very exciting."

"I may need to re-schedule dinner with him," I said.

Cherie's face hardened like plaster in a death mask. "Excuse me?"

"Something came up."

"What?"

I wasn't going to tell her that I'd drunkenly made another date for the same night and that, in my heart of hearts, I'd rather go out with

Garrett. "A work thing."

"Change it."

"I don't know if I can."

My mother stripped her glasses from her face in annoyance. "Julie, this is important to me. You *will* keep this date with Thad, is that understood? I'm not asking much of you."

"No, you just want me to sell West 57, move to Los Angeles, work for you, and marry Thad. Right?"

"Did I ask you to commit to any of those things?"

"Actually, yes," I said.

"It's one night."

"Yes, and it's my life, mother, not yours."

That was the wrong thing to say. It was perfectly true, but it was wrong. Cherie leaned forward, and her dark eyes shot lasers at me, and her volatile temper squirted out of her like she'd stepped on a packet of ketchup. I remembered her fights with Sonny in the old days and how I wanted to cover my ears.

You cross Cherie Chavan at your peril.

"Of course, it's your life!" she roared. "Did I say it wasn't your life? No! What is my sin, you tell me that! Is it a crime to want you to be happy? Foolish me, I set you up with a man you once loved, who is now as rich as Daniel Craig and looks like him, too. So sue me for interfering, Julie Chavan! Do you know how many women want this man? Do you know how many women would strangle a puppy for the kind of opportunity I'm offering you? You are in a rut, rut, rut, rut, daughter of mine, and you will not see the truth until someone tattoos it on your forehead. You are sitting in Sonny's office while the whole publishing industry crashes around you, and you don't know enough to get on a plane and rescue yourself from this Godforsaken place. Well, enough of this, I say. No more of this nonsense. I have sent you your prince on a white horse, and the least you can do is take one night out of your lonely little life and RIDE HIM!"

There were a lot of things I could have said to that speech.

There were a lot of things I wanted to say to that speech.

Instead, I said nothing, because there was nothing to say. My silence was surrender. We both knew I would have dinner with Thad. I couldn't say no to her. Cherie slapped both hands on her legs and gave me the warmest smile a mother can offer, because she was always gracious when she won.

"Well! That's that! It's such a pleasure to see you, my dear. Now into the shower with you. Sarabeth's awaits."

My mother was right about Sarabeth's. The lemon-ricotta pancakes were terrific. I was finally able to get coffee, too. The restaurant is near 80th and Amsterdam, and it was a sea of people squeezed into a tiny space, but they all know Cherie, even though she lives a few thousand miles away. My mother knows how to make an impression. When you get your first hundred-dollar tip, you remember the Indian lady from Hollywood. We got the streetside table by the windows.

After brow-beating me into submission over Thad, Cherie waxed nostalgic. We talked about the past. Me and her. Me and Sonny. Her and Sonny. She had a way of reinventing every story from their marriage to make herself look good, or to make a 15-round knockdown at the Garden as insignificant as a pillow fight. I didn't care. I really did miss my mother. I had lost one parent, but I still had another parent in my life, and the distance between the coasts felt long, particularly when we were seated together across a small wooden table.

It wouldn't be so bad to see her like this every day. Right?

Like I say, she annoys me and dominates me, but that doesn't mean she's wrong.

I don't really remember the good days between my parents. I was too young. People have told me that Sonny and Cherie were a New York glamour couple in the 1970s, and I've seen photographs, and I can see why. They were BPs, cultured and ambitious, dressed to the nines, on the invitation list for every see-and-be-seen party from those days. Both of them came from family money back in India, so they started their Manhattan lives in the right neighborhoods. Sonny became an up-and-coming editor at Knopf, with a personal recommendation from Bennett Cerf, and authors and reporters flocked to him for his XXL personality. Cherie was more than just the beauty on his arm. She was a shrewder businesswoman than Sonny ever was, and she still is. She traveled back and forth between the coasts even then, working up film deals on books that Sonny published. They were the king and queen of the Upper East Side. For a while.

By the time I began to remember things as a child, Sonny had started West 57, and life with Cherie had become a series of royal battles. If gunpowder lives in a house with matches, sooner or later, bad things happen. I hated it. The arguments made me crazy. If truth be told, I blamed my mother. I was Daddy's girl, and she was the one who finally abandoned me and moved west. It didn't take long for me to learn that there was plenty of blame to spread around for the divorce, and most of it wound up at Sonny's feet. Or, more precisely, in his bed.

I made the mistake at Sarabeth's of asking why Cherie stayed as long as she did. It's not like Sonny waited until the 1980s to begin sleeping around. I figured, she was loyal, she was old-fashioned, but that wasn't it at all.

"Oh, no, it was the sex," Mother informed me. She'd rolled one of her pancakes up like a pinwheel and was cutting it into perfect circles. "The man was a horse in bed, my dear."

Oh, wow. Can I rewind and erase the last thirty seconds from my memory?

"I really don't need to know this, mother," I said.

Cherie shrugged. "You asked."

"It wasn't just about sex. I don't believe that."

"Well, of course, who wouldn't love the lifestyle back then? It was an age of giants. People had stature. Year by year, the world has gotten smaller. With the advent of reality television, it has become positively Lilliputian. Yes, I enjoyed being a New York player in those days, but don't fool yourself that I didn't enjoy rolling around in the sheets with that man. Without that, I'm sure I would have left far sooner than I did, even though I loved him. That was an era where women were supposed to turn a blind eye to the affairs, you know. We were all supposed to attend the Rose Kennedy school, where boys will be boys and you have to forgive their little dalliances. Not me."

"He was devastated when you left," I said. "Truly."

"Then he should have stopped sleeping with his authors."

I could see it in her eyes. Thirty years hadn't dimmed the hurt.

"I was devastated, too," I murmured.

Cherie's face melted, and she clutched my hand tightly. "Oh, yes, I know. It was a hole in my heart not to have you with me. You do understand that, don't you? I wanted you to come to L.A., but Sonny was determined to keep you, and in the end, he was right. It wouldn't have been fair to take you out of the world you knew. Not then." She reached out and stroked my hair. "Things are very different, though, aren't they? You're not a little girl anymore."

No, I wasn't, but sometimes she still made me feel that way. Mothers always do.

"I still worry about you," Cherie went on, "no matter how old you are."

"You don't need to."

"But I do. I worry that you are lonely, Julie. I worry that you keep a world of hurt inside and you close off the world to prevent being hurt again. You are a flower, my dear, and beautiful flowers are meant to be open."

I wanted to tell her that she was wrong about me, but she wasn't wrong. Not really.

"I'm fine, mother," I told her, but I wasn't fooling either of us.

"Fine? You can do better than fine. Nothing keeps you here now, Julie. Truly. Why stay? You were the jewel of Sonny's life, but he's gone now. You don't owe him anything except to be happy. It's time to live your own life. It's time for my flower to enjoy the sun."

I swore I wouldn't cry again, but I did. I don't know who I was crying for. Sonny. Her. Me. The past. Everything that once was and couldn't be anymore. My mother pulled her chair next to me and held me and let me grieve. Eventually, I wiped my eyes and pulled away.

"Tell me something honestly, mother," I said. "What kind of a man was Sonny?"

"I don't understand."

"I know he cheated on you all the time. Was that who he was?"

Her brow furled. "Why are you asking me this, Julie?"

"I'm beginning to think I didn't know him at all. Can you be dishonest in one part of your life and a great man in another? Or is a fraud always a fraud?"

"I don't like to hear you talk like that. Sonny was your father."

"Yes, but he lied to me about King's book, mother. He was keeping things from me."

"Why does this matter to you?"

"Because I need to know the truth about him if I'm going to let him go," I said. "Tell me something. Be honest. Irving Wolfe was one of the early investors in West 57, wasn't he? You must know."

Cherie hesitated, but she nodded. "Yes, true. What of it?"

"What of it? He and Wolfe had a relationship going back decades. Doesn't that mean something?"

"No one asserts that Wolfe's crimes go back so far. There was nothing shady about his involvement with West 57. It was a business investment, pure and simple."

"That doesn't matter. Wolfe and Sonny were connected then, and I think they were still connected. I think – I think – that Sonny may have been involved in Wolfe's fraud in some way."

I said it aloud, and it nearly took my breath away, but that was what I was thinking. That was my secret fear. Sonny was a crook. A thief, like Wolfe. And now I was an accessory after the fact, perpetrating a scam with a book called *Captain Absolute.*

My mother sat back in her chair and folded her arms with a you-are-a-child look. She shook her head fiercely. "Never."

"It's the only explanation that makes sense, mother."

"You are wrong. You knew this man, Julie. So did I. He was passionate, and in his passion he sometimes hurt those around him. But he was a good man. A decent man."

"I'm not so sure anymore."

Cherie clutched my hand again, and I heard frustration in her voice. "Why are you doing this to yourself? You're making yourself crazy. This is your sorrow talking, my dear, not you. You are too close to this to think with your head and not your heart. There is only one answer. Let Helmut and the Germans worry about West 57. Walk away. If Sonny were alive, he would have done exactly the same thing."

"I doubt that."

"Trust me, Sonny could read the writing on the wall like anyone else. Forget about King Royal, Julie. Forget about Irving Wolfe. Forget about this book. Trust what you know about your father, and put his legacy in the hands of Gernestier. They are competent businesspeople, and they will make sure West 57 endures for years. You have other things to do with your life. Let it go, and start over."

"I'm not sure I can."

My mother sighed. "You need to get a life, and I am determined you will have one, my dear. Go to dinner with Thad tonight. Okay? You promise me?"

"I will."

"Forget about business. Have fun."

I smiled. "Sure."

"Then do yourself a favor," she told me, "and for God's sake, sleep with him."

21

Let it go.

That was good advice, even if it came from my mother. Unfortunately, I haven't made it to my position in life – late thirties, unmarried, risk-averse, closed off, inadvertently celibate – by taking good advice. No, I didn't let it go. I couldn't help myself. If I were in a horror film where a deranged zombie was carving up rural teenage girls, I would be the one who said, "Now's a good time to have sex in that deserted farm house."

Actually, I was in a horror film once. You will find me in the credits as "Bathtub Victim With Long Hair."

After I left my mother, I flagged down one of the Farouks and shuttled to the other side of the Park to visit Libby Varnay. It wasn't just a social call. She was not only Sonny's friend, she also knew the comings and goings on the Upper East Side better than Liz Smith. Everyone told Libby everything. If anyone could help me unearth the truth behind Sonny's secrets, it was her.

Her nephew and chauffeur, Drew, buzzed me into the building and answered the door on the second floor. He wore a suit that must have been specially made to accommodate his girth. "Hullo, Ms. Chavan," he told me, and his deep voice rumbled like truck tires on the highway. For as young as he was, he'd already lost most of his hair, making him look like a coal-colored Friar Tuck.

"Is she home, Drew?"

"Yes, ma'am."

I glanced around the bejeweled living room, and that was when the reality hit me that Libby was leaving. I'd never really believed that she would abandon New York to go upstate, but she was in the midst of packing up her life. The art had been stripped from the walls. There were open boxes on the floors. Even though she was still here, I felt lonely all over again. I missed her already.

"Are you going with her to Ithaca, Drew?" I asked the boy.

"Oh yes, ma'am. I'd never let Ms. Libby go anywhere without me. She saved me."

"Good."

"I'll get her for you."

"Thanks."

I wandered to the window and looked down at the street below me. Her location on Park Avenue was a prize. The curtains beside me had a musty elegance, like something out of a Victorian romance. I told myself that if I owned such a place, I could never leave it behind. Someplace with character and culture, someplace that was part of my blood.

Someplace like West 57.

Was Cherie right? Could Sonny have let the house go?

Could I?

"Oh, my, you look deep in thought," Libby said to me from the other side of the room. Her eyes twinkled. Her hands were on her hips.

I smiled. "I just had breakfast with my mother. That always gets me thinking."

"Cherie's in town? Lucky you."

"It's not luck. There are no accidents with my mother. She wanted to see me face to face to tell me I should move west." I knew that was why she took that red-eye. It wasn't Bree. It wasn't Thad. It was me.

"And?"

"And I still don't know what to do."

"Well, moving isn't easy, I'll tell you that," Libby said with a sigh.

Her eyes roamed the room as she wandered among the boxes. She wore a form-fitting peach dress that accented her tall, pencil figure.

"But you're doing it."

"Yes, I am. It's working, too. Creatively, that is. I have a chapter done in my book, which is more than I can say for the past six months. Would you like to read it?"

"Of course. I'd be honored."

"I'll have Drew print it out before you go. I have no idea how the printer works. I keep looking for the carriage return at the end of every line when I'm typing on the computer." She came close and touched my shoulder. "How are you, Julie? I felt awful about what happened at the Tavern. Are you okay?"

I nodded. "No harm done."

"Did you find out who this man was?"

"He was another victim of Irving Wolfe. He lost everything in the fraud. It's hard to blame him for being upset."

"Yes, but he had no reason to blame you."

"Maybe," I said. "Or maybe he's right."

"It's just that emotions are running high again about Wolfe because of that book. That's one thing I won't miss. No one around here seems to talk about anything other than *Captain Absolute*."

"What are they saying?" I asked.

Libby frowned and didn't answer right away. She removed a packing box from a Georgian-style sofa and sat down. She crossed her legs, tugged at her hem, and patted the sofa next to her. I joined her there. The sofa seemed made for perfect posture, which Libby always had. "Would you like something to eat?" she asked me. "I can have Drew fix us lunch."

"No, I had a late breakfast with Cherie."

"Sarabeth's?"

"That's right."

"Some things never change. Whenever I see her, that's where we meet."

I was surprised. "I didn't know you two were friends," I said.

"Oh, we get together now and then. I'm not sure Sonny approved. He probably figured she was poisoning me about him, as if Cherie could tell me anything I didn't already know." She added with a wink, "I think she always wanted me as an ally in getting you out to Los Angeles, but I was like Switzerland. Scrupulously neutral."

"I appreciate that."

She studied my face. "You look tired, Julie."

"Late night. Too much wine."

"Ah."

"You saw the interview with King Royal?"

"Yes, I imagine most people around here did. He's an unusual man. I find his attachment to Irving Wolfe a little disturbing. The way he calls him the Captain. Is it real or affectation, do you think?"

"It's hard to tell with King." I added, "I feel like I've unleashed a whirlwind."

"You have."

"What should I do?" I asked.

"Well, my advice is simply to protect yourself, Julie. I don't want to see you hurt."

"Do you think I need a bodyguard?" I asked, only half-joking.

Libby didn't smile. "I meant emotionally, but don't take your security for granted. There are others just like that man in the Tavern who have fallen from a great height. If you feel that everything has been taken from you, you may act as if you have nothing to lose."

"All this because of Irving Wolfe."

Libby nodded. "You have to understand the dimensions of his betrayal. He wasn't simply a thief in the night. He was one of us, part of the Upper East Side community. To have him do what he did, for so long, is a kind of incestuous rape."

"King isn't making it better."

"No, he isn't."

"Sonny had to know what would happen when he published this book," I said.

"Of course, he did."

"So why did he do it?"

"Why? Sonny was a publisher. What would you have him do, censor King Royal? That would have been abhorrent to him. And pointless. Someone else would have printed the book."

Libby made it sound so simple. So did Cherie. Except it wasn't simple. It was one thing to publish a book and another to seek it out. It was one thing to honor the truth and another to hide it. To keep secrets. That was what Sonny had been doing. I knew it was wrong not to trust my father, but I had to believe in my instincts. I didn't think I was wrong about him.

Libby saw the struggle in my face. "What's bothering you, Julie?"

I was tired of keeping it all to myself. I took a deep breath, and I told her everything. I told her about Nick Duggan and the slimy reporter's insinuations about Sonny and Wolfe. I told her about King Royal's blackmail and his hints about what Sonny knew. I told her about the ghost writer's doubts about King's story. I told her about Sonny's partnership with Wolfe going back to the earliest days of West 57.

I told her: "I find myself *believing* the rumors, Libby. I find myself believing Duggan is right. I think, maybe Sonny really did help Wolfe hide a fortune. I think, who knows, maybe Wolfe really is still alive, and Sonny knew it, and King Royal knows it, too."

"Oh, Julie."

"My mother says I'm wrong about Sonny."

"I think you are, too, but it's not about right or wrong for you, is it? This is a crisis of faith. I understand."

Yes, she really did. She knew what I was going through. Being in Libby's presence, it was impossible to forget who she was. You could hear it in her turn of phrase. She knew people's hearts. If you want empathy, talk to a writer.

"That's why I have to know what really happened," I told her.

"Unfortunately, faith is about things you cannot know, Julie. Sonny can't tell you the truth. He can't explain himself to you. He's dead."

"King's not."

"No, but would you really place your relationship with your father in the hands of a man like that? You can't trust him."

"I don't want to," I admitted, "but he knows what happened."

"Even if he does, I'm not sure you should believe what he tells you. All you'll have is more doubt, more uncertainty."

I was frustrated, because she was right. Everyone was right, and yet everyone was wrong. "I guess you're going to tell me what Cherie did. I should let it go and get on with my life."

Libby shook her head. "No, I'm not saying that at all. I trust your judgment, Julie. If you think Sonny was keeping something from you, well, I believe you. What you have to accept is that you may never know exactly what it was or why he chose to keep it to himself. If you're wrong about anything in all of this, it's that you are letting what you *don't know* overwhelm what you *do know*."

"Like what?"

"Like the man you know Sonny to be."

"Maybe he's not the man I thought he was."

Libby pursed her lips. I expected her to lecture me, like my mother. She would chide me for doubting my father. Instead, she said, "Sonny did keep secrets from you, Julie. However, it doesn't make him a bad man that he didn't tell you everything. It makes him human."

"What secrets?" I asked.

"I suppose it doesn't matter now," Libby sighed. "He made me swear that I would never tell you."

"Now you really have me curious," I said.

"Twenty years ago, Sonny asked me to marry him," Libby announced.

I was stunned.

"You and Sonny?"

Libby nodded. "We spent two years as lovers. We did much of the editing of *Morningside Park* in his bed. Cherie knew about it. They were long-divorced, but Sonny told her he was getting serious about me. That's when Cherie came to visit me for the first time. To warn me."

"About Sonny?"

"Yes. About his philandering ways as a husband. She didn't need to bother. I knew all about it. It didn't matter, because I was never going to marry him."

"Why not?"

"I loved Sonny, but I knew we would never be equals in a relationship. He would always try to dominate me. Not out of spite. It's just that he would dominate any woman. It was his nature. All I could see in marrying him was a slow suffocation of my soul. I'm too independent to give that up for a man. I wish I'd found someone I could love who would be a genuine partner, but sadly, I never did. Sonny was the one man I felt that way about, but it wasn't enough."

I stood up, trying to process what she'd told me. I knew what it meant for her to share this with me. She was laying herself bare. "I can't believe he never said anything to me," I said.

"He was proud, Julie. I turned him down. Women don't say no to Sonny Chavan. To tell you about it would diminish himself in your eyes – at least, that was how he saw it. He also knew that you looked up to me, and I imagine he didn't want to risk your misinterpreting my rejection of him. In fact, I'm still nervous about it."

"Don't be, Libby. I understand."

"I hoped you would. You're independent, like me."

"Yes, you're right." Except I wasn't feeling particularly independent right now.

"You see, we can keep secrets for lots of reasons," Libby said. "Don't assume the worst about Sonny. He doesn't deserve that from you."

I returned to the window to stare at the street. I felt a surge of gratitude toward Libby for telling me about her and Sonny. It helped me know him better. I realized I had come here to find my faith again, and Libby, as she always did, had restored a little bit of it for me. It made the idea of losing her even more painful. It made the city feel even emptier. However, I didn't feel quite as alone as I did an hour ago.

Unfortunately, as I watched the sea of people pushing past each other on Park Avenue, I realized that *Captain Absolute* was not simply about me and Sonny. There was more at stake. Lives had been destroyed. Millions had been stolen. Those are big things. Even if I wanted to, I couldn't let it go, because some secrets cannot be kept. I was in the middle of something now, like it or not. So was Sonny.

You see, I saw a woman at a bus stop across the street from Libby's apartment, but she was not waiting for a bus. She was looking up at the window. She was looking at me. I recognized her.

It was the same woman who had been wandering in my footsteps in the meatpacking district as I left the Gansevoort. The woman in the brown pants suit. No doubt about it. This was the same person, some hundred blocks from where I'd seen her last. She was still wearing a brown pants suit like it was a uniform.

She saw me watching her, and she turned away and was gone.

Of course, this is New York, right? You're always bumping into people you know. Ha ha ha. No, if I had that kind of luck in a city of 8 million people, I should be snapping up lottery tickets.

This was no accident.

Much as I hated to admit it, Nick Duggan was right. I was being followed.

22

I didn't know what to tell Garrett about our date.

I slunk into his office in the afternoon like I was doing the walk of shame, and we hadn't even had sex. I'd been avoiding West 57 – and him – all day.

He sat behind his desk among the stacks of manuscripts. I'd kept him up half the night, but he looked none the worse for wear. He always looks great. I knew I should be honest and tell him about Thad. "Can you believe it? A date arranged by my mother. How about a rain check for tomorrow?"

Unfortunately, I was scared of being honest. For lots of reasons.

"Hey," I said.

Garrett put down the page he was reading. "Hey," he said.

"I'm embarrassed," I said.

There was no need to enumerate the reasons for my embarrassment, which would have filled a phone book.

"Don't be," he said.

"Thanks for the rescue."

"Sure."

It would have been better not to mention the whole have-sex-with-me thing, followed by the whole why-not-are-you-gay thing. I had an excuse. I was drunk. I could fake total amnesia, and we would both be fine. Instead, I felt a peculiar need to re-live my humiliation. "About my behavior," I said.

"Julie."

"I'm not Bree. I don't make a particularly good slut."

Garrett held up his hand before I made it worse. "Julie, stop. You don't have to say anything. I don't want you to say anything. Okay?"

I didn't need to thank him. He knew I was relieved to be let off the hook.

"Listen, about tonight," I went on.

I'd decided what I was going to say. I was going to go for it. Lay it on the line. How does this sound?

Listen, about tonight. I'm sorry, I can't make it. I wish I could, but I already scheduled another date. Believe me, it's weird enough for me to have one, but two? I'm seeing Thad Keller. I've told you about him. We used to be engaged a long time ago. I could lie and tell you it's nothing, but I don't know if it's nothing. He says he wants to be back in my life. He's got me off balance. The thing is, it would really help if I knew whether there was a chance of anything happening between you and me. I'm not saying you have to be in love with me. I just want to know what we're doing and whether it could ever turn into anything.

I cleared my throat.

"About tonight," I repeated.

"Yes, about tonight, I'm really sorry, Julie," Garrett said before I could launch into my speech. "I totally forgot I have another engagement, and I can't get out of it."

I blinked. "What?"

"We'll have dinner another time, okay? I know you're preoccupied with the book anyway."

That popping sound was my ego deflating.

"Yes, sure, fine," I said.

"I hope you forgive me."

"No problem," I said. "Actually, my mother is in town. She surprised me today. She wants to take me to dinner."

When in doubt, fall back on a lie.

"So it works out well," he said.

"Perfect."

I stood up. He was smiling at me, and I was smiling back. I realized, however, that I wanted to slap the smile off his face. I wanted to kick him and hurt him for what he had just done to me. I was crushed, destroyed, furious, and bitter. It wasn't that he had beaten me to the punch by canceling our date before I cancelled our date. It was that he so obviously saw it as no big deal. We were work pals. Colleagues going out for happy hour. Catch ya next time, bro.

I could handle being rejected. I couldn't handle being nothing.

I tried to hold myself together, because I didn't want him to see the body blow he had delivered. This was worse than begging him for pity sex. This was worse than laying out my chest to him for open-heart surgery. This took my breath away.

"So," he said.

"So."

"No King today?" he asked. "No Bree?"

"They've got interviews all day. Tomorrow's the big bookstore event on Fifth Avenue."

"Right."

"Right."

I just wanted to leave. This conversation had already lasted six months.

"Do you want me with you at the store tomorrow?" he asked.

"No," I said, too sharply. "No, I've got it covered."

"Okay."

"Okay," I said.

He stared at me. "You all right?"

"Fine."

"About dinner, I'm sorry again."

"Could you please stop shoving that ice pick into me?"

No, I didn't say that.

"No problem," I said again.

"Have fun with your mother."

"I will. You have fun with – whatever it is you're doing."

"Thanks."

He didn't tell me what it was. Another woman. A Yankees game. It could be anything, as long as it wasn't with me.

I finally left like a prisoner released from jail. I hurried back to my office, closed the door gently when I wanted to slam it, and proceeded to put my hands in front of my face and hyperventilate. I did not cry again, because this was beyond crying. If you feel nothing, you can't be hurt. I obviously felt something.

"Do you mind if I point out the obvious, darling girl?"

I opened my eyes.

Sonny was back. He was sitting in his old chair, feet up, arms cocked behind his head. Cigarette smoke floated over his head like a halo. I hadn't driven him away. Or maybe, thanks to Libby, I'd invited him back.

"I can spot the obvious for myself, Sonny."

"Okay, tell me," he said.

"Garrett doesn't have the slightest romantic interest in me. Never did. Never will."

"Hmm." He chewed on this thought as he sucked on his cigarette.

"What, hmm?"

"Oh, I was just thinking that if a man believes a woman he really cares about is going to reject him, he'll usually save his ego by rejecting her first."

"Is that what you would do?"

"Very few women have ever rejected me, darling girl," he boasted with a grin.

"What about Libby?"

My father's grin evaporated.

"Mother rejected you, too," I said.

"You've made your point, Julie. We don't need to review all of my romantic misadventures. Besides, we're talking about you, not me. How did I raise a daughter who doesn't know how to take risks? If your mother and I have one thing in common, it's that we both took big chances in life and love."

"Yes, I wonder what I learned from that," I said.

"Apparently the wrong lesson."

I shook my head. "I'm done with games, Sonny. If a man wants me, he can tell me he wants me. I was with Thad for an hour, and he made a pass at me. I didn't have to get drunk and strip down only to be rejected. Thad knows what he wants, and he's not shy about it. I like that in a man."

"Really? I wasn't shy about asking you to join West 57. That didn't seem to sway you, darling girl."

"That's different."

"Is it?"

I stood in front of the desk. Sonny hadn't moved at all. "You're in my chair," I told him.

"Your chair?"

"My chair," I repeated.

He looked proud of my impertinence. He got up, and I sat down, and I was a little sad because the chair wasn't at all warm. No one had been sitting there. He was already gone, but I talked to him anyway.

"I have a lot of work to do, Sonny," I said. "Then I have a date tonight. So find another ghost to hang out with this evening, okay?"

After all, if you're thinking of having sex with someone, you really don't want your dead father showing up in the bedroom.

23

A limo. That was a good start. Thad sent a limo to pick me up. Not too many limos stop in front of my apartment building. I'd gone home early to get ready for our date, and I went for the killer look. Red is my color, so I wore red, but not much of it. I think my hair was longer than my dress. Spaghetti straps, zipper in the back, push-up bra to push up what God gave me, and my sexiest pair of barely-there panties.

I fidgeted in the limo and calmed myself with champagne. The back seat refrigerator was well stocked. Expensive stuff. I drank two glasses in the time it took to reach Thad's hotel. We were having dinner in his suite, an Asian feast catered by Morimoto's. For privacy, he said.

For convenient access to my vagina, I thought.

Not that I was complaining, because we both had a pretty good idea where this night was going. I am not easy. I am not Bree. Even so, it has been a long time for me, and I'm a realist, and I know how my body reacted to Thad's presence when I saw him after the play. If Bree hadn't interrupted us with her phone call, we would have been naked soon enough and probably would have stayed that way most of the night. I had vivid memories of sex with Thad. I'm pretty conservative in bed, but let's just say that Thad pushed me out of my comfort zones and into some happy places.

The limo pulled into the hotel ramp and stopped near a private elevator. One of Thad's people met me. You know you've made it when you have people. I do not have people. This woman – girl, really, because if your name is "Mandi with an i," you will always be a girl – was blond and perky, and she sized me up in the way that says: I know exactly why you're here. I couldn't help wondering if Thad had slept with her. My instincts said, of course he had. It was the first reminder in my head of what it had been like years earlier, when I dealt with those thoughts on a daily basis.

Mandi escorted me to Thad's suite and then disappeared discreetly.

Thad answered the door. He wore a tux as if we were headed for a night at the opera. Nice look. Thad always liked to be formal, and nothing had changed. He wasn't the kind of guy who dressed down. Garrett, by contrast, lived in his jeans; you couldn't get him out of them. I know this, because last night I tried and failed.

That was a joke.

I found myself comparing my rivals, Thad and Garrett, in my head. Funny that I thought about them like that. The rivals. Garrett probably wouldn't think of himself that way, because he had no interest in me. There was only one man chasing and seducing me, and that was Thad. Thad Keller, millionaire many times over, recognized on the street wherever he went, #84 on the Fortune 100 list of most influential celebs, one of *People* magazine's most eligible bachelors in their Sexiest Man issue the last four years. It occurred to me that I knew way too much about Thad. I'd followed his career over the years with an unhealthy curiosity.

Maybe I'd never really gotten over him.

"Julie," he said, caressing my name with that voice of his. He greeted me with a kiss. It was no peck on the cheek; it picked up right where we'd left off two nights earlier. It was erotic, long, and wet, and it said what we both knew: this date was about us getting into bed. Everything else was foreplay.

His suite was twice the size of King Royal's, and it glittered because of the crystal and mirrors. I think my own apartment would have fit in the hot tub. There was a grand piano, too. Rich people like pianos in their suites, regardless of whether they play, because I guess you never know when Michael Feinstein will show up at your party. You wouldn't recognize the name of the hotel itself, because I'm not sure it has a name. It's one of those private hotels in New York you have to know about, because they have no web site or signage. They specialize in people like Thad. People with endless money and a need for security and privacy wherever they go. People with a taste for perfection and the means to acquire it.

I could hear my mother talking to me in my head. "You could live like this, Julie."

Yes, I could adjust to this lifestyle.

Thad opened more champagne, even better and more expensive stuff than in the limo. He led us out on the balcony, thirty stories up, breathtaking view of the Chrysler building. The New York weather was cooperating this evening with a mild, refreshing breeze. It was as if all the stars had aligned according to some master plan. Of course, the architect of this plan was my mother, not God.

We clinked glasses.

"To you," Thad said.

Yes, to me. Tonight is for me. I sipped. Those little bubbles really do make me feel fine.

"Cherie's in town," I said.

"I know. I saw her." He added with a grin, "She's not invited to dinner. What happens here stays here."

"Don't be so sure. I'd check the room for a web cam."

Thad laughed. So did I. We stood beside each other, watching the view, and he slid an arm around me. It was comfortable, as if no time had passed. I felt at ease with him. I was a little dizzy, but it wasn't just the height or the alcohol. I'd finally pushed the world and the future out of my head, and I was living in the moment, which was a really, really nice moment.

"New York is beautiful up here," Thad said.

"It sure is. I get energy from it when it's not driving me crazy." That's how most New Yorkers feel. We love the city until we hate it.

"I can take a few weeks here with the insane pace, but then I need the ocean again," Thad told me.

"I suppose you have a beautiful beachfront Malibu estate."

"I do."

"Sunshine, surfers, all those amazing bodies."

"Yes." He added, "You should see it sometime. You'd love it. The sunsets are magical."

"Isn't paradise overrated?" I asked.

"No."

"How about earthquakes? I hear there are earthquakes in California."

"You used to like it when the earth moved," he said.

He tried to keep a straight face, but that was so lame that we both smiled.

"You always were a master of the pick-up line," I said.

"Thank you."

"How about the L.A. fires? Can you do anything with the wildfires out there?"

"Too easy," he said, shaking his head. "Something about you being hotter than any fire. Or maybe about how I'd love to make you melt."

"Nice. Do you still practice pick-up lines?"

"I like to stay in shape."

"Just for my own education, what line works best with women?" I asked.

He smiled. "The truth?"

"Sure."

"Hi, I'm Thad Keller."

He said it matter-of-factly. Twenty years ago, his voice would have dripped with ego, but not now. It was what it was. I think he was trying to flatter me, so that I'd think: He could have any woman he wants, and he wants me. I hated to admit it, but it was working. I was flattered.

"You know what line works best for me?" I asked.

"What?"

"Let's have sex."

He nodded. "That probably works with a lot of men."

A lot of men, yes, but sadly, not Garrett.

"It's an astonishing power I have," I said, "which is why I use it so sparingly."

"Like Wonder Woman."

"That's me."

It seemed like the right moment to kiss him again, so that's what I did. For a tall, strong man, he held me with the delicacy of china. By the time our lips parted, I didn't care about dinner. I didn't want to wait or pretend. If he had reached for my zipper, I would have let him strip me there on the balcony, with thousands of people watching us through their binoculars.

Instead, in my purse, my phone chirped for my attention. I was beginning to think my pheromones set the damn thing off.

"If that's Bree, I will shoot her," I said.

"Maybe it's your mother."

Fortunately, it wasn't Bree, and it wasn't Cherie. I checked the phone, and the caller ID said N. Duggan. That was an easy choice right now. I could think of few people I'd rather talk to less at this moment than slimy Nick Duggan. I pressed the Ignore button and let the call go to my voice mail.

"Anybody interesting?" Thad asked.

"Absolutely nobody interesting."

I thought about kissing him again, but the perfect moment had fled for now. We went back inside with our champagne glasses empty. I could smell ginger and an alluring, subtle aroma of fish. I love Morimoto. He's the one chef where I wouldn't even bother looking at a menu. Just bring out anything, Mr. Iron Chef, because I know it will be divine. If I'd taken off my clothes, we would have skipped dinner, but Thad had gone to a lot of trouble to cater my seduction. I might as well make him work for it.

"Are you hungry?" Thad asked.

"Ravenous."

But not for food.

My phone buzzed again. It was a text message this time.

Urgent I see you. Duggan.

No, no, no. Not tonight, Nick. There was nothing urgent tonight outside this suite. There was only me and Thad and what we were going to do to each other. Nick Duggan could wait until the morning when I was back in the real world. I was intent on living a fantasy for a few hours.

"I'm not very good with chopsticks," I admitted, as Thad revealed the sushi rolls waiting for us, which were works of art, little geometric morsels. They were so pretty I hated to ruin them.

"I did a movie in Japan," Thad said. "I became an expert."

"I drop everything I pick up."

"Here, let me show you."

Thad came around behind me at the table to show me, and he molded himself against my back. His arm became my arm. His fingers became my fingers. I let him guide me as he lifted a perfect rainbow circle between the chopsticks, dipped it in a bath of wasabi and soy, and delivered it into my open waiting mouth. The flavors were like a dozen little tongues lapping at my taste buds.

Talk about oral sex.

"Good?" Thad whispered.

I moaned.

We finished the first course that way, him feeding me, me trying to feed him. I wasn't as smooth, but he indulged me. Something sizzling arrived on silver trays, carried by a waiter so unobtrusive that he probably wouldn't have blinked if he'd found us having sex on top of the table. We drank more. We ate things I'd never eaten in my life, fish, vegetables, and fruits that had probably traveled from countries on the other side of the world to arrive between my lips. At some point, the lights dimmed. We were finally alone, and no one disturbed us. I have no idea what time it was. I was in suspended animation.

What was bound to happen began to happen.

I remember us on the sofa, me with my legs pulled underneath me and my head on his chest and his arms around me. His fingered traveled my black hair like raindrops and wound up on my bare thighs. I remember tilting my head back and our mouths finding each other. The pressure of his fingers became one finger, perfectly placed, perfectly soft, a lone castaway adrift in a wet sea.

I was already breathless when we stood up.

"Undress for me," he murmured, helping me by sliding my zipper like a slow-moving train car to the small of my back. He wanted to watch.

It wasn't hard. It didn't take long. There wasn't much to let fall to the floor, but it all fell. I was nude in front of him. I put myself on display, thinking: It's been fifteen years since he saw my body. Dim light is forgiving, but I wondered what he would say.

"You have the cutest little pooch," he told me.

No, he didn't say that. Just kidding. What he did say was very sweet.

If I were Bree, I would now give you all the gory details of what happened next. Him getting naked, us coupling in bed, sweaty and loud. What positions we used. How many orgasms I had. Etc. However, I am not Bree, and I'd prefer to keep those little details to myself. Yes, we had sex. It was beautiful. It was satisfying. It was exactly what I needed. A time out from the world.

By the time we were done, it was still early, just past ten o'clock. I didn't spend the night there. Instead, I took a shower, and as I toweled dry, Thad watched me from the bed, where he was still naked.

"You should stay," he said.

"I know, but I need to go."

If I stayed, I was admitting that we were in a relationship again. Maybe we were. However, if I left, and I woke up in my own bed, then it was only one night. I'd committed to nothing. He didn't look happy with me for leaving. He was used to getting what he wanted. Plus, it's more fun when the clothes are coming off instead of going back on.

"Are you running?" he asked me.

I stopped, zipper halfway up my back. "Yes," I admitted.

"Scared?"

"A little."

He got out of bed, and I drank in the sight of him. My resolve weakened. If he'd said he wanted to go again, I would have unzipped. Instead, he kissed me tenderly and said, "I'll have the limo take you home."

"Thanks."

He zipped me the rest of the way. "See me tomorrow before the show," he said.

"It's a busy day," I said. "I'll try."

"I have some scripts I'd like to show you."

"Scripts?"

"For the new production company. I'd love to get your take on them."

"I don't know, Thad."

"I value your opinion, Julie. So does Cherie."

I nodded. "Okay. Sure."

So maybe it wasn't just one night.

A few minutes later, the limo took me home. I had ten million things running through my head. I felt like a monkey in the jungle, with my hand clutching a new tree and my tail still wrapped around the last one. For now, I was dangling, with a long drop below me. Sooner or later, I'd have to choose to go forward or stay where I was.

Yes, I had a lot on my mind.

I was tired. I was sore, my body sated. I'd used muscles I hadn't used in a long time. It felt good.

I wasn't paying attention to anything except going to sleep. That may be why, as I got out of the limo, I didn't even recognize the click of the paparazzi camera from a doorway across the street.

24

"Nice tits," Bree told me as I opened my apartment door in the morning.

She glided past me, carrying a bag of donuts and two coffees in a foam container. She smelled of cigarette smoke, her highlights were freshly tinted, and her lips were even bloodier red than usual. I wasn't expecting her, but you never really expect Bree. She just appears.

"Excuse me?"

I looked down, thinking I'd had a wardrobe malfunction, but I was wearing a conservative blouse and jeans. Nothing was showing that shouldn't be showing.

"Small but perfect," she went on. "Nice dress, too. Red. Very hot, good choice."

"I'm lost," I said. "What are you talking about?"

Bree plopped down on my sofa. She put down the coffee and donuts and slid a copy of the *Post* from under her arm. "You're a page three girl," she said. "In the UK, that honor goes to a different sweet young thing every day who is willing to bare her perky breasts for the delight of lads in the pub. You put most of them to shame, however."

This couldn't be good. Bree handed me the newspaper, and I ripped it open.

"Shame about them covering up the nips," Bree continued. "We're not so delicate about such things at home. Harden 'em up and point the way, that's our motto. I thought about sending in my photo when

I was 18. Imagine being the wank-of-the-day for all those teenage boys. I could have had the tits that launched a thousand – well, you know."

Page three of the *Post* had a story about a Brooklyn judge on trial for corruption. They could probably run that every day and simply change the judge's name. There was also a story about a raccoon biting off half a finger from a park ranger upstate and a story about a Manhattan cop moonlighting as an Elvis impersonator. The usual Murdoch stuff.

"There's nothing here," I said.

"Oh, right, sorry, I lied. Page six, not page three."

I flipped forward in the paper and laid out page six on the coffee table in front of me. "Oh, balls," I said.

Actually, it was more like: "OH, BALLS!"

There I was. Two of me, actually. One photograph had been taken last night, outside my apartment, me in my red dress, disheveled and post-coital, heels dangling from one hand, and – oh, Lord – my nylons and panties clearly dangling from the other. I may as well have been wearing a sandwich board with the message, "Just Had Sex."

The other photograph was a still from one of my movie roles years ago. As in most of my movie roles, I was nearly naked, in this case, emerging from a swimming pool with bikini bottoms and no top, wet hair, a come-hither smile, and two yellow cartoon daisies discreetly dropped over my nipples by the sensitive editors at the *Post*. It wasn't my proudest moment on screen, although sadly, it was far from my most embarrassing.

Next to the photos of me was Thad's publicity picture from *Rear Window*. The headline read, "Get A Load Of Thad."

Nice.

The article was short, because a picture is worth a thousand words, so there wasn't much to say.

> *What goes around obviously comes around for eight-mil-a-pic actor Thad Keller. In town for a limited run in the lead role of the hot show* Rear Window, *Keller found time on his night off for a steamy hook up with publishing exec Julie Chavan. Word is that*

the two were briefly engaged when both were struggling actors in the 1990s, and when you look at Julie's assets, you can see why Thad was anxious to make another deposit. Hey, Thad, just wondering: did you go in the front door or did you use the "rear window"?

I threw the newspaper across the floor, where it scattered into pages on my carpet like drop cloths for a painter. "I'm going to jump," I told Bree. "Will five stories kill me or just leave me a vegetable?"

"Oh, it's not so bad," she said. "Pretty funny, too, the thing about the rear window. You have to give credit to the boys at the *Post* for that one." She added, "Obviously you did get a load of Thad. Good for you, darling. It's about freaking time. Was it more than one load, by the way?"

"I'm not talking about this," I said.

"Come on, it's just us girls. I want details."

"I'm not going to give you a blow-by-blow account."

"Ah, but there was blowing involved. Good."

"Figure of speech," I said.

"Your mother's going to ask me, you know. She's the one who told me about the newspaper. She called me and woke me up, she was so proud."

"Oh, my God. What is my mother doing reading the *Post?*"

"Good news travels fast, darling. People were already calling. Have you checked your answering machine? I bet you have fans."

I went over to the phone. Bree was right. I had 17 new messages. "Oh, balls," I said again.

"So what does all this mean?" Bree asked. "Are you moving to L.A.? Are you and Thad an item again?"

"I have no idea."

"By the way, what's your batting average? Are you two for two this week? Did you and Garrett get it on when he took you home? If so, you're welcome."

"We did not, and you're not welcome."

"Shame." Bree reached into the white bakery bag. "Cruller? I love donuts. You cannot get good donuts in London unless you go to Harrod's, and even then, they're Krispy Kremes from the States, which doesn't count. I *love* Krispy Kremes."

"I'm not hungry."

"Oh, lighten up. Julie. So you're naked in the *Post*. No big deal. Remember the photo of me cupping that starlet's bare breast at the BFI party a couple of years ago? It went viral all over the world. The *Mirror* dubbed me 'Breast of Show.' I lived to tell the tale, darling."

"That's you, not me. Remember, you're shameless. You live for publicity."

"True enough."

"How did the popzees find me, anyway? How did they know to stake out my apartment?"

"These boys will sit in their own feces for days to get a pic of Jen Aniston, so you're not much of a challenge, darling."

"I bet my mother tipped them off," I said.

"Now you're being paranoid."

"Not with Cherie."

I had another terrible thought. Had *Thad* tipped them off? Was all of this part of a sordid publicity stunt? I told myself that was crazy. Thad didn't need that kind of press attention now. Popzee set-ups were something up-and-comers did, not actors who had already made it to the big leagues. Bree was right. I was being paranoid.

Then again, it's easy to think everybody's after you when your breasts are splashed all over the daily paper. Wherever I went today, I was going to feel like people were staring at my chest. Fortunately, this is New York, so I'm used to it.

"Meanwhile, back to me," Bree said. "While you were getting past your hangover and getting laid yesterday, I was working hard with our friend King. Did you see *The View*?"

"No."

"King killed. The ladies ate him up. He sang, too."

"Oh, please tell me it wasn't Assy McHattie."

"No, but they had to bleep out a few words. It was hysterical. I thought Whoopi was going to wet herself. Thank God, there were no dogs, too."

"You know, you still haven't told me about King and dogs," I said.

"It's only little dogs, darling, and if I don't get details about Thad's load, you don't get details about King and dogs."

I growled at her. Woof.

"Then we did about two dozen more interviews," Bree went on. "Radio, papers, local TV. I've already checked online, and we've got pieces about King in *USA Today*, the Chicago *Tribune*, the *Plain Dealer*, everywhere. It's big, darling. The crowd at Stables & Proud today is going to be SRO."

"I hope so."

"I'm telling you, they better have enough books, because they're going to sell out. And that's before we do *Good Morning America* tomorrow. I am happy happy happy. You should be happy, too. *Captain Absolute* is going to hit the charts at #1, darling."

She was right. The book was a bonafide runaway hit, but I wasn't particularly happy. Bree read my face.

"Julie, you do realize that most ordinary human beings would consider all of this to be good news, don't you? You are sleeping with a rich movie star. You have a job offer to go to Hollywood and make movies. You are publishing a book that's going to sell hundreds of thousands of copies. You are the owner of breasts that can now be considered world famous. What more do you want from life?"

I opened my mouth to reply, but Bree shoved a glazed old fashioned donut between my lips. I bit down, and it was doughy and delicious. "Lethsglotothofix," I said with my mouth full. Translation: Let's go to the office.

"Eat, don't talk. Have some coffee. Relax. Don't worry, be happy."

I stood up, and Bree eyed the girls under my blouse. "They're still looking good, even if you're not twenty-three anymore. Petite but proud. Do they still stand up and say 'howdy do' when you take your bra off?"

"Frku."

It's a good thing my mouth was still full of donut, because I'm not sure that one would have come out as "freak."

Bree had no trouble translating, and she grinned. "Me, as soon as the ladies head south, I'm visiting the emergency clinic to have them propped up. I will not have headlights shining at my feet."

"Let's go to the office," I said again. I didn't want to talk about breasts anymore.

"*Mais certainement.*"

I picked up the strewn pages of the *Post* and crumpled them into a giant paper ball, so that I could deposit them in the trash, which is where they belonged. Bree stopped me in horror.

"Please don't tell me you're throwing the newspaper away!" she cried.

"Yes, I am."

"Julie, in thirty years, you will want to show this to your grandchildren." Her voice rose an octave. "'See, little Thaddy, this is what your gramma looked like before I got all these freaking wrinkles.' 'My gosh, grammy, you had great knockers.'" Bree grabbed the paper out of my hands and smoothed the pages on the coffee table. "This is for *history*, Julie," she told me.

"It's ancient history," I said.

I reached for the pages, and several half-sheets ripped away in my hand. I bent down to grab the rest of the torn pages, and that was when my heart stopped. I really think it skipped several beats and then launched into some kind of malfunctioning arrhythmia. I may even have gone into a coma. I stared at the headline on the *Post* blurb on page two, and I felt paranoid all over again.

Bree saw the expression on my face. "What is it, darling?"

I couldn't speak, so I just pointed. Bree followed the direction of my finger and said, "Well, crap."

HIT AND RUN KILLS REPORTER

It wasn't a long article, and there weren't a lot of details, because the story was only hours old. There was a photo with the article, though. No breasts in this photo. Just a face I recognized.

Someone had run down Nick Duggan.

III

25

"Julie Chavan?" said the woman who'd been following me for two days.

She was waiting in front of my apartment building when Bree and I went outside. She was still wearing a brown pants suit, like she'd been wearing when I saw her near the Gansevoort and outside Libby's condo. Either she has a lightning fast dry cleaner, or she is not an imaginative dresser. She wore beige heels, low and practical. Her hair was mousy and straight, and her face had one of those under-the-UV light fake tans. She was, all in all, a very brown person.

"My name is Goldy Brown," she told us.

Seriously? That can't be true.

"I'm a special agent with the Federal Bureau of Investigation," she added, showing me her FBI identification, which she kept in a tan wallet. "I'm investigating the disappearance of Irving Wolfe."

"Disappearance?" I asked. "Irving Wolfe committed suicide. He threw himself off his boat."

"Were you there?"

"You mean, on the boat?"

"That's right."

"No, of course not," I said.

Ms. Brown gave me a look that said: *Then you don't know anything.* Which was true. All I knew was what was in King's book, and I was beginning to suspect that King was as big a liar as Pinocchio. Except it probably wasn't King's nose that grew every time he made up a story.

"You don't honestly believe Irving Wolfe is alive, do you?" Bree asked, standing beside me. "Only conspiracy nuts believe that."

Ms. Brown's brown head swiveled toward Bree. Even her eyes were brown. "You're the agent who works with King Royal, aren't you? Bree Cox?"

"Yes, I am."

"I have some questions for you, too."

"I can't wait," Bree said brightly. She added with a sly grin, "I love your outfit, by the way. Polyester is the new silk."

Ms. Brown pulled out her gun and emptied her clip into Bree's smiling face. Okay, no, she didn't, but she wanted to.

"What can we do for you, Ms. Brown?" I asked.

"A reporter was killed last night in a hit and run on 131st near the Hudson," she told me.

"Nick Duggan of the *Post*," I replied. "Yes, I read about that."

"His phone records indicate that he called you a few hours before he was killed."

"That's right," I said. When a law enforcement officer asks you a question like that, you want to establish your innocence quickly. "I hope you don't think I rushed up there and ran him down. I don't even know how to drive."

"Besides, she has an alibi," Bree interjected. "She was getting laid at the time."

I winced in embarrassment. Thank you, Bree.

To make matters worse, Ms. Brown said, "Yes, I know."

Great. The FBI was keeping tabs on my sex life. They must be really bored.

"Why did Nick Duggan call you, Ms. Chavan?" she asked me.

"I have no idea. I didn't take the call. I let it go to voice mail."

"Did he leave you a message?"

"No."

"He sent you a text a few minutes later and wanted you to meet him."

"I know. I didn't reply."

"His text said it was urgent."

"I know what his text said, but I was busy." And you already know what I was busy doing.

"So you have no idea what Nick Duggan wanted to talk to you about?"

"No, I don't."

"You've talked to him before, though, haven't you?"

Ms. Brown said this like it was some kind of amazing revelation. She probably watches *NCIS* reruns on Saturday nights. If someone is going to interrogate me, I really want it to be Mark Harmon.

"A couple times, yes. He approached me outside my office building."

"What did he want?"

"He was doing some kind of story about King Royal and his biography of Irving Wolfe, which I'm publishing."

"Did he tell you anything about the story?"

"Reporters don't usually talk about their stories. They're afraid of getting scooped."

"Of course, with Nick, it was usually a pooper scoop," Bree added, laughing.

Ms. Brown didn't laugh. She studied Bree with the eyes of a turkey vulture spotting an even plumper mouse right next to the one she was hunting. "You knew Nick Duggan, Ms. Cox?"

"I know every London reporter," Bree said, which is like boasting that you are intimately familiar with every sexually transmitted disease. It's not likely to enhance your reputation.

"Did Mr. Duggan ever contact *you* to talk about King Royal? Or about Irving Wolfe?"

"No, he knew I'd never tell him a thing."

"Why not?"

"Because the man was a soiled sheet of toilet tissue clinging to the anus of humanity."

"It sounds like you knew him pretty well."

"Nick lived off gossip and innuendo. He didn't care whether any of it was true."

"Even so, you and Mr. Royal stand to make a lot of money on this book, don't you?" Ms. Brown asked. "Neither one of you would want Nick Duggan printing any embarrassing revelations that would hurt sales."

"If you've seen King on TV, you'll know he isn't easily embarrassed," Bree said. "Neither am I."

"I can vouch for that," I said.

"Have you seen or talked to Nick Duggan in the past month?" Ms. Brown asked Bree again.

"I already said no."

"What about your client? Do you know if Duggan made any kind of contact with King Royal?"

"Of course not," Bree said.

I must have made a little *yurp* sound. Ms. Brown looked at me again with her chocolate eyes. "Is there something you want to tell me, Ms. Chavan?"

"Actually, I saw King talking to Nick Duggan two nights ago," I admitted.

"Where was this?" Ms. Brown and Bree asked simultaneously.

"Outside the Gansevoort. It was late, the middle of the night."

"What were they talking about?"

"I have no idea," I said. "I was too far away." I was also drunk, depressed, horny, and flatulent, so I had other things on my mind.

"King didn't kill Duggan," Bree told Ms. Brown. "I happen to know for a fact that he was getting laid last night, too."

I groaned. "Oh, Bree, tell me you didn't have sex with him."

"Not *me*, darling," she replied, rolling her eyes. "The cocktail twins from the bar. Although it's a little tempting to see what that monster would feel like, don't you think? Anyway, I saw them go into his room together, and I'm sure the three of them were doing sticky shots for most of the night. I doubt King had enough time or bodily fluids to rent a car and drive to the other end of Manhattan to meet Nick Duggan."

"What about you?" Ms. Brown asked Bree.

"Me?"

"Yes, you. Where did you go last night after you left King Royal?"

"Last night?"

"Yes, last night."

Bree opened her mouth and closed it like a fish in a tank. She obviously didn't want to say what she was doing. She looked at Ms. Brown, and then she looked at me, and then she looked at the sidewalk, apparently in search of a hole into which she could crawl. "I went back to my hotel room," she said feebly.

Bree?

Her hotel room?

In Manhattan?

No, that was a lie and not a convincing one. Bree Cox did not spend an evening in New York watching *Top Chef* and eating microwave popcorn. A dance club? Maybe. A dinner with Viggo? Also maybe. Getting drunk with the cast of *Jersey Boys*? Equally maybe. Hotel room? No.

"You were in your room all evening?" Ms. Brown asked Bree.

"Yes."

"Alone?"

"Yes."

"Doing what?"

"What difference does it make?" Bree snapped. "I was alone. I was in my room. End of story."

"Did you make any phone calls?"

"No."

Now I really knew she was lying. Bree couldn't spend twenty minutes without making or receiving a phone call, unless she was in the middle of sexual intercourse. Even then, I think she might sneak in a call while changing positions. And, of course, I suddenly realized that's exactly what Bree had been doing. That's why she was lying. She'd had sex with someone and didn't want to tell me who it was.

It wasn't much of a leap to figure out the lucky guy. I was already in bed with one of my ex-fiancés. So Bree called the other.

"Oh, my God, you screwed Kevin Stone last night, didn't you?" I demanded.

Bree groaned. "Oh, balls. Yes, yes, all right, I figured everyone else was getting some, so why not me? I'm so sorry, darling. So much for willpower and giving up married men. You can slap me again if you like. It's a freebie."

"Don't worry about it, Bree," I said. "I don't care."

"Really?"

Really. I didn't care. It surprised me, but I realized that I loved Bree enough to finally forgive her, not just for last night, but for all the mistakes of the past. For all her flaws, Bree was someone I needed in my life. More than that, she was someone I *wanted* in my life. Cherie was right. I held onto grudges too long, and it was time to give this one up.

Bree saw it in my eyes. We were friends again. "Does this mean it's you and me against the world, darling? Like in the old days? Hos before bros?"

I laughed. As always, I couldn't help laughing at everything she said. "You and me," I agreed.

She hugged me. I hugged her. It was a tender, intimate moment, except for the FBI agent standing there, interrogating us about a murder. Ms. Brown looked peeved, probably because no one was hugging her.

"Someone *killed* Nick Duggan," she reminded us, "and it's got something to do with Irving Wolfe."

Bree wiped her eyes. It was odd to see her emotional, and I knew how much it meant to her that we were a team again. "Look, J. Edgar, Nick Duggan had more thumbs in pies than Little Jack Horner. He made enemies with every story he did. Why do you think he was killed because of Irving Wolfe? It was probably some politician or celeb or somebody else who got slimed by one of Duggan's rants. Now leave us alone, okay?"

The FBI agent stared at me. "Is that what you think, too, Ms. Chavan? Do you really believe Duggan's death had nothing to do with *Captain Absolute*?"

"*Captain Absolute* is just a book," I insisted. "A book couldn't possibly be worth killing over."

Right?

That's true, isn't it?

But I didn't believe it, and neither did Ms. Brown.

"Trust me, Ms. Chavan," she said, "anything involving Irving Wolfe is worth killing over."

26

Naked in the *Post*. Dead reporter. Questioned by the FBI.

You'd have to say my day wasn't off to a great start, and it didn't get any better when I arrived at the West 57 building. Bree grabbed a cab south to the Gansevoort to pry King Royal off the twins and get him ready for the bookstore event later that day. I went to the office and hoped I could get inside and close my door before anyone spotted me.

No such luck.

I slipped into the elevator by myself, but as the doors closed, a hand stopped them, and Garrett got inside with me. He was absolutely the last person in the world I wanted to see. He had coffee for one and no bag of Turkish rum babas. I'd already stuffed my face with Bree, but I would have done it again if Garrett had brought breakfast for me, which he usually did. Not today. We stood next to each other, shoulder to shoulder, not saying a word.

It was awkward.

We hadn't parted on the best of terms yesterday. I was mad at him for making a lame excuse and breaking our date, although it was hard to take the moral high ground, because I'd been about to break our date, too. I'd also lied about meeting my mother for dinner and then had sex with Thad. Plus the whole daisies-over-the-nipples photo spread in the newspaper. I was not really covered in glory.

I thought to myself: Garrett is not the kind of man who reads the

Post. He probably didn't even know about the photos. If I was really lucky, no one in the office knew, and Garrett would never find out.

Or maybe not.

"So how's your mother?" he asked.

I heard the acid in his voice. He knew.

"Since when do you read the *Post?*" I asked him.

"Since four of my friends called to ask if I'd seen the hot girl I work with on page six."

"Really? They said I was hot?"

Okay, that's not important.

"Look, I'm sorry I lied," I went on. "I was embarrassed to tell you. Cherie fixed me up with Thad, and I couldn't get out of it."

"Yes, it looked like a mercy date, the way your panties were dangling from your thumb."

Anger bubbled up inside me, turning me red. I'm short, and it doesn't take long for the steam to rise to the top. "That's all you can say to me? Do you realize what I feel like this morning? This was private. This was personal. Those bastards splashed my life all over the newspaper like I was some kind of hooker. And all you can do is take shots at me? Why do you care who I sleep with, anyway?"

"I don't. You don't owe me anything at all."

"Yes, you made that very freaking clear, didn't you?"

Garrett started to shout a reply and then stopped himself. He paced in the elevator car, which smelled like beer. The carpet was stained. The walls were faux wood panels. The space was tiny, and we were never more than a couple feet apart. As he stalked angrily back and forth, our bodies kept brushing together. I wondered how many people had had sex in here.

He leaned back against the metal doors and shoved his hands in his jeans pockets. The toes of our shoes bumped. He looked at me for the first time. "What the hell does that mean?" he asked.

"You know exactly what it means," I said.

"No, I don't."

"*You* were the one who called it off last night, Garrett. You had an important engagement, remember? If you're upset about me lying to you, then tell me the truth. What did you do last night? What was so important?"

Garrett's jaw clenched. He pushed his brown hair out of his face and left it messy, which made me want to straighten it. He looked away and wanted to lie, but I knew he'd tell me the truth. That's who he is.

"I finished reading *Woodham Road* again," he told me. "I put a frozen pizza in the oven. I drank three Summits. I watched the Yankees get clocked. Okay?"

"That sure sounds like an important engagement," I said.

"It wasn't nearly as exciting as your evening."

"From where I'm standing, I don't think you've got much right to judge me."

"Fine. We're both liars."

"I lied because you hurt me," I told him, my voice rising. The elevator car felt small and warm. "I was going to tell you the truth about Thad, because I felt awful about having to cancel, but you cut me off. You dumped our date and made it very clear that it was no big deal to you."

"That's not true."

"Oh, don't try to spare my feelings. The only reason you asked me out at all is because I was drunk and you felt sorry for me. You were being gallant, and then you thought, oh my God, what did I do?"

Garrett came even closer to me. We were breathing the same air. "Don't you put words in my mouth, Julie Chavan."

"Tell me I'm wrong."

"You're wrong."

"Oh, really? So why did you lie? Why did you break our date?"

"Because you came into my office and I could read the truth all over your face. Do you think I'm blind? You got drunk and made a fool of yourself, and when you sobered up, you realized you'd started something that you never meant to finish."

"So what, you're a psychic now? You can read my mind?"

"I didn't need to read your mind. You may as well have been

wearing a t-shirt that said, 'I need an out! Please give me an out!' So I gave you one, Julie. I gave you an out so you didn't have to feel bad about letting me down."

We were both losing it. We shouted like teenagers. The elevator kept creeping toward the floor for West 57.

"I don't need *you* to make decisions for me, Garrett!"

"No, you've got your mother for that. And *Thad.*"

"That's crap!"

"Oh, really? I didn't need to give you an out, but you sure took it, didn't you?"

"What does that mean?"

"I mean, Cherie fixed you up on a date, and you couldn't possibly say no to your mother, who's been trying to run your life since she gave birth to you. You tell me stories for years about Thad Keller suffocating you, and then he's back in your life for one day and you fall into bed with him. Real independent."

"How dare you!" I screamed, because when someone is right, you want to scream at them about how wrong they are. "How dare you talk to me like that!"

"Wake up, Julie!" he shouted back at me. "Everyone is running your life except you! Hell, Sonny's dead, and *he's* still telling you what to do!"

Ding.

The elevator doors finally slid open, freeing us. We had been inside for what felt like hours. Oddly, it was so sweaty and humid where we were, and we were both breathing so hard, that it was as if we had made love together, rather than had a fight that probably ended our friendship.

I was angry, upset, frustrated, and embarrassed, so I did the mature thing. I pushed Garrett hard. He is as tall as a tree, and I am a shrub, but I had adrenaline on my side. He stumbled backward. I shoved past him into the lobby of West 57, where half the staff was staring at the elevator open-mouthed. Sound travels pretty well up those shafts. They'd heard most of it.

I didn't care what anyone thought anymore.

I stormed into my office and slammed the door.

Fortunately, Sonny wasn't waiting to lecture me on my failings. I couldn't deal with him now. Instead, the phone was ringing, and I put on a happy face and answered it as if it were the best day of my life. Rather than one of the worst.

"Julie, it's Helmut at Gernestier."

I don't think Helmut bugged the elevator at West 57, and I don't think he's a reader of the *Post*. Nonetheless, the man is a master of timing. He manages to find me at my weakest moments. I was still trying to catch my breath.

"Hello, Helmut," I said.

"Today is the big day, yes? You have the first bookstore event at Stables & Proud for *Captain Absolute*. I'm sure it will go well."

"I hope so."

"That author of yours, King Royal, he's quite the character."

"Yes, he is, but he's Sonny's author, not mine."

I wondered why I felt the need to make that distinction to Helmut. To Gernestier, there was no difference. Everything was mine now. However, in my heart, I knew that I was beginning to separate Sonny from West 57. They weren't the same thing. Sonny was my father, and West 57 was a business running out of money.

"Of course," Helmut replied, as if he understood my psychology better than I did. "I know you must be busy, but I hoped you might have time to join me in my office today. We could open some champagne."

"To celebrate King's book?"

"To celebrate new beginnings."

They say you shouldn't make important decisions at moments of emotional turmoil. Then again, isn't every crossroad fraught with emotion?

I should have said no. It was a crazy day. I didn't want to fit in a meeting with Helmut, even though the Gernestier building, which is practically around the corner from me, is like visiting the Ritz. He probably has a driving range in his office with a multimedia simulator. You can do book deals around the world and play St. Andrews at the same time. I could work there, if I wanted. I could make a lot of money. I could pick the authors I liked.

Libby Varnay. Not King Royal.

Morningside Park, not *Captain Absolute*.

I didn't know if I would say yes to his offer, and I didn't know if I would say no, but it was my choice. How dare Garrett tell me I was letting other people make my decisions. No one decides for me but me.

"Okay," I said.

"Yes?"

"Yes, let's open some champagne."

"And talk?"

"And talk," I said.

We set a time in the early afternoon. I hung up the phone. I looked up, expecting to hear Sonny bellow at me for betraying him. I couldn't meet with Gernestier. I couldn't dream of handing his house to an accountant like Helmut. *Are you crazy, darling girl?* Instead, I was alone in the office. Just me.

Maybe my little ghost fantasies were over. Maybe I was on my own now, and I had to make my own way.

If only I had a clue where I was going.

27

I arrived at the Gansevoort early to collect Bree and King for the big bookstore event. My phone rang as I was paying Farouk, and it was my mother calling.

"Julie! Where are you?"

"At King's hotel, mother," I said.

"Perfect, so am I. Come see me."

"You're at the Gansevoort? Why are you at the Gansevoort? You always stay at the Pierre."

"That's true, but Bree raved about this place and all the pretty young things, so I decided to try it. It's only a couple nights. Some of us are not locked into routines where we cannot change a single thing in our lives without complaining about it to everyone who will listen."

Ouch.

"I'm pretty busy, mother."

"Room 614, my dear. See you in a minute!"

She hung up. Me being me, I gave in and took the elevator to the 6th floor.

Cherie's door was propped open on one of those metal security rods. I knocked softly and then entered. It was a suite, like King's. Remnants of mimosas and croissants sat on a tray at the dining table. Enya was playing on an iPod dock. I called out, "Mother?"

"In the bedroom, my dear."

I wandered into the king-sized bedroom and said, "Oh!"

My mother lay face-down on a special massage table. She was stark naked except for a towel the size of a postage stamp draped across her backside. Two Swedish masseurs as large as Shrek tended to her body, one placing hot black rocks on her legs, the other sliding his meaty hands down the glistening, greasy skin of her back. The men wore form-fitting shorts and form-fitting t-shirts, and it was impossible not to notice that they had nice forms to fit.

"Hello, Julie!" my mother called cheerily. Her voice was a little muffled, because she was talking through a hole in the table.

"Couldn't this have waited until you were decent, mother?"

"Oh, I've seen you naked often enough, what's the problem? Say hello to Erick and Pieter."

"Hello," I said.

Erick and Pieter smiled at me with very white teeth. I'm not sure they spoke English.

"If you like, they'll do you next," Cherie said. "Strip down, and you can have a shower after."

"No thanks."

"It's very relaxing. They have amazing fingers."

"I'm sure they do, but no."

"Well, I suppose you're already pretty relaxed," Mother said, giggling. "I saw the photos in the paper. It's about time, my dear! Overdue!"

"I really don't want to talk about this."

"Oh, don't be such a prude. There's nothing to be embarrassed about. Was it wonderful? You always used to rave to me about the sex with Thad and what a stud he was in bed."

"I did no such thing," I said.

"No? Well, maybe I just assumed it was wonderful. Anyway, Thad sounded happy when he called me this morning."

"Thad called you?"

"To talk about business, my dear, but I'd already seen the

newspaper. I grilled him for details, but never fear, he was very discreet. He says you're meeting him this afternoon to go over a few scripts. Excellent. Of course, my advice is that you save the scripts until next week in L.A., and you two can get in a quickie before the show."

Ninety seconds with Cherie, and I was already exasperated.

"Do we really need to talk about my sex life in front of Erick and Pieter, mother?"

"Oh, you don't mind, do you, boys?"

They both said "No, ma'am" in unison. I guess they did speak English.

"*I* mind, mother."

"Oh, fine, such delicate sensibilities you have. We'll take a break, shall we? Wait in the living room, boys, and keep your fingers limber."

Erick and Pieter gathered up the rocks from my mother's back and smiled at me as they left. As nimble as a thirty-year-old, my mother pushed herself up on the massage table and sat, nude, with her legs pedaling like a bicycle. She had not a wrinkle to be seen on her golden skin, and her breasts were perkier than mine. However, her body has had plenty of surgical assistance, and mine is still the way God made it.

"Do you want a robe?" I asked.

"No, I'll just get it oily. Really, my dear, when did you become so conservative?"

"I've always been conservative."

"Well, we'll loosen you up on the coast."

"What's this about L.A. next week?" I asked. "We haven't talked about that."

"What about it? I head home tomorrow. Thad goes back to Cali next week when his run in the play is up. I figured you could come with him, and the three of us could talk about the studio."

"I never said I was moving to L.A., mother," I told her.

"Did I say you were? I said talk. It doesn't hurt to talk. Of course, once you spend time at Thad's beach house, you'll never want to leave."

"Thad and I are not an item. It was one night. It probably won't happen again."

"Julie, are you a member of some sect that focuses on self-deprivation? For most of us, there are few problems in life that cannot be eased by the insertion of a male sex organ into one's vagina, but apparently you are an exception to the rule. Was it really so bad?"

"I never said it was bad. It was good. It was what I needed. I'm just saying it doesn't change anything."

"Sex changes everything, my dear. It always does."

I sighed. "Are we done, Mother? I have to go."

"Yes, yes, the bookstore event. Bree is very excited. She's convinced *Captain Absolute* will enter the *Times* list at #1. That's marvelous. Your father would be proud."

I didn't gush about the book, and Cherie noticed my lack of enthusiasm.

"What's wrong? You're not still worrying about this nonsense with Sonny, are you? I told you to give that up."

"It's not that simple. Did Bree tell you that we were grilled by an FBI agent this morning?"

"Oh, she mumbled something about an accident involving some reporter. Sounds like nothing. The death of a tabloid reporter is much like a long-awaited bowel movement. Both involve removing crap from this world, and both are cause for relief."

"Mother!"

"Critics and reporters don't elicit much sympathy from me, my dear."

"This reporter was doing a story about Irving Wolfe, King Royal, and Sonny."

"Well, Sonny hardly came back from the Great Beyond and ran him down, did he?"

"I'm just saying it's suspicious."

"I agree! When we do the movie, we should work it in somehow. Tell the story in flashbacks, use the rumors as part of the script. Is Wolfe alive? Is there a fortune to be found in some musty safe-deposit somewhere? Did this reporter find the truth and meet an untimely end? I like it."

"This isn't a movie."

"I realize that, but you didn't kill the man yourself, did you?" Cherie asked.

"Of course not."

"Then I don't see how it concerns you, my dear."

I sighed again. "I have to go, mother," I repeated. "Was there something else you wanted to tell me?"

"Only that I understand you're meeting *Hellmooooooooooot* again this afternoon, and I wanted to chat to you before you chatted to him."

"Where on earth did you hear that?" I asked.

"From Helmut, of course. I've done deals with him. Remember that weird little Japanese anime film I did that made a fortune? Gernestier had the rights. So Helmut and I go way back. Of course, he knows we're rivals on this deal. He wants you for Gernestier, and I want you for me."

"I'm not a free agent third baseman, mother."

"No, you're much prettier than that, my dear. So what are you going to tell him?"

"I don't know yet."

"Why not?" Cherie demanded.

"I haven't had time to decide. I've had other things on my mind."

My mother clucked her tongue at me. She climbed off the massage table, and even averting my eyes, I couldn't help but notice that she was plucked bare in sensitive places. This is not the kind of thing you really want to know about your mother. She patted my face, and her capped teeth smiled.

"I love you, Julie, and I want the best for you."

"I know that."

"I'm offering you a better life. Money, travel, romance, power. Warm days, cool nights. Truly, it's paradise out there. What's not to love?"

"I didn't say no, mother."

"Then say yes. Look, Julie, I understand this is hard for you. You're still grieving your father. However, sooner or later, you are going to have to make some decisions about your life. You are procrastinating, and you can't walk in place forever, not when West 57 is dying. Helmut is going to want you to decide. I'm going to want you to decide."

"I *will* decide," I said. "But I'll make the decision. Me, not you."

Cherie shrugged. "I wouldn't have it any other way. This is your call, my dear. Just make the right decision, all right? Pack your bags for L.A., and I'll start condo hunting for you when I get back tomorrow."

I hate it when Garrett is right. I wasn't calling the shots in my life. Cherie was.

My mother returned to the massage table and climbed on, stomach down, inserting her face into the hole again. "Send the boys back in on your way out, will you? Good luck at the bookstore today! I hope you get a crowd!"

28

We got a crowd.

You'd have thought that someone really important and influential was in the store. You know, like a Kardashian. Usually, author events at bookstores are depressing affairs. It's the writer, a bookseller or two, the author's spouse, and a couple homeless guys sleeping in the back row among a hundred empty chairs. The author poses for a photo next to a big stack of books, and the store returns them to the publisher the next day. Writer egos are fragile to begin with, and they usually walk out feeling like perfume spritzers in the mall.

Not today.

We had five hundred people bulging out onto Fifth Avenue. Maybe more. It's a two-story store, with an event space upstairs. The crowd filled the upper level, trailed down the stopped escalator, and swelled into a bubble on the outside sidewalk like they were trying to get into the Top of the Standard. You have to give King credit. Most of these people probably didn't know who Irving Wolfe was. They were here for the man who sang Assy McHattie on YouTube and moonwalked with Whoopi on *The View*.

In two days, King Royal had become a pop phenomenon.

"More books," Bree said over and over, like it was her mantra. "We need more books! I'm going to see if they can courier another couple hundred copies from across town. This is freaking amazing!"

Yes, it was amazing. It was chaos on the way to becoming anarchy, and the customers just kept coming.

The crowd swallowed up Bree as she went hunting for a store manager. I stood next to King in the back room, peering out at the sea of people. They'd taken us through the loading dock entrance to avoid being mobbed. King studied the people through a crack in the stockroom door. He had his arms folded over his chest and a solemn expression on his face.

"Nice crowd, King," I said, which was an understatement.

"Yes, the Captain would be proud."

"You don't have to talk if you don't want to," I told him. "You could just sign books."

That was wishful thinking. If King didn't talk, there would be a riot. These people were here because they wanted to hear the next thing out of his mouth. He was like an uncensored love child of Donald Trump and Lady Gaga.

"Oh, no, I must address them," King said.

"Well, it's going to take a few hours just to get through the book line, so keep it short, okay? Fifteen minutes is fine."

"It will take as long as it takes, Julie Chavan."

"We'll start in five," I said.

"Yes, I must ready myself."

"Do you have to pee?"

"No, but I require privacy to gather my thoughts."

"Of course," I said. He probably had to pee.

I left King in the stock room. On the sales floor, the booksellers had erected a velvet rope barrier to keep the crowd back and carve out a little niche with a podium and signing table. The people were impatient. The buzz was loud. I checked out the crowd and saw lots of tattoos and muscle shirts and an odd mix of scantily clad twenty-somethings and middle-aged women who looked as excited as if they were at a Tom Jones concert. I hoped no one tossed panties.

The mob scoped me out as someone in charge and shouted questions.

"Will he sign my breasts?" asked a blonde near the front of the rope.

"No."

"How about my ass?" asked the man next to her.

"No."

They groaned with disappointment. I fought my way to the balcony overlooking the first floor and saw a party going on below me. From Reference to Cooking to Mystery/Thriller, there was hardly an open square foot of real estate inside the store. Most people carried little red bags with their copy of King's book. One of the managers, whom I knew well from other author events, spotted me and waved. He made a little jerking motion with his hand like pulling on an old cash register.

Ka-ching.

"Is it fair to conclude that we are geniuses?" said a voice in my ear. It was Bree. Somehow she'd found me again. She surveyed the rock concert enthusiasm in the bookstore and did a little dance of joy.

"Are we geniuses if we sell a book to people who aren't going to read it, just so they can meet an author who didn't write it?" I asked.

"Yes."

"Then we're geniuses," I agreed.

Our self-congratulations were drowned out by a roar from the upstairs crowd. King Royal marched from the stock room with a copy of *Captain Absolute* under his arm. People whistled and shouted his name. He swayed unsteadily, and I suspected his private time had been used to down a few drinks from a hidden stash. He grabbed the microphone and climbed on top the author's table, next to stacks of books. Not on the floor. On top of the table. He was larger than life, towering over everybody in the store. They could see him downstairs, and they cheered lustily.

As the crowd stared, I heard whispers travel among the people in giggles and gasps. Everyone began to point. I didn't understand what was attracting their attention, and then Bree murmured, "Uh oh, looks like someone crashed the party."

"What?"

I looked at King and murmured, "Oh, crap."

King had traded in his baggy pleats for snug khakis, and let's just say that his robust manhood was impossible to miss. I could have hung a coat on it. Songbirds could have perched on it. Kelly Jax would have swooned.

In front of us, a young woman in the crowd whispered to a friend, loud enough that we could hear: "No way that's real. That's a sock."

Bree, helpful as ever, leaned between them. "It's the genuine article, darlings, take it from me."

They turned to her with big eyes. "You've seen it?"

"In the flesh. It's a thing of beauty. Like a Renoir."

"Wow."

Noticing the buzz, King looked down at himself. *Don't say anything, don't say anything, don't say anything*, I begged him in my head, but that was like asking the wind not to blow and the sun not to rise.

"Yes, I have been blessed in my physical endowment," he announced into the microphone, which broadcast his voice all the way onto Fifth Avenue and probably caused four traffic accidents. He cleared his throat and went on with the solemnity of Lincoln delivering the Gettysburg Address:

> *"A man without a big Johnson*
> *Told his doctor how much he wants one*
> *I'm only at four*
> *Give me six inches more*
> *And I'll bed every girl in Wisconsin!"*

The crowd roared its approval, and King flashed a coy grin and jiggled his curls at their adulation. Welcome to the miracle of modern celebrity. King was definitely in the big leagues now.

I wondered how long the pain would last. I thought about throwing myself over the balcony, but it was like a mosh pit below me, and there were enough people to break my fall. I had visions of several more hours of songs and poems. However, before King could move on to his next X-rated anecdote, I heard a strange noise burbling up from the crowd. I'd never heard anything quite like it. It was a musical sort of growl-howl-snarl-yelp-yip, a combination of braying donkey and Justin Bieber song, and it came from several directions at once. Other people heard it, too, and looked around in confusion. As we listened, it got louder.

"What on earth is that?" I asked.

"Oh, no!" Bree hissed in dismay. "Dogs!"

"What?"

"Dogs! Little dogs!"

This isn't Paris, so you wouldn't expect to find dogs inside a bookstore, but Bree was right. And not just one dog. Somehow, among the crowd, at least six women had smuggled in oversized rats pretending to be canines. Six! The smell of King Royal apparently drew them like raw hamburger. The dogs managed to escape the grasp of their owners and streak toward the table where King was standing. They surrounded it like pixie-sized Orks out of *Lord of the Rings*. A teacup poodle. A Yorkie. Two Chihuahuas. A wiener dog. A little terrier mutt. King saw them and froze in what can only be described as primal loathing.

He *hated* the dogs.

The dogs *loved* him.

The wailing moaning spitting squeaking Bieber concert intensified, and the crazed dogs jumped up and down as if on a trampoline, claws scratching on the legs of the table as they tried to get to King. Their owners screamed their names, which included Giggle, Squink, Taco, Burrito, Magoo, and Queen Latifah. (This is why I do not have pets.) The frantic women pushed through the crowd to retrieve their furry darlings, but the more they pushed, the more others pushed back, and finally, the velvet rope barrier that separated King from his fans crashed to the carpet. Everybody surged forward, rushing King and the dogs. The poodle and one Chihuahua hid under the table. The wiener dog chased his tail in circles. I couldn't see the terrier or the Yorkie, but the second Chihuahua, who was obviously slyer and more determined than the others, used the body of the nearest spectator to claw upward and do a Fosbury flop onto the book table.

King went wild with panic.

The dog attached itself to his leg like a suction cup and would not be dislodged. King danced like Dick Van Dyke, kicking books into the air as his legs flailed, trying to separate himself from the Chihuahua. No such luck. The scraggly brown beast clung to its prize as ferociously as a rodeo star riding a bucking bronco. King spun in circles, he pried at the dog's paws, he swatted its backside with a book, but the dog had found the love of his life and humped King's leg like a Viagra-crazed porn star.

"GET IT OFF! GET IT OFF!" King bellowed into his microphone, announcing his dilemma to half of New York. "GET THIS FREAKING LITTLE MANGY FREAKING PISSANT FREAKING CREATURE OFF ME!"

No, he didn't say "freaking."

He kicked again with his leg in one of the best Rockette imitations I've seen outside Radio City Music Hall. Two things happened. King flew backward off the table like a skydiver as his feet spilled out beneath him, and the Chihuahua soared out in mid-air over the heads of the crowd like a home run headed for the bleachers. People ducked to avoid the canine missile. I heard the dog's owner bleat with fear. As it happened, the dog flew right at me, paws splayed. It was high, and I'm short, but I channeled Brett Gardner, leaped up with both hands above my head, and caught the airborne Chihuahua before it sailed over the railing down to the first floor.

I clutched it to my chest, and the dog, utterly unfazed by its ride into space, happily began to kiss my face.

"EVERYBODY BACK!" Bree shouted with authority.

We couldn't see King anymore. He was completely obscured by the crush of fans. I handed off the dog to its crying owner, and Bree and I squeezed toward the podium to rescue our author. People around us laughed and shouted, but just as quickly, the laughter cut off into terrified screams, and we dove out of the way as the crowd surged backward, nearly trampling us. When we reached King, he was sprawled on the floor on his back, making a big X. I expected to see the other dogs making love to his legs, but this was much worse.

King wasn't alone.

A man stood over him. King stared up at the man with his mouth open, unmoving, as stiff as a corpse. If I had to guess, King was in the process of wetting himself. I didn't blame him. I knew the man standing there. It was the same man who had attacked me with Libby Varnay at Tavern on the Green.

What did Nick Duggan say his name was? Walter Pope.

The man who had lost everything, his life saving, the money for his wife's cancer treatments, to Irving Wolfe.

Walter Pope was pointing a gun at King's head.

Calm people scare me more than angry people. Walter Pope was serenely calm. He wasn't the same angry fanatic he'd been at the Tavern. He'd crossed over to a distant land where nothing mattered anymore.

"Where's my money?" Pope asked.

King, who normally couldn't shut up if you stuffed his mouth with a sock, didn't say a word.

"Where's my money?" Pope repeated in the same monotone.

King made a choking sound reminiscent of the yip of the little dogs. His white skin became even whiter. His eyes grew huge and round.

"I want my money back," Pope told King, and he leaned forward until the barrel of the gun pressed into King's forehead. If he fired, it would make a big hole. "You know where Irving Wolfe hid the money. I want it."

"There's no money," King rasped.

"*Liar.*"

King's skull shook back and forth like a bobblehead. If there had been any money, he would have given it up in a heartbeat. He would have picked pockets on the street and dumped wallets at Walter Pope's feet.

"Mr. Pope," I said, and when the words came out of my mouth, I looked behind me, because I wasn't sure it was me who'd spoken. As a general rule, distracting a man with a gun, who has already attacked you once, isn't a smart idea.

Pope looked at me, and so did the gun. It looked right at me and said hello. I was not happy to make its acquaintance.

"Mr. Pope, I know what you lost," I said. "I'm very sorry."

"This man knows where the money is," Pope insisted. "I want what's mine. I want what was *stolen* from me."

"I understand. I do. It's terrible what Irving Wolfe did to you and so many others. But this won't get you what you want."

Pope waved his gun around the bookstore, and people screamed and ducked. "All of this is because of what Wolfe did! All of you are profiting from that monster! And this freak, this pervert, he's turning my grief into a sideshow."

He pointed the gun at King again. Then back at me. Then at King. It was obviously a tough call, deciding who to shoot first.

"Mr. Pope, I heard about your wife's illness. Please. Don't leave her all alone by doing something foolish."

"It's too late."

The gun. King. Me. King. Me.

"Please, won't you put the gun down?" I asked.

Pope shook his head fiercely. He pointed the gun at King, who began blubbering like a newborn.

"Last chance," Pope said. "Tell me where my money is."

"No!" King wailed. "Stop! Don't!"

I saw Pope's hand trembling, and then he did it. He squeezed the trigger. He fired. He put the gun to King's head, and he fired. I winced, expecting a big bang and lots of blood.

Click.

Nothing happened. He fired again. And again.

Click. Click. Click.

Then click was followed by BONK. From behind, I saw something as big as a concrete block go up and down and land like a hammer on Pope's head. The gun tumbled from his hand. He stuck out his tongue, saw stars, and crumpled to his knees. A second BONK reduced him to unconsciousness. He fell into a limp pile on top of King Royal, who pushed him off and scrambled to his feet and galloped for the stock room.

My unlikely heroine winked at me.

Bree, looking like one of Charlie's Angels, stood there with a ridiculously heavy bargain-priced hardcover copy of Stephenie Meyer's last vampire novel in her hands. For the first and only time in my life, I was grateful that the woman couldn't write a book that was shorter than 700 pages.

29

"If you wanted him unconscious, you could simply have read to him from the book," I told Bree when the excitement was over.

"Well, that's the thanks I get," she replied.

Actually, I'd thanked her profusely after the police took Walter Pope away. I hugged her. I kissed her. I tend to get emotional when I come close to violent death, but I live in New York, so it's not really an uncommon occurrence.

"I guess this won't go down in history as the most successful book signing," I said. "King didn't actually sign any books."

"Are you kidding? This will be the top story on every news show across the country. The video probably has a couple million YouTube hits already. I didn't think this book could get any bigger, but it just did. I'm only sorry I never thought of the crazed gunman idea before."

"The dogs, too," I said suspiciously. "Pretty amazing, all those women showing up at a book event with little dogs. I can't remember that ever happening before."

"Yes, life is full of astonishing coincidences," Bree remarked.

She winked at me. I think she was kidding, but with Bree, you never know.

"Where is King?" I asked.

"I suspect he needed a change of underwear." She wrinkled her nose.

We were still in the bookstore, but the crowd was gone. We sat in armchairs near the children's section with bottles of water in our hands. Bree flipped through a copy of *Walter the Farting Dog*.

"Did you see your life flash before your eyes?" she asked me. "When he pointed the gun at you, that is."

"I'm not sure. Maybe. I was naked a lot, so I think it was *your* life."

"Could be." Bree tapped her water bottle gently against my head. "I'm awfully glad we're friends again, darling."

"Me, too."

"Dinner tonight?"

"I'm seeing Thad before curtain, but I don't think he'll want to eat before the show. So sure, why not?"

"You have better things to do with Thad than eat," Bree said.

"I don't know. We'll see."

"I wish all my lovers approached sex with that kind of rampant enthusiasm," she replied slyly. "Darling, please don't tell me all of your pent-up lust was quenched in a single evening. If so, then I really need to get to know this man."

"I have plenty of lust," I said.

"But not for Thad?" she asked with a knowing stare. "Well, never mind, I'll find a restaurant for us with hot young Spanish waiters. Text me when you're ready to eat, drink, and be merry, okay?"

"I will." Time had zoomed by, thanks to the police and press. I checked my watch. "I've got to go," I said. "I'm meeting Helmut."

"*Ja wohl*," Bree replied. She flipped more pages in the children's book. "I'm going to hang out with this cute little flatulent dog for a while. I like him. He reminds me of my last boyfriend."

"See you later."

I pushed myself out of the chair. I hunted down the store manager and apologized again for the chaos, but he could barely smother the grin on his face. They had sold hundreds of copies of *Captain Absolute* despite the dog attack and the attempted murder, so it was all good. I waved at the counter staff as I headed for the Fifth Avenue door, but I didn't make it out of the store. I bumped into one of the café baristas, who was going in as I was going out, and she recognized me.

"You're from the publishing house, aren't you?" she squeaked in a high-pitched voice.

"That's right."

"So you know that author guy who was here, right?"

"I do."

The girl nodded. She was about twenty-two, ridiculously pretty, like most girls at twenty-two. "Well, I was just over at Victoria's Secret," she said. "You may want to go over there, 'cause there's kind of a problem."

"What's the problem?" I asked.

"That author guy, he's there, and they can't get him to leave."

Great.

I thought about retrieving Bree, but she had already done her heroic deed for the day. This one was mine. I left the bookstore, put on my sunglasses, and made my way down Fifth Avenue to the flagship lingerie boutique, where I was confronted by posters of discreetly topless skinny models. I'm pretty sure that one of the lingerie models in the window displays was the body paint model that Thad used to date. She was beautiful and very sexy. I did not like her.

"Wow, I love your hair," said a clerk inside as she approached me.

"Thank you."

"You want to try something on?"

"No, I'm stocked on power panties, thanks. I'm looking for King Royal. I'm his publisher. Someone said he was here."

Her brow wrinkled in confusion. "King Royal? Oh, the Assy McHattie guy, yeah! Oh, wow, it's good you're here. We were thinking we should call the cops or something."

"Don't do that. He's had a rough day. Where is he?"

"He's in one of our changing rooms. He's fondling the bras. It's a little creepy."

"I'll talk to him."

I made my way to the changing rooms at the rear of the store. "King?" I called.

When no one answered, I tapped on each door and called his name. The voices answering back to me were all feminine, but at the last door, there was no response from inside.

I tried knocking a few more times and then gingerly pushed the door open. The interior was bright under fluorescent light. Several items hung on hangers, including lace teddies, underwire bras, and thongs. King sat on the changing bench, staring into space, kneading the cups of a large pink bra between his fingers. His white dress shirt was untucked, his tie was loose, and his pants were a wrinkled, disheveled mess. His curly mop of hair looked flat. His droopy nose seemed to droop more than usual.

"King, you okay?" I asked.

"Julie Chavan," he replied. "You have found me."

"I was a little worried when you disappeared."

"Yes, I ran. It was cowardly. The Captain would have been disappointed in me."

"Well, you had quite the scare at the bookstore. That would freak anybody out. Why don't you go back to the Gansevoort and rest?"

He studied me with that same faux upper-crust stare he used on Pierce. "I do not need rest. I need money, Julie Chavan. It has become urgent."

"I already told you, King. There's no more money. We're selling a lot of books, so if you stay on the media circuit, you'll earn royalties."

"I am not certain I can stay here," King said. "I may need to disappear."

"King, what are you talking about?"

"My life is in danger. There are those who would kill me for what I know."

I shook my head and sat down next to him. "Look, I'm really sorry about Walter Pope. Irving Wolfe had a lot of victims, and this one went off the deep end. We'll ramp up security. When you do *Good Morning America* tomorrow, we'll have guards on the set to make sure no one gets close to you. Okay?"

"You cannot protect me."

I pried the bra away from his fingers – it was several cup sizes too large for any woman living on Earth – and hung it on a hook, where it dangled like a pink mountain range. "What's really going on here, King?"

"It is better that you not know, Julie Chavan. The best thing for all of us would be if you help me to disappear."

"Exactly what is it you know that could get you killed?" I asked.

King put a finger over his lips in dramatic fashion. "You should not ask so many questions. People who ask questions get hurt. That reporter asked questions, and you saw what happened to him."

"Nick Duggan?" I asked. "Are you talking about Nick Duggan? This is serious, King. If you think you know who killed him, you have to tell the FBI."

"I am the keeper of secrets, Julie Chavan, but I tell no one."

I thought about kicking him in his robust manhood. "Look, I saw you and Nick Duggan talking outside the hotel. What did he want with you?"

"He wanted what everyone wants. The Captain. I'm the keeper of his soul. It's a heavy burden. How I miss him! I loved him, you know, I really did." He opened his mouth and sang in a booming voice:

> Or were I in the wildest waste
> So black and bare, so black and bare,
> The desert were a paradise,
> If thou wert there, if thou were there

In the other changing rooms, women applauded and whistled.

"That's Robert Burns," he said.

"I don't care if it's Robert Pattinson or Robert Goulet. What did you tell Nick Duggan?"

"Nothing," King said. "I told him nothing at all, but Duggan was shrewd. He was getting close to the truth. Too close for his own safety. I warned him that he was on a dangerous path."

"What truth? What are you hiding?"

King shook his head. "No, no, no, Julie Chavan. If I say a word to anyone, I will pay the price, just as Duggan did. If you won't help me, then I need to see to my own protection."

"I want to know what's going on, King," I insisted. "Are the rumors true? Is there a secret stash of cash somewhere?" I thought about what I really wanted to know, and I said: "What was Sonny's role in all of this?"

"Yes, that is what troubles you, isn't it?" he said. "The truth about your father. I already made you a generous offer. You pay me what I need to disappear, and in return, I give you his secrets."

"Forget it. I'm not playing this game."

I turned to leave, and he called after me. "Julie Chavan!"

"What?"

"If you persist in this quest, you will hurt people you care about," King told me. "Remember that."

30

I tried to forget about King and his threats. I had other things to worry about that day. Namely, *Hellmoooooooot.*

I wasn't surprised that Sonny didn't join me in spirit for the meeting at Gernestier. He'd never set foot in that building when he was alive, so I didn't figure he was going to start now. Besides, I think he knew what I was going to do, and he didn't want to be there to see it.

There was only one way to save West 57. Helmut knew it. My mother knew it. I knew it, too.

Helmut greeted me with a smile so blinding I was tempted to put on my sunglasses. Those teeth have to be fake. He hugged me – awkward – and then took me on a tour of the Gernestier executive floor, which was like visiting a wing of the Smithsonian. The entire building is a monument to money. As commercial as they are, they've worked with some of the most successful authors, musicians, artists, actors, and filmmakers in the world, going back decades. I saw first editions, platinum records, Oscars behind glass. I was particularly impressed with the life-sized ice sculpture of James Patterson in a refrigerated case in the lobby.

I'm kidding about that.

The whole place, with its cavernous spaces and high ceilings, had an odd quiet to it, like a library. I felt like whispering. Down below, on the plebeian floors – where the real people worked, where I would work – I'm sure the offices were little hovels crammed floor to ceiling with manuscripts and books, smelling of Subway sandwiches. You drank stale coffee in plastic cups. You plugged your ear against the cacophony of voices from cubicles on either side of you. You filled out expense requisitions when you ran low on pencils and Post-it notes.

You answered the phone: "Julie Chavan, West 57, a Gernestier Division, how may I help you?"

Helmut had the champagne opened and ready for me in the headquarters boardroom. It was Krug, one of the most expensive champagnes you can buy, perfectly chilled. He had two crystal champagne glasses waiting for us on a silver tray. Helmut poured like a sommelier. There were lots of bubbles. I like bubbles.

"To you, Julie," he announced, "and to West 57."

Yes, here's to me. Everyone who wanted something from me was toasting me these days. I didn't feel much like celebrating, but I took a sip. I had to admit that Krug was better than the ten-dollar Korbel I bought myself on New Year's Eve. It probably wasn't protocol to chug the glass, so I paced myself.

Helmut stared out from the floor-to-ceiling windows of the boardroom with a proprietary smile, as if he owned the entire city. He practically did. I stood next to him, looking out across the canyons toward Rockefeller Center and the Empire State Building.

"I have lived in the some of the great cities of the world," he told me. "Berlin, Hong Kong, Tokyo. There is still no city that compares to New York."

"You're right."

"Having lived here now, I'm not sure I could live anywhere else," he said. "You're lucky to have spent your life here."

"Yes, I am."

Helmut pulled back one of the leather chairs from the board table. It looked more like a throne, and there were about forty chairs spaced around a glistening ebony table that was longer than my entire apartment. He wanted me to feel the power of this place. This was where movers and shakers sat. This was where millions were made. Billions. You could be a part of this world, Julie.

We sat down.

"I heard about the fracas at Stables & Proud," Helmut told me. "You are safe, yes? And unharmed?"

"I'm fine."

He shook his head. "A publisher should not be wasting time at such events. A publisher belongs here, seeing the big picture."

"I still like to get my hands dirty," I said. I looked at Helmut's fingernails, which I was sure were never dirty. I thought about asking where he had his nails done, but he was on to other things.

"Tell me something, Julie, does the future worry you?" He eyed me as he sipped his Krug.

"How so?"

"Oh, the publishing world has been turned upside down, and most people in the business are running like frightened cats. They hate that books are finally joining the digital experience that connects everyone on the planet."

"It's probably because book people aren't wired like gamers," I said. "Reading is a more intimate experience. It's not multimedia. It's sitting in the park with a novel by Libby Varnay."

"Who?"

"Libby Varnay," I said.

"I'm sorry, who is that?"

"The author? *Morningside Park*?"

"I've heard of the movie. With Denzel Washington, yes? It was a book, too?"

"It was West 57's biggest bestseller," I said. "That was twenty years ago."

Helmut smiled. "You see, you make my point for me, Julie. The glory days of West 57 are behind it. Sonny was living in the past, not the future. However, you and I can change that."

I couldn't believe that he had never heard of Libby Varnay. "She's writing a new book for us."

He poured more champagne. "I'm sorry?"

"Libby Varnay, author of *Morningside Park*. She's writing another book for West 57."

"Have you seen it?"

"Not yet. I have the first chapter to read."

"What other books has she written?"

"Nothing since *Morningside Park*."

Helmut frowned. "Time marches on, Julie. The future is not about resuscitating a decades-old author. We need fresh young talent. That is where West 57 can make a difference."

I knew what I wanted to do. I wanted to swig the rest of my champagne – you don't leave a half-full glass of Krug – and then get up and walk out the door. I wanted to walk back into the crowded streets of New York to the little family offices at West 57 and get to work saving the business. I wanted to re-build West 57 into the kind of publishing house that would tell stories we would still be reading in a hundred years. That was what I wanted to do.

But I couldn't. I had to live in the real world. Dumbo the Banker had spoken. I didn't have the choice to rescue the house. I only had the choice to keep it alive or let it die.

"So are you still willing to acquire the West 57 brand?" I asked.

"Yes, we are, of course."

Okay. Just say the words, Julie. Just say the hardest words you've ever said in your life.

"Then I'm willing to sell it to you," I said.

I winced, expecting Sonny to breathe fire and smoke into my face. *How could you betray me, darling girl?*

I wondered if he would have understood. I'm not betraying you, Sonny. I'm honoring what you built. I'm assuring that the House of Chavan will live on, even with you gone. West 57 means too much to let it disappear entirely and become nothing but a footnote in the history of publishing. The industry without West 57 would be nothing at all.

Helmut leaned forward and clasped my hand with genuine

enthusiasm. "Excellent! That is wonderful news! I am so pleased!"

"I do have conditions," I said.

Helmut smiled and eased back into the giant leather chair. He seemed amused by my arrogance. I really didn't have any bargaining power here, other than the power to pull the plug and let the water drain out of the bathtub. "Okay. Tell me."

"Any current employees of West 57 who wish to remain after the acquisition will have their jobs guaranteed with Gernestier for two years. No layoffs."

"Six months," Helmut said.

"One year."

He nodded. "Okay, yes. Agreed."

"All existing contracts with authors for undelivered material will be honored."

"Naturally." He added, "That presumes timely delivery per the terms of the contract. We won't float authors forever."

That wasn't likely to help Libby, but there wasn't much I could do. "Yes, of course," I said.

"Anything else?"

"I want Sonny's legacy to be honored."

Helmut's eyebrows made little teepees. "How so?"

"I want a history of West 57 on a permanent page on your web site. I want mention of Sonny in the boilerplate on all press releases. I also want you to contract for, write, and publish a history of the house."

He nodded. "It would be an honor."

The next one came to me off the top of my head. "Oh, and I want his photo here. On this floor in your hall of fame. He'll be part of the history of Gernestier now, so let's make it official."

Besides, I want the Gernestier authors to see Sonny's picture every time they visit Helmut. It'll drive them crazy.

He grinned, as if he could read my mind. "Again, no problem."

"Thank you."

"That's all?" he asked.

"That's all."

"Very good. I will have the contract developed, and I will forward it to you so that you and your attorney can review it. We should be able to proceed expeditiously."

"Fine."

That was all it took to change thirty years of history.

"There is, of course, another matter of great importance, Julie," Helmut said.

Me.

"You," he said.

"You don't want me, Helmut. I'm one of those old-school publishing types. To me it's still about the book, like it was with Sonny."

"I think you underestimate yourself."

"That's flattering, but I don't want to spend the next three years as a figurehead. I want to steer the ship, not be stuck on the prow with a smile painted on my face. Gernestier will own West 57, and you'll run it your way. Let's face it, all you and I would do is butt heads."

Helmut shrugged. "I don't mind conflict. Often better decisions come of it. I'm not *always* right, and I appreciate employees with the courage to tell me so."

"It's a tempting offer," I said, "but no."

"Is it a question of money? Or benefits? We are open to negotiation."

"No, your offer was very generous. This just isn't where I want to go with my life. I hope it doesn't change your interest in acquiring the brand if I'm not part of the deal."

"It doesn't, but I'd like to do a joint press release when we announce the sale. It would be helpful if you could convey your enthusiasm to the industry and your belief that Gernestier represents an exciting new direction for West 57 in the wake of your father's passing." He added, "Our publicity staff will be happy to write something for your approval."

Naturally. He didn't want me on the sidelines sniping. That was fair.

"Of course," I said.

"I'm genuinely sorry, Julie. You may have thought my offer was merely pro forma, but it wasn't. I respect you, and many of us here would have enjoyed working with you."

"That's kind of you to say."

He took my glass and drained the bottle dry. We toasted again with a clink. "If you do not mind my asking, what do you plan to do next?"

He said it in a way that suggested he already knew. He'd talked to my mother. A child of Cherie Chavan does not say no to a maternal directive. If I wasn't going to stay at West 57, then I knew what I had to do.

It was my decision, as long as I made the right one.

"I'm thinking about moving to Los Angeles," I said.

31

I needed to tell everyone at West 57 about the deal, but I wasn't ready. I told myself it was better to wait until the contract was signed, but that was just a way of putting off the inevitable. I hated to drop the bomb, even if it would surprise none of them. They could read the writing on the wall, and the rumors had already spread through the office like a flu virus. They knew what was coming.

The receptionist looked at me strangely. She'd worked for Sonny for 12 years. Ditto the accountant at the files, pawing through contracts and getting ready for a round of royalty payments. He'd been with Sonny for 17 years. The marketing director was a newbie. He'd only been here for six years. They all stared at me as if they knew where I'd been and what I'd done. I'd sold their future. I'd negotiated a year of job security to cushion the blow, but it felt like nothing at all.

I should have said: "Gather everyone together."

Instead, I said: "I'll be in Sonny's – I mean, I'll be in my office. Hold my calls, okay? I don't want to see anyone."

The receptionist nodded at me. She knew. They all knew.

I went inside and closed the door and sat behind the old desk. I stared straight ahead, holding back the tears, but they came anyway. I wanted to see Sonny. I wanted to explain to him why I'd done what I'd done, why I had no choice, why this was the only way. He stayed away, as if he didn't want to see me. He couldn't face me after I'd sold his soul.

When someone knocked at the door, I didn't answer, but the door opened anyway. It was Garrett. He came in and closed the door and watched me. I didn't try to hide that I was crying or wipe my face.

"I want to be alone," I told him.

He ignored me and didn't leave.

"Go away," I said. That was the short way of saying: I don't want you here. I don't want you to comfort me or kiss my head or tell me I did the right thing. I don't want to stare into your brown eyes. In an hour, I will be in Thad's arms. I'll let him make love to me again, and it will be magical, like last night. You have no part in my life, Garrett Wood.

He sat down, reached across the desk, took my hands. "About this morning," he said, "I am so sorry."

"I don't care about this morning," I said. "It doesn't matter to me."

That was a cruel thing to say, but I was in a cruel mood. He absorbed the blow without flinching.

"Fair enough. I just want you to know that I said things I didn't mean."

"That's what people tell you when they accidentally say out loud what they really think," I said.

He didn't deny it. He'd meant everything he said to me.

"Are you okay?" he asked. "I heard about the man at the bookstore. If something had happened to you, I don't know what I would have done. I should have been there."

"I don't need you to take care of me," I said.

Blow number two. He flinched this time. Good.

"Wow, I really screwed things up between us," Garrett replied.

I didn't say anything, but I thought: Yes, you did.

"Is there any way I can make it better?" he asked.

"There's nothing to make better. I'm fine." I got up and went to the office door and held it open. "Could you just leave me alone, please?"

Garrett didn't stand up. He gestured at a manuscript on my desk. "I left you a copy of *Woodham Road*. I thought you'd like to see it."

"You already told me you weren't going to offer on it."

"I said I wasn't going to make promises to an author that I couldn't keep."

"So why should I read it?" I asked. I was just being a bitch now. I don't do that very often, but when I do, I'm good at it.

He shrugged. "It's the best book I've read in years. Sonny would have loved it."

"Sonny's dead," I said.

"Yes, he is."

I waited for him to leave, but he didn't. He knew he could outlast me. Finally, I closed the door and laid my head against the heavy wood and closed my eyes. "I sold the house," I told him. "I sold West 57."

"I figured."

"I sold it to Gernestier," I said. "Sonny must be furious at me. It's everything he wanted to avoid."

"As you just mentioned, Sonny is dead."

I turned around and leaned against the door. "I'm a traitor. I destroyed his legacy."

"It sounds to me like you rescued it," Garrett said.

"It's not the future he wanted for this place."

"Did you have a choice?" he asked.

"No."

"Then why beat yourself up?"

I had no answer for that.

Garrett came to me and leaned against the door beside me. We stood there, shoulder to shoulder. His shoulders were a lot taller than mine. "Look, Julie, it was always a foregone conclusion that Gernestier was going to wind up with West 57. The only real question was whether they were going to get you, too." He cocked his head and asked, "Did they?"

"No," I said. "I turned them down."

"Good for you."

"Everyone here will think I'm a rat swimming away from the ship as it goes down."

"I don't think anyone here would expect you to stay. They'd probably feel worse if you did."

"I negotiated a one-year no-layoff policy for the staff," I said. "Their jobs are secure for now."

"In this economy, that's a good thing."

"West 57 won't be the same."

"Nobody's under any illusions that things will stay the same. Some of the people here will probably do just fine at Gernestier. Maybe better. Others will leave."

"Like you," I said.

"Like me."

"You won't change your mind?"

Garrett shook his head. "I'll stay until you shut off the lights if you want me to, but then I'm gone."

"I'm sorry about this."

"Don't be. I've had a great run here, Julie. I'm like you, I'd stay where I was forever if I didn't get dragged out kicking and screaming. It's probably for the best."

It's true. He and I were so much alike. Both hating change. Both attached to our routines.

"Sonny respected your loyalty," I told him. "He knew you could have left years ago. He knew you stayed because of him."

Garrett shoved his hands in the pockets of his jeans. "I didn't stay just because of him, Julie."

Well, yes, there's the coffee, too. It's great. Sonny bought one of those Keurig single-cup coffee makers. Always a fresh cup when you need one. The location – that's good, too. You've got the N, R, Q, W, and F trains within a few blocks. Eat lunch in the Park whenever you want. And don't forget the hardwood floors. They are smooth and shiny. That's definitely a reason to stick around.

Of course, it's also possible he meant me.

I could have asked: *Do you mean you stayed because of me?*

He could have said: *I stayed because I knew I'd get to see you.*

But that's what normal people would have done. Not us. I didn't ask what he meant, and he didn't volunteer. Don't ask, don't tell.

"I have to go," I said.

"Me, too."

"Are you watching the Yankees tonight?" I asked.

"Yeah, Betances is on the mound. What about you?"

"I have to be somewhere."

"Oh."

Say it, Julie. Tell him the truth. "Actually, I'm meeting Thad."

"Oh," he said again, without enthusiasm.

"He wants me to go to Los Angeles with him. To work with him and my mother. They have a new production company out there."

"That's an exciting opportunity," he said. "Are you thinking about it?"

"Yes."

I thought: *Tell me to stay, and I'll stay. Tell me anything, and I won't go.*

"You'd do well out there."

"You think?"

"Of course. You'd do well anywhere."

"Thanks."

"Have fun tonight," he said.

"You too."

He bent down and kissed me on the cheek. Peck on the cheek, that's all. That was how friends kissed. While his face was in the neighborhood, however, our eyes met, and he gave me a real kiss. A full-on, romantic, tender, God-your-lips-are-soft kiss. It didn't last long – just a couple seconds – and we didn't touch anywhere else, just lips to lips. That was enough. That sucked all the air out of my chest. He slipped out of the office without another word, but I was still floating and flying. I could taste him, and I thought that taste would linger for a long time.

I wanted it to feel like the start of something, but it felt like the end of something. It felt like our first kiss and our last kiss.

It felt like goodbye.

32

Not long after, I was kissed again.

Thad greeted me in his dressing room by caressing my tonsils with his tongue. He lifted me off the floor. He wore a t-shirt and boxers, and his door-knocker sprang up and knocked on my lower door. I'd be lying if I said I wasn't tempted to have it pay a return visit to the area it was rubbing against.

"You are so beautiful," he said, putting me down. "Last night was amazing." His hands had nowhere to go, so his fingertips found their way to my breasts. Unaccustomed to much attention lately from anyone but me, the points immediately hardened, which encouraged more exploration. I didn't really want to have sex, but then again, my hormones had other ideas.

"Yes, it was," I whispered.

His fingers kept roaming like ten little Captain Kirks going boldly where few men had gone before. I found myself drawn into his blue eyes and his sweeping blond hair.

"It means something when two people can take up where they left off as if no time had passed," he said.

"Yes, it does."

"Let's make love again," Thad told me. He didn't really need to say so. His boxers were doing the talking for him. He undid a button on my blouse, and if I didn't say anything right away, I would be naked soon, and he would be naked soon, and nature would take its course. Why was I hesitating?

"Thad," I said.

He heard the turn–off–the–engine tone of my voice and pulled back. "Is something wrong?"

"No, it's just – it's been a difficult day for me. I'm not really in the mood."

"I understand," he said, but he didn't. Men never do.

I glanced southward. "I appreciate your being patient with me."

"I've matured, Julie." He smiled at me. "Anyway, I don't like to have sex before a performance. It takes the edge off. I'm too mellow. If I'm desperately horny, there's more tension for the audience to enjoy."

Thad sat down at a glass table with two comfortable chairs positioned on either side of it. A wildly colorful ceramic teapot sat on a trivet. His dressing room walls were decorated with paintings that could have hung in MOMA. I assume he traveled with them. "Pour out tea for us," he told me. "We'll talk instead of doing other things."

I re-did the button on my blouse. I felt a little off-balance. I sat across from Thad and poured tea for him into a cup with no handle. "Do you have any coffee?" I asked.

"Tea's better for you."

Yes, that's what everyone tells me. I poured tea for myself but didn't drink it. Thad sipped his tea and ravished me with his eyes. I had to admit, I liked it. It's like having a staring contest with a lion. It doesn't hide the fact that it wants to eat you.

"I can't wait for us to be together in L.A.," he said. "Making love beside the ocean is the ultimate experience. Remember sex on the beach in St. Bart's?"

"Of course."

"It's like that, but it's real, not a temporary fantasy."

"Was that what St. Bart's was for us?"

He shrugged. "You know what I mean. You don't have to get away from anything on the coast. You're already there."

"It sounds wonderful."

"It is. I'm very lucky. We both are." He reached across the table to stroke my hair. "Look at you. Your hair is so lush and thick. If you cut it off, you could sell it as a sex toy, like ostrich feathers."

"I'll keep that in mind," I said. "I may need the money."

"You'll never need money again," he said.

I liked that idea. I'm not in love with money, but you tend to notice the lack of it. The nest egg Sonny left me was a hummingbird's nest, enough to cover me for a few months. He'd already poured most of his wealth back into the business.

"Have you ever thought about cutting it?" Thad asked.

"My hair?"

"You'd look so elegant with short hair."

"I like it long," I said.

He smiled. "Everyone in L.A. is doing the short hair thing now. It's the Carey Mulligan look. Very trendy."

"Very not me."

"Well, you may change your mind."

Or maybe I won't.

"You saw the paper today?" I asked, because I didn't want to talk about my hair anymore.

"What, the *Post*? The paparazzi photos? Oh, sure."

"Is there anything you can do about it?" I asked.

"Do? Like what?"

"I don't know. Talk to them. Sue them. Beat them up."

Thad laughed. "I wish I could, believe me. In the early days, the popzees were a useful annoyance. On those rare occasions when *People* printed pictures of someone other than Matthew McConaughey, I wanted it to be me. I dated A-list actresses whenever I could, because I knew the cameras would stake them out. Of course, now they're like mosquitoes, and you just want to swat them. The trouble is, there's always a dozen more waiting to swarm you. After a while, you stop worrying about it."

"I was humiliated," I said.

His face screwed up with concern. He grabbed my hand. "Oh, Julie, I'm sorry. I'm so used to it I didn't even give it another thought. You're right, it must have been awful for you."

"Just tell me you didn't tip them off."

He was genuinely horrified. "Me? How could you think that?"

"I'm sorry. You're right, I know you wouldn't do that to me. I'm just not used to life in the fishbowl. I don't know how you deal with losing your privacy like that."

"It takes time, but you'll learn to live with it. Believe me, there are still days when you want to shove someone's camera down their throat." He added, "I hope that's not why you didn't want to have sex."

I shook my head. "No, I was very tempted."

"Good. You said it was a difficult day. What's going on?"

What's going on?

My list was getting longer. Naked in the *Post*. Dead reporter. Grilled by the FBI. Naked mother. Flying dog. Gun in my face. King with a bra. Garrett's lips and my lips sharing the same space.

Oh, yes, and selling my father's whole life.

"I told Gernestier they could acquire West 57," I said.

Thad tried to paste sympathy on his face, but his delight broke through like sun through the clouds. "I know that was very hard on you, Julie, but honestly, I'm happy to hear it. It was the right call. Now you're free."

"Yes, I'm free."

"Have you told your mother?"

"Not yet, but Cherie's spies have probably already told her."

"Change is difficult, Julie, but you'll look back on this as a turning point in your life. A time when everything began to get better. You'll wonder why you didn't do it sooner."

I wanted to believe that was true. After all, here I was drinking tea with one of the most desirable men on the planet. A man who had made my head spin the previous night with the attentions he paid to my body. A man who wanted to carry me off to his oceanside mansion in the warmth of California. He was a man I once loved and – it was true – could easily love again. Yes, Cinderella, the slipper fits. So stick that shoe on your foot and shut up.

There was only one thing that bothered me. Really, just one thing. I didn't like tea.

"I have a couple scripts for you," Thad told me, getting up. He dug inside a Vuitton satchel and found two thin manuscripts and put them in front of me. One was titled, "The Newest Oldest Profession." The other was titled, "Blowdown."

"What are they?" I asked.

"Honestly? The first one's a teenage fart comedy. Mother joins the adult entertainment industry to make ends meet after a divorce, son's friends hire a hooker for his bachelor party, you can figure out where it goes from there."

"So it's based on a Mamet play," I said.

Thad smiled. "Okay, it's not high art. It will be cheap to produce and is certain to be profitable. A start-up operation needs a couple sure-fire hits under its belt before raising its sights."

"What about 'Blowdown'?"

"Zombies, tornadoes, and blondes."

"No vampires?"

"One, actually," he admitted.

"So what do you want me to do with the scripts?" I asked.

"You've got the editorial eye. Tear apart the stories. Make them better, look for ways to give them more emotional authenticity."

"Emotional authenticity? Mom does nudie dance for junior?"

"Cherie and I were thinking of pitching Jennifer Garner as the mother. She's got the campy chops to pull it off. Besides, it's all tease, no nude scenes, at least not for the mom."

"Ben will be relieved."

"It's a comedy, Julie. Everything sounds like crap when you boil it down to the elevator pitch. The trick is to do crap really, really well. Truly, these can be terrific movies with your help."

"I don't know, Thad."

He put my hands on the script pages. His fingers were warm. "Julie, your input is absolutely essential. Cherie and I trust you implicitly. Give us a few paragraphs on what you would change in the characters and plot. You have full control; whatever you say, we'll do. I promise, if you think the scripts are unsalvageable, then we'll move on. This is the *beginning*, Julie. We're going to be hip-deep in projects in six months. The three of us will do great things, and we'll have fun, and we'll make another fortune for all of us. You cannot imagine the excitement of creating movies from scratch, not just playing one small part."

Yes, I could see the credit on the big screen.

Producer With Long Hair.

"I'll look at the scripts," I said.

"Excellent. I'll let Cherie know. She'll be thrilled."

"I should go," I said. "You have to get ready, and I'm meeting Bree for dinner."

Thad pulled me out of my chair and into his arms. I felt his strength and adrenaline as he folded me into him; it was infectious. Persuasive. He was a man who got what he wanted. "You are an amazing woman," he said.

"Did you tell your body paint model that, too?" I asked impishly.

"No."

"You were too busy scraping off the paint," I said.

Thad grinned. "You're here, she's not."

"True."

"I have to shower before I get into costume. Want to join me?"

"Next time."

I gathered up the scripts and smoothed my hair. I felt the adrenaline, like him. It was almost enough to make me take off my clothes and climb into the shower as a way to celebrate. I thought about my future and imagined sunshine, white wine, warm breezes, film festivals, Oscars, parties, and sports cars. Maybe I would finally learn how to drive.

He saw the excitement in my face. He knew what was going

through my head. "I'm heading west in a few days. You can stay at my place. We can do the first production meetings together. Are you in?"

"I'm in," I said.

I repeated it just to make sure I'd heard myself correctly.

"I'm in."

33

Bree stared at the huge bowl of her margarita glass. She saw her reflection and used her tongue to squeegee her teeth. "I love saying *mar-ga-rita*, don't you? Makes me feel like a flamenco dancer. Makes me want to go ravish Benicio del Toro."

"Do you need tequila for that?" I asked.

"No, no, I would happily do him sober." Bree hoisted her glass in my direction. "Here's to you and your future, darling."

I shook my head. "No, everyone's been toasting me lately. It makes me nervous."

"Oh, well then, here's to me."

"Much better," I said. "Here's to Bree Cox."

Bree sucked up salt from the rim. We drank. I was having white wine.

We were in a tapas joint on 46th not far from the U.N. building. It was still early, and we had the restaurant to ourselves. Spanish restaurants don't really start to crank it up until ten o'clock. Bree had ordered anchovy fillets to get us started. There was a live band tuning up on a stage near us, getting ready for the late-night dancing crowd. The waiters yelled back and forth in Spanish.

Bree flipped through the script pages that Thad had given me for "The Newest Oldest Profession."

"Tasteful," she said.

"Very."

"I like the sushi scene, where they're plucking California rolls off the mother's naked body. That's funny."

"Thad wants emotional authenticity," I said.

"Well, nothing says authentic like someone licking wasabi out of your navel." Bree put down the script and slurped up more margarita. "So Julie Chavan is moving to Los Angeles. That's a shock, but I guess Cherie always gets what she wants."

"What does that mean?" I asked.

"Oh, darling, I wasn't criticizing. Far from it. You know me, I'm envious. I have to go back to wet, dreary old London soon, but you! You'll be in a skimpy bikini on the beach, calling me on your cell phone and saying *ciao* and *babe* and talking about doing lunch in between your oxygen shots and oatmeal facials."

"I don't think so," I said.

"Trust me, in a year you will own the city. It's your destiny." She flagged one of the waiters and shouted across the room. "Fernando, something spicy next, something with chorizo, darling. Make us sweat and take off our clothes." She leaned forward and whispered, "Should I see if he would lie down and let us eat it off his body? You could call it research for the hooker movie. Tapas served on naked muscle boys, that's a killer restaurant concept. I should mention it to Gordon Ramsey."

Bree's brain hops like a grasshopper, but I was still annoyed with what she'd said.

"Do you think I knuckled under to my mother?" I asked.

She gave me one of those annoying knowing smiles of hers. "Do you?"

"No."

"Then why do you care what I think?"

"This is the opportunity of a lifetime. I'd be nuts to say no. No one in my shoes would turn this down."

"Unquestionably," Bree said.

"Would you say no?"

"Me? I'd be on Venice Beach with my teeth capped faster than you can say Paramount Studios."

"So why are you giving me grief?"

"I don't believe I was giving you anything but kudos, darling. I was envious, remember?"

"The sex with Thad has nothing to do with my decision," I went on.

"Nothing at all."

"I have no idea whether he and I are starting something. Right now, it's just physical."

"Absolutely. Physical is good."

"I think I'm going through a grieving process about West 57," I said. "I think that's my problem."

"I wasn't aware you had a problem," Bree told me. "It's all good, isn't it?"

"Yes, it's all good."

Bree finished her margarita and licked her lips with a green tongue. "You know, darling, I will confess that I am just the tiniest bit disappointed. Honestly, I still had visions of our teaming up to form the Cox-Chavan Agency."

"Chavan-Cox. Alphabetical."

"Whatever. Can't you see it? The Cox-Chavan Agency ruling the new media world. Me as queen of the UK, you as queen of the US. It would be a hoot. We'd be like Thelma and Louise."

"We'd kill each other, Bree," I said. "We'd drive off a cliff."

"Oh, eventually, maybe, but we'd have loads of fun along the way."

"I don't want to be an agent anymore. I've done it."

"You're saying it would be emotionally inauthentic for you?"

"Something like that."

"Well, we can't have that. Look at me. I'm an emotionally authentic original. One of a kind, often-imitated, never-equaled Bree Cox. Accept no substitutions."

"That's you," I agreed.

"Of course, no man is an island, right? No woman, either. Think about it, darling. What's Rodgers without Hammerstein? What's Fred without Ginger? What's Levi without Strauss?"

"Levi Strauss was one person, Bree."

"The jeans people? That was one guy? Really?"

"Really."

"I did not know that. Well, never mind. You get my point."

"No, I don't," I said.

"My point is that I don't *need* another agent in my agency. I'm already an agent, and I am the best in the world."

"Except for me."

"All right, except for you. I want a partner, someone to help me build something completely different. Today it's all about owning and developing content, not selling it to someone else. I want a publishing wing, a film wing, a theatre wing, a music wing, a television wing, a gaming wing. I told you, I want to rule the world. I want you and me to find exciting projects, and I want us to do them. Not hand them off to other people. I want to find them, publish them, film them, put them on stage, whatever it takes."

"That takes tons of contacts."

"Which we have."

"And money, which we don't," I said.

"So what? Banks have money. Your mother has money. Gernestier has money. Thad has money. Lots of people have money, and they will invest it with brilliant bitches like us who can turn it into even more money."

"You're crazy, Bree. It's a crazy idea."

"Absolutely true! It would be the craziest and most exciting thing we've ever done. Come on, darling! I can't make it work alone. I want you with me. Can you think of two people better situated to turn the whole industry upside down?"

"No."

"Well, there you go."

"I'm not like you, Bree. I need more security."

"By moving back to your mother's nest?"

"That's a cheap shot."

"Fair enough. I'm sorry. Slap me if you'd like. I just wanted to make my pitch before you jetted off to L.A."

"I appreciate it, but I've made up my mind. Okay? I'm moving west, end of discussion. I'm also done with work talk for the evening. It's a girls' night out, and I just want to celebrate."

"Agreed. Fine. Fernando, another 'rita! And more rioja! We will celebrate the Californization of Julie Chavan."

Our next order of tapas came. It was sausagey and spicey and paprikaey. I loved it. More little plates followed, and we emptied them one after another. The hours flew by, tick tock tick. Other diners joined our private restaurant. The band began playing. I drank more wine. A lot more wine. Regardless of my willpower or inhibitions, I cannot seem to spend an evening with Bree without getting drunk.

We spent the hours talking about nothing. Lady Gaga vs. Madonna. Jonathan Franzen vs. Jodi Picoult. The Yankees – well, that's everything, not nothing. I tried to explain the intricacies of American baseball to Bree, including the infield fly rule. She didn't get it. She tried to explain why the rest of the world is so nuts about soccer and why Chelsea is the world's greatest sports team. I didn't get it. We talked about cats, which we both love. We talked about licorice, which we both hate. We talked about New York taxi drivers (I mean you, Farouk). We talked about everything except me and my day, which was just fine with me.

However, Bree wasn't about to let me off the hook altogether.

"So," she said, when the restaurant was so crowded and loud that we could hardly hear each other, "what's really bothering you, darling? You're supposed to be happy, but you look sad."

"Absolutely nothing is bothering me, and I don't want to talk about it."

"Does it bother you that you're doing what your mother wants for the first time in your life?"

"How is that not talking about it?" I asked.

"Does it bother you that you have a knot in your stomach the size of a basketball?"

"Still not talking about it."

"Does it bother you that you're sleeping with Thad but you're in love with Garrett?"

That one got me. She knew that one would get me. Damn you, Bree Cox.

"I am *not* in love with Garrett," I said.

"I don't know, darling," she said. "You look starry and moon-eyed like a woman in love."

"That's the wine. I'm not in love with Garrett. He's not in love with me. Period, end of story, no sequels. I'm not in love with Thad, either. I'm not in love with anyone."

"Except me, of course."

"Except you," I said.

"Well, good. Come on, then, I know what you need."

"What's that?"

"Let's dance," Bree said. "I haven't danced in ages, not vertically anyway. It'll be like old times. Remember?"

Bree was right. We used to dance together a lot, whenever we were in New York or London. We'd spend hours on the floor. It didn't matter whether it was rock or electronica or soft jazz or country or the boom-boom beat of the clubs. It didn't matter whether it was live or DJ. We'd spend our nights together shaking, hustling, tangoing, boot scooting, whatever. It was our thing, the two dancing chicks. I missed it.

So we danced.

It had been a long time, but it all came back like we were younger and it was yesterday again. The band shot up the tempo for us. We kicked and stomped and wiggled our backsides and jiggled our frontsides and whipped our hair and laughed like schoolgirls. The other dancers eventually gave us the floor. Everyone in the restaurant watched us, smiling and pointing, because it was so obvious we were having a good time with each other. I don't know how much time we spent out there. It was well after midnight when we collapsed back at our table, arms around each other, sweating, grinning, panting like we'd run a marathon. We leaned our heads together, because we could barely prop them up.

People applauded, and we waved and bowed. Fernando brought us liqueurs on the house. Licor 43. It tasted like vanilla ice cream. We downed our shots and licked our lips.

It was great.

"Darling, you've still got the moves," Bree said.

I tried to catch my breath. "So do you."

"You and that swirling hair. Never cut it. It's the sexiest thing imaginable."

I kissed her cheek. "Thank you."

"For what?"

For saying I should never cut my hair, I thought.

"For tonight," I said. "For the whole evening. This is exactly what I needed."

"We've always made a good team, darling."

"When you weren't sleeping with my boyfriends."

"Well, yes."

"Do you know what?" I asked.

"What?"

"I am moving to Los Angeles," I said.

"So you've been telling me."

"I am sleeping with Thad Keller."

"Now you're just rubbing it in."

"I am done with King Royal and Irving Wolfe and *Captain Absolute* and West 57. I don't care about any of it anymore. It is Helmut's problem now."

"It's just a book," Bree said.

"Exactly right, it's just a book."

"So now you can go home and sleep like an angel," she said.

I shook my head, back and forth, back and forth. I wasn't sure if Bree would understand if I told her the truth. I'm not sure I understood myself. I just knew I had something else to do.

"Not quite yet," I said. "I have one stop to make before I go home. There's one more person I have to explain all this to."

34

Lionel the Security Guard looked at me strangely when I arrived at the building so late, dressed for partying, obviously tipsy, my face still flushed from dancing. However, I'm the boss, and I do what I want. I went upstairs into the dark offices of West 57. It was too late even for Garrett to be there, and I was glad. I didn't want to see him. I wanted to be alone with my father.

He was waiting for me. Sonny, I mean. I knew he'd be there.

He wasn't behind the desk. He was in the armchair. I guess he'd decided the desk was mine now. With the lights off, he was a burly silhouette. I sat down, dropping the movie scripts in front of me, next to the manuscript of *Woodham Road* that Garrett had left there and next to the first chapter of Libby's new book.

I turned on the Tiffany lamp, which cast a weak glow. Sonny stared at me with hawk-like eyes. He looked fit and strong, not dead, not gone. His black hair was like a crown. The cigarette in his hand, which sat on the worn armrest of the chair, sent a spiral of smoke toward the ceiling. The lamp reflected on the shiny polish of his leather shoes.

"Drunk again, darling girl?" he asked, amused with me.

"Yes."

"Bree?"

"Yes."

"You two are dangerous together," he said, shaking his head.

"We are, aren't we? I'd forgotten what that was like."

"I always liked dangerous girls," he said.

Sonny cast a nostalgic look around at the bookshelves and sniffed the musty air. He knew the clock was ticking. Our lease was up. "So you did it," he said. "Gernestier."

"Yes, I'm sorry."

"I don't blame you, darling girl."

"I hope that's true," I said, "because I feel guilty."

"No, no, I blame myself. It's all on me." He shook his head and caressed one of the leather-bound books on the end table beside him. "I was a relic by the end, Julie. I was a dinosaur in this world, and when the meteor hit, I was unable to evolve. I wandered through the scorched ruins, thinking everything would go back to the way it was, and it never did."

I got up from behind the desk, and I went to him. I knelt in front of him, at his knees, the way I'd done so many times as a little girl. I didn't touch him. I didn't know what would happen if I did, if he would disappear like a cloud when I discovered there was nothing to feel. I wanted to preserve the image of him in my brain for a while longer.

"That doesn't change the last thirty years, Sonny."

"You're making excuses for me. I don't want them. I became another old man, reminiscing about the glory days, wishing the world hadn't changed so much from what I remembered."

"You would have found another chapter to write," I said.

"Alas, there were no more chapters."

I looked up at my father. He looked vital, a man in his prime, not a man whose heart had expired. "What would you have done, Sonny? I keep thinking I've missed something. There was some other alternative, some other way to save the business. I've gone over it again and again, and I just don't see what else I could have done. And yet I know you, you would have found a way."

"Is that what's bothering you?"

"Yes."

Sonny chuckled softly. "That's sweet. Julie, I do believe you loved

240

me more than anyone else in my life."

"You know I did."

"Even when I tried to rule your life?"

"Even then."

"I'm glad you always stood up for yourself," he told me. "I was proud of you every time you said it was your life and you were going to run it your way. I think I would have been a little disappointed if I actually won."

"Really?"

"Really," he said.

"You didn't answer my question. What would you have done about West 57?"

He smiled at me the way he did when he would hold my hand as we walked through the Park. "I would have done the same thing as you."

"You? You would have sold to Gernestier?"

"Of course."

"You're just trying to make me feel better."

"No, I knew West 57 was dying, darling girl. I did everything I could, but the resources weren't there to turn it around. I wouldn't have shut the doors and put these people on the street and let the name disappear. I would have swallowed my pride and signed on the dotted line and cursed about it to everyone who would listen. That's what I would have done."

"Just like me."

"Just like you. And I wouldn't have been smart enough to get my photo in the lobby at Gernestier. I love that!"

It was good to hear him laugh again. I smiled happily and went back to his desk. My desk. At least for a little while longer. "I wish you'd told me that the business was in trouble," I said. "I'm sorry you went through it alone. Maybe I could have helped."

"There was nothing anyone could do. The writing was on the wall. I was holding the place together with duct tape."

And yet you paid King Royal four million dollars.

I didn't say that aloud, but you can't fool a ghost.

"You haven't asked me the other question," Sonny said. "Come on, I know you want to."

"What question?"

"Oh, don't play dumb. It doesn't suit you, darling girl. You haven't me asked about King. The book. The advance." He paused. "You haven't asked me about Irving Wolfe."

"You're right, I haven't."

"Why not?"

I leaned back in the chair. "Because I don't care about the answer. Not anymore."

"Don't lie to your father."

"No, it's true. I don't want to know. It has nothing to do with me."

I didn't know what else to say or do, so I picked up the first chapter of Libby's new book. I wasn't sober enough to read the whole thing, but I read the first paragraph. It was nothing like *Morningside Park*, but then again, years had passed in the interim. Libby was a different person today than she'd been in her youth. Honestly, I didn't particularly like what I saw. It felt as if she were forcing the words. I put it down, but I thought Sonny would enjoy hearing what she'd written.

"Do you want me to read it to you?" I asked him.

"No."

"It's Libby's work. You love her."

"I know."

"I'm not sure I like it," I admitted.

"Blame me. I pushed Libby to do another book. It was a mistake, and I regret it. *Morningside Park* should stand on its own, not be measured against a second novel."

That was true.

I picked up *Woodham Road* from the desk. This was the novel that Garrett had fallen in love with, and in a single page, I knew why. I was transported immediately to the eighteenth century, into the wilderness, where a scout's horse dies by an Indian's arrow. I felt the animal's suffering.

I felt the scout's sense of loss. Garrett had told me that the book was ultimately not what it appeared on the surface, and I wanted to know its secrets. It was impossible to put down.

"Garrett loves this book," I said to Sonny.

"Then it must be tremendous. Garrett never loves anything that isn't unique and memorable."

I wondered, fleetingly, if he meant me.

"Gernestier will never publish it," I said.

"Then someone else should."

Yes, someone else should. Someone should take it and turn it into a masterpiece, the way Sonny did with *Morningside Park*. Someone should make it into a story heard round the world. A book. A movie. But not me. I will be filming "The Newest Oldest Profession." I will be thousands of miles away.

"You haven't said anything," I told him.

"About what?"

"About Los Angeles. Cherie. Thad. Me."

"If I gave you advice, wouldn't you run the other way?" Sonny asked.

"Probably."

"Then I'll keep my thoughts to myself."

I kept procrastinating. It was late. It was time to go home, but I hated to leave. Every time I left, I wondered if I'd see him again. Sooner or later, he would be gone forever. Sooner or later, I would have to let him go. Not yet.

I saw an empty book box on the floor, and I retrieved it. I began packing up some of the mementos from the desk. It was silly, because I had plenty of time to worry about those things, but I wanted him to see me taking them with me. Things of his. Things I would treasure forever.

I put pictures in the box. "Look at you, this was at the Edgar Awards in 1986," I said. "Nice tux, but who tied your bow tie?"

"You did," Sonny reminded me, smiling.

"Oh, yeah."

There was more. His fountain pen. One of the old-fashioned ones. Norman Mailer had given it to him. "Do you remember the time the pen leaked all over the cover of your first edition of *To Have and Have Not*? You made Mailer get you another copy at an auction."

"I remember."

There was a baseball by Coach, heavy, like a medicine ball. Sonny used it as a paperweight. He used to toss it in the air over and over as he sat in thought. I dug in the drawers of the desk. I found a pulp paperback by Brian Garfield from the 1970s. A letter in pencil from Leon Uris. I found a music box with an inlaid wood top, and when I opened it, it played the haunting movie theme from *Morningside Park* crisply and quickly, as if someone had recently wound it.

Treasures.

In the bottom drawer, I found his calendars. Stacks of them, going back years. Sonny had never relied on Palm Pilots or BlackBerrys or iPhones. To his dying day, he'd written every appointment in the same small 365-day pocket calendars he'd been buying at Duane Reade since the 1970s. I pulled them out of the drawer and began randomly flipping through the pages in each diary, and it was like tiptoeing through Sonny's life. His lunches. His meetings with agents, authors, artists, and booksellers. His notes from each meeting scrawled in the margins like he was editing a book.

His whole life, day by day, year by year, going back to the very beginnings of West 57. I began placing them in the box reverently. Someday, a biographer would want them. Or maybe I would write his biography myself.

One of the calendars, a recent one from last year, fell open in my hand as I was putting it away. It was odd, because the spine was broken. It felt like a used paperback that always opens to the sex scene that people had read a million times. Looking down at the calendar, I saw that a page had been torn out. I could see the frayed edge. Something was missing; something had been taken.

I looked up at Sonny, and he looked at me. His face was dark, as if he were pleading with me to forget what I'd seen. As if he knew I never would. As if he knew, for all my protests, that I couldn't let it go.

"You mustn't let him talk, darling girl," he told me.

"Who?"

"King Royal."

My eyes flew to the calendar page. I looked at the day before and the day after, and I struggled for a moment to place the significance of the missing page – but only for a moment. I'd re-read *Captain Absolute* days earlier. I remembered the chronology. This was the date that Irving Wolfe and King Royal had taken Wolfe's yacht out into the Atlantic waters for the last time. This was the date when King had awakened to discover that he was alone and that Wolfe had taken a final, fatal swan dive from the boat, escaping justice once and for all.

On this date, the missing date in Sonny's calendar, Irving Wolfe died. On this date, King's book was born.

Why would the page be missing?

But I knew why. There was only one explanation. There was an appointment there that Sonny never wanted the world to discover. Or me. It was his secret. His four-million dollar secret.

"You were on that boat, weren't you?" I said to Sonny.

He didn't say a word. He didn't say yes or no. He just sat there in silence with the smoke billowing around his face.

IV

35

Knock knock.

"Who's there?" Bree said through the hotel door at the Gansevoort. It was early. Crazy-early. 5:00 am early.

"Julie."

"Julie who?"

"Bree, just open the door." I was operating on thirty minutes sleep, and I wasn't feeling very funny right now.

Bree opened the door without undoing the chain and peered at me through the crack. She wasn't happy with me. "You couldn't be Julie Chavan. I put Julie Chavan in a cab twenty minutes ago."

"It was three hours ago, actually."

"Like that makes a difference, darling. We should both be in bed. Separately. Sleeping."

"Sorry, but it's important."

"Nothing is important at this hour of the day. Nothing is important until I've had six hours of sleep and two cups of coffee."

"Bree," I said.

"Oh, hell, all right." She undid the chain and opened the door. Her eyes were bleary. She wasn't wearing makeup. Her hair looked like a multi-colored bird's nest, sticking out in little bits of straw. It wasn't a pretty sight. "You were a lot more fun before you started making mature decisions about your life," she told me.

I went into her room and paced anxiously. Bree sat down on the end of her rumpled bed and watched me. She was wearing an oversized I Love New York t-shirt and men's boxer shorts.

"You know, darling, I brought coffee when I invaded your apartment early in the morning," she told me with a yawn. "Donuts, too. Would it have killed you to stop at Krispy Kreme on the way over here?"

"Sorry." I glanced at the boxer shorts. "There's not a guy in the bathroom wearing your panties, is there?"

Bree sighed. "Yes, Fernando came back with me from the restaurant. He asked if he could sleep in my underwear. It's a popular fetish."

"I was just asking," I said.

"Speak, darling, before I pretend you're not here and fall asleep again."

I tried to talk, but I kept walking back and forth like an overwound toy. To the window. To the door. To the window. To the door. Finally, Bree got off the bed and stopped me with both hands firmly on my shoulders.

"Julie, you're making me dizzy," she said. "What is going on?"

"He was there. He was on the boat."

"Who was where on what boat?"

"Sonny. I think he was on Irving Wolfe's yacht with King on the night that Wolfe disappeared. I think that's what King has been covering up all this time."

Bree sat down on the bed again. She ran her hands through her hair, which made it worse. "Aren't you the same girl who told me last night that she didn't care about this anymore? You were done worrying about King and Wolfe and Sonny and the book and the money. Remember? You are out. You are selling West 57 and moving to Los Angeles. It's Helmut's problem."

"If it were your father, wouldn't you want to know the truth?" I asked.

"My father covers Parliament for the *Times*. The bar for scandal is set pretty high. Dad would have to be a cross-dressing necrophiliac before I got too excited about it."

"This is big," I said.

"Fine. Okay. I understand your concerns, and yes, if my Dad were hanging out on a yacht with a billionaire crook on the night the bastard committed suicide, I might have one or two questions about it. However, first things first, okay? Why do you even think Sonny was there?"

I told her about the missing calendar page. She wasn't impressed.

"That's your big revelation? Sonny's calendar? There's no need for your knickers to be up your arse crack, darling. It's probably nothing. Maybe he was at lunch and he needed a piece of paper to scribble out some contract terms."

"There's more," I said. "I checked his cell phone records. Sonny didn't make or receive any calls after nine o'clock that evening. That's impossible, right? He was always on the phone. So either Sonny turned off his phone or he was out of signal range. Like several miles out on the Atlantic."

Bree blinked at me through her fogged brain. "Well, what difference does it make, and what are you going to do about it?"

"I don't know. That's why I came here."

"You came to me for advice?" she asked.

"Yes."

"Darling, you really are desperate."

"I know."

"All right, fine. You want my advice? It seems to me you have two options. The first and clearly the best option is to forget it and get on with your life."

"I can't do that. I thought I could, but I can't walk away."

"Then I guess that means we'll go with the second option, which is to wake up King and throw your suspicions in his face. Okay?"

"Okay," I said.

"Honestly, I'm not sure what you hope to accomplish. If King tells you that you're wrong, you have to decide whether to believe him. If he tells you that you're right, you have to decide whether you want to besmirch your father's public reputation. I'm not sure you'll feel better either way."

"I realize that."

"All right, let me go pee and shower and resuscitate my face, and then we'll go upstairs and see if His Robust Manhood is awake."

"Thank you."

"This is a big favor for someone who arrives at my door coffee-less and donut-less."

"I understand."

Bree hopped off the bed and headed for the bathroom, but as she did, her phone began ringing. "Lord in Heaven, does everyone in this freaking city get up when it's still dark out? In London, people are freaking civilized. We get up at noon and we have COFFEE." She answered the phone with a shout: "WHAT?"

She heard who it was, and she continued more quietly. "Oh, sorry, sorry, darling, it's early, I'm not awake. I know you morning show producers work crazy hours, but those of us in the real world are supposed to be asleep. I confirmed everything yesterday, didn't I, so what's the problem? King's segment isn't for three hours, which means I could be dreaming about Vince Vaughn for another two hours and fifty-eight minutes. Now what the hell is so urgent?"

She took a breath. The producer at *Good Morning America* finally got a chance to talk. When he did, Bree bellowed "WHAT?" again even louder than before. This was followed by a string of expletives that I won't repeat and several more questions.

"He said what?"

"When?"

"Why?"

"Are you freaking kidding me?"

Bree hung up the phone and tried to calm herself with a deep breath. "Apparently, King Royal just called and *cancelled* his appearance on *Good Morning America* today."

"What? When? Why? Are you freaking kidding me?"

"Is that supposed to be funny? That's not funny. Now she wants to be funny!"

"I'm sorry. What did King say?"

"Nothing. He left a freaking voice mail. Awfully sorry, can't make it, hope it's not a problem, blah blah blah. That son of a bitch!"

"We better get up there and find out what's going on."

"I still need fifteen minutes to make myself presentable. While I am showering, please find a murder weapon I can use."

I think she was kidding about that.

Bree needed twenty-five minutes, not fifteen, to finish her ablutions. When she re-emerged from the hotel bathroom, she was pink and naked. It occurred to me that I am seeing way too many people naked these days. I don't even particularly like seeing myself naked. If you are naked as you read this, please put on some clothes.

"How do I look?" Bree asked.

"Naked," I said.

"I was hoping for some variant on 'ravishing' or 'stunning.'"

"Stunning," I said.

"I will consider that a sincere compliment. Did anyone call? Did King call?"

"No."

Bree got dressed quickly. With her makeup and lipstick on, she really did look stunning, in a *True Blood* sort of way. We marched out of her hotel room and took the elevator up to the floor where King had his mammoth suite. At the door, Bree knocked. Well, she pounded actually. There was no answer inside.

"King, it's Bree," she announced pleasantly. "Bree and Julie Chavan. Remember us, darling? We need to chat. Now be a love, and open the freaking door."

Still no answer.

Bree dug in her purse and produced a hotel key.

"You have his room key?" I asked.

"Always get your client's room key, darling. You never know when you will need to wake them, revive them, kill them, or fuck them."

Sorry, that one slipped by me. I'm tired.

She slid the key in the lock and opened the door. We entered the Taj Mahal, and I had visions of finding an orgy inside and seeing more naked people. I wasn't looking forward to it. Instead, the suite was empty and dark. There was litter on the floor. It looked like someone had made a fast getaway.

"King?" Bree called again. She wandered into the other half of the suite and checked the bedroom. The bathroom. The closet. If King were anywhere to be found, I was pretty sure she would have dragged him out by his engorgement. She came back alone, not looking happy, and reported: "He's gone. No luggage, no clothes, nothing."

"He talked about disappearing," I said. "When I saw him yesterday, he was asking for money so he could run away. He was pretty scared."

Bree sat down on the plush sofa and stared at me through her psychedelic bangs. "Darling, don't you think that little bit of news was worth sharing over dinner last night?"

"We were busy dancing. I didn't take him seriously."

"Great. Good. Fine. Okay, we have a #1 bestseller and no author to do the media promos. Let's not panic. If the word goes out that he's disappeared, the rumors alone will sell 50,000 more copies. If he's dead, that's probably 100,000 copies."

"Bree!" I chided her.

"I'm just saying."

"So now what?" I asked.

"Now you both answer some questions," said a voice in the doorway of the hotel room.

We looked up and saw a very brown person staring at us. She was so brown she was Goldy Brown, in fact. Goldy Brown of the FBI.

36

"Where's King Royal?" Ms. Brown asked us without foreplay. "I've been trying to talk to him for two days. He doesn't return my calls. He's avoiding me."

"Maybe he's just not that into you," Bree said.

Ms. Brown's brown face turned cherry red. She'd only met Bree twice, but let's face it, Bree is an acquired taste under the best of circumstances, and we were not in the best of circumstances. Anyway, I think Ms. Brown was calculating whether she could arrest Bree under the Patriot Act and make her disappear.

"I waited for him at the bookstore yesterday," Ms. Brown went on, "and then he sneaked out."

"You were there?" I asked. She could have at least said: Nice catch on the flying dog.

"I was. King was supposed to meet me after the event."

"Well, things got a little crazy," I said. "Maybe you noticed the madman with the gun? The one pointed at my head? Thank God Bree whacked the man with a huge copy of *Breaking Dawn*."

"Yes, if Stephenie Meyer had shown even a hint of editorial restraint, Julie might not be alive today," Bree said.

Ha ha, she's just kidding, Steph. Go, Bella.

"That man, Walter Pope, he needs help," I said. "He tried to kill King."

"Which brings me back to my original question," Ms. Brown said. "Where is King Royal?"

"Gone," Bree informed her. "He's not here."

Ms. Brown looked at me. "Where did he go?"

"I don't know," I replied. "He called and cancelled a major engagement a few minutes ago. We came up to talk to him and discovered he wasn't here. He took everything with him."

"You two are his agent and his publisher, and you don't know where he is? I find that hard to believe."

"If I knew where he was, I'd already have killed him," Bree said.

"Bree, maybe this isn't a good time for jokes," I advised her.

"Who says I'm joking?"

Goldy Brown of the FBI didn't take Bree's word that King was nowhere to be found in the Gansevoort suite. She told us both to sit down, and then she did her own search of the hotel room. She even looked under the bed and behind the shower curtain. When she was satisfied that King was missing in action, she returned to confront us. As tall and brown as she was, she looked vaguely like a #2 pencil.

"I need to find King Royal right now," she told us.

"What's the rush?" I asked.

Ms. Brown wasn't in a mood to share information, so she didn't answer me.

"We're also going to need everything King Royal gave you related to *Captain Absolute*," she went on. "Drafts, notes, tapes, videos, anything he submitted to either of you. And yes, we have a warrant."

"We typically don't get any supporting materials," I said. "We just get the finished manuscript."

"What about you?" Ms. Brown asked Bree.

"Yes, I keep all of that material on a little USB flash drive in my knickers for protection. Do you want me to wipe it off before I give it to you? This is all very exciting, so I'm a little moist down there."

Ms. Brown looked ready to explode. She definitely had an enhanced interrogation planned for Bree. Waterboarding. Toilet swirlies.

Whatever's in fashion at Gitmo these days. (Is that place still open? I've lost track.)

"It would help if we knew what you're looking for," I said to her.

"That's not your concern. Just assemble what you have when you're back at your office. Someone will be in touch with you about it later today. Right now, I want to know what King Royal said before he left."

"He asked me for money," I told her. "He talked about wanting to disappear."

"Did you give him any money?"

"No."

"Did he say where he planned to go?"

"No."

"Why did he want to disappear?"

"He thought his life was in danger. This was right after Walter Pope pointed a gun at us. He was scared. I figured he would calm down. I had no idea he would actually leave."

"Did he mention Nick Duggan's death?" Ms. Brown asked.

I frowned. "Yes, he thought there was a connection between Duggan's death and his investigation into Irving Wolfe."

"What connection?"

"He didn't say."

Ms. Brown didn't look happy. "We found Nick Duggan's research notes. He was digging into Irving Wolfe's death. He was asking around about the last night that Wolfe spent on his yacht. Duggan didn't think it went down the way King Royal describes it in that book. Turns out he was right."

"He was?" we both said.

"Yes, he was," she snapped. "So I need to talk to King Royal. Now. Today. I also want to know if either of you knows what really happened on that boat."

I opened my mouth to tell her about Sonny. He was on the boat. He was there. Instead, before I could say a word, Bree slung her arm around my shoulder and squeezed until I winced in pain. I got the message and didn't say anything.

"King Royal's the only one who knows what happened on the yacht that night," Bree said. "When you find King, you can ask him."

"What about your father?" Ms. Brown asked me. "Did he tell you anything?"

"He didn't," I said, which was true. Alive or dead.

Ms. Brown turned to leave, but Bree called after her. "Whoa, whoa, that's it? You said Nick Duggan was right and that King was lying. We'd like to know what's really going on."

I could see the wheels turning in Ms. Brown's mind. She was debating how much to tell us.

"We found Irving Wolfe," she finally admitted. "It's probably on the news by now, so you'll hear about it anyway."

"He's *alive*?" I asked.

"Not alive," she went on. "Dead. A fisherman in the Atlantic found something in his nets a few days ago. Turns out it was the remains of Irving Wolfe. We've kept it under wraps, but word is leaking out to the media."

"So he's dead," Bree said. "Big deal. King said he was dead, and he's dead. What's the problem?"

"It's not that simple," Ms. Brown told us. "Wolfe didn't throw himself off the boat. He didn't commit suicide. Someone shot him in the head."

37

There were lots of people I could have called for help.

I could have called Cherie. My mother was back in Los Angeles. She would have told me to rub on some SPF 45 and hop a plane to join her. I could have called Thad and poured out my heart to him. I could have called Libby, and she would have sent her nephew, Drew, to pick me up in the limo, and we would have gone to lunch at the Tavern.

They would all have been right there to comfort me in their own ways, but I didn't call any of them. That should have told me something.

I left Bree at the Gansevoort. She was making calls, trying to use her network of reporters, gays, politicians, bartenders, cab drivers, lawyers, and chefs to find King. He wasn't answering his phone. If you want to hide in New York, you've got lots of places to go, but the thing about King is that he is now instantly recognizable. Plus, he can't walk two blocks without singing limericks about girls who kick punts, and people tend to remember that.

Ms. Brown went wherever Ms. Browns go. Probably to the FBI firing range with a photo of Bree on the target.

Me, I went to Battery Park. You can't be more alone than in a place with thousands of people who don't know you. I sat on a bench, ate soggy butter-soaked popcorn, and watched the Staten Island ferries come and go. No one bothered me except the pigeons. The news about Irving Wolfe hadn't broken yet. As soon as everyone heard about it, my phone and e-mail would light up with questions. What was I going to do about King's book? What really happened on Wolfe's boat? Where is King Royal? Is he a suspect in the murder?

Yes, of course, he was a suspect. If two people are alone on a boat, and one winds up with a bullet in his skull, it doesn't take Agatha Christie to figure out whodunit. King killed the Captain.

Except maybe he didn't.

If I was right, and Sonny was on the boat that night, too, then you could connect the dots in another way. Sonny killed Wolfe and paid King four million dollars in a book deal to keep him quiet.

I should have called Helmut at Gernestier to warn him, because when your big bestseller turns out to be a product of the Fictional Memoir Writing School, you owe your soon-to-be parent company a heads up. However, this was still my problem. One way or another, I had to deal with King Royal and *Captain Absolute* myself, but I didn't know how. It's hard to rewrite the ending of a book when you don't know what really happened.

I needed help, and there was only one person in my life who would drop everything to help me. Don't ask me how I knew that, but I knew that. I punched speed dial 1 on my phone, and when he answered, I said, "I need to see you."

Garrett arrived half an hour later.

There is something magical about watching a crowd of strangers, and then, suddenly, miraculously, seeing a familiar face. Well, I suppose it's not miraculous when you know he's coming, but it was still like parting the seas for me. Before he was close enough to recognize, I spotted his unruly brown hair and his lanky stride. He wore jeans and a sport coat and a button-down navy shirt. His hands were in his pockets. I think he was whistling. He whistles a lot, soft, like a distant flute. I like listening to it.

As he came closer, he gave me that little off-synch smile. I was going to miss seeing it every day. He sat down next to me and sighed at the view, because when you're in Battery Park, it's a great view. I wore sunglasses. He didn't need to see that I'd been crying.

"Thanks for coming," I said.

"What's up?"

"King Royal is missing, Irving Wolfe was murdered, and I think Sonny did it," I said.

No, I didn't say that. I thought it, but I didn't say it. You have to ease into these things.

"Popcorn?" I said. I still had half a box.

"Sure."

He dug his long fingers in for a handful and cupped it in his palm. I watched him eat it kernel by kernel as he watched the water, and then he licked the salt and butter off his fingers.

"I could do that for you," I said.

No, I didn't say that, either.

"So," I said.

"So," he said.

I thought I should clear the air. Tell him the truth. Not lead him on. "I'm going to L.A. next week."

He nodded but didn't look at me. "Permanently?"

"I don't know. Maybe, maybe not. Cherie and Thad want my help getting their new production company off the ground."

"That sounds permanent."

"We'll see whether I like it. I haven't given them any guarantees. I'm just looking at scripts now."

"Anything good?"

"No," I said.

"Too bad."

"I love *Woodham Road*, by the way."

"I knew you would."

"Maybe I can turn it into a movie."

"Sure," he said. "Maybe Thad can star in it."

I was listening for sarcasm in his voice. I might have been overly sensitive. Or not. "Maybe so," I replied.

Garrett ate another piece of popcorn and still didn't look at me.

"Are you staying with him?"

"What, in Los Angeles? Probably. I mean, while I'm out there. It's easier that way. He's got a big place."

"I bet he does."

"It's on the ocean in Malibu."

"Nice."

I listened for sarcasm again. Garrett lives in a one-bedroom apartment over a Turkish coffee shop.

When I didn't reply, he finally looked at me. "Whatever you decide you want, I just want you to be happy, Julie."

I should have said thank you. I should have said a lot of things. I didn't. Finally, with the ice broken and me sinking beneath it, I said: "I have a problem, and I don't know what to do."

Concern washed over his face. Everything else was forgotten. That was why I called Garrett.

"Tell me," he said.

So I told him. I connected the dots. I told him about Sonny and the boat and the calendar and the phone calls and King and the FBI and Nick Duggan and Irving Wolfe and the murder and – well, I talked and talked until the only thing left to say was the hardest thing of all.

"I think Sonny killed Irving Wolfe," I said.

Inhale. Breathe. Wait for reply.

"No way," Garrett said.

"What?"

"No way, Sonny did not kill Irving Wolfe."

"How do you know?"

"Because I have faith in him."

"You weren't listening to me," I said. "I think Sonny was on the yacht with Wolfe and King. Wolfe was *murdered*."

"Julie, I don't know what happened out there, so I can't tell you. All I know is that the man I worked for, your father, is not a murderer. I know that in my heart, and you do, too."

That was a nice thought. Cherie and Libby would have said the same thing. Look to your heart. The trouble is, my heart had doubts. I am not one who can turn a blind eye to the facts and pretend they're not real. (Note to self: I really do have a tiny pooch.)

"If Sonny is innocent, then *Captain Absolute* makes no sense," I said. "On the other hand, if he's guilty and needed to cover up a murder – well, everything fits, doesn't it?"

"Not to me. Nothing fits. Sonny wasn't an investor who got taken in the Ponzi scheme. Why on earth would he kill Irving Wolfe?"

"For the money," I said.

"What do you mean?"

"For the money. For West 57. Sonny needed money and a lot of it. So he went to Wolfe to get it. Either Wolfe said no and Sonny got angry, or Sonny knew about the Ponzi scheme all along. He knew Wolfe was embezzling money, hiding it, creating secret accounts. He wanted the money for himself."

"If so, where is it?" Garrett asked. "West 57 is gone. There's no money."

"I don't know. Maybe King knows. He thinks people are trying to kill him because of it, and he may be right. Look at what happened to Nick Duggan."

I saw a cloud in Garrett's face. I realized that my own doubts were infecting him, and I felt guilty. It was becoming real for him, the way it was for me. I shouldn't have called him. He and Sonny were best friends, and I should have left it like that. On impulse, I leaned over and wrapped my arms around his shoulders and hugged him. He held me, too, and our faces pressed against each other. I wasn't sure who needed comfort more.

The hug was nothing at first, but the longer we held it, the more we were conscious that neither one of us had let go. We clung to each other. I think I could have stayed like that for hours. I heard the overlapping voices and laughter of people in the park. If anyone was looking at us, they were probably thinking: Lovers.

Finally, I detached myself, embarrassed. My sunglasses were askew, and I straightened them. His face was flushed. My own cheeks felt hot.

"Next time we do that, let's be naked," I said.

No, I didn't say that. Besides, there wasn't going to be a next time.

My phone rang in my purse. I assumed it was Bree, because she always seems to call when I am cheek-to-cheek with a handsome man. It's like radar. Instead, the name on the caller ID said Gordon Barnes, and it took me a moment, flustered as I was, to remember whether I knew anyone named Gordon Barnes.

I did. He was Dumbo the Flying Banker.

I really had no idea what Mr. Barnes wanted, because after you've told someone that their business is in the crapper, and you've failed to give them their free toaster for opening a checking account in 1994, what else is there to say?

Anyway, based on my track record of the last few days, I knew one thing. Whatever Dumbo wanted, it wasn't likely to be good news.

38

"A safe deposit box?" I asked.

"Yes, that's correct," Dumbo replied.

"This box belonged to Sonny?"

"So it appears. I have to apologize that I didn't tell you about this before. Honestly, I didn't know that Sonny had ever applied for a box. He didn't go through me, and he didn't associate the box with the usual West 57 accounts or his other personal accounts, so it never showed up in my records. Instead, he opened a separate money market account with de minimus funds that have been used only to pay the annual fee. Obviously, if I'd been aware of his interest in a safe deposit box, I would have made sure it was complimentary."

Like my toaster.

"He never mentioned it to me," I said, "and I haven't come across a key in any of his effects."

"Yes, well, that's part of the problem, isn't it?" Dumbo dug discreetly in one ear. It was probably like a seashell where you could hear the ocean.

"Tell me again what happened this morning," I said.

"Of course. Would you like some coffee first?"

"I'd love some."

"Cappuccino? Or just black?"

"Black today."

"Just the way Sonny liked it," he said.

Dumbo flapped out of his office and returned moments later with a cup of coffee. I sipped it, and it was as good as last time.

"I was pleased to hear that you have a buyer for West 57," Dumbo told me, wedging himself back into his chair. "We do business with the Gernestier group. I have great respect for them. You must be relieved to know that the house will again be on a stable financial footing. Sonny would be proud of your leadership."

"Thank you." I added, "The box?"

"Indeed. Well, I wasn't on the floor personally, so I didn't talk with the man myself. However, one of my most experienced tellers handled the request. It seems that shortly after we opened our doors this morning, a gentleman came up to one of our windows and asked to access his safe deposit box."

A gentleman.

"You're sure it was King Royal?" I asked.

"As I mentioned on the phone, his passport identified him as King Royal. Obviously, I don't know him personally, and I didn't see him at the bank myself, but my teller played a YouTube video for me, and she said that the man doing the singing – "

"It's him," I said.

"Ah. Good. As I was saying, Mr. Royal asked to be taken to our deposit box storage area. His demeanor raised some red flags with my teller, because he appeared very agitated. However, he had the key and the box number. It was the correct box number, I should add."

"Where would he get a key?" I said, half to myself.

"From Sonny, I presume."

Yes, that was one possibility. Either that, or King was the one who broke into my office when he arrived in New York. I hadn't come across a safe deposit box key in the time I'd spent at West 57, but Sonny may have hidden it. Whoever had broken in had slashed the spines of numerous books. I'd assumed it was vandalism, but Garrett had insisted they were looking for something.

A key?

"Did you let him into the safe deposit box?" I asked.

Dumbo looked horrified at the idea. "Oh, no."

"Even with the key and the box number?"

"Only the authorized account holder may access the box, regardless of who has the key. That's what my teller tried to explain to Mr. Royal. She looked up the box number he gave her, and then she asked for identification. When she saw that the names didn't match, she told Mr. Royal we couldn't give him access."

"What did he say?"

"He insisted he was authorized to open the box. He said Sonny had given him permission. However, my teller pulled the original hard copy authorization for the box, and it was very clear that Sonny had opened the account himself and had not added any additional agents on the box. Even if Mr. Royal had something in writing – which he didn't – that wouldn't have been sufficient. Sonny had sole access rights. Of course, now those rights are yours."

"What did King do when he was denied access?"

"He blustered. He protested. He may have thought raising a ruckus would change our minds, but naturally, it didn't. After this went on for a while, my teller went to get me. Of course, as soon as she mentioned Sonny's name, I flew out to the lobby."

Yes, he said "flew." I'm not making that up.

"However, Mr. Royal was already gone. He was probably afraid I would have had security detain him."

"Would you have done that?" I asked.

"Over something like this? No, but I would have asked him some questions. Naturally, I knew you would want to hear about this, so I called you right away."

"I appreciate it."

"I'm sorry I didn't know about the box before now. As I say, Sonny did this on his own without talking to me."

Or me.

"Do you know if Sonny accessed the box regularly?" I asked.

"I don't know, but I can find out easily enough."

Dumbo flapped out again and left me with my coffee. I tried to imagine what Sonny would have kept in a safe deposit box. I tried to imagine how King would know about it and why he would rush over here to try to get inside the box after bolting from the Gansevoort. My imagination always carried me back to one word.

Money.

Dumbo came back, and I actually heard a flapping noise, but it wasn't his ears. Mr. Barnes had an old-fashioned white index card in his hand, and he fanned it between his nervous fingers. Obviously, some things are still done the way they were in the old days, with pen and ink, not bits and bytes. He showed me the card. I saw one line, one date, and a signature I recognized. *Sonny Chavan.*

"Sonny accessed the box immediately after he opened the account," Dumbo explained. "He hasn't done so since then. That was the one and only time."

I held the card in my hand. I'd seen my father's signature on contracts and invoices every day for weeks. The familiar scrawl, alone on the card, screamed that this was his secret. This was what he'd been hiding from everyone. This was the truth I'd been trying to find.

I saw the date on the card, which confirmed my suspicions. Sonny had opened the account and the safe deposit box two days after Irving Wolfe died in the Atlantic.

I knew what I wanted to do. Everyone I knew, everyone I loved, would have given me the same advice. Walk away. Don't look inside the box. I could hear them telling me to let it go, and I wished I could listen.

But I had to know. I had to see it with my own eyes.

"I don't suppose King left behind the key to the box," I said.

"No, he took it with him."

"So if I want to look in the box, what do I have to do?"

"Well, the easiest thing would be for you to get the key back from Mr. Royal. He's your author, isn't he? With the key, you can have access in seconds."

"Let's say I can't do that," I said.

"Then we have to drill the box. It will take a couple hours to get a locksmith here, and there is a rather large fee, which I'm afraid we're not able to – "

"Drill it," I said. "I'll wait."

If you lock yourself out of your car, or your apartment, or your safe deposit box, you will wait a long time in New York for a locksmith to rescue you. Dumbo showed me to a comfortable office, where I sat impatiently, drank too much coffee, and read a brochure on the Federal Deposit Insurance Corporation to pass the time. The FDIC, you may be interested to learn, is an independent agency created by the Congress to maintain stability and public confidence in the nation's financial system. Someone should tell them it's not working.

I tried calling Bree but got her voice mail. I tried calling King, but his mailbox was full.

After three hours, when I was ready to bail out a safecracker from Riker's Island to get into the box, Donny the Driller arrived with his tools. Really, that was what his name tag said. He wore a snug t-shirt that read, "Bagels and Locks." The cartoon bagel on his shirt had numbers on it, like a combination dial. It was cute, but my sense of humor was already stretched thin. I didn't laugh.

Donny drilled, with me, Dumbo, and two security guards looking on. Having a man with power tools in your vault makes bankers nervous. The grinding noise of metal on metal covered me with goosebumps, but Donny didn't look bothered by the racket or the flying steel dust. He wore large purple goggles, and as he bent over, his jeans gave us a view of the dark side of the moon. Mr. Barnes didn't look happy.

Fortunately, it didn't take long before the door went *pop*.

"There you go," Donny announced. "You're no longer lockblocked."

He winked at me as if to ask: Anything else you want drilled?

The guards shooed him out of the secure room, leaving Dumbo and me standing next to the wall of locked box doors. Sonny's box, the one with the hole in it, was super-sized, like Sonny. The door was about ten inches by ten inches. When Dumbo opened it, I saw the gray steel box tucked inside the drawer, with a handle to pull it out, like I was opening a lingerie drawer at home.

"Will you be wanting to rent a new box?" he asked me.

I was distracted, staring at the box, wondering what was inside. "I'm sorry, what?"

"Well, obviously, we can't put this box back. There's no way to secure it."

"Oh, of course. I haven't decided yet."

"Fine."

I realized he was waiting for me to remove the box. That was my job, not his. I didn't know what to expect, but this wasn't the time to say, "Oops, changed my mind," not with a hole drilled in the bank's wall. Finally, I tugged on the handle and slid the long box into my arms. I expected it to be heavy, but it was surprisingly easy to carry. With a patient smile, Dumbo guided me to a private room outside the vault. It was small and carpeted, with nothing but a table and chair inside. There was nothing on the walls, not even a photograph or a painting. The bank wants to make sure you know you have complete privacy when you peel back the lid of your box. No hidden cameras. No hidden microphones.

"Just signal me when you're ready," Dumbo said.

"Yes, I will."

He closed the door, leaving me inside. Just me and the box.

I stared at it on the table. I looked around for Sonny, because I thought he would be here to witness the unveiling. I wanted to say to him, "You led me here," but of course, he hadn't. He'd kept this from me. Whatever was inside, he never wanted me to see it.

He wasn't here with me now.

I put my hand on the latch. I thought about what I would find inside. Diamonds. Flash drives. Stock certificates. Gold – no, not heavy enough for that. Maybe a list of bank accounts in countries with a see-no-evil attitude toward wire transfers. Those were the sorts of things you would take from the yacht of a billionaire thief. Those were the sorts of things King Royal would want for himself.

I opened the box. Whatever I expected to find inside, I was wrong, wrong, wrong. This had never been about money. There was no money at all. No hidden fortune. No cash. No jewels. The box was empty except for one ugly, awful thing staring up at me. It made me wish I'd never opened it at all.

Inside the box was a gun.

39

I don't like guns.

I really, really don't like guns. I have never held a gun in my life, and seeing one up close didn't make me want to pick it up. Don't ask me what kind of gun it was. I have no idea. The big kind. The kind that kills people. In this case, the kind that kills a man named Irving Wolfe before his body is dumped in the ocean to be hauled up with a net full of shrimp a few months later.

That kind of gun.

It was in a plastic bag, one of those zipper bags you use for leftovers. I could simply pop it in the freezer and forget about it. Months from now, I would be hunting for something for dinner: Lean Cuisine, Tombstone pizza, garlic shrimp, mother's veggie pie, oh and look, there's that gun, right next to the mocha chip ice cream.

I sat there, paralyzed, staring at it, wondering what to do. I don't know how much time passed, but it could have been an hour or two. I knew I couldn't stay at the bank forever. Sooner or later, Dumbo would check to make sure I was still alive. Of course, maybe he'd forget about me; maybe I could wait until the bank was closed, and when I opened the door, everyone would be gone.

Or not.

I had my shoulder purse with me. This was a day when I was glad I didn't carry a clutch. I put the bag in my purse with my fingertips, like it was something I'd picked up in the park with a pooper scooper. The purse felt heavy as I slung it back over my arm. I closed the lid of the deposit box, opened the door, and signaled Dumbo with a forced smile.

"Did you make a decision about another box?" he asked me.

"Yes, I don't need one."

"We'll close it out then, shall we?"

"Please."

"Well, I'm sorry for all the trouble today," he told me. "I know I'll be seeing you as we wrap up Sonny's affairs, but if I can help in any way, you know where to find me." His ears gave me a final, polite flap.

"Thank you, Mr. Barnes."

I shook his hand and tried not to run for the bank door or fall off my heels as I walked. I just wanted to be out of there, where I could think, where I could decide where to go and what to do next. Sonny's bank is on the Upper East Side on Park Avenue, so I emerged from the revolving door into a pushing-shoving crowd of upscale shoppers. No one paid any attention to me. I was just one more New York woman with an illegal concealed weapon.

You'd think it would be liberating to carry a gun. Bump into me, will you, buddy? Guess what's in my purse?

No, it's not liberating. It was just scary.

I walked two blocks to Fifth and turned north. I didn't know where I was going. Everything I knew and loved was in the opposite direction, so that was as good a reason as any to go the other way. I stayed on the west side of the street beside the park. A horse cop passed me – that's a cop on a horse, not a horse who's a cop – and he eyed my purse and said, "Are you carrying a concealed weapon, ma'am?"

No, he didn't say that. He just smiled at me.

I walked all the way to the Met, where I sat down on the steps. It was late afternoon already. A long, cold, gray day. I was surrounded by tourists taking pictures, teenagers making out, and bearded liberals thinking deep thoughts. There were banners between the columns advertising museum exhibitions. I sat on the steps, heavy purse in hand,

and considered my options.

I could make the gun disappear. Throw it away and wipe my hands. No one knew the gun existed – except maybe King Royal – and no one would miss it. I could board the Circle Line, accidentally lose my purse in the Hudson, and if anyone asked me what was in the safe deposit box, I would say: Nothing. It was empty. Of course, the cops would probably ask Dumbo how long I'd sat inside the bank room, and it was hard to explain spending an hour staring at an empty box. There had to be other options.

You have a gun in your purse, Julie. What are you going to do with it?

I could shoot people. That's what you do with guns. Just flesh wounds, nothing serious. I would only shoot very, very annoying people, like meteorologists.

I could melt it down into a paperweight. A lump of metal on my desk. What's that? Oh, that's the gun my father used to kill Irving Wolfe.

Options. I needed options, but I really had only one option, singular, not plural. There was only one thing to do. I knew that as soon as I opened the box. I knew that as I walked to the Met. I knew that as I sat on the steps. I could go round and round and end up in the same place every time.

I thought to myself: Would it make a difference if Sonny were alive? Would I make a different choice?

No. I'm sorry, Sonny. I only have one choice.

I'd put off the inevitable long enough. I took my phone and did what I had to do. I called Goldy Brown of the FBI.

"You are an honest woman, darling," Bree told me. "I'm very impressed."

"You would have done the same thing in my shoes," I said.

"Me? I don't know. Did you really give the flesh-wounds-for-annoying-people option enough consideration? That's got potential. I can certainly think of some Londoners who deserve a little lead in their buttocks."

"You would have handed the gun over," I repeated. "I know you,

Bree Cox. You're not as criminally subversive as you pretend to be."

She shrugged. "Oh, I know, but it's lovely to dream, isn't it? Besides, the least you could have done is let me *see* the gun before you gave it to Brownie McBeige."

"Sorry."

Bree took my hand as we walked. We used to walk hand in hand in the old days wherever we went. There was just something about it that reminded us we were best friends. Of course, New Yorkers generally *hate* people holding hands, because they take up too much of the sidewalk space. However, as women, we get a free pass, because it's hot.

It was after dark on the New York streets, and the city glowed with light. We were near the Flatiron Building, where I spent most of my career doing deals at the McNally-Brown Agency. It's a beautiful building, but the offices are crummy. Too hot in the summer, too cold in the winter. The place had memories for me, though. Kevin making love to me on his desk. Kevin making love to other women on his desk. Me slapping Kevin. Me slapping Bree.

I didn't say they were all *pleasant* memories.

Bree saw me staring at the building. "Miss it?" she asked.

"No."

"Me neither. I'd never work for anyone again."

"You love being on your own, don't you?"

"I do," she said. "Self-employment is heaven. You get all of the stress and long hours with none of the hassles like security and benefits."

I laughed. I hadn't laughed much today. Bree noticed, and she squeezed my hand.

"You'll weather this storm like all the others, darling," she said. "Next week you'll be in La-La Land canoodling with Thad. You'll be calling up Jen Garner, saying 'Jen, sweetheart, this hooker mother role, trust me, it's emotionally authentic.'"

I laughed again.

We'd had dinner together in Koreatown. I love bulgogi and mandu, and Bree loves kimchee so hot it makes your eyes water. I didn't know where we were going now. Maybe to find a club or a bar. The great thing about New York is that you don't have to know where you're going, and you'll wind up there anyway.

I no longer had a gun in my purse. This made the entire city safer.

"Not to bring up a sore subject," Bree said, "but have you thought about what you're going to do about the book?"

I knew what she meant. *Captain Absolute* was a lie. Do I need to have the ending rewritten to portray my father as a murderer? Do I offer refunds to people who bought the book? Do I pull it off the shelves entirely? There was a lot of money at stake in whatever I chose to do. For West 57. For Helmut. For King. Even for Bree. It's not like I could sue King to get the advance back if Sonny knew that the book was a lie from the start. The real danger is that people would sue *me*.

"I haven't decided," I said, which was true.

"Well, it's our mess together, you and me. We were both conned. You were right about all this nonsense from the beginning, and I was wrong. I will back you up in anything you need to do."

"I have a few options," I said.

"Options? Plural?" Bree smiled and shook her head. "Julie, as long as I have known you, you have been a one-option girl. You pretend you have all these choices competing in your head, and the reality is, you know from day one exactly what you're going to do. It just takes you forever to get around to doing it."

I thought I should complain about that judgment on principle. "That's not true," I said.

"You only had one option on the gun, right?"

"Yes, but that's different."

"Only one option on selling West 57, right?"

"Yes, but that was economic."

"Whatever you say, darling. You are predictable, and I love that about you."

"I never thought I would go to Los Angeles," I protested. "To work with my mother? To start a relationship with Thad?"

"I agree," Bree said, winking at me. "That's not like you at all."

"So you're wrong."

"I'm never wrong," Bree replied cheerily.

"Now you sound like Sonny," I said.

Bree lit a cigarette, and I thought: Sonny.

I'd been trying *not* to think about him, ever since I found the gun. I'd put my mind on hold. However, sooner or later, I needed to confront the reality in front of me. Sonny killed a man – an evil man, an immoral man, but a man. It was still a crime. It was still murder. I wasn't sure I could ever forgive him.

Sonny.

Why did he do it? That was what I really wanted to know. What made him go so far?

Bree blew a cloud of smoke into the street. She eyed me and read my mind. "Don't go leaping to conclusions, Julie. There's a lot we don't know about what happened."

"Irving Wolfe was shot in the head. I found a gun in a secret safe deposit box that had only been opened once, by Sonny, just days after Wolfe died. I'm not naive, Bree."

"Well, I'm not suggesting you put on rose-colored glasses," she told me. "It's suspicious, that's for sure."

"It's more than suspicious."

"Maybe you should take up smoking," she said, taking the cigarette out of her mouth. "Want a suck?"

"No thanks."

"Are you sure? Nothing says 'I love you' like carcinogens."

I laughed again. I was almost tempted to start smoking, but Bree stopped abruptly on the street, with her cigarette dangling from her fingers. "Darling!" she announced suddenly, with a big smile on her face. "How the freak are you?"

I looked around Broadway, but there was no one nearby. Either Bree was talking to herself, or she'd begun to see dead people, like me.

"How's Angie?" Bree went on. "Give that sweetie a kiss for me. Is she with you?"

"What?" I said.

Bree winked and pointed at her ear. She was on the phone. Damn Bluetooth.

"God, yes, darling, the video was a freaking riot, wasn't it? I knew you'd love it. The man is a trip. He's got a voice, doesn't he?" She listened, and her face changed. "Seriously? Are you sure? No, you're right, we've been looking for him. What can I say? As usual, you have saved me in the nick of time. You're a gem. Remember, we need you in the movie of *Paperback Bitch*, darling. You are the cornerstone of the whole thing. Yes, yes, Cherie will call. Ta for now. Kiss kiss."

Bree hung up.

"That was Brad," she said, putting her cigarette back in her mouth.

"Who?"

"Brad Pitt."

"You were just talking to Brad Pitt?" I asked.

"He's filming in Capetown. Freaking fantastic."

"How do you know him?"

"We're mates, don't you remember? He got my arse out of a sling when I was starting out."

That was true. I remembered now. Bree was down to one client and a bench in Hyde Park when Brad Pitt called to save the day by doing a huge deal for a movie that made a fortune.

"So what did he say?" I asked.

"He found King Royal for us."

"Brad Pitt found King? How on earth did he do that?"

"I tweeted the Assy McHattie video to a few people. Brad nearly bust a gut laughing. So did Angelina. He re-tweeted it to half his contact folder, including, as it turns out, one of the old *Law & Order* producers here in New York. I loved that show. Da dum!"

"Bree."

"It was never the same after they lost Orbach, though, don't you think?"

"Bree."

"Right. Anyway, I guess this guy texted Brad a few minutes ago to say that he was listening to King sing the Assy McHattie song right now, live and in person. Brad called me. I guess he saw my post to King about giving me a freaking call before I freaking find him and cut off his motherfreaking you-know-what."

Needless to say, that comment was highly edited.

"So where is he?" I asked.

"The *Law & Order* guy is on his yacht over at the Chelsea Piers. King's on the boat across from him."

"King's on a boat?" I asked.

"Not *a* boat, darling. *The* boat. He's on the *Captain Absolute*."

40

"Julie Chavan!" King shouted to us as we walked up the pier. "Bree of Many Cox! The two loveliest ladies on the planet are here. Captain, my Captain, shall we welcome them as honored guests? Aye aye! Permission to come aboard!"

Yes, King was drunk again. Very drunk.

We climbed the ladder onto the monster yacht, which was like boarding an aircraft carrier. King weaved around the main deck in an unbuttoned silk shirt and boxer shorts. His feet were bare. He wore a white captain's hat, and his curly ringlets bounced under the brim as he swayed.

"Why don't you sit down, King?" I suggested.

King shook his head fiercely and spread his arms wide. In one hand was an open bottle of champagne. Two other empty bottles rolled around the deck as the boat bobbed. "Sit? Sit? No, we must keep moving, my Captain. Move or die, move or die, move or die, like sharks we are! Move or die!"

Bree was right. When I had the gun, I should have spent more time thinking about flesh wounds for annoying people.

We were in the private marina at the Chelsea Piers on the Hudson, surrounded by a smattering of sailboats, catamarans, and floating mansions. These weren't party barges serving Pabst Blue Ribbon on summer Sundays. These were the boats that people bought when they got bored with their Lamborghinis. It was ten o'clock at night. Most of the yachts were dark and empty; it was too early in the season, and too cold, to be at sea or partying. A lot of slips were empty. Their owners were probably docked in some blue-green bay in the Caribbean. I did see one impressive sailboat a hundred yards away, brightly lit, with a lone man in a deck chair sipping white wine. He waved at me. I figured he was Brad's friend, the *Law & Order* guy.

We were aboard the *Captain Absolute*. That was the yacht's name – and, hence, the book's name – but its checkered legacy would be painted over soon. The trustee handling the claims of defrauded investors was in the process of selling the boat to a private charter company, and soon the yacht on which Wolfe died would be re-christened and re-launched to serve as a luxury boat for corporations catering to their top executives and clients. That was the way of the world.

It was a very nice boat. Well over one hundred feet, three levels, glistening in white and black. A helicopter landing pad. Even Thad probably could not afford this boat. Then again, if you have stolen hundreds of millions of dollars, you deserve a nice place to put your feet up on the water.

"What are you doing here, King?" Bree asked.

King wandered around the sharply angled prow and swigged his bubbly like Gatorade. "I am communing with the Captain. His spirit is here." He ripped off his captain's hat and recited in a loud voice: "*No, no, no life! Why should a dog, a horse, a rat, have life, and thou no breath at all? Thou 'lt come no more, never, never, never, never, never!*"

"Shakespeare?" I asked Bree.

"*King Lear.* You have to admit, he knows his stuff."

King spun around and collapsed to his knees with his hat clutched in his fists. I was afraid he was going to sing, but he crawled to the railing instead and threw up into the harbor. I was glad he hadn't done that on the roof of the Gansevoort.

"Let's go, King," I said. "You're not supposed to be here."

King clung to the brass railing, wiping his mouth. He re-positioned the hat on his head, but it was crooked. He wagged a finger at me. "This is where the Captain climbed over the edge. Right here. This is where he offered himself to the goddess of the sea."

I was tired of lies.

"You can cut the crap, King," I snapped. "The FBI recovered Wolfe's body. He was shot in the head. No suicide. I know about the safe deposit box, too. I found the gun. The FBI has it now. So no more fake stories, no more heroic poetry, okay? The game's over."

King flopped down on his backside. "Bollocks," he muttered. He spread his legs wide and put the champagne bottle between them. He gripped the neck of the bottle with both hands. I was glad it was the bottle and not other things.

"I warned you!" he shouted at me. "But did you listen, Julie Chavan? No, you had to keep pushing pushing pushing pushing pushing pushing. And for what? The truth? I told you the truth would only hurt the people you love."

"You want to tell us what really happened?" Bree asked him.

King stared at the stars. He tried to drink more of the champagne but poured most of it down his bare chest.

"The Captain knew the end was drawing nigh," he said.

Nigh? Really?

"He was planning his suicide. He would have done it just like I said. He told me about his wish to lose himself in the sea. He would never let himself be locked up in a cage, not the Captain. That wasn't for him."

"Why kill himself?" Bree asked.

"The rumors had started spreading. The whispers. People were asking questions about the fund accounting for the first time. Investors. Reporters. Attorneys. Private investigators. The government. The net was closing around us. It would only be a matter of days, the Captain said, before everyone knew the truth, that there was no more money, that it was all gone, that it had been a scheme from the beginning. His mood was dark those days. Black even. "

"Get to the last night, King," I said. "Tell us about the boat."

King leaned back against the railing. "The Captain loved this boat.

He was happier here on the yacht than anywhere else on earth. His finest days were at the helm, miles from shore. I suggested we sail off to an island somewhere to escape, him and me, but he said they would follow us. Sooner or later, they would find us."

"The last night," I repeated.

"Yes, the last night. I knew from the beginning that it would be our last night. I knew the Captain would lead us out of harbor but not lead us back. The weather was as grim as his soul, spattering rain out of the night sky. Even so, he had a feast prepared for us. It was like the Shah's table. He wanted a final celebration out on the water."

I was losing patience.

I didn't want to hear about Irving Wolfe.

I didn't want to hear about the Feds closing in.

I didn't want to hear about the boat or the weather or the shrimp cocktails.

"*Tell me about Sonny!*" I said, my voice cracking. "Sonny went out on the boat with you that night, didn't he?"

"The great Sonnymonias! Yes, Julie Chavan. Yes, you are right. He was here."

I closed my eyes. Sometimes you know what you're going to hear, but you still hate it. "What happened?"

"I told you, it was supposed to be a celebration!" King hollered. "A feast! The Captain was joking, laughing, telling stories, as if he had no cares in the world. However, Sonny kept pressing for the truth, kept asking if the rumors were true. Finally, the Captain admitted it. He laid it all out, everything he'd done. It didn't go well, of course. The conversation dissolved into terrible arguing and shouting. It was painful. I had to go below, because I couldn't take it. I covered my ears and tried to drown out their voices."

Oh, Sonny.

"Then I heard the explosion," King went on, his voice slurring with grief, "and I knew what had happened. I ran back up to the deck, fearing the worst, and he was here, right here at my feet." He jabbed at the deck with his finger. "Dead! Shot! My Captain was gone."

That didn't answer my question.

Why? That was my question.

I bent down in front of King. "I know my father had a temper. I know he was desperate, but I still don't understand. What were they arguing about? Why did Sonny shoot him?"

"Sonny?" King asked.

"Yes, of course, Sonny. Why did he kill Wolfe?"

King placed his hat over his heart. He looked sincerely distressed. "Sonny did not shoot the Captain, Julie Chavan. Is that what you thought? If so, then I humbly apologize. No, Sonny tried to stop it. He was a valiant man. I heard him shouting to put down the gun. Sadly, his pleas were in vain."

My father did not kill anyone.

Sonny was innocent.

He was a valiant man.

"Darling!" Bree whispered, hugging me in relief.

I was relieved, too, and I was upset that I had lost my faith. I'd turned my back on everything I knew about Sonny and was willing to believe something awful about him. I should have trusted my father. He was not that man.

I was so caught up in my rush of emotions that I barely heard King's next words. They sounded almost inaudible, drowned by the roar in my head.

"It was that woman," he said.

I thought about plugging my ears and singing. I didn't want to know what he meant. I didn't want to know any more than what I knew already. Sonny didn't shoot Wolfe. End of story. Except it was not the end of the story. There were too many other questions that needed answers. There were still people I loved who would be hurt by the truth.

My voice low and wary, I asked, "What woman?"

"It was that author," King said. "She was on the boat, too. It was her."

That author.

Who?

I wanted him to say it was Stephenie Meyer. I always suspected that pretty little Mormon had a temper.

Or Janet Evanovich. Can't you picture Janet hoisting a big gun and blowing someone away? "Here's one for the money, Wolfie. You don't mess with Janet E."

The trouble is, I knew it wasn't Stephenie or E.L. or Janet or Nora or J.K. or Jodi or Danielle. I knew exactly who it was. I didn't need King to tell me.

41

The next day, we met back at Tavern on the Green. Me and Libby Varnay.

She knew the truth was coming out. I'm not exactly a poker face at hiding my emotions. She probably knew when I called her in the morning and said I needed to see her. My voice was a giveaway.

I arrived early; she was right on time. I watched her approach the table. She was as exquisite as ever as she joined me. Every strand of hair was in place, every lash long and distinct, every fingernail glossy and red. Her silk clothes hung on her in perfect proportion like decorations on a department store Christmas tree. That was Libby – effortlessly elegant. It must be hard to keep up appearances when all your money, all your life savings, everything you've built and treasured, is gone.

Stolen by Irving Wolfe.

Behind her, I saw Libby's nephew, Drew, settle into another table nearby, the way he always did, trailing in her shadow. His suit stretched and strained across his massive shoulders. He had no neck, just a head and torso connected by rolls of fat. Despite his size, he had one of the sweetest, gentlest faces I'd ever seen. He knew the truth was coming out, too. His eyes never left Libby; he was all devotion to her. It made me want to cry.

A waitress hovered over us. She knew Libby; everyone at the Tavern knew Libby. She brought a glass of Viognier to the table without being asked, and Libby gave her a warm smile. "You are a dear."

I ordered nothing at all.

Libby sipped her wine and stared at me. She didn't pretend or play the fool. I was glad. "King told you what happened, didn't he?"

"Yes."

"Of course, he did." She sighed. "I don't like that man."

"Neither do I."

I saw a slight tremble in her fingers as she held her glass of wine. That was the only break in her cool. "I've caused you a great deal of pain, Julie. I'm very sorry."

"Don't worry about that."

"When you came to me and you were so upset about Sonny, so concerned about what he had done, I almost told you everything then. I should have. He would have wanted you to know the truth, and you should have heard it from me, not from a poseur like King Royal."

"I wish I hadn't heard it at all."

"No, it's better this way. It really is. I would hate to think of you living your life having doubts about your father's integrity. Sonny was a wonderful man."

Was he?

He'd covered up a murder. He'd paid King Royal four million dollars to hide the truth. To write a book that was a lie.

"I checked the financial records at West 57," I said. "Your royalty payments went directly into Irving Wolfe's investment fund. Twice a year, ever since *Morningside Park* was released."

Libby nodded. "Sonny told me I should put my money in the hands of a pro. I knew nothing about money, because I never had any. So he introduced me to Irving Wolfe. I liked him. I trusted him. We both did. Every dollar I made with the book and the movie, all these years, I put it in Irving's hands. For me, it was the perfect arrangement. I had no worries. Whenever I needed money, it was there." She frowned. "I was near the bottom of Irving's pyramid. I was one of the lucky ones."

"You never suspected anything?" I asked.

"Suspected anything? No, why would I? There were big numbers on my quarterly statements. I had everything I needed or wanted. That's all I cared about. Whenever I turned on the television, there was Irving, talking about the economy and sharing his stock picks. Everyone else trusted him, too. When the markets went to hell a few years ago, I suppose I should have asked more questions. How was it possible my account balances could seem so stable when everyone else was watching their treasure shrivel? However, like all the others, I persisted in the belief that Irving had the magic touch. He knew things that other people didn't. To be honest, I *wanted* to believe him. It was far better that than to contemplate the horror of the truth."

She was still Libby. Still eloquent in her downfall.

"What happened?" I asked.

Her smile alighted on her face and then flitted away like a nervous bird. "Oh, it's amazing the capacity we have to deny reality until we have no choice. I heard the rumors. I gave them no credence. It was only on that last day, when every newspaper was reporting that an indictment of Irving was imminent, that I finally called to ask him if any of this was true."

"What did he say?"

"He was as charming and persuasive as ever," Libby told me. "He gave no hint that anything was wrong. He told me he was planning an intimate little celebration on his yacht that night, that I should plan to join him. I have to say, for the first time, I felt a ripple of fear. I didn't want to go on that boat by myself. I couldn't confront him alone. I had a premonition of what I would learn."

"So you asked Sonny to go with you," I said.

"Yes, I asked Sonny. He was already concerned by what he'd read in the papers. Naturally, he agreed to accompany me to talk to Irving. He was always there for me."

"You picked him up and went to the boat?"

Libby lifted her wine and put it down without drinking. "Yes."

"Who was there?" I asked.

"Just the four of us. Me, Sonny, Irving, and his odd little man-child, King Royal."

"That's all?"

"That's all," she insisted. "It was intimate, as Irving said."

She repeated: "That was all."

I let her continue without interrupting her. I felt sad, because she wasn't good at hiding things.

"The cruise had a surreal quality," she went on. "There was this sense of disconnection from the world, like Nero partying during the fire. We drank expensive wine. We ate from this elaborate buffet that could have served twenty. Lobsters, caviar, sushi, truffles...everything the condemned man could possibly want for his last meal. That should have told me something. We spent hours talking about nothing. We danced around the subject and pretended everything was fine. Irving wasn't going to bring it up unless we did. So, finally, when we were all a little drunk, I asked him straight out. I had to know. I said, 'Is any of it true?'"

"What did he say?" I asked.

Libby shook her head. "He couldn't have been calmer. He said yes. Just like that. 'Yes, all of it's true.' Then he spread some Russian oscetra on a blini with his mother-of-pearl spoon and ate it as if the news were of no importance at all."

"I'm so sorry, Libby."

"I was speechless. Yes, no, innocent, guilty, it made no difference to him. I realized then that Irving was a man without morals, without any conscience. I didn't even know what to say or what to ask, so Sonny stepped in. He was furious. He demanded to know everything, to know what it meant, to know how much money I'd lost. Irving seemed annoyed to have to explain it, but he did."

"How bad was it?"

Libby stared around the restaurant, allowing its crystal finery to reflect in her eyes. Some people say that when you start with nothing, and then lose everything, the fall isn't so bad because you already know what it's like at the bottom. I don't think so. I think when you start your life as Libby did, in poverty and suffering, you never want to see that place again.

"It was bad," she said. "Inutterably bad. I had all of my money invested with Wolfe. Everything I'd made, it was *all gone*. The account balances were fictitious. More than that, Irving suggested that I would probably find the authorities knocking on my own door. Apparently, because I had been an investor with him for so long, I had profited from his fraud. I had received phantom returns in the millions of dollars, and many investors had seen none at all. So they would be coming to me to recoup what I'd lived on all these years. Not that there's anything left to take."

"That's why you're moving," I said. "Isn't it?"

"Yes." Libby put her hands together as if she were praying. "I hate to leave the city. This is my home, but I can't afford to stay. My tax advisor suggested I keep a mortgage on my condo, but there's nothing left for the payments and taxes. My sister is being charitable in taking me in."

"If there was anything I could do – " I said.

Libby put up a hand to stop me. "Sonny already tried to rescue me, Julie. The new book, that was his idea. It gave him a reason to get me a contract payment to tide me over and pay some bills. The trouble is, I don't have it in me. I have no words. I'm sure you saw that when you read the first chapter. It's not there."

I said nothing. She was right.

"You don't have to soothe my feelings," she went on with an ironic smile. "I know good from bad."

"I'll talk to Helmut about a re-release of *Morningside Park*," I suggested. "A whole new generation could discover it."

"That's sweet of you, but don't worry about me. I have no cares for myself. I've lived with nothing, and I can live with nothing again. What felt so tragic to me was that I can no longer make a difference the way I wanted to. Say what you will about money, but it's awfully useful in this world. The organizations I've supported, I can't fund them anymore. The foundation I planned to establish in my estate, it will never come to pass. That's what Irving took from me. My legacy."

I glanced at the doorway to the restaurant. I saw Goldy Brown of the FBI. The lady in brown. I was running out of time to hear the truth from Libby's lips.

"On the boat, Libby," I said. "What happened when Wolfe told you about the fraud?"

Libby's jaw hardened. Her whole body looked fraught with tension, like a cable holding up a bridge. "You already know what happened. I shot him."

I took her hands across the table and held them in my own. "Oh, Libby, no."

"Sonny tried to stop me, but I lost control. I was staring into a great sea of nothingness, Julie. I couldn't let that man treat his crimes as if they were trivial. I couldn't let him humiliate me."

I shook my head. "Libby, you can't do this."

"I'm telling you what happened."

"No, Libby, you're lying."

"It was me," she insisted. "Didn't King tell you?"

"King wasn't on deck. He didn't see it. You have to tell me the truth. I know you want to protect him, but you can't do that anymore. I found the gun, Libby. Don't try to tell me it's yours. I know better."

I saw Goldy Brown coming closer. She had several burly boys in suits with her. Their suits weren't brown, so it must just be the women who get the beige uniforms.

"It doesn't matter whose gun it is," Libby informed me archly. "I'm the one who pulled the trigger. Me."

"You? Fire a gun? Don't be ridiculous. You *can't* take the blame for this. I won't let you. Are you going to tell me you ran down Nick Duggan, too? Is that your story? The thing is, you're just like me, Libby. You can't drive. You didn't do it."

The FBI team stopped at the table. Not our table. They stopped on every side of Libby's nephew, Drew, surrounding him. Libby heard the commotion behind us, and her head flew around in despair. A strangled cry escaped from her throat. She reached out her hands toward Drew, and her nephew simply offered a patient nod and stood up to accept the handcuffs.

"*Drew*," she murmured.

"I'm so sorry, Libby," I said.

She watched them taking her nephew away. Her face was wrenched with pain. I knew it was worse for her than if they'd put her in prison herself. Libby was a rescuer. A savior. She wanted to raise up everyone. There were no lost causes. It was bad enough that Irving Wolfe had taken away her legacy, but now he'd taken away her pride and joy, too. He'd sacrificed her nephew.

"Drew was just trying to save me," she said.

"I know."

"He was furious about what Irving did to me. He's a good boy. He made a mistake."

"He's not a boy, Libby. He made his own choices."

"Only out of the best intentions, Julie. Only out of love."

"Libby, he killed Nick Duggan, too. There's no excuse for that. No justification."

Libby flinched. "No, no, no, that's my fault. It's all my fault. Duggan contacted *me*. He'd figured out that I was one of Irving's victims. He made the connection to Sonny and the book. He said he'd found someone who saw my limo at the pier the night of that last cruise. When he started asking all of these questions, I panicked. I told Drew we couldn't let the truth come out. Drew said he'd take care of it. I shouldn't have let him go."

I watched her cry. I held her hand, but there was nothing I could do.

I thought about Sonny. Wherever he was, I'm sure he was unhappy with me for letting the truth come out. *Why couldn't you just drop the gun in the river, darling girl?* He'd risked everything to avoid this moment and spare Libby this pain. Instead, I couldn't stop myself from knowing things that my father never wanted me to know.

If I had it all to do over again, if I'd known what I would discover, I would have – I would have –

I would have done the same thing. Bree was right. I'm a one-choice girl.

Sonny and I simply made different choices. His choice was to lie, bribe, cover up, all to protect Libby and her nephew. I knew why Sonny had gone so far. *Only out of the best of intentions. Only out of love.* My father had loved Libby right to the end. She was still the woman he wanted to marry, years after she'd told him no. He still would have done anything for her. And he did.

In the end, Sonny sold his soul to save her. He sold out West 57 the day he agreed to publish *Captain Absolute*. There was no going back.

42

A few days later, I made it official. I issued a press release, short and sweet. I was voluntarily pulling *Captain Absolute* from bookstore shelves and offering refunds to anyone who had already purchased it.

I assumed this would be a popular decision, but you'd think I had asked libraries to burn their copies of *To Kill a Mockingbird*. Bookstore owners called me in droves, begging me to keep the book on the market. It seems that in the wake of all the publicity – Irving Wolfe's body, Drew's arrest, Libby's grief-stricken press conference, King Royal's public *mea culpa* on Jimmy Fallon, complete with a live rendition of Assy McHattie – demand for *Captain Absolute* was at an all-time high. It was like I'd published *The Gone Girl on the Train With the Dragon Tattoo*.

As for refund requests, we got six. Six. This was out of several hundred thousand copies delivered to stores. Everyone else went out on eBay and Amazon and sold their used copies for twice the price. You have to love the American entrepreneurial spirit.

I finally compromised with booksellers. They'd bought the books; they could keep them and sell them. We wouldn't print any more copies, but we weren't demanding that we get the existing books back to be pulped like orange juice. With a finite supply, and seemingly infinite demand, customers flocked to stores, waited in huge lines, and paid full price. Even Wal-Mart didn't discount *Captain Absolute*. As a result, it was the first book in recent memory on which every bookseller in the country made money. Most independents were on track for their best sales month in ten years, and I became an instant industry hero. I was on the cover of *Publishers Weekly* and on the front page of *The New York Times*. The photo caption read, "Publisher With Long Hair."

I'm kidding.

The whole spectacle nauseated me, but Bree pointed out that, in the end, Sonny had been right again. Nobody cared that the book was a lie designed to cover up a murder. Even the big O announced that she was reading it, and with the Oprah Seal of Approval, every book club in the country made *Captain Absolute* their monthly pick. Everyone was happy, including King Royal, who was already in discussions with Fox about a reality TV show. According to Bree, a seven-figure auction was underway for King's next memoir. He was going to be a wealthy man.

For me, the good news was that *Morningside Park* had followed *Captain Absolute* up the bestseller list, thanks to all the news reports about Libby, Drew, and Wolfe. Massive orders started flowing in, and we had to do a huge new print order. Libby was going to make a lot of money with her next royalty check.

Helmut was as giddy as a schoolgirl about the whole thing. When I went to see him at Gernestier, I expected to find him drinking Rostocker beer and dancing to polka music with his buxom secretary. He'd hit a triple jackpot, all 7's lining up on his slot machine. My decision to yank the book enhanced the reputation of West 57 for quality and integrity in its literary line. My decision to let booksellers sell their existing stock was making everyone a pot of money. Naturally, I also knew that as soon as I signed on the dotted line to sell the house, Helmut would quietly reverse my decision and reprint several hundred thousand more copies of *Captain Absolute* to meet the market demand.

It was a win-win-win.

He greeted me with a bear hug in the lobby of the executive floor. Other executives flooded from their offices to meet me. Everyone had to come see Julie Chavan and shake her hand.

"Julie, Julie, Julie," Helmut said as he led me into the board room.

"What a week you've had."

"That's true."

"It's extraordinary. I never expected this book to become such a pop culture phenomenon."

"Neither did I," I said. "I wanted to bury it."

"Ah, but you can't bury something once the culture takes hold of it. Such things have a will of their own. However, I was impressed that you tried to make amends in the marketplace for the dishonesty of the book."

"Thank you."

"Naturally, I would never have done the same thing," he added with a playful flick of his eyebrows. This was definitely the first time I have ever used the word "playful" to describe Helmut.

He pointed me to one of the leather chairs. I was thinking of asking if I could take one with me. It's more comfortable than my bed.

As I sat down, I saw a stack of papers neatly placed on the long conference room table. That was when the reality of this meeting hit me. I tried to keep the sadness off my face, and I don't think I was successful. These were the contracts for selling the brand. I'd had a lawyer review them, and everything was in order. The deal was done. Just sign my name, and I would be free. West 57 would belong to Gernestier.

Just sign my name, and Sonny would really be gone.

If Helmut recognized my discomfort, he was discreet. He looked away as I brushed back the tears. He had champagne ready for us again, and a very nice cheese tray, but I didn't want anything. I wanted it to be over.

I looked around, wanting to see Sonny here, even if it was just one last time. I hadn't seen him in days, not since that late night in the office when I'd first realized he was on the boat with King and Wolfe. Maybe that was the discovery I needed to make; maybe that was the unfinished business we had. You can't keep the dead around forever, right? Sooner or later, heaven wants them. Even so, I was struggling with the idea that I would never see him again. If I'd known, I would have told him what was in my heart. I would have said goodbye.

"I know this is hard for you," Helmut said quietly.

"I didn't realize how hard it would be," I replied, staring at the papers and the expensive Cross pen placed next to them.

"You know, this does not have to be end," he told me. "Our offer still stands. You are welcome to join Gernestier as the director of West 57. I think you would be pleasantly surprised at the autonomy we would give you. With all candor, you are even more valuable to us today, thanks to your high profile, than you were a week ago. With that in mind, we would be inclined to sweeten our offer."

He mentioned a new number.

It was an even nicer number than he'd proposed to me at dinner when all of this started.

Anything to say, Sonny? Any advice for your darling girl? But no. He didn't weigh in or tell me I was crazy or tell me to take Helmut's bratwurst and shove it up his sauerkraut. I was on my own.

"That's extremely generous," I said, "but I have other plans."

"Los Angeles?"

"Yes."

"Well, believe me when I say that your departure is a gain for Hollywood and the movie industry and a sincere loss for New York and the publishing industry."

"That's very kind of you."

I'd made my decision. As always, I really only had one choice to make. I reached for the papers and the pen. Helmut's lawyers had thoughtfully placed little sticky arrows on every page on which I had to sign. There were lots of pages with lots of legalese about intellectual property, fixed assets, reps and warranties, human resources, and other clauses that keep lawyers paying their country club bills every month. I didn't hesitate. I went through the contract page by page, signing every line where I needed to sign. It didn't take long. Not even five minutes. When I was done, I didn't own West 57 anymore.

"Here you are," I said to Helmut.

We shook hands. "You won't regret this decision, Julie," he

assured me. "Gernestier will honor Sonny's legacy."

"I hope so."

"Are you sure I can't offer you something to drink? I could invite some of our other officers to join us."

"No, I need to go."

"I'm sure our paths will cross again," he said.

"I'm sure that's true."

I got up. Strangely, I felt a sense of relief. I'd been dreading this moment for days, but now it was done. I had cut the cord once and for all. I could get on with the rest of my life.

There was absolutely nothing keeping me in New York anymore. No strings. No ties. No regrets. I could leave for the west coast with Cherie and Thad and leave nothing behind me.

Absolutely nothing.

Nothing at all.

Really.

43

"Julie!" Cherie announced happily as I answered my phone. "Where are you?"

"I'm at Thad's hotel, mother," I told her, but she already knew that. I'm sure her GPS tracker was working fine. "The taxi just dropped me off."

"Are you packed? Do you have your bag with you?"

"Of course."

"Wonderful! My dear, this is so very exciting. My assistant will be waiting at LAX to pick up the two of you in a town car and whisk you right back to my office. I will give you the grand tour, show you your space, introduce you to the entire team. We can eat in the cafeteria. You have never seen a cafeteria like ours! We have an Automat with fresh sushi and a salad bar with organic produce grown on-site in our own gardens. Did I mention the running track, too? We will have that pooch gone in no time."

"I don't have a pooch," I said, which was not altogether true.

"Our building is more like a spa than a corporate campus, trust me. Of course, no need to work today. Or even tomorrow, my dear. I want you to get familiar with the area. You and Thad can go see the sights, check out some of the studios, or just lie on the beach if you want. It's going to be 75 degrees and sunny, but of course, that's the forecast every day. Most TV stations out here don't even bother with weather girls. What's there to say about it?"

"It's supposed to pour down rain in New York tonight," I said.

"See? I will be so happy to have you out of there. At long last!"

"It's only a week, mother."

Cherie tut-tutted me. "Julie, California is a drug. Give it a week, and you will be addicted. Trust me, you will never leave. You will be just like Katy Perry, my dear. A California gurl."

I'd made the mistake of telling her about my Katy dream. She was very amused at the idea of wearing a Snoop Dogg goatee.

"Oh, and I've talked to a realtor for you!" Cherie went on. "We'll see him on Friday."

"A realtor? Mother, slow down."

That was a foolish request, because my mother does not do "slow down." She has one speed. Cherie speed.

"You need to meet him, my dear. Lovely little cherub. Gay as the day is long, but he attends all the right parties. That's how you find properties out here. MLS in L.A. stands for Mojitos Lunches Skybar. William will take you around and show you places in all the right neighborhoods, and I assure you, you won't see a For Sale sign outside any of them. Advertising is tacky tacky tacky. Don't worry about prices either. You know I'll make sure you're taken care of."

"That's not what I'm looking for, mother."

"And that's why I'm here to help you, my dear! I can make all the arrangements. We'll find the perfect place in no time. I know you're going to be staying with Thad, and his place is divine, but you *will* want a home of your own, regardless. Even if you're only there a couple days a month, it's useful."

I felt a little like Dorothy, and Cherie was the tornado.

"I have to go, mother," I said.

"Yes, I know, you have a flight to catch. Thank God you're taking Virgin. They understand first class. Oh, one other thing! I almost forgot! I've scheduled you for driving lessons, too."

"Driving lessons?"

"It's Los Angeles, my dear, not New York. People in our business do not take public transportation. We drive. We drive everywhere. We drive to work. We drive to the beach. We drive to our garage to get our car. I'm not letting you on the 405 until you've had a month of lessons. As an incentive, I have my eye on an Audi convertible for you. My dealer owes me a favor. He'll let you have it for a song. A song, my dear, right off the lot. It's yellow."

"I don't like yellow," I said.

"Oh, Julie, yellow is the new red. It's the hot color out here. If you'd like, consider it a welcome-to-Los Angeles gift from me. I'll have it waiting at Thad's, and your driving instructor can run you through the basics. You'll be terrorizing the crosswalks of Malibu in no time."

"Don't buy me a car, mother," I said. "Really."

"We'll call it a loan. How about that?"

"I really have to go," I repeated.

"Yes, yes, safe flight, my dear! Give Thad a big hug for me! Get some sleep on the trip. You've earned it. Tomorrow you'll be on my patio enjoying a cup of tea."

"I like coffee," I said, but Cherie had already hung up.

I know, I know. Tea's better for me.

Thad was on the phone when I arrived in his hotel room. He didn't notice me standing there. I hovered by the door with my roller bag in hand. Meanwhile, Thad's people buzzed around me like worker bees. When Thad relocates, it's not like packing a carry-on and catching a cab. At least ten trunks wheeled by me, pulled by moving men. I saw artwork being taken off the walls. A treadmill. An exercise bike. A filing cabinet. Two espresso machines. Two. I guess that's what they mean by double espresso.

I realized that I was a cog in the wheel of a multi-million dollar enterprise. An international corporation. Thad, Inc.

Mandi with an i, the perky blond who met me at the limo for my date with Thad, was supervising the move. She looked efficient, directing workers, checking items off on a clipboard. She was already dressed for

L.A. in a hot pink dress that showed off her mile-long legs. Her nose was a well-sharpened knife. She had Farrah hair, lips by Botox, and breasts that made me wonder if the U.S. Olympic volleyball team was missing a couple balls.

Mandi saw me and smiled a fake smile with a mouth that had twice the normal complement of teeth. She dodged the parade of workmen and made her way to me at the door.

"Julie," she said smoothly. "It's great to see you again."

I think there was an implied "bitch" somewhere in that greeting.

I smiled back. "Great to see you, too."

"I understand you're traveling with us," Mandi said. "Terrific."

"Thanks."

She eyed my eighteen-inch travel bag like I was traveling with a flatulent sheepdog. "Is the rest of your luggage downstairs? We'll put it in the van."

"This is all of it," I said.

"Wow, really? How cute. I could never travel so light."

"Well, my bras don't take up as much room as yours," I said.

No, I didn't say that.

"It's only a week," I said.

"A week? Really? Thad made it sound like you were making the big move."

"We'll see."

"Well, you should do it. New York is dreary."

"I always thought it was the most electrifying city in the world," I said.

"Oh, it was exciting the first few days, and then I missed the ocean, you know? I'm dying to get in my bikini again and head for the beach."

"I guess you can catch up on your reading there," I said. Yes, I may have tucked a little sarcasm into that comment.

Mandi shrugged. "Who reads anymore?"

I didn't know what to say to that. She said it so matter-of-factly that I was speechless. Of course, maybe she was right. Maybe nobody reads in L.A. Maybe nobody reads anywhere anymore. Except in New York. A lot of us still read in New York.

"Hey, can I get you something?" Mandi asked. "Bottle of San Pellegrino?"

"Sure."

Mandi waved a hand at another of Thad's people. There was obviously a pecking order, and she had graduated beyond water girl. She'd done the polite thing by greeting me, and now she was off to more important matters.

"Julie."

I heard Thad's voice behind me, as seductive as if he were on stage with JJ. He spun me around, grabbed my shoulders with strong hands, and planted a kiss on me. He was genuinely excited to see me.

"Congratulations," he said when we disentangled our tongues. "This is the first day of the rest of your life."

"That's what Cherie tells me," I said.

He laughed in a practiced way, the way people laugh when they have an audience. "Well, listen to her! She's your mother! Mother knows best, right?"

"Sometimes."

"I talked to her today. She's so excited about your coming out there."

"Really? I hadn't picked up on that."

He did a double-take until he realized I was joking, and then he tapped my face in a mock slap. "You are an evil woman. We're going to have our hands full with you." While his hand was in the vicinity of my cheek, he took hold of my hair and twirled it around his fingers like a forkful of spaghetti.

"This hair," he said. "So you really like it long, do you?"

"Yes, I do," I said.

"I have a guy in Malibu. He spent five years in Jamal Hamadi's salon, and now he does his own thing. He is *the* trendsetter right now. I'll make an appointment for you. You'll be amazed at what he can do. He'll convince you to do a bob, I guarantee it."

"Do you have a dentist for me, too?"

"Actually, I do. Why, do you want me to get you in? Your teeth will be as white as an elephant's tusk, I promise."

I'm not sure I want my teeth compared to an elephant's tusk. Anyway, I was joking, but Thad didn't get it.

He gestured at the bag on the floor. "That's all you're bringing?"

"It's just a week," I said again. Maybe someone will believe me.

Thad shrugged. "You don't have to come back here, Julie. Everything can be done long distance. We can get people to pack up your things and ship them. Anyway, don't worry about clothes. Cherie gave me your size. I had my closet stocked with everything you'll need...casual, formal, beach, dancing, premieres, you name it, whatever we want to do. You'll be ready."

"You bought clothes for me?" I asked.

"I had Mandi arrange a wardrobe with one of her gals. I figured you didn't know the L.A. styles. This way, you'll fit right in. It's like having your own personal D&G store."

"Thank heavens for Mandi."

"Yes, she's amazing," he said.

Thad gave an overly-interested look at his perky assistant that went from her blond hair to her sky-high heels. She felt his eyes and returned the stare. I felt a little crackle of electricity between them.

"Are you sleeping with her?" I asked casually.

Thad froze. "What?"

"You heard me."

"Oh, come on, Julie. We're not going down that road again, are we? Now you're sounding like the girl I knew in her twenties. I thought we'd both matured."

"If by matured you think I don't care if you sleep with other women, then no, I haven't matured."

"You were pretty clear to me that you didn't want a relationship," Thad said. "We're in a trial phase, right? So how about you spare me the jealousy until we're really involved?"

He was right. We did sound like we were back in our twenties. Sometimes you can block things out because you're in such a rush to pretend that you've moved on.

Before I could say anything else, he leaned down and whispered, "Look, here's the truth. Have I slept with her? Yes. Am I sleeping with her? No. That's how it is in L.A. Everybody sleeps with everybody else at some point. It doesn't mean anything. If I eliminated everyone I'd slept with from my staff, I'd never hire anyone."

"Well, that's good to know," I said.

"You know what I mean. I'm just saying Mandi and I are *not* involved anymore."

"I'm not questioning your taste, Thad. If I had breasts like that, I'd walk around topless," I said.

"She's beautiful, but everyone in L.A. is beautiful," he told me. "You're beautiful."

"Even with my breasts?" I asked. "Can an A-cup girl find love and happiness on the west coast?"

Thad shrugged. "Who says you have to be an A-cup? If you want implants, I know a guy. Best plastic surgeon in Beverly Hills. He did my eyes. Not to mention a few other things."

Thad's eyes are impressive. They are an eighteen year old's eyes, not a wrinkle or sag anywhere. I wondered where else he'd been nipped and tucked. I was beginning to think that everything about him belonged to an eighteen year old. His ego. His body. Only his wallet had gotten older.

"I don't want implants," I said.

"Then don't get them. I'm just saying, they can help you in L.A. Even on the other side of the camera, it gets you noticed."

"I'll add it to the list. Hair, teeth, boobs. Anything else?"

My sarcasm was lost on him, because Thad wasn't paying attention to me now. He was already on the phone again. It was a busy job, running Thad, Inc. The movers kept moving, but there was almost nothing left in the hotel room to carry out. I expected them to roll up the carpet and take it with them. Mandi with an i waved at us and called, "We're all set, T."

T waved back. I had a brief, blinding vision of their naked bodies entwined. Mandi moaning. Make love to me, T. Harder, T. That's the spot, T.

Thad hung up the phone and gave me one of his very best smiles. The don't-worry-about-anything smile. I almost believed it.

"You ready?" he said.

"Sure, let's go."

We headed for the elevator. The three of us, me, T, and Mandi with an i. Mandi had her clipboard with her, and she was going over plans for the house in Malibu. It must be nice to have such an efficient assistant you can sleep with. She talked about a bedroom for me and winked. That was her way of saying, "You won't need a separate bedroom, will you?"

"I did the deal for West 57 today," I told Thad. "I signed the papers."

Thad didn't reply. He was busy with Mandi.

"It's gone," I said.

Thad finally looked at me. "What?"

"I signed the papers to sell West 57 today."

"Oh, sorry, I thought you already did that. Great. One less thing to worry about, right?"

I blinked. "Right."

The blood, sweat, tears, smoke, and laughter of thirty years of my father's life. One less thing to worry about. It's no big deal. All he did was publish books, and who reads books anymore?

We emerged onto the sidewalk outside the hotel. The limo was waiting for us, its rear door open, its engine running. Across the street, I saw a large van, where Thad's life was packed up for its return voyage to L.A. Mandi bent and slid inside the limo with the grace of someone who does this every day. Her dress stretched tightly across her shapely backside. Thad's eyes followed it. He climbed in behind her and turned and reached out his hand to me like I was dangling from a cliff and in need of rescue.

"Time to go," he said.

Time to go.

I took a breath of the New York air. You could smell everything in the New York air: hot dogs, onions, leather, steam, urine, cologne, horses, soot, roses, sweat, cigars, dog poop, sugar, rain, trash, beer, and musky sex. You could smell everyone in the world doing everything in the world. You could smell conception, birth, life, death, and all of the crazy highs and lows in between. On those rare occasions when I've left the city, I always thought with wonder: the rest of the world doesn't smell at all. I didn't like it. Something always felt missing until I returned to the nose-wrinkling perfume of New York.

"It's going to pour," I said to no one in particular. Soon enough, the horses would smell like wet horses, and the trash would smell like wet trash, and the dog poop would smell like wet dog poop.

"Julie," Thad said impatiently, his hand still waiting for mine. "Climb aboard."

Climb aboard. Climb aboard the express train. Take a ride. I stared at him in the limo, and I had a vision of myself in ten years that was as blindingly clear as a high-def LED Samsung television. I was going to be exactly like my mother. Exactly. I'd be surgically perfect and rich, and Swedish men named Erick and Pieter would give me massages, and I would drive a yellow Audi convertible down the 405. I would be the ultimate California gurl. And Thad? He'd have an even bigger mansion, and Mandi with an i would have been replaced by Candi with an i, and he'd send me big alimony checks and support payments for our daughter, who would tell me she wanted to grow up to be an actress.

"Julie," Thad repeated, with a hint of annoyance.

I shook my head.

"We have to go," he insisted.

No. I don't have to go anywhere. I will go where I want and do what I want. I'm a one-choice girl, and this isn't my choice.

"I'm sorry, Thad."

"Julie, what are you saying?"

"I'm saying goodbye."

He reached for me, but I turned and walked up the street away from him and away from his life. I wondered if he would chase me, but I knew he wouldn't. Not Thad. He had a plane to catch. I heard the slam of the limousine door and the growl of the engine as they left me behind. I just kept walking, smiling at the doormen in the doorways, who tipped their hats to me. The first raindrops began to fall on my head, but I didn't care if my long hair got wet.

44

Bree was in a corner of the rooftop hotel bar under a big, dripping umbrella when I found her. It was ten o'clock at night, but she still had her sunglasses on, and she'd had her hair freshly tinted with rainbow colors. The music and partying went on around her, and she did a little sway with her shoulders to the beat. She sipped a martini and smoked a cigarette.

I sat down across from her with no greeting and no fanfare. She grinned at me without taking her sunglasses off, and she didn't look surprised. "Aren't you supposed to be on a plane, darling?" she asked.

"Nope."

"No Los Angeles for you?"

"Nope."

"No sandy beaches and year-round sunshine?"

"Nope."

"Live forever in stinky, crowded, wonderful New York?"

"Yep," I said.

"Good for you."

"Good for me," I agreed.

"So how did Thad take it?" she asked. "Did he cry?"

"No, he took it well."

"How emotionally authentic of him. How about your mother?"

"Not so well, but she'll get over it. She loves me no matter where I am."

Bree finally stripped off her glasses, where her eyes twinkled at me. "Of course, I knew you wouldn't go," she said.

"No, you didn't."

"Yes, I did. I'm your evil twin, remember? Twins always know what the other one is thinking."

As if to prove her point, a cosmopolitan miraculously appeared in front of me. We clinked our glasses, and we drank. It was strong and smooth and sweet and wonderful. Just like the two of us.

"Are you alone?" I asked, because Bree is never alone.

"Perish the thought," Bree said. "Viggo's in the little boy's room."

"Viggo Mortensen? Are you two dating?"

"Oh, not anymore. It got a little weird when he kept wanting me to call him Aragorn. We're just friends now. Want to meet him?"

"I would, but I have to be somewhere."

"Ah."

"What, ah?"

"Nothing," Bree said, but she smirked at me with that all-knowing, I'm-your-evil-twin Bree smirk. She knew where I was going. "So what are you planning to do with the rest of your life, Julie Chavan?"

"I've been thinking about that," I said. "I have options."

Bree cocked her head and put a finger on her temple, as if she were trying to guess. "Options, hmm? Plural? Let's see. You could go back to your cubicle in the Flatiron building with the McNally-Brown Agency."

"I'm not going to do that."

"You could call up *Helllmooooot* and sign on with Gernestier to run West 57."

"I'm not going to do that, either."

"You could change your mind and jet your way to L.A."

"Definitely not going to do that."

"So what's your plan, darling?" she teased me. "I'm at a loss."

"You know what my plan is," I said. "I want to know if you were serious."

"About what?"

"About you and me. About the Chavan-Cox Agency. About us taking on the world."

"The Cox-Chavan Agency? You know I was serious."

"You really want to be partners."

"Yes, I do."

"You and me. Us."

"You and me."

I took a long, deep breath, like a bungee jumper or a zip liner. Anyone about to take a plunge from a nose-bleed height.

"Okay," I said. "Let's do it."

"Truly?"

"You and me," I said. "Partners."

"This is fab, darling, utterly fab."

We shook hands to seal the deal. We hugged. We kissed. Just like that, we were in business. Julie Chavan and Bree Cox.

"Of course, you know this is probably a bad idea that will never work," I said, when we'd finished celebrating.

"Why is that?"

"Because friends make terrible partners."

"Do they? Well, what about enemies? We've been enemies, too."

"Even worse," I said.

"Then we can agree to be frenemies," Bree replied. "Frenemies make great partners, right?"

"Absolutely." I raised my glass.

We drank. I slugged mine down, and it went right to my head. I could have had six more, but I had somewhere to be.

"I have to go," I said.

"Yes, I know. I'll see you tomorrow, darling. We can plan our takeover of the entertainment industry over coffee and donuts."

"I thought you were heading back to London," I said.

"Actually, I changed my tickets to stay another week. I had a feeling you might be sticking around."

I leaned across the table and kissed her on the cheek. "Life with you will never be dull, Bree Cox."

"Why, thank you, darling."

I headed for the elevators, passing through the drinkers and the dancers with a strange buzz in my head. There was an electricity all around the patio, but mostly, it was inside me. My heart was beating like crazy. That's what happens when you suddenly find you are in love with your future and can't wait to see what it brings.

I stood in front of Garrett's door.

I'd never been to his apartment before, above the all-night Turkish coffee shop. The building smelled of dark-roasted dregs and the inside of an old hookah pipe. I heard twingy-twangy music and a yipper dog yipping. Inside Garrett's apartment, I heard late-night Yankees sports talk on the television.

Everything seemed clear to me while I was walking through the city, but nothing seemed clear when I was about to see his face. What if he wasn't thinking what I was thinking? What if I'd misjudged everything? I thought about what I would say, and my mind drew a blank. I had nothing. I decided I would know what to say when the words came out of my mouth. I'd say something clever and funny. I'd break the ice. Or I'd fall through it.

My nervousness soared as I second-guessed myself. Let's face it, I didn't exactly look like a million dollars. The rain as I left Bree's hotel was a deluge, with animals starting to pair up for the Ark. I was soaked to the bone. I was dripping on the carpet. My hair looked like dreadlocks. Very sexy.

I knocked.

Inside, Garrett turned off the television and answered the door. There he was. He knew it was me; he'd already buzzed me in. We stared at each other, him all warm and casual and sexy with that crooked smile, me as pathetic as a homeless wet dog. I opened my mouth, waiting to say something clever, something funny, something, anything, to explain why I was here.

I couldn't think of a thing to say. Not a word. Nada. Neither did he.

You know what? It was still okay. As it turned out, we didn't need to talk at all. We both knew what we wanted. We both knew why I was there. Words were just going to slow us down.

I got on tiptoes and kissed him, and he bent down and kissed me back, and he pulled me into his apartment and kicked the door shut with his foot, and my arms were around his neck, and his arms were around my back, and I began taking off his clothes, and he began taking off my clothes, and soon enough, there were lots of clothes on the floor, and there were none on us, and we were stumbling into the bedroom and tumbling into the bed, and sorry, that's as far as I go with you.

I think it was two hours later when I finally said something. By then, we'd definitely broken the ice.

I was lying next to him. We were staring at the ceiling fan going around and around and around. We may have been in a sex coma. We were both naked and sweaty, and I was really, really hungry. That's how you know it was good. I could have gone to an all-night deli and scarfed down eggs, bacon, sausage, pancakes, French toast, hash browns, oatmeal, and washed it all down with coffee.

"Did I mention I was staying?" I said to him.

"I was hoping you were staying," he said.

We were quiet for a long time again, holding hands. Being here, under the ceiling fan, with the smell of the Turkish bakery in the vents, listening to the hammering of rain on the windows, was better than any beach in Malibu.

"I've wanted to do that for, like, years," I said.

"Me, too."

"So why didn't we?"

"Because we are stupid, stupid people."

"Yes, we are."

I rolled over onto his body. His skin felt good beneath me. So did other things. I propped myself up on his chest.

"Bree and I are going into business together," I said. "Do you want to work with me?"

"I want to do everything with you."

"I like that," I said.

He opened his mouth to say something more, but I put a finger over his lips and stopped him. We didn't need to say anything else. Not now. When you are naked on top of a naked man, you can find better things to do.

45

I saw him one last time. Sonny.

It was a few whirlwind weeks later. I'd hardly had time to think about the past, because we were so busy making plans for the future. Me. Bree. Garrett. Half the staff from West 57. We were writing contracts, developing strategies, reaching out to clients, talking to publishers, filmmakers, booksellers, advertising agencies, newspapers, and bankers. Dumbo was surprisingly helpful about financing. So was my mother.

I had no idea whether any of our plans would work, but I knew I was having more fun than I'd had in years. We had our first project, too: the book that Garrett and I had fallen in love with, *Woodham Road.* We would publish and market it ourselves. We would produce the film. We would coordinate marketing and publicity. We would do it the way it was supposed to be done. It was a whole new world.

After working together all day, Garrett and I spent every evening together. Sometimes at his place. Sometimes at my place. Talking. Working. Laughing. Reading. Watching the Yankees. Eating take-out. Making love.

In all of the commotion, I'd almost forgotten my father. I'd been thinking of everything else but Sonny. Finally, I had a Sunday morning in which I could break free of the business, so I went for a run through Central Park. It was early, only six o'clock. I started from my apartment in a purple halter and shorts, with my hair tied in the world's longest pony tail. It had been weeks since I ran, so it felt liberating to go all out, pushing myself up and down the hills, panting, sweating.

That was when I thought about Sonny again.

I jogged up one of the hills near Central Park South, in a wooded area, where people liked to lay out on the rocks. That was one of the places where Sonny and I would sit on our summer Sundays. We would bring a picnic, and we would perch on the rocks, and we would both read, and we would chat about life, and he would tell me about authors he'd loved and food he'd eaten and parties he'd attended. He was my hero then.

He was still my hero.

As I remembered those days, I saw him waiting for me, on the rocks, still in his business suit, cigarette dangling from his mouth, as if I were a child again. I stopped on the path. Smiling, breathing heavily from the run, I climbed up the rocks and joined him there. We sat next to each other the way we had in the past.

"It's a beautiful day in the world's most beautiful city," he said to me, which was something he always said back then. It didn't matter if it was snowing or raining or cold or hot. Every day to Sonny was the most beautiful day in the world's most beautiful city.

"Yes, it is," I said.

"You look happy, darling girl."

"I am happy, Sonny. I can't remember when I've been so happy. I'm living my own life. I have friends I love. I have a man I love."

"I'm glad."

"I only wish I still had you," I told him, and I was trying not to bawl.

Sonny laughed in that big way of his, trying to make me feel better. "You do have me, darling girl! You will never be rid of me! Even if you don't see me, I'm always right here."

"I'll remember that."

"The question is whether you can ever forgive me, Julie. I know I disappointed you."

"You didn't disappoint me, Sonny. I'm proud of you."

"Really?"

"Really. How could I not be proud of a father who would sacrifice everything to rescue the woman he loved?"

"I should have told you," he said.

"Maybe. Or maybe this was a journey I needed to take for myself. I know you better now than I ever did when you were alive, Sonny. I know myself better, too. I know what I really care about now."

He winked at me. "You always knew that."

I think he was right, but like Bree said, it takes me a while to figure it out.

I wanted to stay there forever, but I couldn't. It was time to go. It was time to say goodbye. He knew it, too, and he waved his hand toward the path.

"Run, Julie," he told me. "Go on, get on with your life. Turn the page."

"I love you, Sonny."

"I love you, too, darling girl."

I climbed down from the rocks and left him there. I walked for a few steps and then took a last glimpse over my shoulder. The rocks where I'd sat were empty, just as they'd always been. There had never been anyone with me. No ghosts. I waved anyway and blew him a kiss.

I started running again through the Park.

ABOUT THE AUTHOR

In addition to writing witty, romantic novels like WEST 57 and THE AGENCY, B.N. Freeman is well known to readers as bestselling thriller author Brian Freeman. His books include the popular Jonathan Stride and Cab Bolton series. Brian won the award for Best Hardcover Novel from the International Thriller Writers organization.

Lisa Gardner calls him "a master of psychological suspense," and Michael Connelly says, "This guy can tell a story." Nelson DeMille calls him "a first-rate storyteller."

His books are available around the world and in audio editions.

Connect with Brian by e-mail at brian@bfreemanbooks.com or on Facebook at facebook.com/bfreemanfans or Twitter and Instagram using the handle bfreemanbooks. His web site is bfreemanbooks.com. For an inside look at the personal side of the book business, you can also like his wife Marcia's Facebook page: facebook.com/theauthorswife.

NOTE

Everything you have read in this book is 100% fiction. References to real people are purely imaginary, and any such names appear in the book solely as fictional characters. This book is satire, and nothing in here should be taken seriously or considered true.

If you enjoyed this book, please post your reviews on Amazon and Goodreads and share links to the book on Facebook, Twitter, Instagram, and other social media sites!

BOOKS BY BRIAN FREEMAN

<u>The Jonathan Stride Series</u>:

IMMORAL

STRIPPED

STALKED

IN THE DARK

THE BURYING PLACE

SPITTING DEVIL (e-short story)

TURN TO STONE (e-novella)

THE COLD NOWHERE

GOODBYE TO THE DEAD (Available 2016)

<u>The Cab Bolton Series</u>:

THE BONE HOUSE

SEASON OF FEAR

<u>Stand-Alone Novels</u>:

SPILLED BLOOD

THE AGENCY (as Ally O'Brien)

WEST 57 (as B.N. Freeman)

CPSIA information can be obtained
at www.ICGtesting.com
Printed in the USA
LVHW021606030619
619986LV00016B/1226/P